From the Reminiscences of Private Ivanov
and other stories

The translators:

Peter Henry, Professor of Slavonic Languages and Literatures in the University of Glasgow, founder editor of *Scottish Slavonic Review*, is the author of *A Hamlet of his Time: Vsevolod Garshin – The Man, his Works, and his Milieu.*

Liv Tudge, a freelance translator, resident in the United States, holds an M. Litt. (Oxford) for work on Garshin; from 1978 to 1980 she was a translator and editor with Progress Publishers, Moscow.

Donald Rayfield, author of *Chekhov: the Evolution of his Art*, is Reader in Russian at Queen Mary College, University of London.

Philip Taylor has translated Russian opera libretti for Collet's (Publishers).

VSEVOLOD GARSHIN

From the Reminiscences of Private Ivanov

and other stories

Translated by Peter Henry, Liv Tudge,
Donald Rayfield and Philip Taylor

ANGEL BOOKS
LONDON

To the memory of
Grigory Abramovich Byaly (1905–1987)
our mentor in Garshin

First published by Angel Books, 3 Kelross Road,
London N5 2QS

A CIP catalogue record for this book is available from the
British Library.

ISBN 0 946162 08 5 (cased)
0 946162 09 3 (paperback)

Typeset in Great Britain by Trintype;
printed and bound by Woolnough Bookbinding,
both of Irthlingborough, Northants.

Contents

Introduction by Peter Henry   7

Four Days   25
An Incident   36
A Very Brief Romance   52
An Encounter   57
The Coward   74
Artists   93
Attalea princeps   110
A Night   117
Orderly and Officer   134
What Never Was   147
From the Reminiscences of Private Ivanov   151
The Red Flower   197
The Tale of the Toad and the Rose   212
The Legend of Haggai the Proud   218
The Travelling Frog   228
The Signal   233

Notes   242

Translators' Acknowledgement

The generous and valuable assistance of our editor and publisher, Antony Wood, on numerous problems of translation and presentation is gratefully acknowledged.

P. H.

Introduction

I

The first story I read by Garshin, *Four Days*, made a very strong impression on me. I was later intrigued by the reverence in which this unprolific writer has always been held in Russia, during his lifetime and since. As I got to know his fiction – a mere score of published short stories and novellas – his mind and personality, I realised that here is a writer who belongs to 'world literature', although he is known to the English-speaking reader virtually only through the much-anthologised *Four Days*, *The Red Flower* and *The Signal*.

Vsevolod Garshin (1855–88), 'Turgenev's heir' and Chekhov's precursor, was the outstanding new writer in Russia during the period of cultural reorientation that followed the heyday of the realist novel. In the 1880s the towering edifices of Tolstoy and Dostoyevsky were succeeded by fiction of a different kind, and written on a smaller scale. Garshin's dense, subjective, impressionistic, multiple-viewpoint and often allegorical short stories and novellas, which include the best war stories in Russian literature after Tolstoy's, not only pointed the way for Chekhov's fiction but also helped prepare the ground for such new developments as symbolism, expressionism and other manifestations of Russian modernism. A verbal artist of considerable originality and integrity, Garshin moves away from the broad canvas and the solid objectivity of the realist novel towards the introspective and microscopic, the fragmentary and fleeting. His stories make an immediate impact on the reader, many of them having the almost sacred and terrifying quality of a confession. As D. S. Merezhkovsky wrote five years after Garshin's death: 'his absolute, unlimited sincerity . . . arouses the unlimited trust of the reader.'

Most of Garshin's stories express an intense social motivation, a challenge to the social order in strongly personalised terms. He was called 'the Hamlet of our times' by the revolutionary poet P. F. Yakubovich, and indeed he gave voice to the disturbed conscience of his age, of men and women only too keenly aware of the ailments and wrongs of society and their own apparent powerlessness to resolve the urgent social, ethical and existential dilemmas of the time. Beyond this he expressed the elusive vision of a world transformed by the heroic will of martyrs into a new Golden Age. Driven equally by a sense of guilt and a faith in man's inherent potential for achieving the miraculous, he and his heroes attempt to intervene in Don Quixote fashion in the manifestations of evil that they constantly encounter. 'This martyr of the spirit,' a contemporary said of Garshin, 'suffered from an illness from which it is morally wrong to recover, because martyrs have always prevented happy people from becoming spiritually moribund.'

As confirmed by numerous contemporaries, Garshin was a man of charisma and strikingly good looks – 'a perfect model for an icon of Our Saviour', as Ariadna Tyrkova-Williams, the Russian suffragette and feminist writer, put it, recalling the impact he had made on her, then a teenage girl. He was a cult-figure of his age, idolised not only by the young. His public readings evoked ecstatic responses from audiences; people would come up to him in the street, greet him reverently and be happy to accompany him on his way. Many knew his stories by heart. In the 1880s he was a welcome and respected figure in literary, artistic and musical circles, and his advice was sought by writers and publishers.

He was in close contact with the school of painters known as the Itinerants (*Peredvizhniki*), whose broadly popular and 'democratic' aesthetic and social aspirations he shared. In his student days he spent much time with the young artists and was commissioned to write reviews of art exhibitions for St Petersburg newspapers, in which he revealed a sensitive perception of art as such and not merely for its social message, as well as a strong line in irony and wit. His first commentary on art (in verse) was on V. V. Vereshchagin's grimly naturalistic battle canvases (his Turkestan Series, 1874). Some of Vereshchagin's paintings are visual equivalents of Garshin's *Four Days* and other stories on the theme of war. Garshin was on friendly terms with N. A. Yaroshenko, on whose painting *The Furnaceman* he drew in *Artists*; he corresponded with Kramskoy on the 'correct' interpretation of his *Christ in the Wilderness* (1872) as a symbol of the modern idealistic revolutionary. In the 1880s he became a close friend of Ilya Repin who illustrated several of his stories, painted two fine portraits of Garshin and used him as a model for the dying Tsarevich in his huge canvas *Ivan The Terrible and His Son* (1885) which was regarded as both a heretical and a politically subversive work.

Beyond explicit artistic themes, such as in *Artists*, a painterly vision can be perceived in most of Garshin's work, in his pervasive yet subtle use of colours, his visual patterning and composition. His imagery is not confined to the visual plane; his stories also abound in sound images which further enhance the palpable texture and sense of immediacy and reality of his writing, and he displayed a remarkable gift for making the amorphous and the fantastic comprehensible, tangible and meaningful.

Though many of his stories appear to be autobiographical, or to contain a strong subjective element, they are in fact an expression of his empathy, his ability to enter into another's personality and identify with him and to experience his experiences as his own – the essential characteristic of humanist art.

II

Garshin's brief life spanned a time of rapid economic, social and political change and recurring crisis in Russia. The beginning of the modern, capitalist phase in the history of the Russian Empire was marked by two major, interconnected events – the Crimean War (1853–56) and the Emancipation of the Serfs (1861). The former cost Russia a heavy loss of life, finance and international prestige; her defeat ended the myth of the invincible colossus and set in train much social ferment which contributed significantly to the termination of the feudal, serf-based economy. But the Russian peasant was still in a state of economic bondage, and the 'peasant question' continued to be a major, unresolved issue until the end of the century and beyond.

The 1860s saw the rise and crystallisation of the Russian revolutionary movement. It was the age of the new radicals (or revolutionary democrats) dominated by Chernyshevsky, Dobrolyubov and Pisarev, the pioneers of Russian socialism. The first attempt on the life of Alexander II in 1866 signalled the imminence of a head-on collision between autocracy and revolution. In the 1870s populism became the dominant ideology among the Russian intelligentsia. The Populists (*Narodniki*) believed that Russia could, and should, bypass the capitalist phase, thereby avoiding the horrors of industrialisation. Since its historical development differed so profoundly

from that of the rest of Europe, Russia, it was held, had a special path
to pursue; it had a unique, proto-socialist organisation in the village
commune (*mir*, *obshchina*) which could form the nucleus of Russian
agrarian socialism. Hence the intelligentsia's preoccupation with the
Russian peasant, his attitudes and way of life that culminated in the
Movement to the People of the early 1870s, when a large number of
educated men and women, driven by a sense of guilt and compassion
for the peasants, left the cities for the villages, there to share in their
life, aid them in various ways and learn from them the wisdom of life.
From this essentially reformist and educational crusade there
emerged the revolutionary militancy of Land and Freedom (*Zemlya i
Volya*) and, in 1879, the People's Will (*Narodnaya Volya*) whose aim
was the liberation of the Russian people and the end of autocracy, to
be achieved by a policy of political assassination. These 'Nihilists'
were particularly active in the second half of the decade, among them
Vera Zasulich who made an attempt on the governor of St Petersburg
in 1878; the fact that she was acquitted by the jury indicates how
much the educated public was in sympathy with the idealistic young
terrorists.

Russian society reacted sharply to the second major foreign war
in which the country was involved in the latter half of the century –
the Russo-Turkish War of 1877–78. Many hailed its outbreak as a
crusade to liberate the 'Slav Brethren' from Turkish oppression
dramatised by the Bulgarian atrocities in 1876 on the one hand and
the uprisings in Serbia and Herzegovina on the other. For others it
was an opportunity to avenge the humiliating defeat in the Crimean
War, and in Pan-Slavist and government circles there were visions of
creating a Slav Commonwealth under Russian hegemony. At first,
many liberals and democrats supported the war enthusiastically, but
as news of heavy loss of life came in, a process of 'sobering up' took
place, and idealism and patriotism were followed by revulsion and a
feeling of having been duped by Tsarist motives.

The domestic effect of Russia's costly victory (the gains of which
were much reduced by the diplomatic intervention of Bismarck and
the British) was to fan the growing social ferment, which now
developed into a 'second revolutionary situation', as Lenin
characterised the years 1879–81. (The 'first revolutionary situation'
had followed the Crimean War and culminated in 1859–61.) During
this period The People's Will claimed a number of notable victims;
they finally killed Alexander II in March 1881. The ringleaders were

rounded up and publicly executed and their organisation was broken up. The 1880s were a period of uneasy calm and repression, with autocracy apparently firmly in control.

The 1870s had also been a period of great cultural flowering. They saw the establishment of a national school of music – Tchaikovsky, Mussorgsky, Rimsky-Korsakov, Borodin – and a national theatre led by Ostrovsky. In art there emerged the new school of realism, the Itinerants, headed by Kramskoy and Repin. In literature, the pre-eminence of Russian fiction continued with Tolstoy, Turgenev, Dostoyevsky and Leskov. There also emerged a prolific stream of semi-documentary writing by lesser talents describing the lives and hardships of the common people, the peasants and the lower urban classes. The heyday of the Russian novel terminated in the 1880s: after his spiritual crisis of 1879–81, Tolstoy abandoned fiction-writing as a morally indefensible activity, Dostoyevsky died in 1881, Turgenev in 1883, and Goncharov's writing days were over. The 1880s were a transitional period; many new philosophical and aesthetic influences came to bear on Russian culture, such as the ideas of Schopenhauer and Nietzsche and the sociological teaching of Herbert Spencer.

The buoyant optimism of the Russian intelligentsia in the 1860s and the heroic, apocalyptic mood of the 1870s now gave way to the ideology of the so-called 'little deed' advocating social conformism and a sober and prosaic attitude to life on the one hand, and Tolstoy's moral and social teaching on the other. Tolstoyanism preached a practical, demythologised Christianity, non-participation in the political and administrative process, and a refusal to condone, let alone resort to violence on whatever grounds; as such, it acted as a powerful brake on the revolutionary movement.

III

Vsevolod Mikhaylovich Garshin was born on his maternal grand-mother's estate Priyatnaya Dolina (Pleasant Valley), some 200 kilometres south of Kharkov in the Ukraine. His father had been an officer in one of the cavalry regiments but retired prematurely; he was a gentle, lonely and ineffectual man with a bizarre streak that became more and more pronounced (an affectionate portrait of him is given in *A Night*). His mother also had a service background, her father having been a naval officer. There was a disturbing history of hereditary insanity on both sides of the family with a melancholy record of alcoholism and suicides, and the fear of madness haunted Garshin all his life; in fact, he suffered three serious breakdowns.

The family split up when he was five. His mother, a forceful, well-read woman with advanced views – she was a follower of Chernyshevsky – eloped with the boy's tutor, a young radical student and member of a secret society in Kharkov. Vsevolod stayed with his father until 1863 when his mother took him to St Petersburg. Here he attended a modern high school and the Institute of Mining; G. V. Plekhanov, the 'father of Russian Marxism', was a fellow-student with whom Garshin was briefly in contact. His school and student years were spent in straitened and unsettled circumstances; he was lodged with a large number of different families and spent his meagre and irregular allowance from his mother and his earnings from tutoring on books and visits to the theatre and concerts. At school he was accused of having socialist leanings, and he began writing during his student days.

In April 1877 he volunteered for military service in the Russo-Turkish War, not so much out of patriotic motives, 'not to kill, but in order to expose my breast to the bullets', and to share in the hardships endured by the Russian peasants in uniform. As a volunteer-private he marched the 600 kilometres and more from Kishinyov in Bessarabia to the battlefields in Bulgaria. He was wounded in action and returned to Kharkov in September.

His experiences form the basis of *Four Days* which was published in September 1877 in one of the leading journals in St Petersburg and made him instantly famous (the story's relevance to the anti-war camp is evidenced by the speed with which it was published, apparently uncensored – within fourteen days of its receipt by the editor, Saltykov-Shchedrin). Garshin thus entered the literary world of the capital with relative ease, and from 1878 to 1880 he wrote more stories on the war and on social themes.

The year 1880 was a watershed in Garshin's life. The confrontation of autocracy and revolution had reached a crisis point, to which he reacted in a very personal and ambivalent way. Profoundly impress-ed by the heroism of the men and women of The People's Will, he was equally distressed – and mesmerised – by the realities of violence and bloodshed. He was outraged by 'blood, but blood spilt by whomsoever', as he said concerning the explosion at the Winter

Palace in February 1880 that claimed the lives of ten soldiers of the Finnish Life Guards, while the Tsar was unscathed. When a fortnight later the student I. O. Mlodetsky made an attempt on the life of Count M. T. Loris-Melikov, Chairman of the Supreme Administrative Commission that had just been set up to carry out a new policy steering between further repression and reform, Garshin intervened in a highly personal and quixotic way. He wrote an emotional appeal to Loris-Melikov, regarded by many as a humanitarian who might set new standards of governmental behaviour in Russia, pleading with him to spare the life of the young criminal due to be executed the following day; by this act of moral greatness he would 'kill the idea of violence' and usher in an era of all-forgiveness, harmony and peace. He delivered the letter during the night and in fact spent several hours with Loris-Melikov, pleading for Mlodetsky's life. Garshin left ecstatic, believing that the Count had agreed to a stay of execution. But when he saw the scaffolding being erected he experienced a trauma that led to a major mental collapse. He left St Petersburg secretly and went first to Moscow and then to the countryside in Central Russia where he preached the gospel of all-forgiveness to bewildered peasants; he also visited Tolstoy's estate at Yasnaya Polyana where the two writers engaged in a nocturnal conversation on the need for, and ways of, removing violence from life. In due course he was picked up and taken, straitjacketed, to Kharkov where he was placed in a mental institution that was actually no more than a primitive place of detention, with the 'patients' kept behind bars. Here he remained for four months before being transferred to a clinic in St Petersburg, and in November his maternal uncle took him to his estate in Kherson Province near the Black Sea to convalesce. He stayed there for eighteen months, during which time he wrote only one short work – the fable *What Never Was* – and virtually severed all contacts with St Petersburg.

In 1882, his health much improved, he returned to the capital but spent the summer on Turgenev's estate at Spasskoye-Lutovinovo where he wrote *From the Reminiscences of Private Ivanov*, his most sustained and balanced work. He obtained a lowly post at a paper factory and then an undemanding position with the Association of Russian Railways. He married Nadezhda Zolotilova, a qualified doctor, who looked after him with great devotion and provided the stability of married life. Garshin's creative powers were now at a peak – between 1883 and 1887 he wrote his masterpiece *The Red*

Flower, based on his experiences in the mental institution in Kharkov, and completed six more stories. He undertook a number of
translations, notably of Mérimée's *Colombe* and stories by Ouida
and Carmen de Silva, and was active on the Tolstoyan publishing
venture Posrednik that produced cheap editions of 'wholesome'
reading for the common people, and in the writers' organisation
Litfond; he also made considerable headway with a major historical
novel set in the times of Peter the Great and many other projects.
However, in 1887 his health deteriorated sharply and in a fit of
depression he threw himself down a stairwell, dying five days later,
aged thirty-three, on 24th March/5th April 1888.

IV

Garshin's stories reflect the complex moods, anxieties and aspirations of his generation with considerable force and apparent accura-
cy. His war stories did more than that – they contributed strongly to
the rising anti-war mood during the Russo-Turkish War by demon-
strating the butchery and the immorality of war in vivid, sometimes
naturalistic images. Some of his other stories are equally impas-
sioned protests against the institutionalised injustice and cruelty of
the social order. In 1882 he published a slim volume of his early
stories; two years later, it was withdrawn from public libraries as
being 'anti-patriotic' and generally 'harmful'.

In terms of quantitative, completed output a 'minor' writer,
Garshin was in fact an important innovator in Russian literature: he
was a pioneer of the psychological and impressionistic miniature. His
stories show a considerable thematic variety and stylistic range. His
strong personal involvement, and his preoccupation with the fringe
areas of human consciousness, seldom led to a loss of control over his
subject-matter or his language. He was scornful of writers for whom
the provision of factual information was the sole consideration and
who were indifferent to beauty of form. His own idiom is in the
manner of Pushkin's prose – vigorous, compact and well controlled,
yet flexible and varied to suit the atmosphere he is creating; his
'realism' is selective and in sharp focus. Aware that Russian narrative
prose was in urgent need of revitalisation, he fulminated against 'that
realism, naturalism, protocolism and the rest. It's in full flower now,
or rather has reached maturity and the fruit within it is beginning to
decay. I refuse to chew the cud of the past forty or fifty years and I'd

sooner break my skull in my efforts to find something new for myself than trail behind a school which . . . was least likely to become solidly established for years and years.' (1 May 1885.)

Dmitry Merezhkovsky, the theoretician of Russian symbolism, saw Garshin as 'a bold innovator. He created a special, unprecedented language, striking in its brevity. He gives a minimum of characters, a distillation of extensive material which would have sufficed another for an entire novel . . . He simplifies and concentrates [his ideas] into a single artistic image.' (1893.) Garshin's innovatory achievement lies partly in his controlled use of visual and other symbols and images, sometimes amounting to a cryptographic code, notably in *Artists* and *The Red Flower*, where they are escalated and transformed, thereby achieving great concentration; and also in a complex and modern perception of reality beyond reality and the validity of alternative visions. At the same time he could produce the steady epic narrative of *Orderly and Officer* and *From the Reminiscences of Private Ivanov*, where, however, the narrative can suddenly be interrupted by brief impressionistic snatches where the rules of syntax are totally ignored. He was very sensitive to the power of rhythm, which he could control and vary superbly.

In *Four Days* Garshin pioneered stream-of-consciousness writing; this is the first instance of the technique in European literature. In *Artists* he used the technique of alternating diaries, showing the fallibility of human perception and creating the impression that there is no authorial or 'absolute' truth. Garshin's descriptions of dreams and nightmares, in *The Red Flower* and other stories, are always clinically focused. In *The Signal* he employed the naïve simplicity of peasant language and perceptions as required by the Tolstoyanists, together with a subversive semiotic technique for discrediting the main 'Tolstoyan' hero.

V

Garshin was highly regarded by other Russian writers of his time, in whose attitudes is to be sensed a mixture of personal affection and respect for his artistic originality. Turgenev encouraged him in every way. In June 1880 he wrote to him from Paris: 'Ever since your first appearance in literature I have taken note of you as an undoubted, original talent . . . [*Orderly and Officer*] has in my opinion finally confirmed you as holding first place among young writers now starting out . . . Every ageing writer who genuinely loves his craft is happy when he sees he has heirs: you are one of them . . .'

Like all his generation, Garshin was under the spell of Tolstoy's artistic, moral and spiritual leadership. Garshin's war stories have affinities with Tolstoy's *Sebastopol Stories*, but they are not derivative. Ivanov, in *Four Days*, lying wounded on the field of battle, invites comparison with Prince Andrey at the Battle of Austerlitz in *War and Peace*, but their emotions and thoughts are very different. The two writers had, however, similar views on social and moral matters, as came out in their long conversation in 1880; Tolstoy later recalled that Garshin's views were 'grist to my mill'. Garshin's letter to Loris-Melikov strikingly anticipates Tolstoy's letter to Alexander III a year later, begging him to show mercy to the regicides who had killed his father. Two of Garshin's stories, *The Legend of Haggai the Proud* and *The Signal*, are distinctly 'Tolstoyanist' in form and appear to advocate the simplicity, humility and piety demanded by Tolstoy and his followers. However, Garshin did not accept uncritically the tenets of Tolstoyanism, such as that of non-violence and its attitude to science, which he found 'odious' and dismissed as 'silly pomposities'. But his admiration for Tolstoy the man and writer remained undimmed until his death. Tolstoy had a great affection for Garshin and showed much concern for him during and after his illness. He had a high regard for Garshin's writing which, like Turgenev, he rated well above that of other writers of the period. In 1895 he stated: 'If it were possible to combine Chekhov and Garshin, we would have a substantial writer. Chekhov has little of what Garshin had, who always knew what he wanted to say, while Chekhov does not always know what he wants to say.'

Dostoyevsky was a disturbing force for Garshin and he said a number of highly unflattering things about the great novelist and his 'harmful' writing. He was inevitably conscious of living and writing in the shadow of Dostoyevsky's genius, and he dealt with a number of Dostoyevskian themes, such as the insulted and injured struggling to survive in the sub-world of the capital. Though Garshin's work is inferior to Dostoyevsky's, he, too, was inspired by an apocalyptic and resurrectionist vision and a comparable compulsion to portray physical and spiritual pain. While *The Red Flower* is his most Dostoyevskian work, affinities with Dostoyevsky can also be seen in *An Incident*, *Artists* and *A Night*. It is significant that contemporaries arguing with sceptics who thought that men like Alyosha Karamazov 'don't exist', pointed to Garshin as a real-life equivalent of Dostoyevsky's hero, capable of 'either going into the revolution or becoming a monk'.

As a pioneer of the impressionistic novella, with its extreme verbal economy, Garshin was of major importance for Chekhov who knew his writing well and admired his personal and artistic integrity. Garshin was one of the very few who understood and welcomed the innovatory significance of Chekhov's *The Steppe* (1888). Shocked by the news of Garshin's death, Chekhov contributed a story – *A Breakdown* (1888) in which he portrayed 'a man of the Garshinian cast – out of the ordinary, decent and deeply sensitive' – to a commemorative volume published a year after Garshin's death. Garshin was in Chekhov's mind in 1892 when he was writing his asylum story *Ward No. 6*, and there are striking affinities between *The Red Flower* and not only this story but also Chekhov's study of *mania grandiosa*, *The Black Monk* (1894).

A writer who was explicitly indebted to Garshin was Leonid Andreyev (1871–1919), in whose stories Garshinian themes, images and even characters reappear in escalated and often sensationalised form, notably in *The Red Laugh* (1904), inspired by the slaughter of the Russo-Japanese War. Gorky, Bunin and many other Russian writers have acknowledged Garshin's importance in Russian literature. Gorky's *The Mistake* (1895) strongly echoes *The Red Flower*, especially in the main hero's ecstatic vision of the liberation and rebirth of mankind.

VI

This edition of Garshin's stories includes almost all of his mature fiction, placed in broad chronological order of composition. Only *The Bears* and *Nadezhda Nikolayevna* have been omitted, the former because it is structurally unsatisfactory, being composed of a number of disparate pieces; the latter, his longest work, is also his least convincing.

Four Days (1877), the first of Garshin's fiction proper to be published, is an eloquent interior monologue by a wounded Russian soldier lying on a deserted battlefield beside the decomposing corpse of an enemy soldier whom he has killed. He is racked by despair, a sense of personal guilt for his 'crime', and is bitterly aware that, duped by patriotic propaganda, he, the would-be hero-martyr, is to die a common murderer. The staccato, uncoordinated narrative is shot through with stark naturalistic descriptions and swift cinematic changes.

An Incident (1878), a somewhat melodramatic story of prostitution in a dense and fragmentary idiom using multiple viewpoints, is to some extent reminiscent of Dostoyevsky. The heroine, no 'saintly sinner', but an educated and clear-sighted woman, issues a powerful and articulate indictment of society. *A Very Brief Romance* (1878), the story of a young man wounded in the war returning to the woman he loves, is something of a literary pastiche, full of Dickensian allusions and Dostoyevskian imitations, subtle ambiguities and self-parody. In *An Encounter* (1879) two friends of dissimilar type and outlook are confronted – a virtuous young teacher about to take up his first appointment, and a blatantly immoral and cynical engineer living in comfort by means of embezzlement. The subtle process by which 'the covers are stripped away' from each is reminiscent of Chekhov. In *Artists* (1879) the social victim is a workman in a St Petersburg shipyard, dehumanised by the appalling conditions of his work. Here Garshin has refined the structure of the earlier works by telling the story in the form of alternating diary entries by two artists of sharply contrasting kinds. Obsessed with his purpose, the socially committed artist resolves to paint the workman, endowing him with strong Christ-like overtones, and experiences a nightmare in which the workman is a symbol of the despised, who will arise and avenge themselves on an indifferent society.

The Coward (1879) with its ironic title reverts to the war theme. It is told largely in the form of diary entries by a young man driven to despair by the horror of reports from the front and racked by his conscience for having so far avoided sharing in the suffering. The organised slaughter is given a poignant perspective by the naturalistic record of the onset of disease in a friend. The 'Coward' eventually goes to war . . . The hero of *A Night* (1880) has much in common with Dostoyevsky's Underground Men, while the story also contains a number of Faustian and Hamletist echoes. In a merciless survey of his past the lonely and alienated hero becomes aware of his own life-long dishonesty, that he has worshipped false gods, that life is a cruel fraud, and that he must end it all. Told in a subtle blend of interior monologue, third-person narrative, author-narrator, and 'voices' addressing the hero, the story is a cogent statement on the existential dilemmas of modern man. *Orderly and Officer* (1880) is a military still-life in which a simple, retarded peasant lad is juxtaposed with his master, a young ensign whose psychological complexity is described with sympathetic insight. Socially and psychologically so dissimilar, the two men are shown to share an essential identity in the alienating and corrupting stagnation of army life. The story has the deceptive simplicity of an open-ended Chekhovian tale: nothing dramatic happens, no problems are resolved, no one is morally reborn.

Attalea princeps (1879) is the first of several fables that Garshin wrote. It is a heroic allegory on man's indomitable quest for liberty and has always been particularly popular with Russian readers. In this poetic tale an exotic palm-tree imprisoned in a conservatory conceives a determination to break out of captivity; it was seen by some as a prophetic parable on the fanatical determination and defeat of the men and women of The People's Will, but has a deeper and more enduring meaning. Garshin's other fables are *What Never Was* (1882) in Andersen's manner, in which a learned debate by representatives of the insect and animal world philosophising on moral and ethical issues (with, despite Garshin's public denials, a political innuendo) gives an ironic perspective on the Russians' favourite pastime; *The Tale of the Toad and the Rose* (1884), which echoes the theme of Beauty and the Beast and is told in a pervasively melancholy and musical mode (it took shape in Garshin's mind during a piano recital by Anton Rubinstein); and *The Travelling Frog* (1887), the last story Garshin wrote, a humorous, ironic cautionary tale into which a variety of meanings can be, and have been, read.

From the Reminiscences of Private Ivanov (1883) is the high-point of Garshin's writing based on the Russo-Turkish War, a superbly epic account of the Russian peasant army on a march through Rumania to the Danube and the first engagement on Bulgarian soil. The narrative has a convincing, palpable reality and contains a number of sympathetic and perceptive portraits. The portrayal of one of the officers, a man of culture and refinement and yet sadistic in his treatment of his men, is a masterpiece of psychological realism. This work has the elusive qualities that transform a past remembered into art and contrasts with and complements Garshin's earlier stories based on the campaign with their predominantly narrow, intense and inward focus; *From the Reminiscences* fascinatingly sets into perspective Garshin's documentary record (*Action at Ayaslar*, 1877) and his many letters home from the campaign, with their almost schizophrenically unemotional observation of detail.

The Legend of Haggai the Proud (1886) is written in the form and simple language of the ancient Russian legend which it retells. A

powerful ruler is punished by the Lord for arrogance and stripped of
his wealth and power; he lives with the poor in his realm. In what
happens when the term of punishment is over, the influence of
Tolstoy's teaching can be discerned.

VII

It will be worth examining two stories, *The Red Flower* (1883) and
The Signal (1887), in some detail in order to see Garshin's power and
originality at work. *The Red Flower*, set in a mental asylum, is the
artistic summit of his achievement, a vibrant, image-rich, 'surrealist'
narrative, a stylistic tour de force. At the same time it is his most
intimately autobiographical work, and one which epitomises the
kind of writer Garshin is, drawing upon his own experience to the
uttermost, and with meticulous precision and honesty. The anony-
mous hero, obsessed by the belief that Universal Evil is concentrated
in the red poppies in the garden of the asylum, sees his mission as 'to
deliver the world from evil', and we witness the illusory fight
between man and flower. Though told in the third person, this story
has the intensity of a confessional statement, and the hero's insane
quest acquires the validity of a record of heroic martyrdom. This
work is more than the 'perfect study of madness' that Havelock Ellis
found it to be. It is rich in mythic undertones – Classical, Christian,
Zoroastrian – and in it 'the madness of the brave' is presented
complete with its Nietzschean attributes. It is a heightened poetic
statement of the human condition as such, portraying man's instinc-
tive striving to go beyond the confines of his existence into the realm
of the spirit and eternity.

The Red Flower achieves its power by concentration, artistic and
mythical density, an escalatory dynamic and the author's firm control of his 'fantastic' narrative. It is structured on a series of crucial
episodes and circles of action, confined to the hospital and its
grounds. But symbolic treatment opens out the literal setting to far
wider dimensions. The Patient's forcible bathing in the opening
section, for example, is a parody of baptism by total immersion, of a
purification process, an initiation rite, ordeal by torture, preparing
him, like a medieval saint, for an as yet uncomprehended mission.
The world of the hospital, in the fourth section, expanded to fantastic
dimensions in the Patient's mind, 'inhabited by people of all times
and all lands . . . the living and the dead . . .', becomes the world

poised expectantly on the eve of liberation, as on the eve of the Day of Judgement; the Patient may now embark on a metaphysical confrontation. Walking in the hospital garden, he experiences an ecstatic vision of mankind's liberation and of cosmic rebirth. 'Soon, soon the iron bars would fall asunder, all those now incarcerated would rush to the ends of the earth, and all the world would shudder, cast off its threadbare covering, and show itself in a marvellous new beauty.'

There is a deep rhythmic patterning in terms of the alternation of night and day, moments of deathlike calm, lucidity and exhaustion interspersed between vital phases of hectic daytime activity. This nocturnal:diurnal pattern is reversed as the Patient's obsession escalates and his historic task crystallises in his consciousness, and the action moves wholly into his inner world: all three vital, 'spectral' battles with Ahriman, the Lord of Darkness, occur at night, while the world is asleep, unaware that it is in mortal danger. Throughout, there is a constant interaction and transformation of energies, as posited in the chemical allegory enunciated in the Patient's confrontation with the doctor in section three.

The Patient creates a world imbued with his own intensity. He comes to see himself, in solipsist fashion, as the new Redeemer, 'the first warrier of mankind', disguised under a variety of inverted and unheroic guises and attributes. His attire – dressing-gown (*khalat*) standing for negligence and sloth, and cap (*kolpak*) associating with passivity and sleep, as in 'night-cap' and 'fool's-cap' – camouflages his messianic quest.

An important element in the story's imagery is the colour symbolism, part of the Light/Darkness polarisation. White, clarity, visibility and light (moon and stars) are the forces of Good, respite and hope; red, black, obscurity, concealment and darkness are associated with Evil. The bright poppy half-hidden from sight, the black iron bars on the Patient's window blocking the way to liberty, the dark overgrown corner where nobody ever goes and where the last poppy stands, with its 'dusky' head – these represent the hostile world of darkness. The hero associates with the moonlight that penetrates into the hospital and enters his soul, with the stars that understand and sympathise with him.

Notable in the colour symbolism is the pervasive and ambivalent use of red: the ominous, vivid red of the poppy and the paler, neutral red of the red cross on the Patient's cap. The beautiful dahlia, the 'Palladium' of the microcosm, is dappled with red: contamination has already set in. Indeed, contamination, interpenetration and immanence are vital motifs in the story. In death, the Patient – he dies not a victor, but an undefeated hero – is integrally united with his enemy, and the fact that in this union of opposites the poppy has retained its redness is a typically laconic, pregnant Garshinian device, comparable to the epithet 'loaded' at the end of *A Night*, which signals that Aleksey Petrovich has not committed suicide.

The Signal, depicting two railwaymen in a remote part of Russia, is Garshin's most consistently misunderstood work. On one level, this is a parable whose hero is the simple, timid and god-fearing Semyon Ivanov, with the vigorous, irascible Vasily Spiridov as the anti-hero, determined to stand up for his rights. When he fails to achieve redress for the wrong done to him, Vasily resolves to avenge himself on life by tearing up a rail: causing a derailment is his anarchic response to the denial of justice. Semyon seeks to avert disaster, but does not know how to – he has not got a red signalling flag with him. He then hits on the bizarre idea of making one by gashing his arm, soaking his handkerchief in his blood and tying it to a stick, and waves it at the oncoming train. As Semyon collapses from loss of blood, Vasily appears from nowhere, takes over the makeshift red flag, and the train halts just in time. Vasily confesses his sinful intent and surrenders to the judgement of the bewildered passengers: his conversion was achieved by the spontaneous heroism of the meek and simple Semyon.

This is how the story has been generally interpreted. But such a Tolstoyan reading leaves out of account a number of linguistic and semiotic pointers to the deeper levels of the text, where Vasily is the main hero, and Semyon merely his foil. The inner dynamic of the story emanates from Vasily, the dark intruder into Semyon's serene and uncomplicated world. Vasily is a strong man, exuding energy and self-reliance. With tough-minded political perceptiveness he identifies the class enemy who unlawfully pockets a proportion of the railwaymen's pay. Semyon is subtly but insistently discredited, primarily by the tone of the language employed to describe him and his attitudes, which hovers between the simple, the mock-naïve and the ironic. The account of his war service, for example, makes him appear somewhat ridiculous: as a batman he carried tea and a meal to his officer, under fire and terrified, three times a day, finishing the war 'unharmed, but with pains in his arms and legs.' Vasily uses an official inspection as occasion for lodging a complaint, for which he is made to suffer, while Semyon, with mindless docility, polishes his brass badge and reports 'in soldierly fashion. All was found to be in good order.' Semyon's vision is blinkered and philistine. He is clever enough to set up a tiny business in willow pipes; his ambitions are redolent of *poshlost'*, a leading idea in Garshin – the word is applied to someone lacking a spiritual or moral dimension. Semyon's notion of *podvig* (great or heroic deed) is shown as foolish and ultimately unnecessary. This is underscored semiotically by the almost teasing description of how he creates his emblem of *podvig*; it becomes his 'red flag' and, as he falls, a 'red banner', a trivialisation of the militant symbol of insurrection and the *vexillum Christi*. When Vasily takes it over, this lofty symbol is demythologised and seen by the passengers for what it is – 'a bloody rag on a stick'. Here we have a striking instance of Viktor Shklovsky's 'baring of the device'.

Garshin thus offers two models of philanthropy and asks the reader to choose, tilting the balance towards Vasily's. This subversive attack on Tolstoyanism is retrospectively reinforced by the fact that the components of Semyon's emblem – a white cloth, a stick and human blood – were previously attached to Vasily as he sets out for Moscow to seek redress, stick in hand and his cheek bandaged with a piece of white cloth. He is bleeding from an injury inflicted by a representative of the power structure, which he now takes on single-handed, and not from a wound self-inflicted in a moment of quandary. Later, when Semyon dramatically displays his heroic emblem, we are treated to its banalisation in a fake celebration of *podvig*. Garshin's treatment of Semyon is another instance of 'stripping away the covers', reminiscent of his use of this device in *An Encounter*. Garshin has also taken the theme of personal and social liberation a stage further towards its maturer portrayal in a real-life context; he has advanced from the poetical, Lermontovian allegory of lonely rebellion in *Attalea princeps* and from the ecstatic, hallucinatory fight with evil in *The Red Flower*, and has created, in Vasily, an early model of the positive proletarian hero. *The Signal* is a structural *tour de force*, in which Garshin has refined his own brand of cryptography. In the guise of a Tolstoyan tale he has produced a subtle critique of a prestigious social philosophy that he found both misguided and harmful.

The last attempt to render Garshin's work in English of comparable scope to the present volume was made in 1912: R. Smith's translations under the title *'The Signal' and other stories* included *Nadezhda Nikolayevna* but not *Artists* or *The Legend of Haggai the Proud*; the latter would now seem to be translated into English for the first time. *The Scarlet Flower*, eleven stories translated by Bernard Isaacs, was published in Moscow in 1959; it was reissued as *Stories*, with a preface by Alla Latynina, by Progress Publishers, Moscow, in 1982.

One may point to unsureness of touch or narrative immaturity here, lapses into sentimentality or near-hysteria there, but in surveying Garshin's fiction one is struck by the fact that every one of his stories makes its own impact on the reader. Each very decidedly has something to say, each reads like a new departure. Half a dozen of his stories indisputably touch greatness. A hundred years after his death, it is time Garshin found a wider audience.

Peter Henry

Four Days

I remember we were running through a wood, bullets were whizzing past and tearing branches off the trees, we were forcing our way through hawthorn bushes. The firing was becoming heavier. There seemed to be something red flickering along the edge of the forest. Suddenly Sidorov, a young soldier in A Company ('How did he get into our line?' flitted through my mind), squatted on the ground, looking at me speechlessly with big, frightened eyes. Blood was running from his mouth. Yes, I remember that well. I also remember, in the thick bushes just by the forest's edge, seeing – *him*. He was a huge fat Turk, yet I ran straight at him, weak and skinny as I am. Something banged, something flew past me, it seemed enormous; a ringing started in my ears. 'That was him shooting me,' I thought. But with a scream of terror he pressed back against a thick hawthorn bush. He could have gone round that bush, but terrified and uncomprehending, he crawled into its thorny branches. I struck out and knocked his rifle out of his hand, then struck again and rammed my bayonet into something. There was a sound somewhere between a growl and a moan. I ran on. Our men were cheering, falling and firing. I remember firing several shots too when I got out of the wood into a clearing. Suddenly the cheering became louder and we immediately all moved forward. I mean *we* didn't, our unit did, because I stayed behind. I thought that was odd. What was even odder was that everything suddenly disappeared; all the shouting and the firing stopped. I couldn't hear anything and all I could see was something blue; it must have been the sky. Then that too disappeared.

Never have I been in such a strange situation. I must be lying on my stomach and can see nothing ahead of me but a tiny patch of ground. A few blades of grass; an ant crawling down one of them; some stalks of dead grass left over from last year – that's my entire world. And I see it with only one eye, because the other is pressed shut by something hard, probably a branch, with my head resting on it. I'm horribly uncomfortable, I want to move and have no idea why I can't. So time passes. I can hear the chirp of grasshoppers, the

buzzing of a bee. That's all. At last, with an effort, I free my right
hand from underneath me and, pressing both hands against the
ground, try to get up on my knees.

Something sharp and swift as a lightning bolt shoots right through
me, from my knees to my chest and into my head; I slump down once
more. Again darkness, again nothing at all.

I'm awake. Why do I see stars shining so brightly in the blue-black
Bulgarian sky? How can I not be in my tent? Why did I crawl out of
it? I move and there's an agonising pain in my legs.

That's right, I've been wounded in battle. Is it serious or not? I feel
for my legs where they hurt. Both legs are caked with dried blood. I
touch them and they hurt even more. It's like tooth-ache: a persistent, soul-wrenching pain. There's a ringing in my ears, my head
feels heavy. Dimly I realise that I've been hit in both legs. Whatever
happened? Why haven't they picked me up? Surely the Turks haven't
beaten us? I begin recalling what happened to me, at first vaguely,
then more clearly, and come to the conclusion that we haven't lost
the battle at all. Because I fell (though I actually don't remember this,
but I do remember everyone running forward and I couldn't and all I
was left with was something blue before my eyes) – I fell in the
clearing on the brow of the hill. Our little battalion commander had
pointed out this clearing to us. 'Make for there, lads!' he'd shouted in
his ringing voice. And we made it, so we can't have been beaten . . .
But why haven't they picked me up? I mean, it's quite open here in
the clearing; you can see everything. Surely I'm not the only one
lying here. There was so much shooting. I must turn my head and
take a look. It's easier to do that now, because when I came round last
time and saw the blade of grass and the ant crawling down it, when I
tried to get up I fell in a different position, on my back. That's why I
can see those stars.

I haul myself into a sitting position. It's a hard thing to do with
both legs smashed. I all but give up several times; at last, with tears of
pain in my eyes, I'm sitting up.

Above me, a scrap of blue-black sky with a big star and a few small
ones shining in it, and there's something dark and tall round it.
Bushes. I'm lying in the bushes: that's why they haven't found me!

I can feel the roots of my hair crawling.

But however could I have got into the bushes, when I was hit in the
clearing? I must have crawled here after I was wounded, and out of

my mind with pain. The odd thing is that now I can't move at all, yet I managed to drag myself all the way to these bushes. Perhaps then I'd only been hit once, and a second bullet got me here.

Faint pink spots are swimming before my eyes. The big star has faded, and some of the smaller ones have vanished. Here's the moon rising. How I wish I were at home now! . . .

Strange sounds are coming to my ears . . . like somebody moaning. Yes, it is moaning. Is there somebody lying near me, also forgotten and hit in both legs, or perhaps with a bullet in the stomach? The moans are so close, yet there doesn't seem to be anyone near me . . . My God – it was me – me! Low, plaintive moans; does it really hurt that much? It must do. Only I can't really feel this pain, because my head is foggy and heavy as lead. Best to lie back again and get some sleep, sleep, sleep . . . Would I ever wake up, though? Who cares.

Just as I'm about to lie down again, a broad pale strip of moonlight clearly lights up the spot where I'm lying and I can see something large and dark four or five paces away. I can see specks of moonlight glittering on it here and there. Buttons or cartridges. It's a corpse, or a wounded man.

Who cares, I'm going to lie down . . .

No, it can't be true! Our men can't have withdrawn. They're here, they've driven back the Turks and they're holding this position. Then why can't I hear talking or crackling camp-fires? I expect I'm too weak to hear anything. They must be here.

'Help! Help!'

Weird, mad, hoarse screams burst from my chest, but there's no answer. They echo loudly in the night air. All else is silence. Only the grasshoppers chirp on tirelessly. The moon's round face looks at me mournfully.

If he's wounded, wouldn't a shout like that have brought him round? It's a corpse. One of ours, or a Turk? Oh God! As if it matters. And sleep descends onto my inflamed eyes.

I'm lying with my eyes closed, though I've been awake for some time. I don't want to open my eyes, because I can feel the sunlight on my closed lids: it will burn them if I open them. Better not to move . . . Yesterday (I *think* it was yesterday) I was hit, a day has passed, more days will pass, I shall die. Who cares. Better not to move. Keep

my body still. If only I could stop my brain working, too! But I just
can't hold it back. Thoughts and memories jostle in my head. Still, it
won't last long, it'll all be over soon. There'll be just a few lines in the
papers about our casualties being insignificant: 'Wounded – so many;
killed in action – Ivanov, Volunteer Private.' No, they won't even
print my name; they'll just say: 'Killed in action – one.' One private,
like that wretched little dog . . .

The whole scene flashes vividly into my mind. It happened long
ago; but then everything, my whole life, that *other* life, before I came
to be lying here with shattered legs, was so long ago . . . I was
walking along a street, and a bunch of people pulled me up short. The
crowd was just standing there and looking silently at a little white
bloodstained thing that was whining pitifully. It was a nice little dog;
it had been run over by a horse-drawn tram. It lay dying, as I am
now. A caretaker pushed through the crowd, grabbed the little dog
by the scruff of its neck and carried it away. The crowd dispersed.

Will somebody carry me away? No, I'll just lie here and die. And
yet, how good life is! . . . That day when the little dog was run over
I'd been happy. I'd been quite tipsy, and with good reason, too.
Don't torment me, memories, leave me alone! The happiness that
was, the torments that are . . . If only there were just physical
torture, not the memories that torment me, force me to draw
comparisons. Heartache, heartache! You're worse than wounds.

But it's really getting hot. The sun is burning me. I open my eyes –
the same bushes, the same sky, only now in the light of day. And
there's my neighbour. Yes, it is a Turk, a corpse. How huge he is! I
recognise him, it's the same one . . .

Before me lies the man I've killed. Why did I kill him?

There he lies, dead and bloodstained. Why did fate drive him here?
Who is he? Perhaps he has an old mother, the same as I have. She will
be sitting many an evening by the door of her wretched hovel looking
towards the distant north, waiting for her beloved son, her worker
and breadwinner, to come home . . .

And me? Yes, me too . . . I'd gladly change places with him. He's
lucky: he can hear nothing, feel no pain from his wounds, no deathly
heartache, no thirst . . . The bayonet went straight into his heart . . .
There's a big black hole in his tunic, with blood all round it. *I did
that.*

I didn't mean to do it. I meant no harm to anyone when I went to
fight. The idea that I too would kill people somehow escaped me. I

only saw *myself* as exposing *my* breast to the bullets. And I went and did that.

And now what? Idiot, idiot! And this poor *fellah* (he's in Egyptian uniform) – he's even less to blame. Until they were packed into a ship like herrings in a barrel and taken to Constantinople he'd never heard of Russia or Bulgaria. He was ordered to go and he went. If he hadn't, they'd probably have given him a flogging and, who knows, some Pasha might have put a bullet into him. He made the long, hard march from Istambul to Rustchuk. We attacked and he tried to defend himself. But when he saw what terrible men we were, not in the least afraid of his patented English Peabody-Martini rifle, pushing on and on regardless, he was terrified. Just as he was going to run for it, some little chap whom he could have killed with one blow of his black fist popped up and stuck a bayonet into his heart.

How was he to blame?

And even though I've killed him, how am I to blame? Why am I to blame? Why am I tormented by this thirst? Thirst! People don't know the meaning of the word! Even when we were marching through Rumania, doing fifty versts a day in sweltering forty-degree heat, even then I never felt what I'm feeling now. Oh, if only somebody would come!

My God – there must be some water in that huge flask of his! But how do I get to it? What would it cost me! All the same, I must get to it.

I start crawling. My legs drag, my weakened arms can hardly move my inert body. The corpse is fifteen feet away, but to me that's more – not more, but worse – than dozens of versts. Anyway, I must keep on crawling. My throat is burning, searing me like fire. But I'll die sooner without water. But still, maybe . . .

And I keep on crawling. My feet catch on the ground and every movement is unbearable pain. I scream, scream and howl, but keep on crawling. At last I'm there. Here's his flask . . . there *is* water in it – lots of it! It feels over half full. Oh, that water will last me a long time – till I'm dead!

You, my victim, you are saving me! . . . Leaning on one elbow I start unstrapping the flask, and suddenly I lose balance and fall, my face on my saviour's chest. He is already beginning to give off the heavy stench of death.

I've drunk my fill. The water is tepid but not foul, and there's lots of it as well. I'll live for a few more days. I remember that in *The Physiology of Everyday Life* it says that a man can survive without food for over a week as long as he has water. Oh yes, and there was a story about a suicide by starvation. He lived for a very long time, because he took water.

And now what? What if I do live another five or six days? Our men have retreated, the Bulgarians have scattered. There's no road nearby. So I'll die just the same. All I've done is ensure myself a week of death-agony instead of three days. Better to end it all? My neighbour's rifle is lying beside him, a fine English product. I only have to stretch out my hand – and in an instant it'll all be over. His cartridges are here in a heap. He didn't have time to fire them.

Well, should I end it all, or should I wait? For what? Rescue? Death? Wait for the Turks to come along and strip the skin off my wounded legs? Better do the thing myself . . .

No, I mustn't give up; I'll fight to the last, until my strength is gone. I mean, if they find me I'm saved. Perhaps my bones aren't broken and they'll patch me up. I'll see the homeland again, my mother, Masha . . .

Please God, may they never know the whole truth! Let them think that I was killed outright. How could they stand knowing that I suffered for two, three or four days!

My head is spinning; that journey to my neighbour has worn me out completely. And there's that horrible stench. He's gone quite black – what will he be like tomorrow or the day after? I'm only lying here because I haven't the strength to drag myself away. I'll rest for a while and then I'll crawl back to where I was before; and besides, the wind's coming from that direction and it will carry the stink away from me.

I'm lying here totally exhausted. The sun is burning my face and hands. I've nothing to cover myself with. The sooner night comes the better; I think it'll be the second.

My thoughts get confused and I pass out.

I must have slept for a long time, because when I woke up it was night. Nothing has changed: my wounds are hurting, my neighbour's still there, huge and motionless as ever.

I can't stop thinking about him. Did I really give up everything that's sweet and dear to me, everything I love, and did I do that thousand-verst march, go hungry, suffer cold and intense heat, did I end up lying here in this torment – just so that this poor wretch should stop living? How have I furthered our cause in any way, except by committing this murder?

Murder, murderer . . . Who is? I am!

When I got it into my head to sign up, my mother and Masha didn't try to stop me, though they wept for me. Blinded by an idea, I didn't see their tears. I didn't realise – now I do – what I was doing to my nearest and dearest.

But why look back? What's done can't be undone.

It's odd the way some of my acquaintances reacted to my decision. 'What a crackpot! Doesn't know what he's in for!' How could they talk like that? How does that fit in with their ideas of heroism, patriotism and that sort of thing? Because to them I embodied all those noble virtues. And yet – I'm a 'crackpot'.

So I go to Kishinyov; I'm loaded up with a pack and all sorts of equipment. Off I went with thousands of others, among whom you might have found only a few who were going from choice, like me. The others would have stayed at home, if they had been allowed to. Still, there they march, like us few 'thinking ones', they march thousands of versts and fight every bit as well as us, better even. They do what they've got to do, even though they'd drop it all and go back if only they were allowed to.

A keen morning breeze has blown up. The bushes stir and a sleepy bird flies off. The stars are fading. The dark-blue sky has turned grey and is specked with soft, feathery clouds; grey twilight is lifting from the earth. So this is the third day of – what shall I call it? – life? or death-agony?

The third . . . How many more left? Not many, that's for sure . . . I feel very faint and I doubt I can move away from this corpse. Soon we'll be quits and won't bother each other any more.

I must have a good drink. I'll drink three times a day: morning, noon and evening.

The sun is up. Its enormous disc, criss-crossed and broken up by the black branches of the bushes, is blood-red. Looks like it's going to be hot today. My neighbour – what's it going to do to you? You're ghastly enough as it is.

Yes, he was ghastly to look at. His hair had begun to fall out. His skin, dark to begin with, had gone pale and yellowish; his face had swollen, drawing the skin so tight that it had burst behind the ear. Maggots were squirming around there. His feet, wedged into his boots, had swollen and enormous bubbles oozed out between the hooks. His whole body was bloated enormously. What will the sun do to him today?

It's unbearable lying so close to him. I've got to crawl away from him, no matter what. I can still lift my hand, open the flask and take a drink; but can I drag my heavy, inert body away? Yet move away I must, a tiny bit at a time, a couple of feet an hour.

I spend the whole morning in this manoeuvre. The pain is intense, but I don't care about that now. I can't remember, or even imagine, how it feels to be well. I seem to have got used to pain. This morning I've managed to crawl those fifteen feet or so back to where I was before. But I haven't enjoyed the fresh air for long – as if it could be fresh nine or ten feet from a putrefying corpse. The wind changes and wafts towards me a stink so strong that it makes me want to vomit. My empty stomach goes into sharp, painful spasms; all my insides heave. And the stinking, tainted air washes over me.

I give up completely and burst into tears . . .

I lie there semi-conscious, shattered and stupefied. Suddenly – is it my confused imagination playing tricks? I don't think it is. Yes, it's the sound of human voices. The clatter of horses' hooves and human voices. I almost call out, but check myself. What if they're Turks? What then? Other, more ghastly tortures would be added to those I'm already suffering – just reading about them in the papers makes your hair stand on end. They'd skin me alive, roast my wounded legs . . . I'd be lucky if that were all – they're highly inventive. What would be better – to end my days in their hands, or die here? But what if they're Russians? Oh, you damned bushes! Why did you have to grow in such a thick wall around me? I can't see anything through them; only in one place the branches form a sort of window that looks out on a hollow in the distance. I think I can see the little stream that we drank from before the battle. Yes, there's the huge sandstone slab placed across the stream like a bridge. They'll probably ride over it. The voices are dying away. I can't make out the language they're speaking: even my hearing is going. Oh Lord! Supposing they're Russians . . . I'll shout to them; they'll hear me, even from the stream. That'll be better than to risk falling into the clutches of those Bashi-bazouks. But why are they taking so long? The suspense is wearing me out; I don't even notice the smell of the corpse, though it's as strong as ever.

And suddenly some Cossacks come into view on the crossing of the stream. Blue uniforms, red stripes down their trousers, lances. Half a squadron of them. In the lead, a black-bearded officer on a superb mount. The moment his unit has crossed the stream, he turns right round in his saddle and shouts:

'At the trot, for-ward!'

'Stop, stop, for God's sake! Help, lads, help!' I shout; but the clatter of the sturdy horses, the rattle of sabres and the Cossacks' noisy talk drown my hoarse shouts – they can't hear me!

Damnation! I slump down to the ground exhausted and sob. I've knocked the flask over and out pours the water, my life, my salvation, my deferment of death. By the time I notice it there's no more than half a glass left, the rest has soaked away into the dry, thirsty earth.

How am I to recapture the numbed feeling that came over me after that horrible event? I lay motionless, my eyes half-shut. The wind kept changing, sometimes blowing pure, fresh air my way, sometimes enveloping me in the stench. That day my neighbour became so hideous as to beggar description. Once when I opened my eyes to look at him, I was appalled. His face was gone. It had slid off the bones. His frightful bony smile, his eternal smile, struck me as more revolting, more awful than ever, though I've often held skulls in my hands and even prepared whole heads in anatomy class. This skeleton in uniform with its shiny buttons made me shudder. 'This is war,' I thought, 'this is how it looks.'

And the sun goes on searing and scorching me. My arms and face were burned badly some while back. I drank what water was left. I was so tortured by thirst that I swallowed it all in one gulp, though I'd only meant to take a sip. Oh, why didn't I shout to the Cossacks when they were so close to me? Even if they'd been Turks, it would have been better than this. They would just have tortured me for an hour or two, but now I have no idea how much longer I've got to lie here suffering. Oh mother, my dear mother! You'll tear out your grey hair, you'll beat your head against a wall, you'll curse the day you bore me, you'll curse the entire world for inventing war to make people suffer!

But you and Masha will probably never hear of my torment.

Farewell, mother, farewell, my sweetheart, my love! Oh, it's so hard, so bitter! I feel something clutch at my heart . . .

That little white dog again! The caretaker showed no pity for it, knocked its head against a wall and threw it into a pit where they threw rubbish and poured slops. It was still alive. And it suffered for a whole day. I am worse off than it was, because my suffering has gone on for three whole days. Tomorrow is the fourth day, and then the fifth, and the sixth . . . Death, where are you? Come, come, take me!

But death doesn't come and doesn't take me. And I lie under this terrible sun, without a drop of water to ease my burning throat, and the corpse is infecting me. It has disintegrated completely. Myriads of maggots are dropping from it. How they squirm! When they've eaten him up and only his bones and uniform are left, then it'll be my turn. And I'll end up the same way.

The day passes, then the night. Nothing changes. Morning comes. Nothing changes. Another day passes . . .

The bushes stir and rustle, like people talking softly. 'You'll die, die, die!' they whisper. 'You can't see, can't see, can't see!' reply the bushes on the other side.

'You can't see them here!' a loud voice says nearby.

I give a start and come to instantly. The kindly blue eyes of Yakovlev, our lance-corporal, are looking at me through the bushes.

'Shovels!' he shouts. 'There's two more here, one of ours and one of theirs!'

'Not shovels, don't bury me, I'm alive!' I want to shout, but only a faint groan escapes from my parched lips.

'Good God! He can't be alive! It's Barin Ivanov! Over here, lads, our Barin's alive! Someone get the surgeon!'

Half a minute later they are pouring water and vodka and something else into my mouth. Then everything fades.

The stretcher moves, rocking rhythmically. The rhythmic movement lulls me to sleep. I wake up and doze off again. My wounds are dressed and they don't hurt; a feeling of inexpressible well-being flows through my entire body . . .

'Ha–alt! Lower stretcher! Orderlies, fourth detail, one step forward! Hands on stretcher! Lift!'

Our medical officer, Pyotr Ivanych, is giving the orders. He's a tall, thin, very kindly man. He's so tall that when I turn my eyes his way I can still see his head, his long, sparse beard and his shoulders, although my stretcher is on the shoulders of four strapping soldiers.

'Pyotr Ivanych!' I whisper.

'What is it, old fellow?'

Pyotr Ivanych leans over me.

'What did the surgeon say to you, Pyotr Ivanych? Will I die soon?'

'Come now, Ivanov, enough of that! You're not going to die. All your bones are intact. You're really a lucky chap! Bones fine, arteries fine. But however did you manage to survive for three-and-a-half days? What did you have to eat?'

'Nothing.'

'And drink?'

'I took the Turk's flask. Pyotr Ivanych, I can't talk now. Later.'

'That's quite all right, old fellow, you get some sleep.'

Sleep again, oblivion . . .

I've come round in the divisional hospital. Doctors and nurses are standing over me, and among them I can see a familiar face, that of a famous St Petersburg professor, who is bending over my legs. His hands are covered in blood. He's doing something to my legs that doesn't take long, then he turns to me and says:

'Well, Somebody's on your side, young man! You'll pull through. We had to take off one leg, but that's nothing much. Can you talk?'

I can and I tell them everything that's written down here.

1877   *Translated by Peter Henry*

An Incident

How it happened that I have started to think, after not thinking at all for almost two years – that I'll never know. Certainly that gentleman couldn't have got me thinking this way. Because one encounters so many gentlemen of that sort that I am quite used to their sermonising by now.

Oh yes, almost every one of them – except the complete habitués or the very clever ones – invariably starts talking about quite unnecessary things, both from his point of view and mine. He'll start by asking what my name is and how old I am, and then, more often than not putting on a gloomy face, he'll get to inquiring if it is 'not somehow possible to take leave of such a life'. At first that sort of questioning tormented me, but I am used to it now. You can get used to a great deal.

But for the past two weeks, whenever I am not cheerful – that is, not drunk (for have I any hope of being cheerful unless I am drunk?) – and when I am quite alone, I start thinking. I'd rather not, but I have no choice: these oppressive thoughts will not leave me be. There is only one way to forget – to go where there are plenty of people getting drunk and rowdy. And then I start drinking and getting rowdy as well; the brain gets fuddled and you don't remember a thing . . . That makes it easier. Why has this not happened before, not since that day when I washed my hands of it all? For more than two years I have been living here, in this foul rom, spending my time in the same old way, frequenting places like the Eldorado and the Palais de Crystal, and all the time, although things have not been really cheerful, at least I never thought they were miserable. And now it has all changed, changed completely.

How tiresome and foolish it is! I shall never get myself out of it, no matter what; I shall never get myself out of it simply because I shall never want to. I got myself into this life and I know where I am going. In *The Dragonfly* (one of my gentlemen friends brings me a copy quite often, and he always does when there is something *piquant* to show me) – well, I saw an illustration in *The Dragonfly*, with a pretty little girl holding a doll in the centre and two rows of figures leading away from her. The row leading upwards from her was a little high-school girl or maybe a private boarder, then a demure young miss, a motherly woman and, finally, an old lady, such a venerable old dear, and the row leading downwards, in the opposite direction, was a young girl with a package from a shop, then me, me, and me again. The first was me as I am now; the second was me sweeping streets; and the third was an utterly repulsive, vile old hag. Only I won't let myself come to that. Another two or three years, if this life doesn't do for me sooner, then I'm off to the Yekaterinovka. That I can do; I won't be afraid.

That illustrator was a strange one, though! Why must it inevitably follow that a girl at a boarding-school or a high-school becomes a demure young maiden, a respected mother and grandmother? Then what about me? Praise be, even I can flaunt my French or German out on the Nevsky! And I don't think I've forgotten how to draw flowers, and I can remember 'Calypso ne pouvait se consoler du depárt d'Ulysse.' And I can remember my Pushkin and my Lermontov and everything, everything . . . the examinations, and that fateful, terrible day when I was left alone, dimwit, complete dimwit that I was, with my great-hearted relatives who made such a fuss over 'taking in the orphan', and the ardent, trite declarations of that popinjay, and how stupidly delighted I was, and all the lies and filth of that 'polite society' out of which I fell to this place where I now numb myself with vodka. Yes, I have even taken to vodka. '*Horreur!*' as *cousine* Olga Nikolayevna would cry.

And indeed, isn't *horreur* just the word for it? But am I really to blame for it all? Now supposing – when I was a chit of seventeen, cooped up inside those four walls since the age of eight and seeing only other chits like myself and their *mamans* – supposing I had chanced not on someone like him, that charming friend of mine, with his hair dressed *à la Capoule*, but someone else, a good man . . . Then, like as not, things would have turned out differently . . .

Foolish thought! What good people are there? Have I ever seen any, before or after my catastrophe? Why should I think there are good people, when out of the dozens of people I know, there isn't a single one I could bring myself not to hate? And can I believe that there are any, when I receive here husbands with young wives, and children (all but children – fourteen and fifteen years old) from 'good families', and old men, bald men, paralytics and dotards?

And when all is said and done, what can I do but hate and despise, though I myself am a despised and despicable creature, when I see amongst them ones like that German whippersnapper with a monogram tattooed on his arm just above the elbow? He explained to me it was his fiancée's name. *'Jetzt aber bist du, meine Liebe, allerliebstes Liebchen,'* he said, gazing at me with oily little eyes, and to cap it all he quoted Heine at me. And he even proudly explained to me that Heine was a great German poet, that the Germans have greater poets still – Goethe and Schiller – and that only the great, gifted German people could bring forth such poets.

Didn't I just want to dig my nails into his foul, slick, blond little mug! But instead, I tossed off the glass of port he treated me to and forgot everything.

Why should I be thinking about my future, when I know well enough what it will be? Why should I be thinking about my past, either, when there is nothing there to put in the place of my present life? Oh yes, that is true. If this very day I were offered the chance to go back to refined society, to those people with their refined hair-partings, *chignons* and turns of phrase, I would not go back. I would stay and die at my post.

Oh yes, even I have a post! I too am necessary, am essential. Not long ago a young lad came to me, a very talkative sort he was, and he quoted an entire page off by heart from some book or other. 'That's our philosopher, our Russian philosopher,' he said. This philosopher was saying something very obscure and very flattering to the likes of me, something to the effect that we are 'the safety-valves of social passions'. The words were disgusting, and the philosopher was probably a foul man, but worst of all was that little shaver going on about those 'safety-valves'.

And still, that very same thought came into my head not long ago. I was in court, getting fined fifteen rubles for indecent conduct in a public place.

And at the very moment sentence was being passed, with everyone in the place standing, this is what I thought: 'Exactly why are all these fine folk giving me such despising looks? What if I am in a sordid, repulsive line of business, performing the most despicable duty? It is a duty, all the same! That magistrate is performing a duty too. And I think that we both . . .'

I think nothing, all I feel is that I am drinking, that I don't remember a thing, that I'm getting fuddled. Everything is jumbled in my head – that foul hall where I shall dance shamelessly this evening, and the Lithuanian Castle, and this foul room where only a drinker could live. My temples are pounding, my ears are ringing, something is leaping and rushing about in my head, and I too am rushing away somewhere. I want to stop and take hold of something, if only a straw, but there isn't even a straw for me.

I am lying – there is! And not just a straw, perhaps something better. But I have sunk so low that I have no wish to stretch out my hand to grasp that support.

It happened at the end of August, I suppose. I remember it was such a glorious autumn evening. I was walking in the Summer Gardens when I met this 'support'. There was nothing at all special about the man, except perhaps that he was an amiable chatterbox. He told me about practically everything he did and everyone he knew. He was twenty-five years old; his name was Ivan Ivanovich. He was neither unattractive nor good-looking. He chatted to me as if I were some acquaintance of his, even told me stories about his superior and explained who was in favour in his department at the moment.

He went away and I forgot about him. A month later, though, he showed up. And he showed up sombre, sorrowful and gaunt. When he entered the room, his unfamiliar, louring face even frightened me a little.

'Do you remember me?'

At that instant I did remember him, and told him so.

He blushed.

'I just thought you might not, because so many . . .'

The conversation stopped short. We were sitting on the sofa, me in one corner and him in the other, looking as if he were paying the first social call of his life, bolt upright, even holding his top hat in his hands. We sat for quite some time; at last, he got to his feet and bowed.

'I'll be saying goodbye, then, Nadezhda Nikolayevna,' he declared with a sigh.

'How did you find out my name?' I cried, flaring up. 'My working name is not Nadezhda Nikolayevna: it's Yevgeniya.'

I shouted at Ivan Ivanovich so crossly that he was actually frightened.

'But I didn't mean any harm by it, Nadezhda Nikolayevna. I won't . . . not a single soul . . . But Pyotr Vasilyevich, the police inspector, is an acquaintance of mine, and he told me everything about you there is to tell. I wanted to call you Yevgeniya, but my tongue wouldn't obey me, and I said your real name.'

'Just tell me why you've come here.'

He was silent, and gazed sadly into my eyes.

'What for?' I went on, getting heated. 'What possible interest can you have in me? No, you'd better not come here: I will not strike up an acquaintance with you, because I have no acquaintances. I know why you came here! Your curiosity was roused by that policeman's story. You thought, "Now here's a rarity – an educated girl come to such a life . . ." You've got a mind to save me? Get away from me – there's nothing I need! Better leave me to breathe my last alone rather than . . .'

Then I glanced at his face, and stopped. I saw that I was belabouring him with every word. He said nothing, but the very look of him forced me into silence.

'Goodbye, Nadezhda Nikolayevna,' he said. 'I am very sorry I distressed you. And myself too. Goodbye.'

He stretched out his hand to me (I could not but give him mine) and left with slow steps. I heard him descending the stairway and watched through the window as he crossed the courtyard, his head bent low, with a slow, unsteady stride. At the gate he looked back, glanced up at my windows, and vanished.

And that, now, is the man who could be my 'support'. I need only drop a hint, and I could be a legally wedded wife. The wedded wife of a poor but noble man, and I could even become a poor but noble mother, should the Lord, in his wrath, still see fit to send me a child.

II

Today Yevsey Yevseich said to me, 'Listen to what this old man's going to tell you, Ivan Ivanych. The way you've started acting isn't sensible, my dear sir. You mind our superiors don't get wind of it.'

He said a lot more (hinting around the real point at issue) about work and respect for rank, about our General, about me, and finally started getting to my misfortune. We were sitting in a tavern where

Nadezhda Nikolayevna often came with her friends.

Yevsey Yevseich had long ago perceived everything and long since dragged many of the details out of me. I could not keep a check on my stupid tongue, blabbed it all out and on top of that nearly started bawling.

Yevsey Yevseich grew angry.

'Oh, you womanbody – you sentimental womanbody! A young man, a good clerk, and what a song and dance he's making over a piece of trash! Spit on her! What possible concern of yours can she be? Now if it was some decent little lass, but this, if you don't mind my saying so . . .'

Yevsey Yevseich actually spat.

After this episode he frequently harked back to the subject of his distress (Yevsey Yevseich was sincerely distressed on my behalf), but was more careful with his language, because he had noticed that I took it badly. But he couldn't restrain himself for long, and, though at first he tried to talk neutrally about it, in the end he unfailingly concluded that I should rid myself of her, 'spit on her', and so on in that vein.

Strictly speaking, I quite agree with the point that he dins into me daily. How often have I too thought that I should rid myself of her, 'spit on her'? How often! And just as often, after thinking that, I've left the house and my feet have carried me to that street . . . And here she comes, with rouged cheeks and blackened eyebrows, in a velvet jacket and a modish little sealskin hat – making straight for me; and I cross to the other side, so that she won't notice I am on her trail. She reaches the corner and turns back, boldly and proudly eyeing the passers-by and sometimes speaking to them. I follow her on the other side of the street, trying not to lose sight of her, and hopelessly watch her tiny form in the distance, until some . . . swine comes up to her and addresses her. She answers him, she turns and goes off with him . . . And I follow. If the path were studded with sharp nails it could not pain me more. And I walk on, hearing nothing and seeing nothing save those two figures . . .

I don't look where I am going, I don't look around me, I walk on goggle-eyed, bumping into people, being reproached, cursed and jostled. Once I knocked a child over . . .

They turn right and then left, and go through the doorway – first her, then him; almost always some strange kind of civility prompts him to cede her the way. Then I go in too. Opposite the two windows that I know so well there is a barn with a hayloft that can be reached by a light iron ladder which ends in an unrailed platform. And I sit on that platform and look at the drawn white curtains . . .

Today again I was standing at my strange post, although it was pretty frosty out there. I was frightfully cold; my feet had gone dead under me, but still I stood there. Steam rose from my face; my whiskers and beard had frozen; my legs had started to stiffen. People passed through the courtyard, but they did not notice me and, conversing loudly, went on their way. Sounds carried from the street: a drunken song (it is a cheerful street!), a squabble, scrapers clattering where the caretakers were clearing the pavement. All these sounds filled my ears, but I paid them no more attention than I did the cold that pinched my face or the chill in my feet. All this – the sounds, my feet, the cold – seemed to be far, far away from me. My feet ached intensely, but something inside me ached more intensely still. I am not strong enough to go to her. Does she know that there exists a man who would count himself happy just to sit in the same room with her and, without even touching her hands, simply gaze into her eyes? A man who would cast himself into the flames if that would help her to get out of this hell, if only she wanted to? But she doesn't want to . . . And even now I don't know why she doesn't want to. I just cannot believe that she is rotten to the core; I cannot believe that because I know it is not so, because I know her, because I love her, I love her . . .

The waiter went up to Ivan Ivanych, who had put his forearms on the table and his face on his forearms and was shuddering fitfully, and poked at his shoulder.

'Mister Nikitin! Now this'll never do . . . All these folk here . . . It'll make the master angry . . . Mister Nikitin! You can't carry on like this here. Kindly get up!'

Ivan Ivanych raised his head and looked at the waiter. He was not at all drunk, which the waiter realised the moment he saw that sad face.

'It's nothing, Semyon. It's all right. You just bring me a half-carafe of your best.'

'And what'll you have with it?'

'With it? A glass! No, don't be stingy – not a half-carafe, a full carafe. Here – this'll cover it, and here's forty kopeks besides. In an hour's time, send me home in a cab. You know where I live, don't you?'

'That I do . . . Only what's all this, sir?'

He was obviously bemused; never in all his long years of service had he been faced with a case like this.

'No, wait. I'll manage on my own.'

Ivan Ivanych went into the vestibule, put on his coat, stepped outside, and turned into a shop with a squat window where there glinted, vivid in the gaslight, the multicoloured labels of bottles neatly and tastefully arranged on a bed of moss. A moment later he emerged with a bottle in each hand, went back to the rooms that he rented in Zuckerberg's furnished lodging-house, and locked the door behind him.

III

Again I've been in a stupor, and again I've awoken. Reeling every single day for three weeks! How can I ever bear it? Today my head aches, my bones ache, my whole body aches. Profound melancholy, tedium, aimless and agonising brooding. If only someone would come!

As though in answer to that thought, the bell rang in the hallway. 'Is Yevgeniya in?' 'She is, sir, come in,' the cook's voice replied. Erratic, hurried steps sounded in the corridor, the door was flung open, and in the doorway appeared Ivan Ivanych.

He bore no resemblance to the timid, sheepish man who had come two months previously. His hat askew, a colourful tie, a self-confident, insolent gaze . . . and on top of that a stagger in his step and a strong smell of wine.

Nadezhda Nikolayevna sprang to her feet.

'Well, hello!' he began. 'Thought I'd just drop in.'

He sat on a chair by the door without removing his hat, and sprawled back. She was silent; so was he. Had he not been drunk, she would have known what to say, but now she was at a loss. While she was thinking what to do, he started talking again.

'Mmm-yes! Just dropped in . . . Got evv-ry right!' he yelled in a sudden rage, and stretched himself to his full height.

His hat had fallen off, his tousled black hair had tumbled over his face, his eyes glittered. His whole figure expressed such rage that Nadezhda Nikolayevna was momentarily afraid.

She tried taking a gentle tone with him.

'Listen, Ivan Ivanych, I shall be very glad to see you another time, but go home just now. You've had a bit too much. Be a good fellow, my dear – go home. Come back when you're feeling well.'

'She's in a funk!' mumbled Ivan Ivanych, as if to himself, sitting down again. 'Now she's docile! But what are you chasing me away for?' he wailed, frantic again. 'What for? Why, you're the one who drove me to drink – I used to be a sober man. How do you lure me? Tell me that!'

He was weeping. The drunken tears choked him, streamed down his face and trickled into a mouth contorted with sobbing. He could scarcely speak.

'Any other woman would be only too happy to be quit of this hell. I'd work like a mule. You'd live a carefree, peaceful, honourable life. Tell me what I've done to deserve your hatred!'

Nadezhda Nikolayevna was silent.

'Why don't you talk?' he yelled. 'Speak – say anything you like, only say something. I'm drunk – it's true . . . I had to be drunk to come here. Do you know how afraid I am of you when I'm in my right mind? Why, you can twist me round your little finger. Tell me to steal and I'll steal. Tell me to kill and I'll kill. Do you know that? I'm sure you know. You're clever, you see everything. If you don't know . . . Nadya, my dearest, have pity on me!'

And he crawled across the floor on his knees before her. But she stood motionless by the wall, her head braced against it and her hands behind her back. Her gaze was fixed on some point in space. Did she see anything, did she hear anything? What did she feel at the sight of that man prostrate at her feet and begging for her love? Pity? Scorn? She wanted to pity him, but felt incapable of pity. He aroused only revulsion in her. And what other feeling could he have aroused in this pitiful condition – drunk, dirty, abjectly pleading?

He had been absent from work for several days now. He drank every day. Finding comfort in wine, he was less absorbed by his obsession; he sat at home and drank, mustering his strength to go to her and tell her *all*. What he was to tell her, he did not know. 'I'll tell her all. I'll bare my soul,' was the thought that kept flickering through his drunken head. At last he had plucked up courage, come to her, and begun to speak. Even in his inebriated haze he realized that what he was saying and doing rendered him anything but lovable, yet he carried on talking, feeling that with every word he was plunging deeper and deeper, drawing a noose tighter and tighter around his own neck.

His long, disjointed declaration continued. His words came more and more slowly, until at last his drunken, swollen eyelids closed and, his head flopping over the back of the chair, he fell asleep.

Nadezhda Nikolayevna continued to stand in the same position, aimlessly staring at the ceiling and drumming her fingers on the wallpaper.

'Do I pity him? No, I don't. What can I do for him? Marry him? Would I dare? And would that not be just another kind of sale? Oh Lord, no – it would be even worse!'

She did not know why it would be worse, but she felt it to be so.

'As things are, at least I'm open about it. Anyone can strike at me. The humiliations I bear! But if I . . . How would that make me better than I am? Would it not be just the same debauchery – only not straightforward? There he sits, drowsing, his head lolling back. His mouth open, his face pale as death. His clothes are dirty – he probably took a tumble somewhere. He is breathing so heavily . . . even wheezing now and then . . . Oh yes, this will pass and he'll be proper and respectable again. But that wouldn't be the whole story – I suspect that if I gave him power over me, this man would torture me with just the memory . . . And I wouldn't be able to endure that. No, I had best stay as I am . . . And anyway, I shan't stay as I am much longer.'

She threw a wrap over her shoulders and went out, slamming the door. The noise woke Ivan Ivanych; he looked round with senseless eyes and, finding the chair an uncomfortable place to sleep, staggered to the bed, collapsed on it and was soon dead asleep. He awoke late that evening, with a headache but sober, and seeing where he was, immediately took to his heels.

I left the house with no idea where I was going. The weather was foul; it was a dark, overcast day; sleet fell on my face and hands. It would have been far better to stay at home, but how could I stay there? He is wholly beyond help. What support can I offer him? Can I change my attitude towards him? All my soul, everything inside me is aflame. I don't know why I don't want to seize my chance to give up this terrible life and be free of this nightmare. Supposing I married him? A new life, new hopes . . . Could the pity that I do after all feel for him perhaps turn into love?

No! At this moment he is ready to lick my hand, but then . . . then he would trample me underfoot and say, 'You actually opposed my wishes, you despicable creature! You scorned me!'

Would he say that? I think he would.

I do have one means of salvation, of deliverance – an excellent means. I made up my mind about it long ago and I shall doubtless resort to it in the end, but I feel it isn't time yet. I am too young, I feel too much life in me. I want to live. I want to breathe, to feel, to hear, to see; I want to be able, if only once in a while, to look at the sky, the Neva.

I am on the embankment. Immense buildings on one side, and on the other the Neva, dark now. Soon the ice will be breaking, and the river will be sky-blue. The park on the opposite bank will turn green. The islands will be covered with green too. A Petersburg spring, but spring none the less.

And suddenly I remember my last happy spring. I was seven years old, living with my mother and father out in the country, on the steppe. No one watched me too closely, and I scampered about wherever and however I pleased. I remember how in early March, along the steppe ravines around us, rivers of melted snow began to flow and murmur, the steppe darkened, the air grew so astonishingly moist and delightful. The brows of the hills were uncovered first, and the grass showed green there. Then the whole steppe turned green, although snow still lay dying in the ravines. Rapidly, in just a few days, clumps of peonies seemed to spring up from nowhere ready-formed, and shot up, and they had resplendent, bright purple flowers. Larks began to sing . . .

Lord, what have I done to be cast alive into hell? Surely what I am enduring is worse than any hell?

A stone descent leads directly down to a hole in the ice. Something has drawn me downwards, to look into the water. But it isn't time, is it? Of course not. I shall wait a while.

And yet it would be good to stand on the damp, slippery edge of that hole in the ice. So I would slip in, just like that. It's only cold . . . After a second you're floating downstream under the ice, beating insanely on the ice with your hands, feet, head, face. I wonder if daylight penetrates as far as that?

I lingered, standing motionless over the hole in the ice, already in that state where all thought ceases. My feet had long been soaked through, but I didn't move from the spot. The wind, though not cold, cut right through me, making me shiver from head to foot, and still I stood there. And I don't know how long I would have remained in that torpor, if someone hadn't called to me from the embankment, 'Hey, Madam! Lady!'

I didn't turn round.

'Lady, back on the pavement, please!'

Behind me, someone started down the steps. There was the sound of feet scraping on the sand-strewn flagstones and also a dull clattering noise. I turned round: a constable was on his way down, his sword clattering. When he saw my face, his polite expression promptly turned into one of coarse insolence, and he came up to me and tugged at my shoulder.

'Clear off out of it, you trash. Gallivanting all over the place! You drop yourself through the ice, you silly woman, and it's us as 'as to answer for wrong 'uns like you.'

My face had told him what I was.

IV

The same and more of the same . . . I cannot be alone for so much as a moment before deep melancholy grips my soul. What can I do with myself to make me forget?

Annushka has brought me a letter. Who is it from? I haven't had a letter from anyone for such a long time.

Dear Madam, dear Nadezhda Nikolayevna,

Although I well understand that I am of no consequence to you, yet I consider you a kind girl, who will not wish to offend me. For the first and last time in my life, I ask you to visit me, since today is my name-day. I have no relatives and no acquaintances. I implore you to come. I give my word that I shall say nothing offensive or unpleasant to you. Have pity on your devoted

Ivan Nikitin

P. S. I cannot think of my recent conduct in your apartment without a sense of shame. Visit me today at six o'clock.
I enclose the address.   I. N.

What is the meaning of this? He has brought himself to write to me.
This is less simple than it appears. What does he want with me? Shall I
go or not?

How strange to be wondering whether to go or not. If he is trying
to trap me, it's either to kill me or . . . But if he kills me, at least that
will settle it all.

I will go.

I shall dress simply and modestly, and wash the rouge and powder
from my face. That will be nicer for him. I shall do my hair simply.
How thin my hair has become! I did my hair, put on a black woollen
dress, white collar and cuffs, and a black shawl, and went to the
mirror to look at myself.

I almost burst into tears when I saw a woman who bore no
resemblance to the Yevgeniya who does her sordid dances 'so well' in
various dens of iniquity. What met my eye was no brazen, berouged
coquette with a smiling face, rakish, fluffed-out *chignon* and painted
lashes. This broken, suffering woman, pale-faced and with such a
haunted look in her big, black eyes set in dark circles – this is
something quite new, not me at all. Or perhaps it really is me? And
that Yevgeniya whom everybody sees and knows is something alien
that has settled on me, that is crushing me, killing me.

And I did burst into tears, and wept long and hard. From my
earliest years it has been dinned into me that tears bring relief. Only
that can't be true for everyone. I was not relieved; I felt even worse.
Every sob brought pain, every tear was bitter. Those who still have
some hope of recovery and peace – to them, perhaps, tears can bring
relief. But what hope have I?

I wiped away my tears and set off.

I had no difficulty in finding Madame Zuckerberg's lodging-
house, and the Finnish maidservant directed me to Ivan Ivanovich's
door.

'May I come in?'

From inside the room came the sound of a box being slammed shut
in haste.

'Come in!' Ivan Ivanych hastily called out.

I went in. He was sitting at a writing-desk, sealing an envelope. He
did not even seem glad to see me.

'How do you do, Ivan Ivanych,' I said.

'How do you do, Nadezhda Nikolayevna,' he replied, rising to his feet and holding out his hand to me.

A tenderness flitted across his face when I put out my hand to him, but it disappeared instantly. He was serious, even stern.

'Thank you for coming.'

'Why did you ask me to come?' I inquired.

'My God, do you really not know what seeing you means to me! However, this conversation must be unpleasant to you.'

We sat in silence. The maidservant brought in a samovar. Ivan Ivanych handed the tea and sugar to me. Then he set jam, biscuits, sweets and a half-bottle of sweet wine on the table.

'Please pardon me for these refreshments, Nadezhda Nikolayevna. Perhaps you find this unpleasant, but don't be angry. Be so kind as to make the tea and pour it. Take something to eat – there are sweets here, and wine.'

I began to preside over the table, while he sat opposite, keeping his face out of the light, and took to scrutinising me. I sensed his constant, fixed stare, and I felt myself blushing.

I raised my eyes for a moment, but lowered them immediately, because he continued to gaze earnestly at my face. What was the meaning of this? Could the setting, the modest black dress, the absence of impudent faces and vulgar conversation have affected me so strongly that I had changed back into the demure, bashful girl I had been two years previously? It was vexing.

'Do tell me, if you please, what you're gawping at me for,' I said, with an effort but sharply enough.

Ivan Ivanych sprang to his feet and paced about the room.

'Nadezhda Nikolayevna – don't speak so coarsely! Stay as you were when you came in, if only for an hour.'

'But I don't understand why you asked me here. Surely not just to stare at me in silence!'

'Yes, Nadezhda Nikolayevna – just for that. It doesn't cause you any great distress, and it comforts me to look at you for this last time. It was so kind of you to come, and dressed as you are too. I didn't expect this and I am all the more grateful to you for it.'

'But why for the last time, Ivan Ivanych?'

'Because I am going away.'

'Where to?'

'Far away, Nadezhda Nikolayevna. It's not my name-day today at all. I just wrote that and I don't know why. I simply wanted to look at you once more. At first I thought of coming and waiting until you left the house, but then I somehow decided to invite you here. And it was so kind of you to come. May God reward you with all that's good.'

'There's little good in store, Ivan Ivanych.'

'Yes, there's little good for you. But then you know better than I do what is in store for you . . .' Ivan Ivanych's voice trembled. 'I'm better off,' he added, 'because I'm going away.'

And his voice trembled even more.

I felt inexpressibly sorry for him. How fair had I been to think such bad things about him? Why had I thrust him from me so coarsely and so brusquely? But now it was too late for regrets.

I got up and began to put my coat on. Ivan Ivanych sprang up as if he had been stung.

'You're leaving already?' he asked in an agitated voice.

'Yes, I must go . . .'

'You must . . . Back there! Nadezhda Nikolayevna – best let me kill you here and now!'

He said this in a whisper, seizing my hand and staring at me with large, bewildered eyes.

'It would be best, wouldn't it? Tell me!'

'But Ivan Ivanych – they would send you to Siberia. I certainly don't want that.'

'To Siberia! . . . You actually think I couldn't kill you because I'm afraid of Siberia? That has nothing to do with it . . . I couldn't kill you because . . . But how could I kill you? How could I kill *you*?' he declared, panting. 'Why, I . . .'

And he seized me and lifted me into the air like a child, squeezing the breath out of me and raining kisses upon my face, my lips, my eyes, my hair. And then suddenly – as suddenly as he had begun – he set me on my feet again and said rapidly:

'Well, go then, go . . . Forgive me, but it's the first and last time. Don't be angry with me. Go, Nadezhda Nikolayevna.'

'I'm not angry, Ivan Ivanych . . .'

'Go, go! I thank you for coming.'

He saw me out and immediately locked the door. I made my way downstairs. My heart was aching even more than before.

Let him leave and forget me. I shall stay here and live out my time. Enough of this sentimentalising. I shall go home.

I hastened my step and was already thinking what dress I would put on and where I would go that evening. And so ends my romance, a brief pause on the slippery path! Now I shall lurch on unhindered, with no more pauses, down and down.

'*But he's shooting himself!*' something within me suddenly cried out. I stopped, rooted to the spot. Everything went dark before my eyes; cold shivers ran down my spine; my breath caught . . . 'Yes, he's killing himself!' He slammed that box shut . . . That was a revolver he was looking at. He was writing a letter . . . For the last time . . . Run! Perhaps there's still time! Lord, stop him! Lord, don't take him from me!

I was gripped by mortal terror such as I had never known. I ran back like a madwoman, colliding with people. I don't remember running up the stairs. I remember only the maidservant's stupid face as she let me in, I remember the long, dark corridor with all its doors, I remember flinging myself towards his door. And as I seized the handle, a shot rang out behind the door. People sprang out from everywhere, swirled frenziedly round me, together with the corridor, the doors, the walls. And I fell . . . and in my head too everything swirled and vanished.

1878   *Translated by Liv Tudge*

A Very Brief Romance

Bitter, freezing cold . . . January is here, and is taking its toll of all poor folk, the janitors and the constables, and everyone who cannot nuzzle into some warm place. It is taking its toll of me too, of course. Not that I have no warm corner to go to – that was just my whimsical turn of phrase.

Why, then, am I wandering along this deserted embankment? The street lamps are blazing brightly with all four burners, though the wind is gusting into them and making the gas-lights dance. Their brightness gives the dark bulk of the ornate *palazzo*, its windows in particular, an even gloomier air. The huge shining panes reflect the whirling snow and the gloom. The wind is howling and moaning across the Neva's icy wastes. A 'ding-dong, ding-dong' comes pealing through the blizzard. Those are the chimes of the Fortress Cathedral – mournful cadences that beat steadily in time with my peg-leg as it raps on the frozen granite flagstones and with my sick heart as it pounds against the walls that hem it in.

I should introduce myself to the reader. I am a young man with a wooden leg. Perhaps you will declare that I am imitating Dickens: do you remember Silas Wegg, the literary gentleman with a wooden leg in *Our Mutual Friend*? No, I am not imitating anyone. I really am a young man with a wooden leg. Only I've not been so for very long . . .

'Ding-dong, ding-dong!' The bells ring out their mournful 'Lord a'mercy', then toll the hour. Still only one o'clock! Still seven hours until daybreak! Then this black, sleet-laden night will depart and give place to a grey day. Shall I go home? I don't know: it's absolutely all one to me. I need no sleep.

Last spring, too, I was much given to strolling the nights away along this same embankment. Ah, what nights they were! What could be finer? They are so unlike the stifling southern nights, with their fervid black sky and big stars that pursue you with their gaze. Here everything is limpid and elegant. The multi-coloured sky is chill and lovely; the 'dawn through the night', made famous by the almanac, gilds the north and east; the air is fresh and keen. The Neva rolls on, proud and pure, her little waves lapping serenely against the embankment stones. And on that embankment I stand. And on my arm rests a girl. And that girl . . .

Ah, my dear ladies and gentlemen! Why have I begun to tell you all about the injuries I have borne? But such is the poor, stupid human heart. Once injured, it frantically confronts any passing stranger, seeking relief. And finds none. Which is perfectly understandable, for who has any need of a worn-out, undarned sock? Anyone would try to kick it away, and the further the better . . .

My heart was in no need of darning last spring when I met Masha, without doubt the best of all Mashas in the world. I met her on this very same embankment, which was certainly not as cold as it is now. And I had a real leg instead of this wretched peg – a real, presentable leg, just like the left leg I still possess. I was altogether quite presentable, not in the least like the spraddle-shanks I am now. An ugly word, but now words don't matter . . . Anyway, I met her. It all happened as simply as can be. I was walking; she was walking. (I certainly don't traipse after women – that is, I *didn't* traipse after women, since now I have this peg-leg . . .) Something – I don't know what – prompted me to start talking to her. First of all, of course, about certainly not being one of those saucy chaps and so on, then about the purity of my intentions, etcetera and so forth. My genial features (now stamped with a heavy furrow just above the bridge of my nose, and a very gloomy furrow too) restored the young lady's poise. I accompanied her to Galernaya Street, right up to the door of her house. She was returning from a visit to her old grandmother, who lived by the Summer Gardens. She went there every evening to read novels aloud to the poor old lady, who was blind.

Now the grandmother is dead. This past year such a lot of people have died – and not all old grandmothers, either. Even I could have died, very definitely – take my word for that. But I endured. Gentlemen, how much suffering can a man endure? You don't know? Nor do I.

Very well. Masha commanded me to be a hero, so I had no choice but to enlist . . .

The age of the crusades is over; knights in armour are no more. But if the girl you love says to you, 'This ring is me!' and flings it into a blazing fire, even into the most terrific blaze – like the time Feigin's flour-mill burned down, for instance (how long ago that was!) –

surely you would fling yourself after it? 'Oh my, isn't he a one! No, of course not!' you reply. 'I'd take myself off to Butz's and buy her another, ten times the price.' And will she say that the original ring is not her any longer, but the new one, the expensive one? That I will never believe. Anyhow, I'm not one of your sort, dear reader. Perhaps the kind of woman you like would say that. I mean, you probably own hundreds of shares and maybe you are even on the board of Gröger & Co. You'll even have copies of *The Dragonfly* sent out to you in Bucharest, to keep you amused. You perhaps remember, when you were a child, how you once watched a moth that had flown into a flame? That amused you too. The moth lay quivering on its back, fluttering its scorched little wings – you found that interesting. Then when you got bored with the moth, you squashed it with your thumb and the poor little creature was put out of its misery. Ah, gracious reader – if only you could squash me with your thumb and put me out of my misery!

She was a strange girl. For several days after the declaration of war she was gloomy and taciturn, and nothing I could do seemed to amuse her.

'Listen,' she said one day. 'Are you an honourable person?'.

' I presume so,' I replied.

'Honourable people practise what they preach. You were in favour of this war, so you should go and fight.'

She knitted her brow, and her little hand grasped mine tightly.

I looked at Masha and responded with an earnest 'Yes!'

'When you come back, we shall be married,' she said to me at the station. 'So do come back!'

Tears stopped my breath; I all but burst out sobbing. But I held firm and found the strength to reply, 'Remember, Masha, honourable people . . .'

'. . . practise what they preach,' she completed the sentence for me.

I clasped her to my heart for the last time and flung myself onto the train.

I went to fight because of Masha, but I also honourably discharged my duty to my country. I marched cheerfully across Rumania through rain and dust, in heat and cold. I selflessly gnawed soldier's hard-tack. In our first engagement with the Turks I didn't turn coward. For that I was decorated and promoted to NCO. In our second engagement there was a thud, and I thudded to the ground. A moan, a haze . . . A surgeon in a white apron, with blood-stained hands . . . Nurses . . . My amputated leg with the birthmark below the knee . . . It all flew by me like a dream. A hospital train with extremely comfortable berths and a supremely elegant lady in charge whisked me back to St Peterburg.

When you leave a town in decent condition, with two legs, and return to it with one leg and a stump – that's quite something, believe me.

They put me in a military hospital; that was in July. I asked the address bureau to find me the address of Marya Ivanovna G., and the attendant, a kind-hearted old soldier, brought me it. Still the same, on Galernaya Street! . . . I wrote a letter, then another, and yet another – but no answer came.

Gentle reader, I have nothing further to relate. Of course you don't believe me. An unlikely tale indeed: a knight in armour and a faithless deceiver. 'Some old romance, word for word!' My astute reader, you do wrong to disbelieve me. Knights in armour still exist; I am not the only one . . .

At last they fitted me with this peg-leg, and I could discover the cause of Masha's silence for myself. I took a cab to Galernaya Street, and started hobbling up the long flight of stairs. How I had soared up them eight months before! At last, the door. As I rang the bell, my heart stood still . . . Footsteps sounded behind the door. Avdotya, the elderly maidservant, opened it and, deaf to her cries of delight, I ran (if running is possible on unevenly calibrated legs) into the drawing-room. Masha!

She was not alone. She was sitting with a distant relation, a very handsome young man, who had been completing his studies at the same time as myself when I was last in St Petersburg, and now had every expectation of securing a very good appointment. They both gave me a most tender welcome (on account of the peg-leg, of course), but they were both ill-at-ease. Within fifteen minutes I understood everything.

I did not wish to stand in the way of their happiness. My astute reader gives a spiteful smile: do you really expect me to believe all this twaddle? Whoever would relinquish the girl he loved to some ne'er-do-well, without rhyme or reason?

Well, in the first place, he is certainly not a ne'er-do-well, and in the second place . . . I could perhaps point out to you that in the second place . . . but you wouldn't understand. You wouldn't understand because you do not believe that goodness and truth exist in our day. You would prefer to see three people unhappy rather than just yourself. You don't believe me, my astute reader. Then don't believe me, and good luck to you!

The wedding was the day before yesterday. I was best man. I proudly performed my duties in a ceremony in which the most precious creature in my life gave herself to another man. Masha threw me a timid glance now and then. And her husband treated me with oh-so-solicitous embarrassment. It was a jolly wedding. There was champagne. The German relations shouted '*Hoch!*' and called me '*der russische Held*'. Masha and her husband are Lutherans.

'Ah-hah!' my astute reader hoots. 'Now you're caught, Mr Hero! What did you need to bring in the Lutheran church for? Why, for the simple reason that there are no Orthodox weddings in December! That's the size of it, sir. So all this twaddle is pure fabrication.'

Think what you like, my astute reader. It's absolutely all one to me. But if you spent these December nights pacing the Palace Embankment with me, listening with me to the tempest and the bells and the rapping of my peg-leg, if you felt what I am feeling in my inmost soul on these winter nights, you would believe . . . 'Ding-dong, ding-dong!' The bells are tolling four o'clock. It's time to go home, fling myself onto my cold and lonely bed, and sleep. Reader, farewell!

1878   *Translated by Liv Tudge*

An Encounter

Into the far distance stretched a broad and tremulous band of silvery moonlight; the rest of the sea was black; the muted, rhythmic sound of waves rolling to the sandy shore carried up to the figure standing on the rise; blacker than the sea itself were the silhouettes of ships rocking at anchor; one huge steamer ('English, I'll be bound,' thought Vasily Petrovich) settled in the bright band of moonlight and hissed out ragged jets of steam which evaporated in mid-air; damp, salty air wafted from the sea. Vasily Petrovich had never seen the like before; he gazed in delight on the sea, the moonlight, the steamers and other craft, and drew rapturous breaths of sea air, the first of his life. He lingered, relishing these novel sensations, standing with his back to the town where he had arrived only that day and where he was to live for many a year. Behind him a colourful crowd was strolling along the promenade; the ear caught Russian speech and foreign tongues, the quiet, urbane tones of local dignitaries, the twittering of young ladies walking in twos and threes, and the loud, cheerful voices of big high-school boys clustered around them. A burst of laughter from one of these groups made Vasily Petrovich turn. A jaunty crew was trooping by; one of the boys was saying something to a pretty young schoolgirl; his companions were boisterously interrupting his heated, evidently self-vindicatory declamation.

'Don't believe it, Nina Petrovna! He's a dreadful fibber! He's making it all up.'

'But truly, Nina Petrovna, I'm not one bit to blame!'

'If you ever take it into your head to deceive me again, Shevyryov . . .' the girl declared in an affectedly prim young voice.

Vasily Petrovich did not catch the end of the exchange before the troop had passed. Half a minute later, another burst of laughter floated through the darkness.

'There it is – the soil I am to cultivate, like any humble ploughman,' thought Vasily Petrovich, first because he had been appointed to the local high-school and secondly because he was given to casting his thoughts, voiced or not, into figurative forms. 'Yes, this is the humble sphere where I am to work,' he thought as he seated himself on a bench again, facing the sea. 'And my dreams of a professorship, of political journalism, resounding fame? That kind of enterprise is a bit beyond you, Vasily Petrovich, old chap – so just try your hand here for a while.'

And beautiful, gratifying thoughts began to stir in the new teacher's head. He saw himself detecting the 'divine spark' in the boys from their first year in school, sustaining those special individuals who were 'striving to cast off the yoke of darkness', watching over fresh young energies as they unfolded, 'shunning vulgar life's besmirchment'; and in the fullness of time seeing his pupils become exceptional men . . . His imagination even painted such scenes as he, Vasily Petrovich, now a grey-haired old teacher, sitting in his humble apartments receiving his former pupils, one of them a university professor famous 'at home and in Europe', another a writer, a famous novelist, and a third a public figure and likewise famous. And they all treat him with respect. 'It was the good seeds you sowed in my soul when I was a boy, my dear Vasily Petrovich, that made me a real human being,' says the public figure, and, greatly touched, he presses his old teacher's hand.

But Vasily Petrovich did not spend long on such elevated topics; his thoughts soon passed to matters that impinged more directly on his present situation. He drew a new wallet from his pocket, and, having counted his money, began to consider how much he'd have left after paying his essential expenses. 'How annoying that I spent so much without thinking on the journey,' he thought. 'Lodgings . . . Well, let's say about twenty rubles a month, my board, linen, tea, tobacco . . . I'll be able to save a thousand rubles in six months, in any event. I'm sure I'll be able to give tuition at a good rate here – four or five rubles an hour . . .' A sense of satisfaction came over him, and he felt the urge to reach into the pocket containing two letters of recommendation to local worthies, and to read the addresses for the twentieth time. He drew out the letters and carefully unfolded the paper they were wrapped in, but could not read the addresses, the moonlight being too feeble to afford him that pleasure. A snapshot was enclosed with the letters. Vasily Petrovich turned it directly towards the moon and tried to discern the familiar features. 'Liza, oh my Liza!' he declared almost aloud, and sighed, not without a certain gratification. Liza was his fiancée; she would remain in St Petersburg until Vasily Petrovich had saved the thousand rubles which the young couple deemed essential for their first domestic establishment.

With a sigh, he slipped the snapshot and the letters into his left-hand side pocket and launched into dreams about his future married life. And those dreams were even more gratifying than those of the public figure who would come to thank him for sowing the good seeds in his heart.

The sea was pounding far below; the wind was freshening. The English steamer had left the band of moonlight, which now glittered unbroken and iridescent with the dull lustre of a myriad wavelets and grew ever brighter as it extended into the boundless reaches of the sea. Vasily Petrovich had no desire to rise from the bench, tear himself away from this tableau and return to the cramped hotel room he had taken. It was late, however; he stood up and made his way along the promenade.

A gentleman wearing a lightweight raw silk suit and a straw hat with a length of muslin wrapped around the brim (the summer finery of the local swells) got up from a bench as Vasily Petrovich was passing and asked:

'May I have a light, please?'

'By all means,' replied Vasily Petrovich.

The red glow lit up a familiar face.

'Nikolay, old friend! Can it be you?'

'Vasily Petrovich?'

'None other . . . Oh, I'm so glad! I never thought, never guessed . . .' said Vasily Petrovich, hugging his friend and kissing him three times. 'What brings you here?'

'Work, pure and simple. And you?'

'I've been appointed at the high-school here. I've only just arrived.'

'Where are you staying? If it's a hotel, then please come to my place. I'm very glad to see you. You don't know anyone here, I suppose? Come to my place, we'll have supper and a chat about old times.'

'Let's do that, let's,' Vasily Petrovich responded. 'I'm very, very glad to see you! I arrive here, like a man in the wilderness, and all of a sudden meet you – delightful! Cab!' he cried.

'No need to shout. Sergey, let's have you!' Vasily Petrovich's friend said in a loud, nonchalant voice.

A dandyish barouche drove up to the kerb; its owner jumped in. Vasily Petrovich stood on the pavement, staring in astonishment at the carriage, the ebony horses and the plump coachman.

'Kudryashov – are these horses yours?'

'They are indeed. Surprised?'

'Astonishing . . . This isn't like you!'

'Who else? Come now, get in – plenty of time to talk later.'

Vasily Petrovich got in and seated himself next to Kudryashov, and the carriage set off, rattling and jouncing along the road. Vasily Petrovich sat on the soft cushions, swaying from side to side, and smiled. 'What a how d'ye do!' he thought. 'Seems like only yesterday Kudryashov was the poorest student in the place and now – a barouche!'

Kudryashov, his feet up on the seat opposite, smoked his cigar in silence. Five minutes later, the carriage halted.

'Well, dear fellow, out you get. Let me show you my humble hovel,' said Kudryashov, descending from the footboard and handing Vasily Petrovich down.

Before entering the humble hovel, the visitor cast an eye over it. Since the moon was behind it and shed no light on it, he could make out only that the hovel was a one-storey stone building with ten or twelve large windows. An awning set on columns with gilt-dashed scrolls hung over a heavy oak door with panels of mirrored glass, a bronze handle in the shape of a bird's foot holding a cut glass sphere, and a glittering brass plaque engraved with the owner's name.

'Quite a hovel you've got, Kudryashov! This is no hovel – it's a real *palazzo*,' said Vasily Petrovich as they entered a vestibule with oak furniture and a black-mawed fireplace. 'Have you bought it?'

'No, dear chap, I haven't come to that yet. I rent it. It's not expensive – fifteen hundred.'

'Fifteen hundred!' Vasily Petrovich dragged out.

'It makes more sense to pay fifteen hundred than fritter away capital that can earn much higher interest if it's not tied up. And I need a great deal of money. I mean, when I build for myself, it won't be trash like this.'

'Trash!' Vasily Petrovich exclaimed, thunderstruck.

'Certainly it's not much of a house. Well, come now, come quickly . . .'

Vasily Petrovich, who had already removed his coat, followed his host. The appointments of Kudryashov's home fed his amazement still further. It comprised a succession of high-ceilinged rooms with parquet floors and expensive, gold-patterned wallpaper; a dining-room of imitation oak with badly executed replicas of game on the walls, a huge carved sideboard and a large circular table drenched in light that streamed from a suspended bronze lamp in a milk-glass shade; a drawing-room with a grand piano, a profusion of sundry bent-beech furniture, little sofas, little backless settees, tabourets and chairs, with expensive lithographs and nasty oleographs in heavily gilded frames; and a sitting-room according to expectations, with silk upholstery and a plethora of superfluous objects. It was as though the owner of this house had had a sudden windfall – had won two hundred thousand or thereabouts – and had furnished his apartments hand over fist, in grand style. Everything had been purchased pell-mell, purchased not because it was needed but because there was money to burn, which had found an outlet in the purchase of a grand piano, on which, as far as Vasily Petrovich knew, Kudryashov could at best pick out a one-finger tune; an unprepossessing old painting, one of tens of thousands attributed to some second-rate Flemish 'master' to which, doubtless, no one ever paid the slightest attention; a Chinese chess set which could not be used, so ethereally dainty were the pieces, whose heads were carved to form three interlocking spheres; and a welter of similar superfluities.

The friends went into the study. This was a more comfortable room. A large desk, cluttered with various bronze and ceramic trifles, littered with papers and drafting and drawing materials, occupied the centre of the room. On the walls hung huge coloured diagrams and maps, and below them stood two low ottomans with little silk bolsters. Kudryashov, with one arm around Vasily Petrovich's waist, led him straight to an ottoman and sat him on the overstuffed seat.

'Well, I'm very glad, very glad to meet an old comrade,' he said.

'So am I . . . You know, I arrive here, like a man in the wilderness, and all of a sudden meet you! You know, Nikolay Konstantinovich, when I saw you, so much stirred in my soul, so many memories revived in my mind . . .'

'What of?'

'What of! Our student days, the times we lived so well – if not in the material sense, then certainly in the moral sense. Do you remember . . .'

'What is there to remember? Tucking into disgusting sausages? Enough, dear chap, the boredom of it . . . Do you want a cigar? Regalia Imperialia or whatever it is – all I know is that they cost fifty kopeks each.'

Vasily Petrovich took the precious offering from the box, drew a tiny penknife from his pocket, sliced off the cigar's tip, lit it, and said:

'Nikolay Konstantinovich, I really feel I'm in a dream. To have got a post like yours, in such a short time.'

'A post like mine! It's not worth a damn.'

'What do you mean? How much do you make?'

'How much what? Wages?'

'Yes – your salary.'

'I, Kudryashov Secundus, civil engineer and provincial secretary, receive a salary of one thousand six hundred rubles per annum.'

Vasily Petrovich's jaw dropped.

'What do you mean? Where does all this come from?'

'My dear chap, you're simplicity itself! Where from? From the water and the earth, the sea and the dry land. But chiefly from here.'

And he tapped his index finger on his forehead.

'You see those pictures hanging on the wall?'

'Yes,' replied Vasily Petrovich. 'What of them?'

'Do you know what they are?'

'No, I don't.'

Vasily Petrovich rose from the ottoman and went up to the wall. The blue, red, brown and black shading was as unintelligible to him as the mysterious numerals penned in red ink along the dotted lines.

'What are they – diagrams?'

'Diagrams, of course. But what of?'

'Truly, old friend, I don't know.'

'Those diagrams represent, my dear Vasily Petrovich, a projected mole. You do know what a mole is?'

'Well, of course. I do teach the Russian language, after all. A mole is a . . . how can I put it? . . . well, it's a breakwater of sorts . . .'

'A breakwater, precisely. A breakwater that serves to create a man-made harbour. Those diagrams represent a mole that is presently under construction. Did you look down at the sea?'

'Yes, of course I did. It's an extraordinary view! But I didn't notice any construction.'

'No wonder,' Kudryashov said with a laugh. 'Not very much of the mole is in the sea, Vasily Petrovich – it's here, on dry land.'

'Where do you mean?'

'Here, in the keeping of myself and the other engineers – Knobloch, Puytsikovsky and the rest. This is strictly between you and me, of course – I'm telling you because we're friends. What are you staring at me for? It's all perfectly normal.'

'But listen, that's terrible, and you know it! Surely you can't be telling the truth! Can you really stoop to dishonest means in order to acquire this luxury? Can it really be that all your past has served just to bring you to . . . to . . . And you speak so calmly about it . . .'

'Wait, wait, Vasily Petrovich! Please let's do without the strong language. You say "dishonest means"? First, tell me the meaning of "honest" and "dishonest". I'm sure I don't know it – perhaps I've forgotten, but I think I never did know it. And it occurs to me that you, strictly speaking, don't know it either – you just struggle into it like some kind of uniform. Just drop this whole subject. It's not polite, above all. Allow others their opinions. You say "dishonest". Say it, if you wish, but don't rail at me. After all, I don't rail at you for not sharing my view. It's all a matter of personal opinion, dear chap, the individual point of view, and since there are so many different points of view, let's say to blazes with the whole business and go into the dining-room for a drop of vodka and a chat about something pleasant.'

'Oh Nikolay, Nikolay – it pains me to look at you.'

'That's your privilege – be pained to your heart's content. So what if you're pained? It'll pass. You'll get used to the sight, your eyes will adapt and you'll say, "What a fathead I've been, after all." You *will* say that, mark my words. Come on, let's have a nip and forget about erring engineers. That's what brains are for, chum – to err with . . . And you, my gentle teacher, how much will you be earning, eh?'

'It wouldn't interest you.'

'But more or less?'

'Well, about three thousand, with private lessons.'

'There, you see – for a paltry three thousand you're going to trudge through life giving lessons! And I just sit here and look around, doing what I want if I want and not if I don't. If I got a whim to spend the whole day spitting at the ceiling, I could. And money . . . so much money that "'tis for us of no account . . .""

They went into the dining-room, where supper was already laid out. A cold roast of beef reared up like a rosy mountain. Jars of preserves sported multi-coloured English lettering and vivid designs. An array of bottles was lined up on the table. The two friends had a glass of vodka, then set to their supper. Kudryashov ate slowly and carefully, completely engrossed in his task.

Vasily Petrovich ate and thought, thought and ate. He was in a great quandary, and had absolutely no idea what to do. In obedience to his convictions, he ought to have made a hasty exit from his old friend's house and never set foot in it again. 'This very forkful is stolen,' he thought, putting the forkful into his mouth and taking a sip of the wine poured by his dutiful host. 'And surely what I'm doing is no less than a disgrace?' Numerous reasonings of this sort stirred in the poor teacher's head, but reasonings they remained, while a furtive voice lurked behind them, countering each with 'Well, and what of it?' And Vasily Petrovich felt himself in no fit state to settle that question, and did not budge from his seat. 'Ah well – I shall observe,' flashed through his head by way of justification, which made him feel ashamed of himself. 'What do I need to observe for? Am I a writer or something?'

'Meat like this,' Kudryashov began, 'cannot – just note this – cannot be found anywhere in this town.'

And he told Vasily Petrovich a long tale about how he had dined at Knobloch's, been struck by the quality of the roast beef he was served, found out how it could be procured, and finally procured some.

'You've come at just the right moment,' he said at the conclusion of his story. 'Have you ever eaten anything like it?'

'It certainly is excellent roast beef,' Vasily Petrovich replied.

'It's superb, dear fellow. I like having everything just so. But why aren't you drinking? Wait, I'll pour you some wine.'

There followed a no less interminable tale about the wine, involving an English skipper and a London merchant, Knobloch again and the customs. While telling this tale Kudryashov took a sip at his wine now and then, and became more animated as he drank. Spots of high colour appeared on his flabby face, his speech quickened and grew more lively.

'But why are you so silent?' he finally asked Vasily Petrovich, who was indeed maintaining a dogged silence as he listened to the sagas of the meat, the wine, the cheese and the various other godsent delicacies that graced the engineer's table.

'Somehow, my friend, I just don't feel like talking.'

'"Don't feel like talking" – what nonsense! I can see you're still upset by that confession of mine. I very, very much regret I told you. We'd have had such an agreeable supper without that damned mole . . . But you'd best put it out of your mind, Vasily Petrovich, drop it . . . Eh, Vasenka? To blazes with it, really! What's to be done, dear fellow – I didn't live up to expectations. Life isn't a school-room. And I don't know how long you'll stick to your chosen path.'

'Please don't make any conjectures about me,' said Vasily Petrovich.

'You're offended? . . . Of course you won't stick to it. Are you such a model of unselfishness? Are you really at peace with yourself now? Surely every day you wonder if your actions are in accordance with your ideals, and surely every day you conclude that they aren't? That's true, isn't it, eh? Drink your wine – it's good stuff.'

He filled his own glass too, held it up to the light, tasted it, smacked his lips and drank it off.

'And you, my gentle friend, are thinking that I don't know what's going through your head right now? I know exactly. "Why," you're thinking, "am I sitting in this man's house? A lot of use he is to me! Surely I can get by without his wine and cigars?" Wait now, wait – let me finish! I don't think you're in my house for the wine and cigars at all. Not at all. Even if you had a craving for those things, you still wouldn't bow and scrape for them. Bowing and scraping is a very hard business. You're sitting in my house and talking to me simply because you can't decide if I really am a criminal or not. I don't shock you, and that's that. Of course, you find that very offensive because your head is full of principles arranged under various headings and according to them I, your former comrade and friend, turn out to be a scoundrel, but for all that you can't feel any hostility towards me whatsoever. Principles are all very well, but take me for what I am, I'm a comrade and a good sort and even, you could say, a good man. I mean, you know I'm incapable of harming anyone . . .'

'Stop, Kudryashov – how have you come by all this?' Vasily Petrovich waved his hand around. 'You say yourself that it belongs to someone else. Well, you've harmed whoever it's been stolen from.'

'It's very easy for you to say "whoever it's been stolen from." I'm thinking and thinking whom I could have harmed, and for the life of me I don't understand who it might be. You don't know how it's done. I'll tell you and then perhaps you'll agree with me that it's not so easy to discover who's been "harmed".'

Kudryashov rang the bell. An impassive figure in black tails appeared.

'Ivan Pavlych, bring me a diagram from the study. The one hanging between the windows. You'll see, Vasily Petrovich, it's quite a magnificent business. Truly, I have even begun to perceive poetry in it.'

Ivan Pavlych carefully carried in a huge sheet of paper backed with calico. Kudryashov took it, pushed aside the plates, bottles and glasses, and laid the map on the tablecloth, which was spattered with red wine.

'Look here,' he said. 'This is a cross-section of our mole and this is its longitudinal section. You see that blue shading? That's the sea. At this point it's so deep that we can't start building directly on the sea-floor. So as a starting-point, we lay a bed for the mole.'

'A bed?' Vasily Petrovich queried. 'That's a strange term.'

'A stone bed made up of huge cobbles each not less than one cubic foot in volume.' Kudryashov unscrewed a tiny silver compass from the head of his watch-key and with it traced a little line on the diagram. 'Look, Vasily Petrovich – that's a sazhen. If we measured across, the bed would be just under fifty sazhens wide. Not exactly a narrow cot, is it? So, we have a mass of stone that wide coming up from the sea-floor to within sixteen feet of the surface. If you consider the width of the bed and its enormous length, then you'll have some conception of the massive amount of stone involved. Sometimes, you know, barge after barge goes out to the mole, all day long, barge after barge drops its load, and when you come to measure it, the increment is practically negligible. It's like tipping the stone into a bottomless pit . . . The bed is shown here on the plan in a muddy-grey shade. As it proceeds forwards, a new phase of work begins on it from the shore. Steam cranes start putting down gigantic man-made stones, cubic blocks of cobbles and cement onto the bed. Each of them is over one cubic sazhen in volume and weighs many hundred poods. The crane lifts them, turns them, and lays them in rows. It's a strange sensation when the gentle pressure of your hand on a lever can make a huge mass like that rise and fall as you wish. When a mass like that obeys you, you have some idea of what mankind can do . . . See, there they are, those cubes.' He pointed with the compass. 'They're laid almost to the surface, and then, on top of them, goes the uppermost layer, which is dressed stone. So that's what it's all about – a good match for any Egyptian pyramid. Now you have a general idea of the work that has been going on for a number of years already, and will last Lord only knows how many more. As long as possible, preferably . . . Still, if it all goes on as it has been doing recently, it could well last out our lifetime.'

'What happens next?' asked Vasily Petrovich after a long silence.

'Next? Well, we sit tight and make as much as we can from it.'

'From what you've told me, I still fail to see how you can make anything from it.'

'The innocence of youth! Though come to think of it, we're the same age. It's just the experience you lack which makes me older and wiser. This is the point. You know that every sea has storms? They do the job. They sweep the bed away, year after year, and we lay down another.'

'But I still can't see how you . . .'

'We lay it down,' Kudryashov continued serenely, 'on paper, here on the diagram, because the storm damage only occurs on paper.'

Vasily Petrovich was all bewilderment.

'Because waves of up to only eight feet can't really sweep the bed away. Our sea is no ocean – and even in the ocean, moles like ours hold. And here, at a depth of something over two sazhens below the surface, which is as high as the bed comes up, it's as still as death. This is how it's done, Vasily Petrovich – listen. In spring, when the dirty weather of autumn and winter is over, we meet and consider how much bed has been swept away this year. We mark it on our diagrams. Well, and then we write to the relevant quarters, saying that this and that many cubic sazhens of construction work have been swept away by the storms. And back comes the answer – build on, patch it up, deuce take you! So we patch it up.'

'But what do you patch up?'

'Our pockets!' quipped Kudryashov, laughing at his own witticism.

'No, that's impossible! Impossible!' Vasily Petrovich cried, jumping up from his chair and dashing about the room. 'Listen, Kudryashov, it'll be the ruin of you . . . The immorality aside . . . I'm only trying to say that you'll get caught at it, and you'll suffer for it, you'll be sent to Siberia. God, oh God, the hopes, the aspirations! Capable and honest in schooldays, and then . . .'

Vasily Petrovich spoke long and fervently, in a transport of emotion. But Kudryashov, perfectly composed, smoked a cigar and observed his friend pacing to and fro.

'Yes, without question you'll be sent to Siberia!' declared Vasily Petrovich, rounding off his diatribe.

'It's a very long way to Siberia, my friend. You are a caution, Vasily Petrovich – you don't understand a thing. Am I the only one who . . . how can I put it politely . . . benefits? Everything around, the air itself – even the air, by all accounts, does its share of pilfering. Not long ago some new boy arrived here and was about to start writing reports about "honesty". What happened? We covered up . . . And we always will. All for one and one for all. Do you think that a man is his own worst enemy? Who would dare touch me if it could bring about his own undoing?'

'Then, as Krylov put it, you've all got fluff on your snouts?'

'Precisely. Everyone gets everything he can out of life, no Platonic idealism about it . . . Now, what had we started talking about? Oh yes, about whoever I'm supposed to have harmed. So tell me – who is it? Our less fortunate brethren, maybe. How though? It's not as though I'm drawing on some wellspring – I'm taking what has been made available, what has already been taken, and if it doesn't come to me, then perhaps it will go to someone worse. I don't live like a pig, at least – I do have certain intellectual interests. I subscribe to heaps of newspapers and journals. They rant on about science, about civilisation, but where would that civilisation be without us, without people of means? And who is it that enables science to progress, if not people of means? And those means have to be got from somewhere. By the so-called honest ways . . .'

'Oh, don't go on, don't say it all, Nikolay Konstantinovich!'

'And why not? Would you like it better, you shifty old soul, if I took to lying and justifying myself? We steal, do you hear me? And if the truth were told, you're stealing now yourself.'

'Now listen here, Kudryashov . . .'

'I'm not going to listen to you,' Kudryashov said with a laugh. 'My dear chap, under your mask of virtue you're a thief. School-teacher – what kind of occupation do you call that? Will your labour really give a good return for even the miserable pittance you're paid now? Will you turn out a single decent man? Three-quarters of your charges will come out like me and one-quarter like you – well-intentioned milksops. So tell me frankly, aren't you taking money for nothing? Is there such a distance between you and me? And then he has the gall to preach about honesty!'

'Kudryashov – believe me, this conversation is extremely unpleasant to me.'

'Not to me – not a bit.'

'I didn't expect to find what I have found in you.'

'And no wonder. People change and I've changed, and you couldn't have predicted how. You're no prophet.'

'One needn't be a prophet to hope that an honest youth will become an honest citizen.'

'Oh, lay off! Don't use that word to me! "Honest citizen"! And what textbook did you dredge up that museum-piece from? It's high time you stopped sentimentalising. Look, you're not a child . . . Now Vasya,' and Kudryashov took Vasily Petrovich's hand, 'be a friend, let's have done with this "accursed question". Let's drink like good comrades instead. Ivan Pavlych! Fetch us a bottle of this, my man.'

Ivan Pavlych instantly reappeared with a new bottle. Kudryashov filled the glasses.

'Well, let's drink to the flourishing of . . . what? No matter – to yours and mine.'

'I drink,' said Vasily Petrovich earnestly, 'to your coming to reason. That is what I most devoutly wish for.'

'Be a friend, don't harp on . . . Besides, if I came to reason, there'd be nothing to drink; belts would have to be tightened. See where your logic leads? We'll just drink, without wishing anything for anyone. Let's have done with this tedious maundering: we'll never agree on anything: you won't bring me to the straight and narrow and I won't out-argue you. And anyway, it's not worth trying – your own wit will bring you to my way of thinking.'

'Never!' Vasily Petrovich exclaimed heatedly, banging his glass down on the table.

'Well, we'll see about that. But look now – I've told you all about me and you haven't said one word about yourself. What have you been doing and what do you intend to do?'

'I've already told you – I have a post as a teacher.'

'Is it your first appointment?'

'Yes, it is. I only gave private lessons before.'

'And you intend to give them here too?'

'If they're to be had, why not?'

'We'll get them, dear chap, that we will!' Kudryashov clapped Vasily Petrovich on the shoulder. 'We'll put all the local youth into your learned hands. What was your hourly rate in Petersburg?'

'Not enough. It was very difficult to get good terms. A ruble or two, no more.'

'And a man torments himself for a pittance like that! Well, don't

you dare to ask less than five here. It's hard work! I remember
scampering around giving measly lessons in my first and second year.
There were times when you'd get fifty kopeks an hour and be glad of
it. It's the most thankless, difficult work. I'll introduce you to the
whole set here – there are some quite delightful families, with young
ladies too. You play your cards right and I'll arrange the marriage for
you, if you like. Eh, Vasily Petrovich?'

'No thank you – I don't need that.'

'Betrothed already? Truly?'

Vasily Petrovich's expression betrayed his embarrassment.

'I can see in your eyes it's the truth. Well, dear chap, I congratulate
you. Wasn't that quick! Good show, Vasya! Ivan Pavlych!' shouted
Kudryashov.

Ivan Pavlych appeared in the doorway, his face sleepy and cross.

'Fetch us some champagne.'

'There is no champagne. It's all gone,' the servant replied glumly.

'Never mind Kudryashov – there's really no need.'

'Shut up – I'm not asking you. Do you want to make me angry or
what? Ivan Pavlych, don't come back without champagne, do you
hear? Off with you!'

'But everywhere's shut, Nikolay Konstantinovich.'

'Don't answer back. You've got money. Off you go and get some.'

The servant left, muttering something under his breath.

'He's always answering back, the brute! And you with your "no
need". If one doesn't drink at a time like this, then what's champagne
for? . . . Well, who is she?'

'Who?'

'Why, your fiancée . . . Poor, rich, good-looking?'

'You don't know her anyway, so why tell you her name? She has
no fortune, and beauty is in the eye of the beholder. She's beautiful to
me.'

'Have you got a snapshot?' Kudryashov asked. 'Carry it near your
heart, I'll bet! Show me!'

And he stretched out his hand.

Vasily Petrovich's face, already flushed with the wine, grew
redder. He unbuttoned his jacket, not knowing why he did so, took
out his pocket-book and removed the precious photograph. Kudryashov snatched it and inspected it.

'Not bad, dear chap! You know how many beans make five.'

'Can't we do without that kind of talk?' Vasily Petrovich snapped.

'Give it back and let me put it away.'

'Wait – let me feast my eyes. Well, God grant you love and good counsel. Here, take it and lay it on your heart again. Oh, what a man!' Kudryashov exclaimed, and burst into laughter.

'I fail to see what you find so funny.'

'Just a funny thought, dear fellow. I had a vision of you in ten years' time – you in a dressing-gown, the wife plain and pregnant, seven children and you short of the ready for their little shoes, pants, caps and all that. A prosaic existence, in short. Will you carry that photograph in your side-pocket then, eh? Ha, ha, ha!'

'Why don't you tell me about your poetic future? Making money and spending it – eating, drinking and sleeping?'

'Not eating, drinking and sleeping, but living. Living in the full awareness of my freedom, and even a certain amount of power.'

'Power! What power do you exercise?'

'Money is power, and I've got money. I can do what I want . . . If I wanted to buy you, I'd buy you.'

'Kudryashov! . . .'

'Stop striking silly poses. Surely you and I, old friends as we are, can rag each other a bit? Of course I've no intention of buying you. Live as you will. But still, I can do anything I want. Oh, what a fool, what a fool I am!' cried Kudryashov suddenly, slapping himself on the forehead. 'We've been sitting here all this time, and I still haven't shown you the main attraction. You say "eat, drink and sleep"? Now I'll show you something that will make you take back what you said. Come. Bring a candle.'

'Where to?' asked Vasily Petrovich.

'Follow me. You'll see where.'

Vasily Petrovich got up from his chair feeling that all was not quite right with him. His legs were not completely obedient and he couldn't hold the candlestick without dripping wax on the carpet. He established some control over his recalcitrant limbs, however, and followed Kudryashov. They passed through several rooms and a narrow corridor, and arrived in a damp, dark place. Their feet clumped dully on the stone floor. Somewhere, a stream of falling water sounded a perpetual harmony. From the ceiling hung stalactites of tufa and bluish volcanic glass; great artificial cliffs dominated the scene. A mass of tropical greenery covered them, and dark mirrors glittered here and there.

'What is it?' asked Vasily Petrovich.

'An aquarium to which I have dedicated two years of my life and a great deal of money. Wait – I'll light it.'

Kudryashov vanished behind the greenery, while Vasily Petrovich went up to one of the mirror-like panes of glass and tried to make out what was behind it. The feeble light of the single candle penetrated only a little way into the water, yet fish large and small, drawn by the spot of light, gathered in the glow and stared vacuously at Vasily Petrovich with their round eyes, opening and closing their mouths and fluttering their gills and fins. Behind them were the dark contours of water plants. Something reptilian was moving in there, but Vasily Petrovich could not make out its shape.

A sudden blinding flood of light made him close his eyes for an instant, and when he opened them again, the aquarium had changed beyond recognition. Kudryashov had switched on two electric lamps whose light permeated an expanse of azure water teeming with fish and other creatures and full of plants whose blood-red, drab brown and muddy green silhouettes stood stark against an indeterminate backdrop. The cliffs and tropical plants, looking darker now in contrast, set off to perfection the thick, mirror-like panes of glass and the view they gave into the depths of the aquarium. Everything was now darting and swarming about, alarmed by the dazzling light. A whole shoal of big-headed little gobies was speeding to and fro, wheeling as if on a word of command; sinuous sterlets stuck their mouths against the glass and rose to the surface or sank to the bottom as if trying to work their way through the solid, transparent barrier; a sleek, black eel burrowed into the sand, raising a great cloud of sediment; a comical, stubby cuttlefish detached itself from the outcrop where it had been resting and swam in fits and starts across the aquarium, tail end first, its long tentacles trailing. It was all so lovely and novel that Vasily Petrovich was thoroughly entranced.

'How about that, Vasily Petrovich?' Kudryashov asked, emerging.

'Marvellous, dear chap, astonishing! What a job you've done! What taste, what effects!'

'And – what knowledge. I went to Berlin specially to see the marvel they have there, and without conceit I can say that my aquarium, while nowhere near as big, of course, is not a bit less elegant or interesting. It's my pride and comfort. When I feel low, I come here, sit down and stare for hours on end. I love all these creatures because they're open and straightforward, not like us humans. They tuck into each other without the slightest embarrassment. Look, look over there – see, a chase!'

A little fish was darting fitfully upwards, downwards and from side to side, trying to escape some elongated predator. In mortal terror it flung itself out of the water into the air and hid under rocky ledges, but those sharp teeth pursued it everywhere. The predator was just about to seize it when another one pounced from the side and snatched the prey and the little fish vanished down its gullet. The pursuer stopped in bewilderment; the robber hid in a dark corner.

'Beaten to it!' said Kudryashov. 'The fool's left with nothing to show for it. Was it worth the chase, to have the morsel whipped away from under its nose? . . . If you knew how many of those little tiddlers get gobbled up. Put in a whole host of them today, and they're eaten by tomorrow. They eat without a thought for the morality of it. And us human beings? I've only recently left all that balderdash behind myself. Vasily Petrovich! Surely you agree that in the end it *is* balderdash?'

'What is?' Vasily Petrovich asked, not detaching his gaze from the water.

'Why, all those compunctions. What use are they? With or without compunctions, if a nice morsel presents itself . . . Well, so I sent them packing, those compunctions of mine, and now I try to model myself on these brutes.' He pointed at the aquarium.

'Freedom for the free,' sighed Vasily Petrovich. 'But Kudryashov – I take it these are all sea plants and fish?'

'Indeed. And that's sea water too, you know. I had a special conduit built.'

'From the sea, really? But that must have cost a colossal sum.'

'Quite a bit. My aquarium cost me about thirty thousand.'

'Thirty thousand!' Vasily Petrovich exclaimed in horror. 'On a salary of one thousand six hundred!'

'Stop acting so horror-struck. If you've seen enough, let's leave. No doubt Ivan Pavlych has brought the necessary . . . Just a minute while I switch off the power.'

The aquarium was plunged into darkness once more. The candle which was still burning looked to Vasily Petrovich like a faint, smoky glimmer.

When they came back into the dining-room, Ivan Pavlych was holding a napkin-swathed bottle at the ready.

1879   *Translated by Liv Tudge*

The Coward

The war won't give me any rest. I can see only too clearly that it is dragging on and it's very hard to say when it will end. Our men are still the same fine soldiers they always were, but the enemy has turned out to be nothing like as weak as was thought; it's four months since war was declared and our side still has not had a real success. Yet every extra day carries off hundreds of men. I don't know whether it's my nerves, but the casualty lists from the front affect me far worse than they do everyone around me. Others can calmly read, 'Our losses were negligible, the following officers have been wounded . . . other ranks – 50 dead and 100 wounded', and they can even be glad casualties were so low, whereas I see before my eyes, the moment I read a report, a picture of utter carnage. Fifty dead, a hundred mutilated, and that's negligible! Why are we so outraged when the newspapers report a murder with a mere handful of people killed? Why is it that the sight of corpses lying on a battlefield riddled with bullets does not fill us with as much horror as the scene of a house after burglary and murder? Why did the Tiligul railway disaster, which cost several dozen lives, cause an uproar all over Russia, when no attention is paid to action at the front with 'negligible' losses of another few dozen lives?

Vasily Lvov, a medical student I know, with whom I often argue about war, said to me the other day:

'Right, you peace-lover, I'd like to see what you'll do with your humanitarian beliefs when you're called up and have to shoot at people yourself.'

'I won't be called up, Vasily: I've been put in the reserves.'

'If the war drags on they'll take the reserves too. Don't pretend you're not afraid, your turn will come.'

My heart missed a beat. Why had I not thought of that before? Of course they will take the reserves, there is nothing to stop that happening. 'If the war drags on' . . . and it very likely will. Even if this war does not last very long, another one will be sure to start. Why not make war? Why not do great deeds? I feel this war is only the beginning of wars to come that neither I nor my little brother nor my sister's little baby boy will escape. And my turn will come very soon.

What will become of you then? You protest will all your being against war, but war will make you put a rifle on your shoulder and go off to kill and die. No, no, that's impossible! Here am I, a peaceful, easy-going young man who so far has only known his books, the lecture-room, his family and a few close friends, who has planned to devote himself to serious work in a year or two for the cause of truth. I, used to looking at the world objectively, to standing back from it; I, who thought that I could identify its evil anywhere and so avoid it – I can see my edifice of tranquillity being destroyed and myself squeezing into that rough shirt whose tears and stains I have just been examining. And no amount of education, self-knowledge or knowledge of the world, no amount of spiritual freedom, will give me the pathetic physical freedom to dispose of my own body as I will.

Lvov tends to laugh when I start telling him why I am outraged by war.

'Take a simpler view of things, old man, you'll find life easier,' he says. 'Do you think I like this slaughter? Apart from being a calamity for everyone, it's affecting me personally, it's cutting short my studies. They'll arrange accelerated graduation and send us away to cut off soldiers' arms and legs. All the same, I don't go in for pointless reflections on the horrors of war, because no amount of thinking on my part will do anything to abolish it. Really it's best to stop thinking and get on with whatever you're doing. If they send me off to look after the wounded, I'll go and do it. What else can you do, in times like these you have to make a sacrifice. By the way, did you know that Masha is off to the front as a nurse?'

'Really?'

'She made up her mind a couple of days ago; today she's gone to practise bandaging. I didn't try to put her off; I only asked what she was going to do about her studies. "I'll finish them later," she said, "if I'm still alive." All right, let my sister go, she'll learn something useful.'

'And what about Kuzma?'

'Kuzma is saying nothing, he's just going about looking furious and gloomy. He's given up his studies altogether. I'm glad for him that my sister is going away, really: the man's simply a wreck, torturing himself, following her like a shadow, doing nothing. That's love for you!' Vasily jerked his head emphatically. 'He's just run out to walk her home as if she hadn't been out on foot alone all her life!'

'Vasily, I feel it's not a good idea to have him living with you.'

'Of course it's not, but who could have foreseen this? The flat is too big for me and my sister: there's a spare room – why not let some decent fellow have it? And the decent fellow has gone and fallen head over heels in love with her. To be quite honest, I'm annoyed with her too: I mean, why should she look down on Kuzma? He's kind, no fool, a nice fellow. And she doesn't pay him the slightest attention . . . Anyway, you'd better clear off out of my room – I'm busy. Wait in the dining-room if you want to see my sister and Kuzma, they'll be back soon.'

'I won't, Vasily, I'm in a hurry too, goodbye.'

No sooner had I gone into the street than I saw Masha and Kuzma. They were walking in silence: Masha walked ahead with an expression of laboured concentration, with Kuzma a little to one side and behind her as if he dared not walk next to her, occasionally glancing sideways at her face. They passed without seeing me.

I can't do anything and I can't think about anything. I've read about the third battle of Plevna. There were twelve thousand Russian and Rumanian casualties alone, not counting Turks . . . Twelve thousand . . . Sometimes I visualise this figure as a row of digits, sometimes as an endless chain of corpses lying in a row. If they were to be laid shoulder to shoulder, they'd make a road five miles long . . . What is this?

I was told about General Skobelev, how he'd rushed somewhere, attacked something, taken a fortress, or lost one . . . I can't remember which. There's only one thing I can remember and see in this horrible business: a mountain of corpses used as a pedestal for grandiose deeds to be set down on the pages of history. Maybe this is how it has to be – I don't intend to judge – I can't, anyhow. I don't reason about war, I react to it directly with my emotions that are outraged by the mass of blood spilt. Probably a bull experiences something similar when other bulls like itself are slaughtered before its eyes . . . It can't understand what use its death is and just gazes, its eyes bulging with horror, and utters a desperate, heart-rending roar.

Am I a coward or not?

Today I was told that I am. True, it was a very shallow person who heard me express my worry that I might be called up and my reluctance to go to war. The lady's opinion didn't upset me, but it provoked the question: am I not in fact a coward? Perhaps all my outrage against what everyone else considers a great cause can be traced to fear for my own skin? Indeed, is one unimportant life worth worrying about when such a great cause is at stake? Am I in fact capable of risking my life for a cause?

I did not bother with these questions for long. I went back over my life, recalling all the times – admittedly few – when I had had to face danger, and I could not accuse myself of cowardice. I had not been afraid for my life then, and I'm not afraid for it now. Therefore it can't be death that frightens me . . .

More battles, more deaths, more suffering. After reading the paper I'm in no state to get on with anything: in books there are no letters, only rows of falling men; my pen is like a weapon inflicting black wounds on the white paper. If I go on like this I shall end up with real hallucinations. But actually I do have a new worry now, which has distracted me a little from that one agonizing thought.

Last night I went to see the Lvovs and found them having tea. Brother and sister were at the table. Kuzma was walking rapidly from one corner of the room to another, holding his hand against his face which was swollen up and tied with a handkerchief.

'What's wrong with you?' I asked him.

He didn't reply, just waved his hand and went on pacing.

'He had a bad toothache and it's turned into an inflammation and an enormous abscess,' said Masha. 'I did ask him to go to a doctor in good time, but he wouldn't listen, and now see what it's come to.'

'The doctor will be here soon, I've asked him to come,' said Vasily.

'There was no need for that,' said Kuzma through clenched teeth.

'There certainly was – you could have an internal discharge. And here you are, still walking about though I did tell you to go to bed. Do you know what that can lead to?'

'I don't care what happens,' muttered Kuzma.

'Of course you do, Kuzma; don't be silly,' Masha said quietly.

These words were enough to calm Kuzma down. He even joined us at table and asked for tea. Masha poured him a glass and passed it to him. As he took the glass from her hands a truly ecstatic expression came over his face, an expression so incongruous with his comically misshapen, swollen face that I couldn't help smiling. Lvov grinned too; only Masha gave Kuzma an earnest and compassionate look.

The doctor arrived, a jovial man as fresh and healthy as an apple. He examined the patient's neck, and his normal jovial expression changed into one of concern.

'Let's go to your room: I need to have a really good look at you.'

I followed them to Kuzma's room.

The doctor made him get in to bed and began examining the upper part of his chest, touching it gently with his fingers.

'Right now, you stay there like a good lad and don't get up. Have you any friends who would sacrifice some of their time for you?' asked the doctor.

'I think so,' Kuzma replied in a rather puzzled tone.

'I would ask them,' said the doctor, turning invitingly to me, 'to watch over the patient from today and to send for me if there's any change for the worse.'

He left the room. Lvov went to the hall to see him out; they spent a long time there talking in barely audible voices, and I went back to Masha. She was sitting pensively with her head propped on one hand, slowly stirring her tea with the other.

'The doctor's told us to stay with Kuzma all the time.'

'Is he really in danger?' Masha asked in alarm.

'He must be. Otherwise there would be no need for us to stay with him. You won't mind looking after him, will you, Masha?'

'No, of course not. There, I haven't been to the front yet and here I am being a nurse already. Let's go in and see him; it must be very dreary to lie there all alone.'

Kuzma met us smiling as much as his swollen cheek would let him.

'Thank you,' he said, 'I was beginning to think you'd forgotten me.'

'No, Kuzma, we shan't forget you now: we've got to stay with you . . . Now you can see,' said Masha with a smile, 'what comes from not listening to me.'

'You'll do that?' Kuzma asked shyly.

'Yes I shall, but you must do as I say.'

Kuzma shut his eyes and blushed with pleasure.

'Now,' he said suddenly, turning to me. 'Could you hand me the mirror please? It's on the table there.'

I handed him the little round mirror; Kuzma asked me to shine the light for him and examined the swelling in the mirror. His face clouded over and although we all tried to involve him in conversation he uttered not another word for the whole of the evening.

Today I was told for certain that the reservists will be called up soon; I had been expecting it and therefore wasn't particularly surprised.

I could have escaped the fate I dread so much, I could have used influential connections to do my service here in Petersburg. I could have got myself fixed up here, to do clerical work, for example. But I find that sort of thing distasteful, and besides, there's something I can't define inside me, assessing the situation and forbidding me to dodge the fighting. 'It's wrong,' my inner voice tells me.

Something I never expected has happened.

This morning I went to take Masha's place by Kuzma's bedside. She met me at the door, pale and worn out after a night without sleep, and her eyes were red with crying.

'What is it, Masha, what's the matter?'

'Quiet, quiet, please,' she whispered. 'It's all over.'

'What's over? He hasn't died, has he?'

'No, he's not dead yet . . . but there's no hope. Both the doctors . . . you see, we called in another one . . .'

Tears were choking her voice.

'You go and have a look . . . Let's go in to him.'

'Dry your tears first and have a drink of water, or you really will upset him.'

'It doesn't matter . . . Do you think he doesn't know? He knew yesterday when he asked for the mirror; he was going to be a doctor himself soon.'

The room where the sick man lay was filled with the heavy smell of a dissecting room. His bed had been moved to the centre of the floor. Under the blanket could be seen the sharp outlines of his long legs, his large body and his arms stretched out along his sides. His eyes were shut, his breathing was slow and heavy. It seemed to me that he had grown thinner overnight; his face had taken on a nasty sallow hue and was moist and clammy.

'What's the matter with him?' I asked in a whisper.

'He'll tell you . . . You stay with him; I've had enough.'

She covered her face with her hands and left the room, shaking with stifled sobs; I sat by the bed and waited for Kuzma to wake up. There was a deathly silence in the room, punctuated only by the pocket watch on the bedside table ticking its quiet song and the sick man's heavy intermittent breathing. I looked at his face and couldn't recognise it; it wasn't that his features had changed drastically – they hadn't. But I saw him in a completely new light. I had known Kuzma for a long time and we were friends (though we had never been on particularly intimate terms), but never had I put myself in his place as I did now. I thought about his life, his failures and his joys, as if they were my own. Up till now I had seen mostly the comic side of his love for Masha, but now I realised what agonies this man must be enduring. 'Is his life really in such danger?' I wondered. 'Surely not. A man can't die of a stupid toothache. Masha is crying over him now, but he'll recover and all will be well.'

He opened his eyes and saw me. Without changing his expression he began to speak slowly, pausing after each word.

'Hello . . . There, you can see how I am . . . It's the end. It crept up on me so unexpectedly . . . so stupidly . . .'

'Kuzma, do tell me what's the matter with you. Perhaps it's not so bad after all.'

'Not so bad, you say? No, old man, it's bad all right. I wouldn't be wrong about something so obvious. Come here, have a look.'

Slowly and deliberately, he turned back the blanket, unbuttoned his nightshirt and an unbearable smell of putrefaction assailed me. Starting at the right side of his neck, over an area the size of a hand, Kuzma's chest was black as velvet with a slight grey-blue tinge. It was gangrene.

For four days now I've been at the sick man's bedside without a wink of sleep, either with Masha or with her brother. There seems to be barely a flicker of life in him, yet it won't leave his powerful body. They've cut a piece of black dead flesh out of him and thrown it away like a rag and the doctor has told us to bathe the great wound left by the operation every two hours. Two or three of us approach Kuzma's bed every two hours, turn and lift his enormous body, lay bare the terrible wound and pour a carbolic solution on it through a gutta-percha tube. The liquid is sprayed over the wound and Kuzma sometimes summons enough strength to smile 'because it tickles', as he puts it. Like anyone who is hardly ever ill he very much enjoys being nursed like a small child and he is particularly pleased when Masha takes what he calls 'the reins of government' – the gutta-percha tube – into her hands and sets about irrigating the wound. He says that nobody can do it as skilfully as she does, despite the fact that the tube is often shaking in her hands because she is so upset and the whole bed gets splashed with water.

How their relationship has changed! Masha used to be quite unattainable for Kuzma, he was afraid even to look at her; she would seldom take any notice of him; now she often cries quietly as she sits by his bed when he is asleep and nurses him tenderly, and he calmly accepts her care as his due and talks to her as if she were his little daughter.

Sometimes he is in great pain. His wound burns and he is racked by fever . . . At those times some weird ideas come into my head. I see Kuzma as a unit, as one of the units making up the tens of thousands reported in despatches from the front. I try to use his illness and the pain he is suffering as a measure of the evil caused by war. How much torture and anguish we have here in this one room, this one bed, this one breast – and all that is but a drop in the ocean of grief and pain suffered by that enormous mass of men who are being sent into battle, pulled back and stacked in the fields in piles of bodies, dead and bloody, some of them still groaning and writhing.

Lack of sleep and oppressive thoughts have completely exhausted me. I must ask Lvov or Masha to take my place while I go and get a couple of hours' sleep.

I slept the sleep of the dead, curled up on a tiny little divan, and was awoken by someone shaking my shoulder.

'Get up, get up,' Masha was saying. I leapt up completely bewildered at first. Masha was whispering in a rapid and frightened voice.

'Patches, more patches,' I finally made out.

'What patches, where are the patches?'

'Oh my God, he doesn't understand a thing. Kuzma's got more patches. I've sent for the doctor.'

'Well, maybe it means nothing,' I said with the indifference of someone who's just been woken up.

'Means nothing? Have a look yourself.'

Kuzma lay there, his limbs sprawled out, in a heavy, restless sleep; he kept tossing his head from side to side and gave out occasional muffled groans. His chest was exposed and I could see two small black patches about two inches below the bandaged wound. The gangrene had penetrated further beneath the skin, spread under it and come out in these two places. Although I had held out little hope for

Kuzma's recovery, these new and unmistakable tokens of death made me turn pale.

Masha was sitting in a corner of the room, with her hands in her lap, looking at me silently with despairing eyes.

'You mustn't despair, Masha. The doctor will come and have·a look; perhaps it's not the end yet. Perhaps we'll still pull him out of it.'

'No we won't, he'll die,' she whispered.

'All right, we won't and he'll die,' I answered just as quietly. 'It will be a great loss for all of us, but you mustn't let grief destroy you: these past few days you've looked more dead than alive yourself.'

'You don't know the torment I've been through these few days. I can't even explain it to myself. I didn't love him and even now I don't think I love him the way he loves me, but if he dies my heart will break. I'll always remember him looking at me so intently, never speaking when I was there even though he had plenty to say and loved talking. I'll never be rid of the reproach deep down that I had no pity for him and didn't value his mind, his heart and his affection. You may think this is ridiculous, but I'm tormented all the time now by the thought that if I'd loved him our lives would now be quite different, everything would have turned out differently and this terrible, absurd thing might never have happened. I keep thinking and thinking, finding excuses for myself, but deep down inside me something keeps repeating: it's your fault, it's your fault.'

At this point I looked at the sick man, afraid that he would be woken by our whispering, and I saw a change in his face. He was awake and had heard what Masha was saying, but was trying not to show it. His lips were quivering, his cheeks were burning, his whole face seemed to be lit up by the sun, the way a damp and cheerless meadow lights up when the lowering rainclouds part and let a ray of sunlight glimpse through. He must have forgotten both his illness and her fear of death; one single feeling filled his soul, causing two tears to pour from under his closed, quivering eyelids. Masha stared at him for a few moments, she seemed to be startled, then she blushed, a tender expression flitted over her face and, bending over the poor man who was half a corpse, she kissed him.

Now he opened his eyes. 'My God, I want so much not to die,' he said. And suddenly the room resounded with strange, quiet sobbing sounds that were quite new to my ears, for I had never seen this man cry before.

I left the room. I was on the point of bursting into tears myself.

I do not want to die either, nor do all those thousands out there. At least Kuzma is being granted some comfort during his last hours – but what about them? Besides the fear of death and his physical pain, Kuzma is feeling something so good that I doubt he would exchange these moments for any others in his life. No, this is something altogether different. Death will always be death, but it's one thing to die among those who are close to you and love you, and another to lie there in the mud and your own blood, waiting to be finished off at any moment or run over by field-guns and squashed like a worm . . .

'I'll tell you frankly,' the doctor said to me in the hall as he put on his fur coat and galoshes, 'even with hospital treatment, ninety-nine per cent of such cases die. I can only count on the painstaking nursing, the patient's excellent spirits and his very strong desire to recover.'

'Everyone who's sick wishes to recover, doctor.'

'Of course, but in your friend's case there are certain factors which strengthen the desire,' said the doctor with a little smile. 'Anyway, we'll do an operation tonight, we'll make another incision, put in drainage tubes so that the water will do more good, and we'll keep hoping.'

He shook my hand, wrapped his fur coat tight around him and went off on his rounds. That evening he turned up with his instruments.

'Perhaps you would like some practice, my colleague-to-be, and do the operation?' he said turning to Lvov.

Lvov nodded, rolled up his sleeves and set to, with a grave and sombre expression. I watched him inserting into the wound a peculiar instrument with a triple-edged blade, saw the blade cut through the body, and Kuzma clutching the bedclothes with his hands and gnashing his teeth with pain.

'Now come on, be a man,' Lvov said to him morosely as he placed the drainage in the new wound.

'Does it hurt very much?' Masha asked gently.

'Not so much, my dear, but I feel very weak and exhausted.'

The wound was bandaged, Kuzma was given some vodka and he calmed down. The doctor left. Lvov went to his room to study, while Masha and I started to put the room in order.

'Tuck the blanket in,' said Kuzma in a flat and toneless voice. 'I can feel a draught.'

I began to adjust his pillows and the blanket as he instructed, which he did very peevishly, insisting that there was a small gap by his left elbow that was letting in a draught. He asked me to tuck in the blanket properly. I tried to do so as best I could, but for all my efforts to please him Kuzma still felt a draught, now on his side, now on his legs.

'You're not doing it properly,' he grumbled in a low voice. 'There's another draught down my back; let her do it.' He looked at Masha and I realised very clearly why I was useless at pleasing him.

Masha put down the phial of medicine she was holding and came to the bed.

'Shall I do it?'

'Yes please . . . That's good . . . now I'm warm . . .'

He watched her arranging the blanket, then he closed his eyes and fell asleep with an expression of childlike happiness on his worn-out face.

'Are you going home?' asked Masha.

'No, I've had a good long sleep and I can sit up; but I'll go if I'm not needed.'

'Please don't go, let's talk just a little. My brother's always shut away with his books and I find it so sad and depressing to be alone with a sick man when he's asleep and to think that he is dying.'

'You must be strong, Masha; nurses aren't allowed to have depressing thoughts or cry.'

'I shan't cry when I'm a nurse. After all, it won't be as depressing to nurse wounded men as someone so close to me.'

'You still intend to go, then?'

'Of course I do. Whether he recovers or dies, I'll still go. I'm used to the idea now and I can't give it up. I feel like doing something good and giving myself some good bright days to remember.'

'Oh Masha, I'm afraid you won't see much brightness in the war.'

'Why not? I'll be working – and that's all the brightness you need. I want to do my share in the war.'

'Do your share! Aren't you horrified by the war? This doesn't sound like you at all.'

'I mean exactly what I said. Who told you I like the war? Only . . . how can I put it to you? War is an evil; you and I and many others share that opinion. But it is something inevitable; it makes no difference whether you like war or not, it will happen and if you don't go off to fight, they will take someone else and some human being will be maimed or worn out by the fighting just the same. I'm afraid you don't understand me; I'm not expressing myself very well. What I mean is that I think war is a *universal* misfortune, it's a *universal* suffering, and while it may be permissible to back out of it, I don't like doing that.'

I said nothing. Masha's words expressed very clearly my own vague objections to backing out of fighting. I myself *felt* as she felt and thought, only I *thought* differently.

'Now you seem to be thinking all the time about trying to stay here,' she went on, 'if you're called up to fight. My brother was telling me about it. You know I'm very fond of you, you're a decent man, but this is something about you that I don't like.'

'I'm sorry, Masha: it's a matter of viewpoint. Why should I be held responsible? I didn't start the war, did I?'

'You didn't – nor did any of those who have died and are dying out there now. They wouldn't have gone either if they'd had the choice, but they didn't have it, and you do. They're off to the war and you're going to stay in Petersburg, alive, healthy and happy, just because you know people who'd be sorry to send a friend of theirs to the war. It's not for me to judge, maybe it's forgivable, but I don't like it, no, I don't.'

She shook her curly head vigorously and fell silent.

At last it has happened. Today I put on my grey greatcoat and had a taste of basic training . . . rifle drill. My ears are still full of 'Atten – tion! . . . Form fours! Present arms!'

And I have been standing at attention, forming fours and crashing about with my rifle. Eventually, when I have divined enough of the mysteries of forming fours, I shall be assigned to a contingent, we shall be put in carriages, sent off in a train, posted to regiments and allocated the places vacated by the dead . . .

Well, none of that matters . . . It's all over; I don't own myself any more, I'm floating with the current; now the best thing is not to think, not to reason, but to accept all the chance events of life uncritically and only scream when it hurts . . .

I have been put in a special section of the barracks reserved for the privileged classes; it's special in that it has beds, not bunks, but it's still pretty filthy. The non-privileged recruits have a really rough time. Until they're posted they live in a huge shed which used to be an

indoor riding school; it was made into two storeys by putting boards
on the rafters, piles of straw were put in and the temporary inmates
have been left to get on with it as best they can. In the gangway
through the middle of the shed snow and mud have been tramped in
from the yard by a constant stream of men coming in; it's got mixed
with the straw and has created an unimaginable slushy mess, and even
the straw at the sides is not all that clean either. Several hundred men
are standing, sitting and lying in the straw in regional groups: a real
ethnic exhibition. I found some men from my own area: tall, gangly
Ukrainians in new svitkas and Astrakhan hats lying huddled together
and silent; there were about a dozen of them.

'Hello, lads.'

'Hello.'

'How long have you been away from home?'

'It'll be two weeks now. And who might you be?' one of them
asked me. I gave my name which they all turned out to have heard of.
Now they'd met a fellow-countryman they came to life a bit and
opened up, chatting in Ukrainian.

'Fed up?' I asked.

'Of course we're fed up. It gets you down. If only they fed us
properly, but the grub is bleedin' awful, my God it is!'

'Where are they going to send you?'

'How would we know? They say, to fight the Turks . . .'

'What do you think about going?'

'I've seen it all before, haven't I?'

I began asking about our town, and memories of home loosened
their tongues. There were stories about a recent wedding for which a
pair of oxen had been sold and how soon afterwards the groom had
been called up, about the court bailiff ('a hundred devils on horseback down his throat'), about how short land had become and how
this year several hundred people had left the village of Markovka for
the Amur in Eastern Siberia . . . The conversation was entirely
confined to the past; nobody talked about the future, the labours,
dangers and suffering that lay in store for all of us. Nobody wanted to
know about the Turks, the Bulgarians, or the cause for which he was
going to die.

A tipsy young soldier from a local unit came along and stopped by
our group; when I mentioned the war again, he declared categor-
ically:

'Them Turks have got to be taught a lesson.'

'Why must they?' I asked. I couldn't help smiling at his certainty and confidence.

'They've got to, sir, them heathens has got to be wiped out without a trace. It's their trouble-making has put us all to such misery. Now if them Turks had done like they ought, decent and quiet like, without making trouble, I'd be at home now with my parents, safe and sound. But they're stirring up trouble and we've got the misery of it. Don't you worry, I'm telling you straight. Let's have a cigarette, sir.' He broke off abruptly, stood to attention and saluted me.

I gave him a cigarette, said goodbye to my fellow-countrymen and went home, since I was off duty now.

'They're stirring up trouble and we've got the misery of it', the drunken voice was ringing in my ears. Brief and vague, but that sentence pretty well says it all.

At the Lvovs' house there is an air of hopelessness and misery. Kuzma is very poorly – although his wound has cleared up now, he has a terrible fever, and is delirious and groaning. Brother and sister have not left his bedside all the days I have been busy joining the army and training. Now they know I am going to the front the sister has become sadder still and the brother more sullen.

'In uniform now,' he said gruffly when I went to see him in his room which stank of tobacco smoke and was littered with books. 'You people, you people . . .'

'What do you mean, Vasily?'

'You won't let me get on with my studies, that's what! I've no time, they won't let me finish my course, they'll send me to the war. There's a lot of things I'll never find out, and to cap it all I've got you and Kuzma.'

'I know, Kuzma is dying; but what about me?'

'Aren't you dying too? If they don't kill you you'll go mad or put a bullet through your head. Don't I know you, and hasn't it all happened before?'

'What do you mean "happened before"? Do you know anything about it? Tell me, Vasily.'

'Leave it, the last thing I want is to upset you even more. It won't be good for you. I don't know anything about it, I don't know why I said that.'

But I persisted and he told me what had happened before.

'A wounded artillery officer told me this. They'd marched from Kishinyov in April, just after the war was declared. It was raining constantly, the roads had disappeared; there was just mud, so bad that the guns and the carriages were up to their axles in it. It got so bad that the horses couldn't get a grip; so they attached cables and the men had to pull the guns. On the second day the road was horrific: sixteen versts with twelve hills and nothing but quagmires between them. They got stuck. The rain was lashing down on them, not a dry thread on their backs, they were starving and exhausted, but they had to keep on pulling the guns. Naturally they kept on pulling and then falling unconscious face-down in the mud. In the end they were stuck in such a morass that they just couldn't get any further and still they kept on straining away. "I'm frightened to remember what it was like," the officer said. They had a medical officer, just qualified, a highly strung chap. He said, "I can't stand the sight of this; I'm going on ahead." He rode off. The soldiers cut down a load of branches, practically made a whole causeway and finally got moving. They dragged the battery to the top of a hill – and there was the medical officer hanging from a tree . . . That's what's happened before. That man couldn't stand the sight of such suffering, so how on earth are you going to put up with it all?'

'Vasily, isn't it easier to bear the torments yourself than to kill yourself like that medical officer?'

'Well, I don't know what's so good about being put in the shafts of a gun-carriage.'

'My conscience won't be tormenting me, Vasily.'

'Now that's a bit too subtle for me, old man. You have a talk to my sister about that: she's an expert on subtle points like that. If you want to go through *Anna Karenina* with a fine-toothcomb or have a chat about Dostoyevsky, she can do all that; I'm sure that conundrum's been sorted out in some novel. Farewell, philosopher.'

He gave a good-natured laugh at his joke and offered me his hand.

'Where are you going?'

'Across the river, to the clinic.'

I went into Kuzma's room. He was awake and feeling better than usual, as Masha, who spent all her time sitting by his bed, explained to me. He hadn't seen me in uniform before and the sight made a disagreeable impression on him.

'Are they letting you stay or sending you off with the army?' he asked.

'They're sending me off; didn't you know?'

He said nothing.

'I did know, but I'd forgotten. I don't remember a lot these days, old man, and I can't make sense of things . . . Right, off you go then. You have to.'

'You too, Kuzma!'

'What do you mean "me too"? Do you mean I'm wrong? What have you done to deserve being let off? Go and die. More useful men than you and better workers than you are going . . . Can you straighten my pillow? . . . That's it.'

He was talking in a low irritable voice as if to take it out on me for his illness.

'That's all true, Kuzma, but I'm going, aren't I? I'm not just protesting on my own behalf. If I were, I'd stay here without any more fuss: that could easily be fixed. I'm not doing that, I've been called up and I'm going. But at least let me be allowed to have my own opinion about it.'

Kuzma lay there, his eyes fixed on the ceiling as if he wasn't listening to me. At last he slowly turned his head towards me.

'Don't think there's anything real in what I say,' he murmured. 'I'm worn out and irritated and I really don't know why I pick on people. I've become very bad-tempered: my time must be up soon.'

'Stop it, Kuzma, cheer up. Your wound's cleared up, it's healing, and things are taking a turn for the better. You should be talking about life now, not death.'

Masha's big sad eyes looked at me and I suddenly recalled her telling me a fortnight before, 'No, he won't get better, he'll die.'

'Suppose I really did come back to life? That'd be good,' said Kuzma with a faint smile. 'You'll be sent away to fight and Masha and I will come, she as a nurse, me as a medical officer. And when you're wounded I'll be fussing round you as you are round me now.'

'Stop chatting, Kuzma,' said Masha. 'It's bad for you to talk too much. Anyway, it's time to begin your torture.'

He submitted to us; we undressed him, removed his bandages and began working on his large mutilated chest. And as I directed the stream of water at the bared bloody places, the exposed collar-bone which shone like mother-of-pearl, the vein which ran right through the wound lying clear and free, as though this were not a wound in a living human being but an anatomical specimen, I thought of other wounds, of a far more horrible kind, appalling in their quantity and inflicted, moreover, not by blind, senseless chance but by deliberate deeds of men.

I have not written a word in this notebook about what is happening at home and what I'm going through there: my mother's tears when I come or go; the heavy silence when I join them all at table; my brothers and sisters being so kind and considerate – it's all too sad to see or hear, and sadder still to write about. The thought that in a week I shall have to lose the most precious thing in the world makes me choke with tears . . .

And now at last it's goodbye. Tomorrow at first light our unit is boarding the train. I have been allowed to spend my last night at home; and I am sitting in my room alone, for the last time. The last time! Does anyone who hasn't experienced that 'last' time know the bitterness of those words? For the last time my family have gone off to bed, for the last time I've come into this little room and sat down at the table with its familiar low lamp and its untidy piles of books and paper. I haven't touched them for a whole month. For the last time I pick up a piece of work I've begun and take a close look at it. It has been abandoned and is lying there dead, aborted, senseless. Instead of finishing it you are going with thousands of men like you to the edge of the world because history has decided it needs your physical strength. Forget about your mental powers: nobody wants them. What does it matter that you've nurtured them for many years and prepared to apply them to something or other? A vast organism that you know nothing about, of which you are a minute and insignificant particle, has decided to cut you off and throw you away. And what can you do to stop that decision, 'you, the great toe of this assembly'?

But no more of this. I must try to get some sleep: tomorrow I have to get up very early.

I asked them all not to come to the station to say goodbye. Farewells mean just more tears. But by the time I was in the carriage packed with people I felt such soul-piercing loneliness that I think I would have given anything to spend those last few minutes with someone close to me. At last the appointed hour came, but the train didn't move – there was some hold-up. Half-an-hour passed, then an hour, then another half-hour, and it still hadn't moved. I could have gone home and back again in that hour-and-a-half . . . Perhaps

someone would find it too much to stay away and would come . . .
No, they'd all think the train had left; nobody would count on it
leaving late. All the same, they might . . . And I looked out in the
direction somebody might come from. Time had never dragged so
slowly.

I was startled by a shrill bugle sounding the muster. The soldiers
who had got out of the carriages, huddled on the platform, scrambled
back on to the train. The train was about to leave and I shouldn't see
anybody.

But I did. The Lvovs, both of them, came almost running towards
my carriage and I was terrifically glad to see them. I can't recall what I
said to them; I can't recall what they were saying to me, but for one
phrase, 'Kuzma's dead'.

Those are the last words in the notebook.

A broad snow-covered field. It is surrounded by white hills with
white, frosted trees. The sky is overcast and low; there is a thaw in the
air. The crackle of rifles and the heavy pounding of the guns is
constant; smoke covers one of the hills and slowly drifts off it into the
field. Through it you can see a black moving mass. If you look harder
you can see it is made up of separate black dots. Many of these dots
are motionless now, but others keep on moving forward, although
they are a long way off their goal, which can be detected only from
the mass of smoke swirling off it, and although their numbers are
dwindling all the time.

The reserve battalion lying in the snow has not piled arms; rifles in
hand, it is watching with all its thousand eyes the movement of the
black mass.

'They're off, lads, there they go . . . Oh no, they won't make it!'

'But why are they holding us back? They'd take it in no time if they
were given a hand.'

'Bored with life, are you?' an elderly regular soldier said gruffly.
'Lie there if you've been told to and thank God you're in one piece.'

'I'll stay in one piece, dad, don't you worry,' a young soldier with
a cheerful face replied. 'I've been in four attacks and it's not bothered
me one bit. It's only scary right at the beginning, and after that you
don't turn a hair. It's the first time for sir here, so I'll bet he's saying
his prayers now. Isn't that right, sir?'

'What's up with you?' a lanky black-bearded soldier lying beside
him chimed in.

'Do look a bit more cheerful, sir!'

'I'm quite happy as I am, lad.'

'You keep close to me if anything starts. I've been through it, I know the score. Anyway he's brave enough, our sir, he won't run for it. But we had another volunteer once, and when we went in and the bullets started flying about, he threw down his pack and his rifle and ran for it, but he stopped a bullet, it got him in the back. You can't do that – the oath, you know.'

'Don't you fear, I shan't run,' replied 'sir' quietly, 'you can't run away from a bullet.'

'Of course you can't – no sense in doing that. A bullet's dead cunning . . . Holy saints, our lot aren't moving!'

The black mass had stopped, covered in wreaths of smoke. 'They're getting a hammering now, they'll be falling back soon . . . No, they're going forward. Save them, Holy Mother of God! Go on then, go on, there they go . . . Lord, look how many have been hit. And no-one's there picking them up.'

'A bullet! A bullet!' The words echoed all round. Indeed, something had come whistling through the air. It was a stray bullet flying high above the reserves. Then came a second, and a third. The battalion began to stir.

'Stretcher!' someone shouted.

One of the stray bullets had done its work. Four stretcher-bearers rushed to the wounded man. Then suddenly on one of the hills, away from the point under attack, little figures appeared, men and horses, and at once a thick round puff of smoke as white as snow burst out there.

'The bastards are aiming at us!' the cheerful soldier cried out. A shell whined and crashed, a shot rang out. The cheerful soldier plunged his face into the snow. When he lifted his head he saw that 'sir' was lying face downwards next to him, arms flung out and his neck bent unnaturally. The second stray bullet had made an enormous black hole above his right eye.

1879   *Translated by Donald Rayfield*

Artists

I

Dedov

Today I feel as though a ton weight has fallen from my shoulders. What unexpected bliss! Away with my engineer's epaulettes! Away with my instruments and calculations!

Isn't it rather shameful, though, to be so overjoyed at my poor aunt's death, just because I have been able to resign my position on the strength of what she left me? True, on her deathbed she urged me to commit myself entirely to the pursuit I love so, and now, apart from anything else, I am delighted that I can honour that most ardent wish. It was only yesterday . . . The look on our chief's face when he heard that I was resigning! And when I explained to him my aim in so doing, he simply gaped.

'For love of art? . . . Hmm! . . . Put in your resignation, then.'

And he said nothing more; he just turned and walked away. But I needed nothing more. I am free! I am an artist! Is this not the pinnacle of bliss?

Wanting to get right away from people and from Petersburg, I hired a wherry for a turn around the bay. The water, the sky, the distant city glittering in the sun, the blue woods bordering the Gulf, the mastheads in the Kronstadt anchorage, the dozens of steamers scudding along and sailing boats and two-masted *laivas* gliding by – I saw it all in a new light. It was all mine, all under my mastery, all there for me to capture, to dash onto a canvas and set before the crowd, stunning them with what art can do. True, I ought not to sell the skin before I have killed the bear; as yet, after all, God only knows what kind of great artist I shall make . . .

The wherry briskly sliced through the smooth water. The wherry-man – a strapping, hearty, handsome lad in a red shirt – plied the oars tirelessly, bending forward and throwing himself back, propelling the boat powerfully with each movement. The setting sun played on his face and his red shirt, making such an effect that I felt an urge to sketch him in colour. My little box with its tiny canvases, paints and brushes is always at my side.

'Stop rowing and sit still a minute while I paint you,' I said.

He dropped the oars.

'No – look as though you're taking an upstroke.'

He picked up the oars, flourished them like a bird flapping its wings, and settled in a splendid pose. I quickly pencilled in the outlines and started to paint. Mixing the colours was a rare delight. I knew that nothing would tear me away from them as long as I lived.

The wherryman soon began to tire; his devil-may-care expression turned listless and dreary. He started to yawn and once even wiped his face on his sleeve, dropping his head towards one of the oars to do so. The folds in his shirt were completely lost. What a nuisance! I cannot abide it when my subject moves.

'Do sit still, my good fellow!'

He grinned.

'What's so funny?'

He gave a bashful grin and said, 'Well, it's a rum do, sir.'

'What's rum about it?'

'Well, painting me like I was a curiosity. Like a picture or something.'

'And a picture there shall be, my good friend.'

'What would you want with that?'

'It's for practice. I'll paint small ones and more small ones, then I'll start on the big ones.'

'Big ones?'

'Up to three sazhens across.'

He said nothing, then asked solemnly, 'So you can do icons as well?'

'That I can. Only I paint pictures.'

'Aye.'

He thought a bit, then asked, 'What good are they?'

'What?'

'Them pictures . . .'

Naturally I was not going to start lecturing him on the meaning of art, I just told him that good money can be made with these pictures – a thousand rubles, two thousand, and up. The wherryman was completely satisfied and said not another word. The study turned out splendidly (very lovely, the fiery tones of the red calico in the light of the setting sun), and I went home pleased with everything.

II

Ryabinin

Before me old Taras the model, standing in the strained posture demanded by Professor N., 'with 'is 'and on 'is 'ead', that being 'a vairy classical pozz'. Around me, a crowd of classmates, each sitting, like me, at an easel, with palette and brushes in hand. Right at the front is Dedov, painting Taras zealously, landscape man though he is. A smell of paint, oils and turpentine in the room, and a deathly hush. Taras is allowed to rest every thirty minutes; he sits on the edge of the wooden box that serves him as a pedestal, and turns from a 'life' into an ordinary, naked old man. He stretches arms and legs numb with long immobility, makes do without a handkerchief, and all the rest of it. The students congregate round the easels, eyeing each other's work. There is always a crowd around mine. I'm a very able Academy student and am confidently expected to be among 'our coryphæi' – to use the felicitous expression of Mr V. S., the well-known art critic, who declared a long while ago that 'Ryabinin will amount to something'. That is why everyone looks at my work.

Five minutes pass, then we all take our places again. Taras clambers back onto his pedestal, puts his hand on his head, and on with the daubing . . .

And so it goes, day after day.

Tedious, isn't it? I convinced myself a long time ago that it's all very tedious. But a locomotive with a full head of steam can do one of two things – speed along the rails until the head of steam is gone, or leap the rails and transform itself from a flawless iron-and-copper marvel into a heap of debris. My choice is the same . . . I am on rails that clasp my wheels tight, and if I run off them – what then? I must speed on to the station, come what may, and never mind if to me that station is a black pit where nothing shows clear. Other people say that my destination is artistic accomplishment. It will be somehow artistic, no question of that – but as for accomplishment . . .

When I go to an exhibition and look at paintings, what do I see in them? A canvas overlaid with paint, which is so disposed as to create impressions similar to those evoked by real objects. People walk round and marvel – my, how ingeniously the colours are placed! And that's that. Whole books, whole mountains of books have been written on this subject, and I have read many of them. But all the Taines, the Carrières, the Kuglers, all those who have written about art, including Prud'hon, leave us none the wiser. They all hold forth on the meaning of art, but as I read them, the thought unfailingly stirs in my head: 'If indeed it has any.' I have never seen a good painting exert a good influence on any man: why then must I believe that it could?

Why must I believe it? I need to believe it, I sorely need to – but *how* can I believe it? How can I convince myself that I will not dedicate my life exclusively to the doltish curiosity of the crowd (and thank goodness if only to curiosity and not, for instance, to the arousal of base instincts) and to the vanity of some *nouveau-riche* belly-on-legs that casually walks up to one of my paintings – one that I have lived through, suffered through and hold most dear, that I have created not with brush and paint but with nerves and blood – and growls 'Not too bad, that', thrusts its hand into its bulging pocket, tosses me a few hundred rubles and takes my painting away from me? Takes it away, with all the agitation, the sleepless nights, the grief and the joy, the delusions and the disappointments. And once again you walk alone in the crowd. Mechanically you draw the model in the evenings, mechanically you paint him in the mornings, amazing your professors and your class-mates with your rapid progress. Why are you doing all this? Where are you going?

It has been four months since I sold my last picture, and I still have no ideas for a new one. How excellent it would be if something bobbed up in my head . . . Utter oblivion: to retreat into that painting as into a monastery, to think of nothing else. The questions 'where?' and 'why?' vanish while the work is there; one has a single thought, a single aim in mind, and there is delight in bringing it into being. A painting is a world in which you live and to which you are answerable. Wordly morality vanishes there: you create a new morality in your new world, and in that world you sense your rectitude and your worth or your paltriness and falsehood in your own way, without reference to real life.

But you cannot paint forever. In the evenings, when dusk halts work, you return to life and again hear the eternal question 'Why?' – the question that banishes sleep and keeps you tossing feverishly in your bed, staring into the darkness as if the answer were written there somewhere. At first light you fall into a dead sleep, and on awakening you descend once more into another world of dreams, peopled only by images that arise from within yourself, taking shape and growing distinct on the canvas before you.

'Why aren't you working, Ryabinin?' my neighbour asked loudly.

I was so preoccupied with my thoughts that the question made me jump. The hand holding the palette had dropped; the hem of my jacket had got into the paints and was all smeared; my brushes were on the floor. I glanced at my sketch: it was done, and well done. A lifelike Taras stood there on the canvas.

'I've finished,' I told my neighbour.

The class had finished too. The model had stepped off the box and was dressing. All the students were noisily gathering their belongings. A general chatter arose. People came and complimented me.

'A medal, a medal . . . Best sketch of all,' some said. Others said nothing; artists don't care to compliment each other.

III

Dedov

It would appear that I command the respect of my fellow students. Of course, my riper years – relative to theirs, that is – might have something to do with that. In the entire Academy, only Volsky is older than I. Yes indeed, art has an astonishing power of attraction! This Volsky is a retired officer, a gentleman of about forty-five and quite grey. To enrol in the Academy at his age, to start studying again – is that not an act of heroism? What a dogged worker he is: in summer he is out doing sketches from morning to night in all weathers, self-sacrifice personified; in winter he paints all the time while it is light, and draws in the evenings. In two years he has made great progress, though fate has not endowed him with exceptional talent.

Now Ryabinin is a different prospect – devilishly talented, but a terrible idler. I don't think he will ever amount to anything serious, though all the young artists revere him. The oddest thing about him, to me, is his predilection for those so-called 'realistic' subjects: he paints bast shoes, leg-cloths and sheepskin coats, as though we didn't see enough of them in life. But the odd thing about him is that he hardly does any work at all. Sometimes he gets down to it and in a month he'll complete a painting that everyone hails as a miracle, while admitting that the technique leaves something to be desired (in my view, his technique is exceedingly feeble). Then he stops painting, even stops sketching, walks round with a long face and won't speak to anyone, not even to me, although he seems to hold himself less aloof from me than from his other class-mates. A strange lad! I am astonished by people who fail to find full satisfaction in art. They cannot seem to understand that nothing elevates a man like the act of creation.

Only yesterday I finished a painting, exhibited it – and today was asked to price it. I will not let it go for less than three hundred. I've already been offered two hundred and fifty. I am of the opinion that one should never retreat from one's stated price. That wins respect. And here I am especially determined not to give way, because my picture is sure to find a buyer. The subject is attractive and saleable: winter, sunset, black tree-stumps in the foreground, stark against the red glow. That is K.'s style, and look how his go! This winter alone, I hear, he made twenty thousand or so. Not bad at all. I cannot understand how some artists contrive to be poor. Take K. – not a single little canvas of his goes to waste. Everything finds a buyer. It is simply a question of going about it the right way: as an artist, a creator, when you are painting a picture – as a trader when it's painted. And the more adroit you are on the business side, the better. The public has a way of trying to swindle us artists.

IV

Ryabinin

I live on Fifteenth Street, off Sredny Prospekt, and four times a day I go walking along the quay where the foreign ships put in. I love that place for its motley colours, its teeming life, its jostling and noise, and for the abundant subject-matter it has offered me. Here, watching the day-labourers hauling sacks, turning windlasses and winches, and steering pushcarts with all kinds of loads, I learned to paint the working man.

I was walking home with Dedov, the landscape painter . . . He's as genial and innocuous as a landscape himself, and passionately enamoured of his art. Now he surely knows no doubts of any kind. He paints what he sees – he sees a river and he paints a river, he sees sedge

in a marsh and he paints sedge in a marsh. And what do that river and
that marsh mean to him? He never gives it a thought. Apparently he
is an educated man – a qualified engineer, at least. He gave up his job,
being the lucky recipient of some inheritance or other which freed
him from having to work for a living. Now he just paints and paints:
in summer he sits from morning to night in a field or wood,
sketching; in winter he tirelessly composes sunsets, sunrises, noontides, and first and last moments of showers, winters, springs and so
forth. He has forgotten all his engineering, with no regrets. But when
we walk by the wharves, he often explains to me the purpose of
the huge lumps of iron and steel, the machine components, boilers
and all the omnium-gatherum that has been offloaded from the
ships.

'Look at this great boiler they've shipped in,' he said to me
yesterday, knocking his cane against the ringing metal.

'Don't we know how to make those here?' I asked.

'We do make them, but not many and not enough. See what a pile
they've brought in? But it's nasty workmanship – it'll have to be
repaired here, see where the seam's splitting? The rivets have worked
loose here too. Do you know how they make these things? It's hellish
work, I can tell you that. A man sits in the boiler and holds the rivet
from inside with tongs, pressing his chest against them for all he's
worth, and outside the boilersmith bangs the head of the rivet with a
hammer and flattens it into a little cap like that.'

He pointed to a long row of raised metal circles running down the
seam.

'But, Dedov – that's the same as pounding on his chest!'

'Just the same . . . I once had a go inside a boiler, and after four
rivets I was hard put to get myself out. My chest was shaken to bits.
But they get used to it somehow. True, they die like flies. They can
take it for a year or two – after that, if they're still alive, they're
seldom good for anything. Just you try taking the blows of a
whopping great hammer on your chest for a whole day, and inside a
boiler at that, in that stifling air, bent completely double. In winter
the iron is icy, in the cold, and he's sitting or lying on it. In that boiler
over there – the red one, see, the narrow one – there's no room to sit:
you have to lie on your side and give 'em your chest. Tough work
they do, those stone-lugs.'

'Stone-lugs?'

'Yes – that's what the workers call them. They often go deaf with the clanging. And do you think they earn much for that sort of hard labour? Kopeks! Because this job demands no skill, no artistry – just brawn . . . You see such heartrending sights at those ironworks, Ryabinin, if only you knew! I'm so glad to be done with them forever. At first it was hard just to get through the day with such suffering before your eyes . . . How different Nature is. She harms no one, nor need one harm her in exploiting her, as we artists do. Oh look, just look at that greyish tone!' he suddenly interrupted himself, pointing to a corner of the sky. 'Down there, below that little cloud . . . How charming! That greenish tinge it has! And if you painted it like that – I mean, exactly like that – nobody would believe you. But it's not bad, is it?'

I said something nice about it, although, to tell the truth, I saw nothing at all charming about a mucky-green scrap of St Petersburg sky, and I stopped Dedov short just as he started rhapsodising about another 'little tinge' near another little cloud.

'Tell me – where can I see one of those stone-lugs?'

'We can go to an ironworks together. I'll show you all sorts of things. Tomorrow, if you like. But you're not thinking of painting a stone-lug, are you? Don't, now – it's not worth it. There must be something jollier than that! But if you like, we can go to an ironworks tomorrow.'

Today we went to an ironworks and looked everything over. And we saw a stone-lug. He was sitting there, curled into a ball in the corner of a boiler, offering his chest to the blows of a hammer. I watched him for half an hour; during those thirty minutes the hammer rose and fell hundreds of times. The stone-lug writhed. I am going to paint him.

V

Dedov

Ryabinin has thought up something so idiotic that I don't know what to make of it. The day before yesterday I took him to an ironworks. We spent the whole day there and looked at everything, with me explaining the various procedures to him (to my amazement, I have forgotten very little of my trade). Finally, I took him into the boiler-shop. They happened to be working on an enormous boiler.

Ryabinin crawled inside and spent half an hour watching a labourer holding rivets in his tongs. He crawled out pale and shaken; all the way back he never said a word. And today he announced that he has already started painting that stone-lug. There's an idea for you! There's poetry in muck for you! Here I can say without fear or favour something that I would obviously never say outright: as I see it, this entire peasant tendency in art is sheer monstrosity. Who can be bothered with Repin's infamous 'Volga Boatmen'? They are splendidly drawn, indisputably – but that's all. Where is the beauty, the harmony, the grace? And why does art exist, if not to convey the grace that is in Nature?

Now, take what I am doing. Just a few more days' work and my tranquil 'May Morning' will be finished. The water in the pond barely stirs; the willows bend their boughs over it; the east is catching fire; the tiny, feathery clouds are tinted with pink. A female figure descends the steep bank with a pail, to draw water, and startles a flock of ducks. That is all: it seems simple enough, yet I can distinctly sense that there is no end of poetry in that painting. Now that is *art*! It inclines a man to quiet, gentle reverie; it soothes the soul. While Ryabinin's 'Stone-lug' will not move anyone at all. Everyone will promptly run away from that eyesore, those unsightly rags, that grimy face. How strange! In music, unpleasant, ear-splitting dissonances are not permitted – why, then, should we painters be allowed to produce downright unsightly, repulsive images? I shall have to talk to L. about it. He will write a little piece and by-the-by slate Ryabinin for that painting of his. And rightly so.

VI

Ryabinin

I have not been to the Academy for two weeks; I stay at home and paint. The work has thoroughly exhausted me, although it's going well. I should have said 'especially since', not 'although' it's going well. The closer it comes to completion, the more fearsome seems this thing that I have painted. And furthermore, I think this will be my last painting.

There he sits before me in a dark corner inside a boiler, a man wrenched double, dressed in tatters, panting with fatigue. He would not be visible at all but for the light that comes through the round rivet holes. Small pools of this light dapple his clothes and face, golden specks shimmer on his tatters, on his shaggy, sooty beard and hair, on his dark-red face that streams with a mixture of sweat and dirt, on his sinewy, straining arms and tormented, broad, sunken chest. And the fearsome blows ceaselessly crash down on the boiler, forcing the wretched stone-lug to muster all his strength to hold that incredible pose. Insofar as that tension and effort can be expressed, I have expressed it.

Sometimes I lay down my palette and brushes and sit some distance from the painting, directly facing it. I am satisfied with it; nothing of mine has ever succeeded as has this dreadful thing. The misfortune of it is that this satisfaction does not comfort me; it tortures me. It is not a finished painting, it is a raging disease. And how it will resolve itself I do not know, but I feel that after this there will be nothing more for me to paint. Fowlers, fishermen, hunters, with all their various telling expressions and their supremely typical physiognomies, the whole 'fertile domain of the genre style' – what is it to me now? I will never move people more than with this stone-lug of mine . . . if I move them at all.

I tried an experiment: I invited Dedov round and showed him the picture. All he said was, 'Well, well, old man!', and spread his hands. He sat down, looked at it for half an hour, then bade me a silent farewell and left. It seemed to move him. But then, he is an artist after all.

And I sit before my painting, and it moves me. I look at it and cannot tear myself away; I feel for that tormented figure. Sometimes I can even hear the hammer blows . . . It will drive me mad. I must cover it up.

A cloth hangs over the painting on the easel but I am still sitting before it, thinking still of that same indeterminate and fearsome thing that tortures me so. The sun is setting, and casting a slanting strip of yellow light through the dusty panes onto the cloth-draped easel. Just like a human figure. Just like a German actor's version of the Earth Spirit in *Faust*. 'Who summons me?'

Who summoned you? It was I, I who created you in this place. I called you forth, though not from some 'sphere' but from inside a dark, stifling boiler, so that the sight of you may appal the clean, sleek, odious crowd. Come, you who are fettered to the canvas by the force of my will; glare out at those morning coats and trains, shout at them, 'I am a festering sore!' Belabour their hearts, deprive them of their sleep, stand like a spectre in their sight! Murder their tranquillity, as you have murdered mine!

Not a hope of it! The painting is finished and fitted with a gilt frame, and two attendants will carry it off to the Academy on their heads. And there it will stand amongst the 'Noontides' and the 'Sunsets', alongside a 'Girl with Kitten' and not far from a three-sazhen 'Ivan the Terrible Piercing Vaska Shibanov's Leg with his Staff'. I can't say that it will be overlooked; they will look at it and even praise it. Artists will analyse the line. Critics will listen to them and start scribbling away in their notebooks. Only V. S. is beyond plagiarism: he will look, approve, praise and shake my hand. The art critic L. will descend upon the poor stone-lug in a fury, yelling, 'But where's the grace in this? Tell me, where's the grace?' And he will give me a good tongue-lashing. The public . . . the public will walk by impassively or with a wry face. The ladies – they will merely remark, '*Ah, comme il est laid, ce* stone-lug,' and sail on to the next painting, to the 'Girl with Kitten', and, looking at her, will say 'Sweet, very sweet,' or something in that vein. Worthy gentlemen with bovine eyes will gawp at it, bury their noses in their catalogues, emit something between a moo and a snort, and proceed unscathed. And perhaps at best some young lad or girl will stop, their attention caught, and will discern in the exhausted eyes that stare out, martyred, from the canvas the howl of pain that I have put into them.

Well, what next? The painting has been exhibited, bought and carried off. What will happen to me then? Will all that I have undergone these last few days perish without trace? Will it all prove nothing more than a passing upset, to be followed by a peaceful search for some inoffensive topic? Inoffensive topic! There suddenly comes into my mind the memory of a gallery keeper I know, compiling a catalogue, calling out to his clerk:

'Martynov, write this down – No. 112. First Love Scene, Girl Plucks Rose.

'Martynov, write this down now – No. 113. Second Love Scene, Girl Smells Rose.'

Shall I smell the rose, as I did before? Or shall I run off the rails?

VII

Dedov

Ryabinin has almost finished his 'Stone-lug' and today he invited me
to view it. I went to see it with preconceptions which, let it be said, I
was forced to abandon. A very powerful impression. Splendid line.
Three-dimensional modelling. Best of all is the bizarre yet absolutely
correct illumination. The painting would doubtless be commend-
able, were it not for the odd, uncouth subject-matter. L. is in full
agreement with me, and his article appears in the newspaper next
week. We shall see what Ryabinin will have to say then. L. will not
find it easy to take issue with the picture in terms of technique, of
course, but he can deal with its significance as a work of *art* – and art
will not abide being pressed into the service of base and foggy ideas.

Today L. came to see me. He was full of praise. He made a number
of observations on various minutiae, but on the whole he was full of
praise. I only hope the professors will look at my painting with his
eyes! Surely, in the end, I'll get what every Academy student is
striving after – the Gold Medal? The medal, four years abroad, on a
government bursary, and then – a professorship . . . No, I made no
mistake when I resigned from that cheerless, humdrum job, that
dirty job where you run across one of Ryabinin's stone-lugs at every
turn.

VIII

Ryabinin

The painting has been sold and taken to Moscow. I have received my
fee for it and, at the insistence of my fellow students, was obliged to
put on a celebration for them in the Vienna. I don't know how long
this has been the custom, but practically all young artists hold their
festivities in the corner salon of that hotel. It is a large, high-ceilinged
room, with its chandelier and bronze candelabra, carpets and furnishings all blackened by time and tobacco smoke, and a grand piano
put to much hard labour under the rampaging fingers of impromptu
pianists. Only the huge mirror is new, since it is replaced twice or

three times a year – on each occasion that merchants, instead of artists, celebrate in the corner salon.

It was quite a gathering: genre painters, landscape painters, sculptors, two reviewers from minor newspapers and some outsiders. The drinking and chatting began. Within half an hour everyone was talking at once, because everyone was rather merry. Including me. I remember being bumped and making a speech. Then I kissed a reviewer and drank to eternal comradeship with him. We drank, talked and kissed a great deal, and finally went home at four in the morning. Apparently two of our number settled down for the night in the corner salon of the Vienna Hotel.

I scarcely managed to drag myself home and tumbled fully dressed onto the bed. I felt a swaying motion as if I were on a ship; the room seemed to be swaying and spinning along with the bed and me. That went on for a couple of minutes; then I fell asleep.

I fell asleep, and woke very late. My head aches; my body feels full of molten lead. I can't open my eyes for a long while, and when I do, I see the easel – empty, with no painting on it. It reminds me of the days I have lived through, and then it starts all over again, from the beginning . . . Oh dear God, I must put a stop to this!

My head aches more and more; a fog drifts over me. I doze off, wake, and doze again. And I don't know whether there is a deathly silence all around me or a deafening noise, a pandemonium of sound, strange and fearsome to the ear. Perhaps it is silence, but in that silence something rings and knocks, whirls and flies. Like a huge thousand-horsepower pump drawing water from a bottomless abyss, it sways and rackets and I can hear the dull rumble of falling water and the machine pounding. And above it all, one note, unending, droning, tormenting. And I want to open my eyes, get up, go to the window, fling it wide and hear living sounds – a human voice, a rattling carriage, a barking dog – and to escape this eternal din. But I have no strength. I was drunk yesterday. So I must lie here and listen, listen endlessly.

And I wake, and doze off again. And again that knocking and thundering somewhere – sharper now, closer and more distinct. The blows come closer and pound along with my pulse. Are they inside me, in my head, or outside me? Ringing, piercing, precise . . . one-two . . . one-two . . . Beating on metal and on something else too. I can hear the blows on the iron; the iron clangs and trembles. First the hammer makes muffled, squelching noises, as if falling on a viscous mass, then it rings more and more vibrantly, and finally the huge boiler begins to clang like a bell. Then a pause, silence again; louder and louder, and once more that unbearable, deafening noise. Ah yes, that's it: first they are pounding on red-hot, viscous iron, then it cools. And the boiler clangs when the rivet head hardens. I understand. But that other sound – what is it? . . . I try to understand what it is, but my brain is hazed. It seems so easy to recall, whirling in my head, agonisingly close, but what it is I don't know. I can't grasp it . . . Then let it knock – we shall leave it be. I know, but I just don't remember.

And the noise waxes and wanes, mounting at times to an agonisingly grotesque pitch and at times seeming to vanish altogether. And I fancy it's not the noise that vanishes, but I vanish, hear nothing, cannot lift a finger, raise my eyelids, or cry out. Numbness holds me fast and horror overwhelms me, and I awake all in a fever. I am not entirely awake, but in some other dream. I fancy that I am back in an ironworks, only not the one I visited with Dedov. This one is much larger and darker. On all sides, the eerie, unearthly shapes of giant furnaces. Sheaves of flame soar from them, smutting the ceilings and walls, which have long been black as coal. The machines sway and shriek, and I can scarcely make my way between their whirling wheels and racing, trembling drive-belts. Not a soul anywhere. Somewhere, though, a knocking and a crashing; work is going on over there. There, too, a frenzied clamour and frenzied blows; I'm afraid to go to it, but I'm caught up and carried along, and the blows grow louder and the clamour more fearsome. And then it all converges in a roar and I see . . . I see a weird, misshapen creature writhing on the ground under blows that come raining down on it from all sides. A whole crowd is battering it with whatever comes to hand. Everyone I know is here, with wild faces, pummelling with hammers, crow-bars, sticks, fists, that creature for which I have found no name. I know that it is – him again . . . I throw myself forward, wanting to cry, 'Stop! Why this?' and suddenly I see a pallid, distorted, terrible face – terrible because that face is my own. I see myself, another myself, raising a hammer to deal a frenzied blow.

The hammer descended on my skull. Everything vanished; for a while I was aware of darkness, silence, emptiness and immobility, and soon I vanished too . . .

Ryabinin lay completely insensible until dusk. Finally, his Finnish landlady, remembering that her tenant had not been out all day, had the wit to enter his room, and, seeing the poor young man flailing about in a raging fever and mumbling all kinds of nonsense, she took fright, let out an exclamation in her incomprehensible dialect, and sent her young daughter to fetch the doctor. The doctor came, examined, palpated, listened, grunted, sat at the desk, and, his prescription written, departed – while Ryabinin continued to rave and thrash.

IX

Dedov

Poor old Ryabinin has fallen ill after yesterday's romp. I went to see him and found him unconscious. His landlady is taking care of him. I had to give her money, since there was not a kopek in Ryabinin's desk. I don't know if that confounded female has pinched it all or if perhaps the Vienna has the lot. True, we did have quite an evening; it was very jolly. Ryabinin and I drank to eternal comradeship. I drank with L. too. A splendid soul, that L., and such artistic discernment! In his latest article he showed a more subtle understanding of what I meant my painting to convey than anyone else, for which I'm profoundly grateful to him. I really ought to paint some little thing, *à la* Klever you know, and present it to him. Incidentally, his name is Alexander; isn't tomorrow his name-day?

But things could go very badly for poor Ryabinin: his big competition painting is far from finished, and the closing date is not exactly over the far horizon. If he is ill for a month or so, he will not get his medal. Then he can bid his foreign studies farewell! I am glad of one thing, though – that as a landscape painter I am not trying to rival him, but I'll bet his class-mates are rubbing their hands. Why shouldn't they – one more chance for them.

Still, I must not leave Ryabinin to the mercy of fate. I have to get him to hospital.

X

Ryabinin

Today, coming round after being unconscious for several days, I was
a long time deciding where I was. At first I could not even understand
that the long white bundle extending before my eyes was my own
body, wrapped in a blanket. With great difficulty I turned my head to
right and left, making my ears hum, and saw a long, dimly-lit ward
with two rows of beds on which lay the swathed forms of other
patients; a knight in copper armour standing between two big
windows with lowered white blinds – which turned out to be simply
a huge copper wash-stand; an icon of the Saviour in the corner, lit by
the feeble glimmer of a little lamp; and two colossal glazed-tile
stoves. I heard my neighbour's quiet, irregular breathing, the rattling
sighs of a patient further away, someone else's peaceful snuffling, and
the stentorian snores of an attendant, no doubt assigned to watch
over the bed of a gravely ill patient who might still have been alive or
had perhaps already died yet was lying there like us, the living.

Us, the living . . . 'Alive,' I thought, and even whispered the
word. And suddenly, an uncommonly fine, joyful and serene feeling, such as I had not felt since childhood, swept over me, and with it
the awareness that I was far from death, that before me stretched my
whole life – a life I can certainly shape in my own way (oh, most
certainly I can!), and, albeit with difficulty, I turned over onto my
side, drew up my legs, cradled my cheek in my hand and fell asleep –
just as, in childhood, you would awake at night beside your sleeping
mother, when the wind rattled the windows, and the storm wailed
dolefully down the stove-pipe, and the beams of the wooden house
cracked like pistol-shots in the fierce cold, and you began to weep
quietly, fearing yet wanting to wake your mother, and she awoke,
kissed and blessed you drowsily, and, lulled, you curled up tight as
tight and fell asleep, your little soul at ease.

Dear Lord, how weak I am! Today I tried getting up and walking
to the bed opposite – my neighbour is a student of some kind who is
recuperating from a fever – and I nearly collapsed on the way. But the
head is recovering faster than the body. When I first came round, I
remembered virtually nothing, and had a struggle to recall even the

names of my close acquaintances. Now it has all come back – not as a real past, though, but as a dream. Now it doesn't torture me, no. The old days are gone forever.

Today Dedov brought a whole stack of newspapers that had high praise for my 'Stone-lug' and his 'Morning'. Only L. had no praise for me. But anyway, that's all one now. It's all so far, so far from me. I am very glad for Dedov; he has won the big gold medal and is off on his foreign studies soon. He is indescribably happy and content. His face shines like a buttered pancake. He asked me if I intended to compete next year, since illness had prevented me this time. You should have seen his eyes pop when I told him 'No.'

'Are you serious?'

'Absolutely serious,' I replied.

'Then what are you going to do?'

'I shall have to see.'

He went away in absolute perplexity.

XI

Dedov

I have lived through these last two weeks in a haze, in agitation and impatience, and have calmed down only now that I am on the Warsaw train. I cannot believe what is happening to me! I am an Academy stipendiary, an artist, on my way to spend four years abroad perfecting my art. Vivat Academia!

But Ryabinin, Ryabinin! Today I saw him in the street, as I was getting into a carriage to drive to the station. 'Congratulations,' he says. 'And you can congratulate me too.'

'Whatever for?'

'I've just passed the entrance examination for the teachers' seminary.'

The teachers' seminary! An artist, a man of talent! He'll just go to waste, he'll perish out in the countryside. The fellow is out of his senses.

For once Dedov was right. Ryabinin, it turned out, did not succeed. But more of that some other time.

1879   *Translated by Liv Tudge*

Attalea princeps

In a certain big city there was a botanical garden, and in the garden was a huge palm-house made of iron and glass. It was very handsome: the whole building was held up by fine wreathed columns supporting light, decorated arches which were intertwined with a veritable spider's web of iron framework to carry the glass panes. The palm-house was especially beautiful in the evening when lit by the red glow of the setting sun. Then it was all on fire, the red reflected light played and bounced back as in a huge finely polished gemstone.

Through the thick transparent glass the captive plants could be seen. Despite the palm-house's size they were very cramped. Their roots intertwined and took away each other's food and moisture. Branches mingled with enormous palm leaves, bent and broke them, only to bend and break themselves when they came up against the iron framework. The gardeners were constantly pruning branches, wiring back leaves to stop them growing as they wanted, but it was little use. The plants wanted wide open spaces, their homelands and freedom. They were natives of hot countries, they were tender, luxuriant beings, they could remember their homelands and yearned for them. For all its transparency, a glass roof was not the open sky. Sometimes, in winter, the panes froze over; then it became completely dark in the palm-house. The wind howled, beat at the panes and made them all shiver. The roof became covered with wind-blown snow. The plants stood there and listened to the wind howling and remembered a different wind, warm and moist, that gave them life and health. And they wanted to feel it waft over them again, wanted it to sway their branches and play with their leaves. But the palm-house air was still; only occasionally might a winter storm smash a pane and a cutting cold current, full of frost, enter the vault; wherever the current struck, leaves went pale, shrivelled and withered.

But the broken panes were very quickly replaced. The botanical garden had an excellent, very learned director who insisted on immaculate order, even though he spent most of his time at his microscope in a special glass booth within the main palm-house.

Among the plants was one palm taller and more handsome than

any of the others. The director, sitting in his booth, called it by its Latin name, *Attalea*. But this was not its native name: botanists had invented it. The botanists did not know its native name and it was not written in charcoal on the white board nailed to the palm's trunk. Once a man who came from the hot country where the palm had grown visited the garden; when he saw it he smiled, because it reminded him of his homeland.

'Ah,' he said, 'I know this tree.' And he called it by its native name.

'I'm sorry,' the director shouted from his booth as he carefully sliced a stalk into sections with a razor, 'you're wrong. The tree you mentioned doesn't exist. This is *Attalea princeps*, a native of Brazil.'

'Oh yes,' said the Brazilian, 'I quite believe you when you say that its botanical name is *Attalea*, but it also has a native, real name.'

'Its real name is the one given to it by science,' said the director drily and bolted the door of his booth so as not to be bothered by people who didn't understand that if a man of science has spoken, they must be quiet and not argue.

The Brazilian stood for a long time looking at the tree and he grew sadder and sadder. He recalled his homeland, its sun and sky, its luxuriant forests with marvellous animals and birds, its wilderness, its wonderful southern nights. He also recalled that he had never been happy anywhere except in his homeland, and he had travelled the whole world. His hand touched the palm in what seemed a gesture of farewell and he left the garden: the next day he was on his way home by boat.

But the palm had to stay where she was. Now she felt even worse, although she had felt bad enough before. She was completely alone. She towered thirty feet above the tops of all the other trees and they disliked her and envied her, thinking her too proud. Attalea's height gave her nothing but trouble; apart from the fact that all the others were together and she was alone, she remembered her native skies better than they remembered theirs, and felt more yearning for them, because she was the nearest to what they had for a sky: that vile glass roof. Sometimes they could see something blue through it: it was the sky, albeit alien and pale, but still the real blue sky. While the other plants chatted to each other, Attalea kept silent, yearning and thinking only how good it would be to stand outside even under this pallid sky.

'Can someone please tell me if we're going to be watered soon?' asked the sago palm which was very fond of moisture. 'I really think

I'm going to be quite parched today.'

'I'm amazed to hear you say that, dear,' said a pot-bellied cactus. 'Isn't the vast amount of water they pour on you every day enough for you? Look at me: I get very little moisture and yet I am fresh and succulent.'

'We're not used to counting every drop,' the sago palm replied. 'We can't grow in this poor dry soil like you cactuses. We're not used to living just anyhow. And I must tell you that nobody asked for your comments anyway.'

This said, the sago palm fell into a sulky silence.

'Personally,' the cinnamon tree intervened, 'I'm pretty satisfied with my situation. I admit it is rather tedious here, but at least I can be sure nobody is going to strip my bark off.'

'But we haven't all been stripped,' said the tree fern. 'Of course, many may consider even this prison a paradise after the wretched existence they led when they were free.'

At this the cinnamon tree, which had forgotten that it had been stripped, took offence and became argumentative. Some plants took its side, some the tree-fern's, and a heated exchange of abuse began. If they had been able to move they would certainly have come to blows.

'Why are you quarrelling?' said Attalea. 'What good will that do you? Your irritation and spite are only increasing your unhappiness. You should stop your arguments and think about doing something. Listen to me: grow higher and wider, fling out your branches, press against the frames and the glass; our palm-house will collapse into little bits and we shall be free. If only one branch pushes against the glass, of course it will be cut off, but what can they do with a hundred strong, bold trunks? All we have to do is work in harmony and victory will be ours.'

At first nobody answered the palm: they all said nothing, not knowing what to say. Finally the sago palm plucked up courage.

'That's all nonsense,' it declared.

'Nonsense, nonsense,' all the trees joined in and at once set out to prove to Attalea that what she was putting forward was utterly absurd. 'An impractical dream,' they shouted. 'Absurd! Ridiculous! The framework is solid and we'll never break it, and even if we did, what then? Men will come along with knives and axes, they'll cut off our branches, mend the frames and everything will go back to how it was before. All we'll have to show for it will be whole bits of ourselves cut off . . .'

'Have it your own way,' replied Attalea. 'Now I know what I have to do. I'll leave you in peace: live as you like, grumble at each other, argue over your water ration and stay under your glass hood for ever. I can find my way alone. I want to see the sky and the sun, and not through these grids and panes – and I shall!'

And the palm's green top looked proudly down on the forest of her comrades sprawling beneath her. None of them dared say anything to her; only the sago palm said quietly to a neighbouring cyclad: 'Well, we'll see, we'll watch you getting your big block chopped off, you'll be cut down to size, you stuck-up thing!'

Despite their silence the others were annoyed with Attalea for her proud words. Only one little grass plant was not angry with the palm and not offended by what she had said. It was the most wretched and despised of all the plants in the house: coarse and pallid, a creeper with thick limp leaves, there was nothing remarkable about it and its only use in the palm-house was to cover the bare ground. It wound round the foot of the great palm as it listened and it thought that Attalea was right. It did not know the south, but it, too, loved the open air and freedom. It, too, found the palm-house a prison. 'If I, a dull little grass plant, suffer so badly without my grey skies, pale sun and cold rain, what must this fine and mighty tree be going through in captivity?' So thought the grass plant as it tenderly wound itself round the palm and pressed caressingly against her. 'Why am I not a big tree? I would follow the palm's lead. We would grow together and reach freedom together. Then the others would see that Attalea was right.'

But it was just a dull little grass plant, not a big tree. All it could do was wind itself round Attalea's trunk still more tenderly and whisper its love and its wish for Attalea's attempt to succeed.

'Of course, our weather isn't nearly as warm, the sky isn't as clear, the rain isn't as soft and plentiful as in your country, but we still do have the sky, the sun and the wind. We don't have any gorgeous plants like you and your comrades with those huge leaves and beautiful flowers, but some very fine trees do grow in our country – pines, firs and birches. I'm just a little grass plant and I'll never gain my freedom, but you are so great and strong. Your trunk is hard and you don't have far to grow before you reach the glass roof. You'll break through it and get out into the wide world. Then you can tell me if it's still as beautiful there as it used to be. That will be enough for me.'

'Little grass plant, why don't you want to come with me? My trunk is hard and strong: lean against it and climb up me. It's no trouble for me to carry you.'

'No, how could I? Look how floppy and weak I am: I couldn't lift even a single little twig. No, I'm no match for you. Grow, and good luck to you. I only ask you – when you reach freedom, remember your little friend sometimes.'

Then the palm set about growing. Even before, visitors to the palm-house had been amazed by its enormous height; now it was getting taller and taller every month. The director of the botanical garden attributed such fast growth to good management and was proud of the skill with which he had planted out the palm-house and was doing his job.

'Yes indeed, you should look at *Attalea princeps*,' he would say. 'It's not often you find a specimen as well grown as that even in Brazil. We've put everything we know into ensuring that the plants develop just as freely in the glasshouse as they would in their natural state, and I think we have had some success in this.'

At this point, looking pleased with himself, he would whack his stick against the solid tree-trunk and the blows would echo through the palm-house. The blows made the leaves of the palm quiver. Oh, if only she could have groaned, what a roar of wrath the director would have heard!

'He thinks I am growing just to please him,' Attalea thought. 'Let him think so.'

And she went on growing, depriving her roots and leaves of every drop of sap just to stretch upwards. Sometimes she felt that the distance to the vault was getting no smaller, and then she would harness all her strength. The framework drew nearer and nearer; at last a new leaf touched the cold glass and iron.

'Look, look,' said the plants. 'Look where she's got to! Will she really dare?'

'How frightfully tall she's grown,' said the tree fern.

'Growing tall is nothing! What's new about that? Now if she could get as fat as I am,' said the stout cyclad with a trunk like a barrel. 'Why stretch upwards? She won't get anywhere. The grids are solid and the glass panes are thick.'

Another month passed. Attalea rose higher and higher. Finally she pushed right up against the framework. There was nowhere left to grow. Then her trunk began to bend. Her leafy crown was crumpled, the cold bars of the framework bit into the tender young leaves, cut through them and disfigured them, but the palm was stubborn and would not spare her leaves, no matter what; she pushed against the grids and the grids began to give, even though they were made of strong iron.

The little grass plant watched the struggle and was faint with emotion.

'Tell me, doesn't it hurt you? If the frames are so solid wouldn't it be better to retreat?' it asked the palm.

'Hurt? What does being hurt mean when I am seeking freedom? Wasn't it you who were encouraging me?' replied the palm.

'Yes, I did, but I didn't know it would be so hard. I'm sorry for you – you are suffering so much.'

'Be quiet, weak little plant. Don't pity me. I shall die or free myself.'

At that very moment a metallic bang rang out. A stout iron band had snapped. Glass splinters rained down with a ringing noise. One of them hit the director's hat as he was leaving the palm-house.

'What is this?' he cried with a shudder as he saw pieces of glass flying through the air. He ran a few yards out of the palm-house and looked at the roof. Above the glass vault the palm's green crown, now straightened, towered proudly.

'Is this all?' she thought. 'Is this all I was longing and suffering for all that time? Was achieving this my highest goal?'

It was well into autumn when Attalea straightened her crown through the opening she had made. Sleet was coming down in a fine drizzle; the wind drove grey clumps of cloud low over the ground and Attalea felt they were trying to wrap themselves around her. The trees were bare and looked like hideous corpses; only the pines and firs had their needles of dark green. The trees stared sullenly at the palm. 'You'll freeze to death,' they seemed to be telling her. 'You don't know what frost is. You won't be able to bear it. Why did you leave your hothouse?'

And Attalea realised that it was all over for her. It was beginning to freeze. Should she go back under the roof? But she could not go back now. Attalea had to stand there in the cold wind, feel its buffets and the sharp touch of the snowflakes, look at the grimy sky and the pitiful countryside, the filthy back-yard of the botanical garden, the huge dreary city which she could see through the mist, and wait for people down below in the hothouse to decide what to do with her.

The director ordered the tree to be sawn down. 'We could build a special hood over it,' he said, 'but how long would that last? It'll grow again and smash it all. Anyway, it would cost far too much. Take it down.'

The palm was tied with ropes to stop it smashing the palm-house when it fell, and they sawed it through, low down, right at the roots. The little grass plant wrapped around the tree-trunk was reluctant to leave its friend and also fell victim to the saw. When the palm was dragged out of the palm-house, there were little stalks and leaves, bruised and lacerated by the saw, sprawling over the stump that was left.

'Tear that rubbish out and throw it away,' said the director. 'It's gone yellow and the saw's ruined it. Plant something else here.'

With a deft stroke of the spade one of the gardeners tore up the grass plant in one clump. He threw it into a basket, carried it outside and flung it into the back yard straight on top of the dead palm tree which was lying in the mud, already half-buried in snow.

1880   *Translated by Donald Rayfield*

A Night

The pocket watch lying on the desk was hurriedly and monotonously singing out its two notes. Even a good ear would have found it difficult to distinguish between them, but to the owner of the watch, a pale man sitting at the desk, the ticking sounded like an endless song.

...What a cheerless, gloomy song... said the pale man to himself. ...Time itself is the singer, and this monotonous singing is probably intended for my edification. Three, four, ten years ago, this watch was ticking away just as it does now, and in ten years' time it will still be ticking in the same way, precisely the same way...

The pale man glanced at it listlessly and immediately turned his eyes back to the spot at which he had just been staring with a vacant expression.

...All my life, with its seeming variety – its sorrows, joys, despairs, raptures, hatreds and loves – has passed to the time of its ticking. And only now, tonight, when everything in this huge town and this huge house is asleep and there isn't a sound but the beating of my heart and the ticking of the watch – only now do I see that all these adversities, joys and raptures were nothing but hollow spectres. Some of them I pursued without knowing why, from others I fled also not knowing why. I didn't realise then that there is only one thing that really exists in life, and that is time. Time passing with merciless regularity, not halting where hapless man, who lives but for the moment, would like to dwell, nor lengthening its pace by one iota when reality becomes so oppressive that he would willingly make it a past dream: time which knows only one song, the one I hear now with such agonising clarity...

These thoughts passed through his mind as the watch went on doggedly hammering out the eternal song of time. That song brought many things back to his mind.

...Yes, it's very strange. It can happen that a particular smell, some object with an unusual shape, or a catchy tune can bring back a whole scene from one's distant past. I remember once being with a man who was dying: an Italian organ-grinder happened to stop outside the open window, and at the very moment when the man had already uttered his last incoherent words and, with head thrown back, was in his death throes, I heard the strain of a trite little tune from *Martha*:

> Maidens shy
> For birds in the sky
> Have arrows of flame...

Ever since that time, whenever I hear this tune – I hear it sometimes even now, vulgarities die hard – the crumpled pillow and on it the pale face immediately appear before me. Whenever I see a funeral, that little barrel-organ instantly begins to play into my ear:

> Maidens shy
> For birds in the sky...

How vile and nasty! Anyway, what was I thinking about? Ah yes, why is it that this watch, whose ticking I ought by now to have become used to, reminds me of so much? My whole life! 'Remember, remember, remember...' I remember! I remember only too well, even all the things that are best forgotten. My face contorts with these memories, my fist clenches, and I thump it down on the desk in a frenzy... There, that blow has drowned out the song of the watch and for a moment I can't hear it, but only for a moment, and then it ticks away again insolently, doggedly, obstinately: 'Remember, remember, remember...' ...

'Oh yes, I remember all right. No need to remind me. It's all here before me as plain as day. Here's something to admire!'

He shouted this aloud in a choked voice, and felt his throat tightening. He thought he saw before him his whole life; he remembered a series of ugly, grim scenes in which he himself had been the principal actor. He recalled all the filth of his life, turned over all the filth in his soul and could not find a single pure or bright speck in it. He was certain that there was nothing but filth left in his soul.

...Not so much nothing but filth – there never was anything else... he corrected himself.

A faint, timid voice from a remote corner of his soul said: 'Stop! Are you sure there was nothing else?' He could not make out what that voice was saying, or at least he pretended to himself that he could not, and continued to torture himself.

...I have been over everything in my mind, and I believe I was right: I have nothing worth dwelling on, nowhere to get a foothold and take the first step forward. Forward – where to? I don't know, but I must somehow break free from this evil spell. There is nothing to sustain me in my past, because everything is falsehood and deception. I have lied and deceived myself at every turn. That's how a swindler deceives others, by pretending to be rich and speaking of his wealth which is somewhere 'out there', 'not yet to hand', but which exists, whilst he borrows money right and left. All my life I've been in debt to myself and now the reckoning has come – and I'm bankrupt, a plain fraudulent bankrupt...

He kept thinking these words over, with a certain strange enjoyment. He seemed almost to be proud of them. He did not perceive that by calling his entire life a deception and by smearing himself with filth he was in fact lying with the worst kind of falsehood in the world, that of lying to himself. Because he really did not have such a low opinion of himself at all. If someone had said to him just one tenth of what he had said to himself that long evening, his face would have flushed, not from shame in realisation of the truth of such reproaches, but from anger. He would have retaliated against the offender who had wounded his pride, which he now appeared to be trampling so mercilessly himself.

Was he really himself? He had reached such a state that he could no longer say of himself: 'I am myself.' Several voices were speaking in his soul; they were saying different things and he could not make out which of them really belonged to his 'self'. One voice, the clearest, lashed him with precise, even elegant phrases. A second voice, unclear but persistent and nagging, sometimes drowned out the first: 'Don't torture yourself,' it said. 'What's the point? Better to go on deceiving all the way, deceive them all. Pretend to others to be what you are not, and you'll be all right.' There was yet a third voice, the one that had said: 'Stop! Are you sure there was nothing else?', but this voice spoke timidly and was barely audible. He did not try to make out what it was saying.

...Deceive them all... Pretend to others to be what you are not. But haven't I tried to do that all my life? Haven't I deceived, haven't I been acting out a part in a farce? And have things turned out 'all right'? The way it's turned out is that even now I'm parading as an actor because I'm not being who I really am. But do I know what I really am? I am too confused to know. But it doesn't matter, I feel that I've been posturing for a few hours and saying pitiful words to myself which I don't really believe, and that I am saying them just now before my death. But am I really on the point of death?...

'Yes, yes, yes!' he shouted aloud, smashing his fist viciously down on the edge of the desk with each word. 'I must get out of this muddle once and for all. The knot is tied so tightly that it can't be untied: it will have to be cut. Why ever did I delay, and lacerate my soul which is already torn to shreds? Once my mind was made up, why have I sat here like a statue since eight o'clock?'

And he hastily pulled a revolver from the side pocket of his fur coat.

II

He had indeed sat without moving from eight o'clock in the evening until three in the morning.

At seven in the evening of this, the last day of his life, he had left his flat and taken a sleigh. Sitting huddled in it, he had driven to the other end of town, where an old friend of his, a doctor, lived; he knew he had gone to the theatre with his wife that day. He knew that they would not be in, and he wasn't really going to see them at all. As a close friend of the doctor, he would certainly be allowed into the study, and that was all he wanted.

...Yes, I'm sure to be allowed in. I'll say I have to write a letter. I just hope that Dunyasha doesn't hang around in the study...

'Hurry along there, old fellow!' he shouted to the driver.

The driver – a little man with a back hunched with age, a very thin neck swathed in a coloured scarf sticking out of a very broad collar, and grey curly hair flecked with yellow strands protruding from beneath his enormous round cap – clicked his tongue, drew back the reins, clicked his tongue again, and began to speak hastily in a broken voice:

'We'll get there, sir, you can be sure. Come along, you spoiled animal! Oh Lord, forgive me, but what a horse! Get along there!' He clipped the horse with his whip, to which it responded with a slight flick of the tail. 'Myself, I'd be pleased to oblige you, but the master only let me have this horse... I tell you, it's such a... The gentlemen get annoyed, but what can you do? The master says: "Well, Grandad, you're old, and you and that old nag make a good pair." The lads just laugh at me. They're fond of bawling their heads off; what's it to them? Of course, how can they understand?'

'Don't they understand?' asked the passenger, who was thinking how he would prevent Dunyasha from coming into the study.

'They don't understand, sir, that they don't, how could they! They're stupid, these young folk. I'm the only old man at the yard. Is it right to go insulting an old man? I'm over seventy and they laugh at me. Twenty-three years I served as a soldier. They're stupid, right enough... Hey there, old girl! Have you frozen stiff?'

He clipped the horse again with his whip, but since it took no notice at all, he added:

'What can you do with her? She must be over twenty... Just look at her flicking her tail...'

The hands showed half past seven on the illuminated face of a clock in one of the windows of an enormous building.

...They must have left by now... thought the passenger... but perhaps they haven't... 'Not so fast, Grandad, slow down, I'm in no hurry.'

'That's right, sir,' said the old man with obvious delight. 'Better to take it slowly. Hey there, old girl!'

For a while they went on in silence, then the old man plucked up courage to speak.

'Can you tell me, sir,' he said suddenly, turning towards the passenger and showing his wizened little face with its wispy grey beard and red eyelids, 'why there's this curse on mankind? We had a cabbie called Ivan. A young fellow he was, couldn't have been more than about twenty-five years old, maybe less. Who's to know what can have made him do hisself in?'

'Who was that?' asked the passenger in a low and husky voice.

'Our Ivan, Ivan Sidorov. He was one of us cabbies. Cheerful lad he was, and a good worker, I'll tell you. This is how it happened. It was a Monday, we'd had our supper and gone to bed, but Ivan went to bed without eating anything. Said he had a bad headache. In the night when we were fast asleep, he gets up and goes off. Only no one saw any of this. The next morning we went to harness the horses up, and there he was in the stables hanging from a nail. He'd unhooked the harness from the nail and put it down nearby, then he'd put up a rope... Oh Lord! It was enough to break your heart. What reason could a cabbie have for hanging hisself? Why would a cabbie go and hang hisself? Strange business!'

'Why did he?' asked the passenger, clearing his throat and with trembling hands wrapping himself more tightly in his coat.

'They don't have thoughts like that, cabbies don't. The job's hard going: in the morning before the light of dawn you harness your horse and leave the yard. It's cold and frosty, as you know. All you can do at the end of the day is to warm yourself at the inn, sort out the takings so that you get your two rubles twenty-five, and then it's off to your lodgings to sleep. There isn't much time for thinking. With people like you, sir, well, all sorts of things can get into your head the way you live.'

'How do you mean?'

'The life you lead. You gentlemen get up, put on your dressing-gown, drink tea and walk about the room. You walk about, but sinful thoughts are lurking. I've seen it, I know. In our regiment, the Tenginsk Regiment – I was serving in the Caucasus then – there was a lieutenant called Prince Vikhlyayev. I became his batman...'

'Stop, stop!' said the passenger suddenly. 'Pull up by the street-lamp over there. I'll walk from here.'

'Just as you like, sir; you walk if you wish. Thank you, sir.'

The driver turned round and disappeared in the snowstorm which was starting up whilst the passenger walked on with sullen steps. Ten minutes later he made his way up the front staircase of a house of ordinary appearance and, reaching the second floor, rang the bell at a door upholstered in green baize and with a highly polished brass name-plate. The few moments he waited for the door to open seemed like an eternity to him. Blank oblivion took hold of him; everything disappeared – the agony of the past, the strangely apposite prattling of the half-drunk old man which had impelled him to walk the rest of the way on foot, even his purpose in coming to this place. All he could see was the green baize door with its black braid held in place by bronze nails, and that was all that existed in the world for him.

'Oh, Aleksey Petrovich!'

Dunyasha, holding a candle, had opened the door.

'The master and mistress have just gone out; they've just this minute gone downstairs. How is it you didn't see them?'

'They've gone out? What a nuisance, to be sure,' he said with feigned annoyance and in such a strange tone of voice that Dunyasha, who was looking him straight in the eye, was bewildered. 'I needed to see them. Listen, Dunyasha, I'll just go into the master's study for a moment... may I?' he asked in a timid voice. 'I'll only be a moment, to write a note... It's just something...'

He looked at her with an imploring expression in his eyes, without taking his coat off or moving from the spot. Dunyasha felt ill at ease.

'What do you mean, Aleksey Petrovich, I mean, have I ever... After all, it's not the first time!' she said in an offended tone. 'Come in.'

...Yes indeed, why all this? Why am I saying all this? She will come in after me. I must get her away. Where can I get her to go? She will guess, I'm sure she'll guess, she has guessed already...

Dunyasha had not guessed anything, although she was extremely surprised by the visitor's strange appearance and behaviour. She was alone in the flat and was glad of the company of another living person, if only for five minutes. Setting down her candle on the table, she stood by the doorway.

...Go away, for God's sake, go away... Aleksey Petrovich begged her in his thoughts.

He sat down at the desk, and, feeling Dunyasha's eyes on him and imagining she was reading his thoughts, took a sheet of paper and wondered what he should write.

'Pyotr Nikolayevich,' he wrote, stopping after each word, 'I came to see you on a very important matter, which...'

'Which, which...,' he whispered. ...She's still standing there... 'Dunyasha!' he said suddenly in a loud and abrupt voice, 'Go and get me a glass of water.'

'Certainly, Aleksey Petrovich.'

She turned and went out.

The visitor got up from the chair and swiftly tiptoed over to the sofa, above which the doctor had hung his revolver and sabre, souvenirs of the Turkish campaign. He deftly unbuttoned the holster flap, took out the revolver and thrust it into the side pocket of his fur coat; then he took some cartridges from a little pouch attached to the holster and slipped them into his pocket as well. Three minutes later he had drunk the glass of water that Dunyasha had brought him, sealed the unfinished letter and set off home. The thought 'I must put an end to it all!' kept spinning around in his head. But he did not put an end to it all immediately he arrived home. Entering the room, he locked the door and without removing his overcoat threw himself into an armchair, glanced at a photograph, a book, the wallpaper

design, listened to the ticking of his watch which he had left on the
desk, and lost himself in thought. He sat without moving a muscle far
into the night, right up to the moment when we found him.

III

It was some time before he could get the revolver out of his narrow
pocket; then when it lay on the desk he found that all the cartridges
except one had fallen through a small hole into the lining of his coat.
Aleksey Petrovich took off his overcoat and was about to pick up a
paper-knife to slit the seam and get them out when a new thought
dawned on him; a wry smile curled one corner of his parched lips and
he stopped.

...Why bother? One is enough!...

'Yes, just one of these tiny things is quite enough to make
everything disappear for ever. The whole world will disappear; there
will be no regrets, no wounded vanity, no self-reproach, no people
full of hatred and pretending to be good and simple, people you can
see through and you despise, and with whom you yet pretend to be
loving and well-wishing. There will be no self-deception, no deception of others, there will be the truth, the eternal truth of non-being.'

He heard his own voice; he was no longer thinking, he was talking
aloud. And what he was saying seemed to him to be repellent.

'It's the same old story... You are dying, you are killing yourself,
and you can't even do that without a lot of talk. Who are you
showing off to? Yourself. Oh, enough, enough, enough...,' he
repeated in a tortured, exhausted voice, and with his trembling hands
he tried to open the unyielding revolver.

The revolver opened at last; the tallow-smeared cartridge slipped
into the chamber; the hammer cocked almost by itself. Nothing
could prevent his death now. It was a standard issue officer's
revolver, the door was locked and no one could get in.

'Well now, Aleksey Petrovich!', he said squeezing the handle
firmly.

...Shouldn't I write a letter?... he thought suddenly. ...I can't die
without leaving a word, surely? – But why, for whom? Everything
will disappear, there will be nothing; what concern of mine is it
that...But that's how things are done. I'll write one. Why not just for
once speak absolutely freely, without feeling ashamed of anything,

least of all of myself? This is a rare opportunity, a very rare one, my only one...

He put the revolver down and took a little pad of writing paper from the drawer. He tried several pens, but they would not write, broke and spoiled the paper. After spoiling a number of sheets he finally wrote down: 'St Petersburg, 28th November 187*.' Then his hand glided over the page, producing words and phrases which he scarcely understood himself.

He wrote that he was dying calmly because he had nothing to regret; that life is a never-ending lie; that the people whom he had loved – if in fact he had ever loved anyone at all and not merely pretended to himself – could not bind him to life because they were 'played out'. No, it was not even that, because 'there was nothing that could be played out', people had simply lost interest for him now that he understood them. He wrote that he understood himself as well, understood that there was nothing but falsehood in him; that if he had achieved anything in his life it was not from the desire to do good, but out of vanity; that if he had not done anything wicked or dishonourable it was not from an absence of wickedness but from his cowardly fear of people. That none the less he did not consider himself any worse than 'you who remain to go on lying to the end of your days', he was not asking for their forgiveness, but was dying with a contempt for others no less than for himself. At the end of the letter a harsh, senseless phrase burst out of him:

'Farewell, people, farewell, you bloodthirsty, grimacing apes!'

He needed only to sign his name. But when he had stopped writing he felt hot; his blood had surged to his head and was pounding against his sweat-bathed temples. Forgetting the revolver, and also forgetting that once he was rid of his life he would also be rid of the heat, he got up, went to the window and opened it. A cloudy stream of frosty air blew in on him. It had stopped snowing and the sky was clear. On the other side of the street a dazzling white garden all covered in hoar-frost glistened in the moonlight. A few stars looked down from the clear distant sky, one brighter than the others, shining with a reddish hue...

'Arcturus,' whispered Aleksey Petrovich. 'It must be years since I last saw Arcturus. When I was still at school...'

He could not take his eyes from the star. Someone huddled in a thin coat passed quickly along the street, stamping frozen feet on the flagstones. The wheels of a carriage squealed on the lightly frosted snow, and then a cab drove past carrying a fat gentleman, but Aleksey Petrovich stood still as though rooted to the spot.

'It must be done,' he said at last.

He walked towards the desk. The distance from the window was only a few paces, but it seemed to him that he had been walking much further. He had reached the desk and already picked up the revolver when through the open window the distant, tremulous but clear sound of a bell was heard.

'A bell,' exclaimed Aleksey Petrovich in surprise, and replacing the revolver on the desk, sat down in the armchair.

IV

'A bell,' he exclaimed again. …Why a bell?

…A church bell, I suppose? Call to prayers…church…stuffy air…wax candles. Old Father Mikhail, the village priest, performing the service in his plaintive, cracked voice, and the deacon droning in his low bass. I feel sleepy. Dawn is only just glimmering through the windows. My father, standing beside me with his head bowed, makes hurried little signs of the cross, and behind us, constant prostrations amongst the crowd of peasant men and women… How long ago that was!…So long ago that I can't believe it was real or that I myself ever saw it, and didn't read it somewhere or hear about it from someone. No, no, it all happened, and things were better then. And not just better, but good. If things were only like that now, I needn't have gone for the revolver…

'Put an end to it!' the thought whispered to him. He looked at the revolver and reached out for it, but instantly drew back.

'Scared?' whispered the thought.

…No, I'm not scared, that isn't it. There's nothing to be afraid of any more. But that bell – what's it for?…

He glanced at his watch.

…It must be matins. People will be going to church; many of them will feel better. At least that is what they say. I remember that I used to feel better too. I was a boy then. Now all that has passed away, turned to dust. And nothing has made me feel better. That's the truth.

The truth! What a moment to find the truth!…

And the moment seemed inescapable now. He turned his head

slowly and looked at the revolver again. It was a large, standard one, a Smith and Wesson. At one time it had been burnished, but was now shiny as a result of rubbing inside the doctor's holster for so long. It lay on the desk with its handle pointing towards Aleksey Petrovich, who could see only the worn wooden handle with its ring for the cord, a part of the chamber with the hammer raised, and the tip of the barrel pointing towards the wall.

…There is death. I need only to pick it up, turn it round…

The street was quiet: no one was walking or driving past. And amid the silence the distant ringing of the bell resounded once more; waves of sound burst in through the open window and reached Aleksey Petrovich; they spoke to him in an alien tongue, but they were saying something enormous, vital and solemn. Peal followed on peal, and when the bell sounded for the last time and the quivering sound melted away into the air, Aleksey Petrovich felt a sense of loss.

The bell had performed its work: it had reminded the confused man that there was something outside his own narrow little world, which had tortured him and was driving him to suicide. An uncontrollable wave of memories burst over him, fragmentary and jumbled, and as if completely new to him. This long night he had thought over many things, had recalled much, and imagined that he had remembered his whole life and seen himself in a clear light. Now he suddenly felt that there was another side to himself, the side about which the timid voice of his soul had spoken.

V

…Do you remember yourself as a little boy, when you lived with your father in that remote, forgotten little village? He was an unhappy man, your father, and he loved you more than anything on earth. Do you remember how you used to sit together on long winter evenings, he busy with his accounts and you buried in a book? The tallow candle would burn with a reddish flame, which gradually grew duller until, armed with snuffers, you trimmed the wick. That was your task, and you would perform it with such an important air that your father would lift his eyes from his big ledger and look at you with his usual sad, tender smile. Your eyes would meet.

'Look how much I've read, Papa,' you used to to say, and you would show him the pages you had read, squeezing them between your fingers.

'Go on reading, my little man, go on!' your father would say, encouraging you, before immersing himself again in his accounts.

He let you read everything, thinking that only goodness would remain in his beloved boy's mind. And you read and read, without understanding any of the arguments, although in your own child's way you vividly absorbed the images.

Yes, everything then really was as it seemed. Red was red and not the reflection of red rays. In those days there were no ready-made moulds for one's impressions, none of the ideas into which man pours all his feelings without worrying whether the mould is right and hasn't cracked. And when you loved, you knew that you loved, there was no doubt of it...

A beautiful, mocking face looked into his eyes and vanished.

...And her? Did you love her too?. Ah well, we've played with feelings long enough. But I believe my words and thoughts were sincere enough at the time... What torment it was! And when happiness came along it proved false, and if at that moment I had been capable of saying to time: 'Wait, stop a while, it's good here', I should still have wondered whether to give the command or not. But afterwards, very soon afterwards, I should have needed to drive time on... But best not to think about that now! I must think about how things actually were, not how they appeared to be...

But there had not been much: only childhood. And all he remembered of it was fragmentary snatches, which Aleksey Petrovich began to piece together avidly.

He remembered their little house, the bedroom where he had slept opposite his father. He remembered the red rug hanging above his father's bed. Every evening as he fell asleep, he used to look at this rug and find new shapes in its fantastic patterns — flowers, animals, birds, human faces. He remembered the mornings with their smell of straw, which was burnt to heat the house. Good old Nikolay would have dragged in enough straw to fill the hall and would be stuffing armfuls of it into the stove. It would burn brightly and cheerfully, and though acrid, the smell of the smoke was still pleasant. Alyosha could have sat in front of the stove for an hour, but his father would call him to drink his tea, which was followed by his lesson. He remembered how he couldn't understand decimals and how his father grew heated as he tried his utmost to explain them.

...I don't think even he understood them properly... thought Aleksey Petrovich.

Then came the scripture lesson. Alyosha liked that best of all. All those immense, amazing and fantastic characters. Cain, then the story of Joseph, the Pharaohs and the wars. The ravens bringing bread to the prophet Elijah. And there was an illustration of this: Elijah was sitting on a stone with a big book and two birds were flying down to him, holding something round in their beaks.

'Look, Papa: the ravens brought the bread to Elijah, but our Vorka takes everything from us.'

Their own tame raven with its feet and beak painted red – that was Nikolay's idea – would leap sideways along the back of the sofa and, craning its neck, try to pull a shining bronze frame from the wall. This frame contained a miniature watercolour of a young man with smooth temples, wearing a dark-green uniform with epaulettes and a very high red collar with a cross on the lapel. It was Papa twenty-five years earlier.

The raven and the portrait appeared for a moment and then disappeared.

...What else? There were stars, a cave and a manger. I remember that that word 'manger' was quite new to me although I had previously known it in connection with the stables and the cattle-shed. This manger seemed to be something special...

The New Testament was not taught like the Old, not from a thick book with pictures. Alyosha's father told him about Jesus Christ and he often used to read whole pages from the Gospels.

'"...whosoever shall smite thee on thy right cheek, turn to him the other also." Do you understand, Alyosha?'

And his father would begin a long explanation to which Alyosha did not listen. He would suddenly interrupt his teacher:

'Papa, you remember when Uncle Dmitry Ivanych came? It was just like that then: he struck his Foma in the face, but Foma just stood there; and Uncle Dmitry Ivanych struck him on the other side; Foma still didn't move. I felt sorry for him and cried.'...

'Yes, I cried then,' said Aleksey Petrovich, getting up from the armchair and pacing up and down the room, 'yes, I cried then.'

He felt terribly sorry for the tears of that six-year-old boy, for the times when he could cry because he had seen a defenceless man beaten.

VI

All this time the frosty air had been streaming in through the window. A swirling mist seemed to be pouring into the room, which had already become quite cold. The large low lamp with its opaque shade standing on the desk burned brightly, but it lit only the surface of the desk and part of the ceiling, forming on it a round, trembling pool of light; the rest of the room was in semi-darkness. All that could be distinguished was a book-case, a large sofa, some other furniture, a mirror on the wall reflecting the illuminated desk, and the tall figure restlessly pacing from one corner of the room to the other; eight steps forward and eight back, each time appearing briefly in the mirror. Sometimes Aleksey Petrovich paused at the window and the cold, misty air streamed over his feverish head, his exposed neck and chest. He shivered, but did not feel refreshed. He continued to delve into fragmentary and jumbled memories, remembering hundreds of tiny details, lost himself in them and could not understand in what way they were linked or meaningful. He knew only one thing: that until the age of twelve, when his father had sent him to high-school, he had lived a completely different inner life, and he remembered that things had been better then.

...What is it that draws you back into your early life? What was so good about those childhood days? A lonely child and a lonely man, an 'unsophisticated' man, as you called him after his death. Yes, you were right, he was an unsophisticated man. Life quickly and easily deformed him, and destroyed all the good that he had stored up in his youth; but it did not make him evil. He lived out his days, impotent and with an impotent love, which he lavished almost exclusively on you...

Aleksey Petrovich thought about his father, and for the first time in many years felt that he loved him despite all his lack of sophistication. He would have liked, even for a moment, to return to his childhood, to the village, to the little house, and snuggle up to that broken man, snuggle up to him simply as children do. He longed for that pure and simple love which only a child knows, and perhaps the very pure, unsullied amongst adults.

...Must it be impossible to regain that happiness, that capacity for knowing that you are speaking and thinking the truth? How many years have gone by since I last felt that! You speak passionately, with apparent sincerity, but in your soul there is always a worm which gnaws away and sucks at it. This worm is the thought: 'Now my friend, isn't all this just a tissue of lies? Do you really believe what you are saying now?'...

One more phrase, that seemed senseless, had taken shape in Aleksey Petrovich's mind: 'Do you really think what you are thinking now?'

It was senseless, but he understood it.

...In those days I used to think just what I thought. I loved my father and I knew that I loved him. Oh God, if only I could find some real, natural feeling inside my 'self', that will not perish! There is a whole world outside! The bell reminded me of that. When it sounded I remembered the church, I remembered the crowd, I remembered the vast human mass, I remembered real life. That is where I must go to get outside myself, that is where I must love. And love as children do. As children... It's written down here...

He went over to the desk, pulled open one of the drawers, and started rummaging inside it. A small dark-green book he had once bought as a cheap curio at some nation-wide exhibition lay in the corner. He seized it joyfully. The pages, printed in small type and arranged in two narrow columns, turned swiftly beneath his fingers, and familiar words and phrases rose up in his memory. He began on the first page and read all the way through, even forgetting the particular phrase that had sent him to the book in the first place. It was a phrase familiar to him from long ago and long ago forgotten. When he got to it, he was struck by the vastness of its meaning, expressed in nine words:

'Except ye be converted, and become as little children...'

He felt that he understood everything.

...Do I understand what these words mean? '...be converted, and become as little children!...' They mean not putting yourself first in everything. They mean tearing from your heart this hideous idol, this monster with its bloated stomach, this repulsive Self, like a tapeworm sucking your soul dry and still demanding more food. But where shall I find it? You have eaten everything already. All my strength, all my time have been sacrificed to serving you. First I nurtured you, and then I worshipped you; though I hated you I still worshipped you, sacrificing all the good I was given to you. 'But now

I've worshipped, worshipped, worshipped you enough!'

He went on repeating these words as he paced the room, but now with feeble, unsteady steps, and with his head lowered onto a chest heaving with sobs; he did not bother to wipe the tears from his face. His legs refused to obey him; he sat down, huddled up in one corner of the sofa resting his elbows on the arm, and lowering his fevered head into his hands, wept like a child. This state of collapse lasted for a long time, but there was no longer any suffering in it. All that raging, feigned malice had been assuaged. Soothing tears flowed and he did not feel ashamed of them; if anyone had walked into the room at that moment, he would not have restrained his tears which were carrying away all his hatred. He now felt that the idol which he had worshipped for so many years had not devoured everything, that there still remained some love and even selflessness, and that it was worth living to pour out this remnant. Where, in what cause, he did not know, and now he did not need to know where he should lay down his guilt-stricken head. He remembered the grief and the suffering which it had been his lot to see in life: the real grief of life, compared to which his lonely sufferings meant nothing, and he understood that he had to go there, into the midst of that grief and take his own share of it, and only then would there be peace in his soul.

'It's terrible, I can't go on living and fearing for my own sake. I must, I absolutely must bind myself to the common life, suffer and rejoice, hate and love not for my own "self" which consumes everything and gives nothing in return, but for the truth common to all men, which exists in the world and which, however I may have raved in that letter over there, speaks to the soul in spite of all attempts to stifle it. Yes, yes!' repeated Aleksey Petrovich in tremendous excitement, 'all this is written in the little green book, truly and for all time. I must "reject my self", annihilate my "self", cast it aside...'

'What good will that do you, madman?' whispered a voice.

But the other voice, previously timid and inaudible, now thundered in reply:

'Silence! What good will self-laceration do him?'

Aleksey Petrovich leapt to his feet and drew himself up to his full height. This reasoning had driven him to ecstasy. Never before had he known such rapture, either from life's successes or from woman's love. This rapture was generated in his heart, burst from it and gushed forth in a huge hot wave, poured through his limbs and briefly gave warmth and life to his numbed, unhappy being. Thousands of bells rang out in triumph. The blinding sun flared, lit up the whole world, and vanished.

The lamp which had been burning all through this long night grew duller and duller and finally went out altogether. But it was no longer dark in the room: day was beginning to dawn. Its calm grey light gradually filled the room, dimly lighting the loaded weapon and the letter with its wild curses lying on the desk – and the happy and peaceful expression on the pale face of the corpse lying in the middle of the room.

1880   *Translated by Philip Taylor*

Orderly and Officer

'Strip off!' said the doctor to Nikita, who was standing stock-still, his eyes fixed on some undisclosed point in the distance.

Nikita shuddered and hastily began unbuttoning.

'Look lively, man!' the doctor yelled impatiently. 'See how many of you I've got here.'

He gestured towards the crowd that thronged the assembly hall.

'Get a move on. . . he's not all there. . .', the NCO with the measuring rod observed helpfully.

In greater haste, Nikita shed his shirt and pants and finally stood stark naked. There is nothing more lovely than the human body, as someone or other has said on numerous occasions, somewhere, sometime; yet had the individual who first pronounced that dictum been alive in the seventies of this century and seen Nikita with nothing on, he would most likely have taken it all back.

Before the conscription board stood an undergrown man with a disproportionately large stomach (inherited from several dozen generations of forbears who never tasted good bread) and long, flaccid arms endowed with enormous, blackened, callused hands. His long, ungainly torso was supported by two very short bow-legs, and the entire form was crowned with a head. . . but what a head! The facial bones had developed wholly at the cranium's expense. The forehead was low and narrow; the eyes, bereft of brows and lashes, were the merest slits; on the huge, flat face a tiny button nose sat orphaned, its retroussé turn not only failing to impart a haughty expression to the face but actually serving to render it more pitiful still. The mouth was at odds with the nose, being enormous – an amorphous cleft around which, despite Nikita's twenty years, there was not a single hair. Nikita stood with head hanging, shoulders hunched, arms dangling loose, toes turned slightly in.

'What an ape,' said the commandant, a spry, chubby little colonel, bending towards a young, lean and exquisitely bearded rural district councillor. 'What an absolute ape.'

'An excellent corroboration of Darwin's theory,' the latter ground out. The colonel mumbled his agreement and turned to the doctor.

'Well, yes, of course he'll do! The lad's hale enough,' the doctor said.

'Only he'll never get into the Guards!' The colonel gave a burst of resounding, good-humoured laughter. Then, turning to Nikita, he added in a sober tone, 'Report back here in seven days. Next – Parfyon Semyonov. Strip off.'

Nikita sluggishly began to dress, his arms and legs defiantly refusing to go where they were supposed to. He was whispering something to himself, but even he probably did not know what it was; he understood only that he had been passed for military service and that in two weeks he would be driven from his home, not to return for several years. That solitary fact filled his head; that solitary thought pierced the haze and torpor that enveloped him. At last he conquered his sleeves, fastened his belt and left the room where the medical inspections were being held. A little old man of sixty-five or so, very stooped, was waiting for him in the vestibule.

'Have they sheared thee?' he asked.

Nikita did not reply, and the old man understood that they had, and questioned no further. They left the chambers and went out into the street. It was a clear, frosty day. A crowd of peasant men and women, come with the young men, was standing expectantly about. Many of them were beating their hands together and stamping; the snow crunched under boots and bast shoes. Steam billowed from the muffled heads and the shaggy little horses; smoke rose straight up from the chimneys of the little town in lofty columns.

'Taken thine, have they, Ivan?' a burly peasant in a new tanned-leather coat, a big sheepskin hat and good boots asked the old man.

'Aye, Ilya Savelich, they've taken him. The Lord would treat us ill. . .'

'What'll tha be doing now then?'

'Nowt to do. . . 'tis the Lord's will. . . One breadwinner in the family, and gone now. . .' Ivan spread his hands.

'If tha'd've adopted him afore now,' Ilya Savelich said reprovingly, 'the lad would have been safe and sound.'

'Who was to know it? The likes of that is not in our ken. And you see he's like a son to me, the one working-man in the family. . . I was thinking that the masters would mind that. "No matter," says they. "That cannot be, for such is the law." "Your honour," I says, "how is it the law, when his wife is expecting? And you see, your honour," I says, "I cannot shift for myself. . ." "No matter," he says. "We know nowt of that, old 'un, but by the law, since he is an orphan, without kin, so he must serve. Who is to blame," he says, "if he has a wife and son – you'd be marrying off lads of fifteen next." I wanted to speak more, but he wouldn't hear me. He got angry. "Give over," he says. "We've enough to do without thee." What can us do? 'tis the will of God!'

'He's an obedient one, that lad of thine.'

'Obedient and hard-working, God's my witness! I've never had a contrary word from him. I'll say this, Ilya Savelich, he's been better to me than my own flesh and blood. What a misfortune for us. . . The Lord giveth and the Lord taketh away. . . Farewell, Ilya Savelich. Happen they'll be looking yours over soon?'

'It's up to the authorities! Only mine'll not be passed, being as he's lame.'

'Lucky for you, Ilya Savelich.'

'Fear God, tha rattletrap! Luck – a son born lame?'

'Well – it's for the best, Ilya Savelich. The lad'll stop at home at least. Farewell, and good health to you.'

'Fare thee well, lad. . . Now then, hast forgotten thy little debt, eh?'

'I cannot, in no way, Ilya Savelich – that is, you see, I just cannot, it's impossible. Please just wait a bit. This misfortune that's come upon us!'

'Very well, then, very well. We'll talk it over later. Fare thee well, Ivan Petrovich.'

'Farewell, Ilya Savelich, and good health to you.'

Nikita had meanwhile unhitched the horse from the post. He and his foster-father got into the sledge and drove off. It was some fifteen versts to their village. The little nag trotted briskly along, her hooves sweeping up clumps of snow that scattered in mid-air and covered Nikita. Nikita lay near his father, bundled up in his cloth coat, and said not a word. The old man spoke to him once or twice, but he did not respond. He seemed to have frozen solid, and stared at the snow immobile, as if searching it to find the point he had left behind in the assembly hall.

They arrived home, went into the hut, and told all. The family – which besides the two men consisted of three women and the three children left by Ivan Petrovich's son, who had died the year before – began to wail. Nikita's wife, Paraskovya, dropped in a faint. The women wailed all week.

How that week passed for Nikita, only God above knows, since he was silent all the while, and the frozen expression of docile despair never once left his face.

At last it was all over. Ivan drove the new conscript to town and handed him over at the mustering point. Two days later, Nikita and a squad of new conscripts were tramping through the snowdrifts along the highroad to the provincial capital where his assigned regiment was quartered. He was fitted out in a new, short sheepskin jacket, wide trousers of thick black cloth, new felt boots, a cap and mittens. In his knapsack, with two changes of linen and some pies, lay a one-ruble note, carefully wrapped in a kerchief. All this Ivan Petrovich had bestowed on his foster-son after begging another loan from Ilya Savelich to equip Nikita for his military service.

Nikita proved to be an execrable recruit. The old soldier who had been instructed to put him through basic training was in despair. Notwithstanding all the inducements he applied to Nikita, including a certain amount of head-cuffing and face-slapping, the pupil could not manage to attain a proper grasp of even such uncomplicated lore as doubling ranks. The figure Nikita cut when arrayed in his uniform was pitiful in the extreme: standing to attention, he either let his stomach bulge out or drew it in and thrust his chest out, slanting his entire body in a manner that threatened to pitch him flat on his face. Officers and NCOs, toil as they might, were unable to turn Nikita into even a mediocre soldier of the line. During company drills, the commanding officer would yell at Nikita, then give the platoon sergeant a dressing-down, and he would take it out on Nikita all over again, putting him on extra fatigue duty. Before long, however, the platoon sergeant realised that extra fatigue duty was not a punishment for Nikita, but a pleasure. He was a fine worker, and being put on such tasks – which, besides hauling firewood and water and stoking the stoves, primarily entailed keeping the barracks clean by constantly slopping a wet mop over the floors – suited him perfectly. While he was working, he was at least not obliged to think how not to get muddled and do a left turn on a command of right turn, and he felt, moreover, completely free of those fearsome questions – 'What is a soldier?' 'What is a standard?' – that belong to that branch of high erudition that soldiers call the catechism.

Nikita knew perfectly well what a soldier was and what a standard

was; he was prepared to discharge his soldierly obligation with all
possible zeal, and would most likely have given his life in defence of
the standard; but to state, with the bookish precision required by the
catechism, the exact meaning of 'standard' was too much for him.

'*The standard is that which gonthal. . . gonfal. . .*' he would
babble, striving to hold his ungainly body at something resembling a
position of attention, poking his chin up into the air and blinking his
lashless lids.

'Booby!' the consumptive NCO who took the catechism drills
would yell. 'You vipers! What are you trying to do to me? Will I have
to suffer you forever, you blockheads, you clodhopping yokels?
Pah! How many more times will I have to tell you? Now then –
repeat after me: *The standard is a sacred gonfalon. . .*'

Nikita could not even repeat those few words. The NCO's
menacing mien and his loud voice had a stupefying effect on him: his
ears rang; standards and sparks capered before his eyes; he could not
hear the abstruse definition of 'standard'; his lips would not move.
He would stand in silence.

'Devil take you – say something! *The standard is a sacred gonfalon. . .*'

'*The standard. . .*'

'Well?'

'*Gonthal. . .*' Nikita would go on, his voice trembling, his eyes
filled with tears.

'*Is – a – sacred – gonfalon. . .*' the NCO would yell, beside
himself.

'*Sacred that which. . .*'

The NCO would run from corner to corner of the parade-floor,
spitting and cursing. Nikita would remain standing on the same spot
and in the same position, following the infuriated soldier with his
eyes. He did not resent the abuse and the insults; he just regretted
with all his heart his inability to 'do right' by his superiors.

'Three extra duties!' the NCO would say in a sinking voice, having
shouted himself hoarse and worn himself out, and Nikita would
praise the Lord for releasing him, however briefly, from the hated
catechism and drills.

When it was noticed that the punishments meted out to Nikita not
only failed to distress him but actually delighted him, he began to
find himself under lock and key. Finally, having tried all ways to set
the unfortunate man to rights, they washed their hands of him.

'We can't do a thing with Ivanov, sir,' the sergeant-major told the company commanding officer almost every day in the course of his morning report.

'Ivanov?. . Yes, yes. . . what's he done now?' the captain would reply, sitting in his dressing gown, smoking a cigarette and sipping tea from a glass in a nickel-silver holder.

'He hasn't done anything, sir. He's obedient enough, only he doesn't understand a blessed thing.'

'Keep trying,' the company commanding officer would say, pensively emitting a smoke ring.

'We have been trying, sir, but nothing comes of it.'

'Well then, what am I to do with him? You will grant, Zhitkov, that I'm not God Almighty? Eh? Well, you booby, what is to be done with him? Dismissed!'

'Yes sir, very good, sir.'

At last the company commanding officer tired of hearing the sergeant-major's daily complaints about Ivanov.

'Will you stop talking about Ivanov!' he yelled. 'Just excuse him from drill, to blazes with him. Do what you like, only spare me from him in future. . .'

The sergeant-major tried to transfer Nikita Ivanov to a non-combatant company, but it was already over-manned. An attempt at making him an orderly failed too, because every officer already had one. Then they started charging Nikita with the most menial tasks, abandoning all efforts to turn him into a soldier. So it was for a year, until a new subaltern, Ensign Stebelkov, was posted to the company. Nikita was given into his charge as a 'permanently appointed runner', or to speak plainly, an orderly.

Alexander Mikhaylovich Stebelkov, Nikita's new master, was a very decent young man of middle height, with a clean-shaven chin and a moustache magnificently drawn out into two sharp little stakes which he stroked lightly with his left hand from time to time, not without a certain satisfaction. He had just graduated from the Military Academy, in which institution he had displayed no particular partiality towards book-learning, though he had gained a perfect mastery of parade-ground drills. He was perfectly happy with his present situation. Two years in the Academy on a government stipend, under the stern scrutiny of the officers; a complete dearth of acquaintances in whose homes he might escape the Academy's martial discipline on leave-days; not a kopek of his own to spend on any diversions whatsoever. . . it had all wearied him to death. And now, seeing himself an officer on pay of up to forty rubles a month, a half-company of soldiers under his command, and an orderly at his exclusive disposal – for the moment he wished nothing more. 'Good, very good,' he thought as he fell asleep, and when he woke, the first thing he remembered was that he was an officer, no longer a cadet, that he no longer had to leap straight out of bed and start dressing, in fear of being hauled over the coals by the duty officer, that he could instead lie abed and indulge in the luxury of a cigarette.

'Nikita!' he yelled.

Nikita, in a faded pink calico shirt and black broadcloth trousers, his bare feet stuck into a pair of old light-blue rubber overshoes of unknown provenance, appeared in the doorway between the single room of Stebelkov's quarters and the hallway.

'Is it cold today?'

'I wouldn't know, sir,' Nikita replied timidly.

'Go and have a look, and let me know.'

Nikita promptly sallied forth into the bitter cold, and a minute later appeared again in the doorway.

'It's powerful cold, sir.'

'Any wind?'

'I wouldn't know, sir.'

'You oaf – what do you mean, you "wouldn't know"? You've just been in the yard. . .'

'Not a smitch in the yard, sir.'

'"Not a smitch, not a smitch"! Get out into the street then!'

Nikita went into the street and returned to report that there was a 'lusty wind'.

'No drill today, sir, so Sidorov was saying,' he ventured to add.

'Very well. Dismissed,' said Alexander Mikhaylovich.

He rolled himself into a ball, pulled up the warm flannelette blanket and fell into a drowsy reverie as the brightly burning stove, stoked by Nikita, crackled away. His cadet days seemed like a disagreeable dream to him now. 'And it wasn't all that long ago – they'd be banging that drum right in my ear, I'd be leaping up, shivering with cold. . .' After these memories arose others, also not particularly agreeable: poverty, the straitened circumstances of low-grade clerks, his eternally morose mother, a tall, gaunt woman with a stern expression on her thin face which seemed always to say, 'Pardon me, but I will not permit any Tom, Dick or Harry to insult me!' A whole brood of brothers and sisters, the squabbles they had, his mother's complaints about her fate, the harsh words between her and his father when he came in drunk. . . The high-school where studying had been so difficult, despite all his efforts; the classmates who had persecuted him and given him, for some unknown reason, the highly insulting nick-name 'Herring'; the failed Russian language examination; the grievous, humiliating scene when he had come home expelled from school, in tears. His father was on the oilcloth sofa sleeping off the drink; his mother was busy at the kitchen stove preparing dinner. One look at Sasha coming in with his books and in tears told her what had happened, and she fell on the lad and scolded him roundly, then dashed to her husband, woke him, forced him to understand what was wrong, and the boy got a beating from his father.

Sasha had been fifteen at the time. Two years later he had become a volunteer cadet, and before the age of twenty he was a man of independent means, an ensign in an infantry regiment. . .

'Good,' he thought under his blanket. 'The club this evening . . .there'll be dancing. . .'

And Alexander Mikhaylovich pictured the main hall of the officers' club, full of light, heat, music and young ladies sitting in clusters along the walls, each waiting for a nimble young officer to invite her for a few turns of the waltz. And Stebelkov, clicking his heels ('Damned shame I've got no spurs!'), would bow nimbly to the major's pretty young daughter with a graceful sweep of his arms and say '*Permettez*!', and the major's daughter would lay her hand beside his epaulette and they would whirl and whirl. . .

'Yes, this is a far cry from your "Herring". How stupid, anyway – why was I a Herring? The others weren't Herrings but they're sitting out their first year at some university, starving, while I. . .And why were they so set on university? Granted, a doctor or a court investigator earns somewhat more than I do, but then how long does it take to get there. . .and paying their own way too? How different with us – once you're into the Academy, you're off. Serve creditably and you can end up a general. . . Ah, then I'd give 'em what for!. . .' Alexander Mikhaylovich did not tell himself precisely who would be getting what for, but the memory of 'the others who weren't Herrings' did flit through his soul at that moment.

'Nikita!' he yelled. 'Have we got any tea?'

'None at all, sir. It's all gone.'

'Pop out and get a quarter.'

He drew a new purse from under his pillow and gave Nikita the money.

Nikita went to buy the tea. Alexander Mikhaylovich continued his musing, and by the time Nikita came back with the tea, his master had dropped off again.

'Sir, sir!' Nikita whispered.

'Eh? What? Got it? Good, I'll get up now. . . Help me dress.'

Alexander Mikhaylovich had never, either at home or at the Academy, been dressed by anyone but himself (except, of course, in infancy), but once he had an orderly at his disposal it took him only two weeks to forget completely how to put on and take off his own clothes. Nikita drew socks and boots onto his master's feet, helped him into his trousers, draped over his shoulders a summer greatcoat that served him as a dressing-gown. Alexander Mikhaylovich, not bothering to wash, sat down to morning tea.

A lithographed regimental order was brought, and Stebelkov, perusing it from beginning to end, was pleased to see that his turn for sentry duty was still far away. 'And what's this all about?' he thought, reading on:

'In the interests of maintaining Gentlemen Officers' educational standards, I propose that as of next week Staff-Captain Yermolin and Lieutenant Petrov begin courses of lectures, the former on tactics and the latter on fortifications. The time of these lectures, which will be held in the officers' mess, will be announced in a special regimental order.'

'What the deuce is this for? Lectures on tactics and fortifications!' thought Alexander Mikhaylovich. 'As if we hadn't had a bucketful of that at the Academy! And besides, they won't say anything new, they'll just read out their old notes. . .'

Having read the order and finished his tea, Alexander Mikhaylovich called Nikita to take the samovar away, then sat down to roll some cigarettes, continuing his endless musing on his past, present and future, in which he descried, if not a nice fat pair of general's epaulettes, then at least the thick ones of a staff-officer. And when the cigarettes were rolled, he lay on the bed and perused a previous year's issue of *The Cornfield*, looking at all the well-thumbed illustrations and not missing a single line of text. At last, what with lounging so long and reading *The Cornfield*, his head started to feel muggy.

'Nikita!' he yelled.

Nikita jumped up from the greatcoat spread near the stove on the hallway floor, which served him as a bed, and sprinted to his master.

'Look what the time is. . . No, better give me my watch.'

Nikita carefully took the silver watch with its chain of new gold from the table, handed it to his master, and went back to his greatcoat in the hallway.

'Half past one. . . Time for dinner, perhaps?' thought Stebelkov, as he wound the watch with a little bronze key – a recent acquisition, with a tiny snapshot set into the head that was magnified when viewed against the light. Alexander Mikhaylovich looked at the photograph, screwing up his left eye, and smiled. 'Upon my word, they do some capital things these days! However did they manage. . . to get it so small?' he pondered briefly. 'Still, time I was off. . .'

'Nikita!' he yelled.

Nikita appeared.

'Bring me the washing things.'

Nikita brought into the room a tub and a wash-jug balanced on an unpainted stool. Alexander Mikhaylovich started to wash. At the first touch of the icy water, he shrieked:

'How many times have I told you, blockhead, to stand the water in the room overnight? You'll freeze my face off. . . you oaf. . .'

Nikita kept his silence, profoundly conscious of his guilt, and zealously poured water over his irate master's hands.

'Did you brush my tunic?'

'Yes, sir, I did,' Nikita said, as he handed his master his brand-new officer's tunic with glittering gold epaulettes embellished with a numeral and a single silver star, which had been hanging on the back of a chair.

Before putting it on, Alexander Mikhaylovich scrutinised the dark-green fabric closely, and found a piece of fluff.

'What's this, then? Is this what you call brushing? Is this the way to perform your duties? Get out, you oaf, and brush it again.'

Nikita went into the hallway and began to produce with the brush and tunic the kind of sound generally termed 'rasping'. Stebelkov, aided by a folding mirror in a yellow wooden frame and a jar of *pommade hongroise*, began to bring his moustache to the utmost conceivable perfection. At last the moustache was in fine trim, but the rasping in the vestibule continued unabated.

'Give me the tunic, or you'll be brushing it till Kingdom Come. . . I'm going to be late because of you, you oaf. . .'

He carefully buttoned the tunic, then put on his sword, galoshes and greatcoat, and went into the street, his scabbard clattering on the frozen paving boards.

The remainder of the day was taken up with dinner, reading *The Russian Invalid*, and chatting with fellow-officers about army life, promotion and pay; in the evening Alexander Mikhaylovich took himself to the club and tore round in a 'whirlwind waltz' with the major's daughter. He came back to his quarters late in the evening, tired and slightly tipsy from the several drinks he had had in the course of the evening, but contented. . . The only variations in this life were drill, sentry duty, summer bivouacs, an occasional field manoeuvre and an infrequent lecture on fortifications or tactics which could under no circumstances be cut. And so it continued for years, leaving no traces on Stebelkov except that the colour of his complexion changed and a bald spot began to spread, and in place of the one star on his epaulettes there appeared two, then three, then four. . .

But what was Nikita doing all this while? Well, Nikita lay on his greatcoat by the stove most of the time, jumping up in answer to his master's endless demands. In the morning there was a fair amount to do: he had to stoke the stove, set up the samovar, fetch water, brush the boots and clothes, dress his master, sweep and tidy the room. (Admittedly, the last task did not take much time, since the entire furnishings of the room consisted of a bed, a table, three chairs, a set of shelves and a trunk.) Still, Nikita did have some semblance of work to do. His master's departure ushered in the endless day, which consisted almost entirely of enforced thumb-twiddling, interrupted only by a sortie to the barracks to fetch dinner from the company kitchen. When he had been living in barracks, Nikita had learned something of the cobbler's trade – how to patch, sole and heel – and after his move to Stebelkov's quarters he had it in mind to continue this pursuit, hiding his sack behind the hallway door whenever anyone knocked. For several days his master had detected a strong smell of shoe-leather in the hallway, then, discovering the source of the smell, he had given Nikita a severe telling-off and told him 'not to let it happen again.' So Nikita was left with nothing to do but lie on his greatcoat and think. And he would lie on it and think for evenings on end, finally dropping off moments before there came the knock on the door that announced the master's return; Nikita would undress him, and soon the little room would be plunged into darkness, the officer and the orderly sound asleep.

The wind drones and wails, buffeting snowflakes against the window. And it sounds to the sleeping Ensign Stebelkov like thunderous dance music; he is dreaming of a brightly lit hall, such as he has never seen before, thronged with finely attired strangers. But he feels no embarrassment – on the contrary, he senses that he is the hero of the evening. Some of his former superiors are also present; their demeanour towards him is one of rapture, very different from before. The colonel, rather than offering him two fingers to shake, clasps both chubby hands around his; Major Khlobushchin, who has always looked askance at Stebelkov's attentions to his daughter, brings her to him with a humble bow. What great thing he has done to be thus lionised, he does not know – but unquestionably he has done something. He looks at his shoulders and sees on them a set of general's epaulettes. The music thunders, the couples speed by, and he too is speeding on and on, higher and higher. The glittering hall is far from him now; it looks like a bright little speck. He is surrounded by a press of people in various uniforms; they are all seeking orders from him. He doesn't know what they are asking, yet he gives out orders, orderly officers tear towards him and away from him. Cannon thunder in the distance; marching bands play; regiment after regiment troops by. All this is moving on, with him; the thunder of the cannon is closer now, and Stebelkov is afraid. 'I'll be killed!' he thinks. And fearsome cries go up on all sides; strange, hideous, ferocious men, such as he has never laid eyes on before, run at him. Closer and closer they come; Stebelkov's heart shrinks, in the clutches of the sort of nameless terror that only dream can bring, and he yells 'Nikita!'

The wind drones and wails, buffeting snowflakes against the window. And it sounds to the sleeping Nikita like real wind and foul weather. He dreams he is lying in his hut, alone, with no wife, no father, no other member of his family near. He has no idea how he got home, and fears that he may have deserted from the regiment. He fancies that a search party has been formed and senses that it is closing in, and he wants to run and hide, but cannot stir a limb. Then he cries out, and the hut fills with people; they are all people he knows from the village, but there is something eerie in their faces. 'Hail, Nikita!' they say to him. 'Your folk are all gone, brother, God has gathered them in. Passed on, every one. Here they are, look now!' And Nikita sees his entire family in the crowd – Ivan, his own wife, Aunt Paraskovya, and the little ones. And he realises that, although they are standing amongst the rest, they are dead, and all the other villagers are dead too; and that is why their laughter is so eerie. They come towards him, lay hold of him, but he tears himself loose and runs through the snowdrifts, stumbling and falling, pursued now not by the dead but by Ensign Stebelkov and the soldiers. And he runs on and on, while the ensign yells, 'Nikita, Nikita, Nikita!. . .'

Stebelkov *is* yelling 'Nikita!'

Nikita wakes, jumps up and gropes his way into the room, his bare feet scuffing the floor.

'Are you making fun of me or what, confound you? How many times have I told you to leave the matches within my reach? How he can sleep, the blockhead! I've been calling for half an hour. Can't rouse him at all. Give me a light!'

The sleepy Nikita fumbles on the table and the window-ledges until he finds the matches. He lights a candle set in a copper holder covered with verdigris and, squinting, hands it to his master. Alexander Mikhaylovich lights his cigarette and fifteen minutes later the officer and the orderly are once again deep in slumber.

1880   *Translated by Liv Tudge*

What Never Was

One fine day in June – fine indeed, because it was 28 degrees Réaumur – one fine day in June it was hot everywhere, but nowhere more so than in a clearing in a certain orchard where there stood a shock of new-mown hay, because this spot was sheltered from the wind by a thick, thick cherry grove. Almost everyone and everything slept; people had eaten their fill and were occupied full-length in after-dinner occupation, birds had fallen silent; many insects even had hidden away from the heat. As to the farm animals, there is nothing to be said. The livestock large and small were sheltering under a lean-to. The dog had settled into a hole that he had dug up against the barn and was lying there panting, his eyes half-shut and his pink tongue stuck out almost half an arshin; now and then, evidently feeling wretched in the stifling heat, he yawned such a yawn that a reedy little whine came out with it. The pigs – a mamma and thirteen little ones – had taken themselves off to the river bank and settled into the rich black mud which covered everything from view save piggy snouts with two little holes that snorted and snuffled, elongated, mud-drenched backs, and huge, drooping ears. Only the chickens, undaunted by the heat, were managing to kill time by clawing up the dry ground in front of the kitchen porch, where, as they knew perfectly well, there was not a single grain left; but the rooster must have been in a bad way, since from time to time he took on a foolish expression and gave a full-throated 'For shame, for sha-a-ame!'

But now we are out of the clearing where it was hottest of all. In that clearing, however, sat a whole gathering of ladies and gentlemen, wide-awake. Not all of them were sitting, mind you. The old bay horse, for instance, who had been chancing his flanks to Anton the coachman's whip by tearing at the shock of hay, could not sit at all, being a horse; and some sort of caterpillar was not sitting either but, rather, lying on its belly. But the word itself is neither here nor there. Under a cherry tree there had gathered a small but very serious company: a snail, a dung-beetle, a lizard, the aforementioned caterpillar; and a grasshopper came jumping up to join them. Nearby stood the old bay attending closely to their observations, bending towards them one bay ear that bristled from the inside with grey hairs. And on the bay sat two flies.

The company was conducting a decorous but fairly spirited debate in which, as is proper, no one was agreeing with anyone else, since each set great store by the independence of his own character and viewpoint.

'I hold,' the dung-beetle was saying, 'that any decent creature must concern himself first and foremost with his progeny. Life is labour for the coming generation. He who wittingly performs the duties laid upon him by Nature stands on firm ground. He knows what he is about, and, come what may, he is in no way answerable. Look at me – does anyone labour harder than I do? Does anyone, day in day out, without a moment's rest, roll a ball as heavy as this – a ball that I myself have so tastefully fashioned from dung, with the noble aim of enabling new dung-beetles like myself to grow? And yet I think that no-one could have so calm a conscience or could say with so light a heart, "Yes, I have done all I was able and obliged to do" – which is what I shall say when new dung-beetles emerge into the world. That is the meaning of labour!'

'Get away with you, my lad, you and your labour!' said an ant that had come by during the dung-beetle's speech, dragging a monstrous length of dry stalk, in spite of the heat. He stopped for a minute, sat back on his four rear legs and wiped the sweat from his exhausted face with two front feet. 'I labour too, and more than ever you do! But you work for yourself – or for your young, which amounts to the same thing. Not everybody is so fortunate. . . You should try hauling logs for the State, like me. Even I don't know what forces me to work until I drop, and in heat like this too. Nobody will give me any thanks for it. We poor worker ants labour away, and where's the beauty in our lives? Such is fate!'

'Your view of life is too cut and dried, dung-beetle, and yours is too gloomy, ant,' retorted the grasshopper. 'No, beetle – I love to chirrup and jump, and there you have it! My conscience doesn't trouble me one whit. And besides, you haven't even touched on the question that Madam Lizard posed. She asked, "What is the world?" – and you're talking about your dung-ball. How very ill-mannered. The world. . . The world, in my opinion, is a very good thing, because it holds new grass, sun and breeze all for us. And how huge it is! You here, among these trees, cannot begin to comprehend how huge it is. When I am in the open field I sometimes jump up as high as I possibly can – and that, I assure you, is enormously high. And from that height I can see that the world is endless.'

'Just so,' the bay agreed sagely. 'But not one of you could hope to see even a hundredth part of what I have seen in my time. It is a pity that you cannot understand what a "verst" is. . . A verst from here there is a village called Luparyovka, where I go every day with a barrel to fetch water. But they never feed me there. In the other direction lie Yefimovka and Kislyakovka, which has a church with bells. And then Svyato-Troitskoye, and then Bogoyavlensk. In Bogoyavlensk they always give me hay, but the hay is bad there. In Nikolayev – that's a town, you know, twenty-eight versts away – well, the hay is better there and they give you oats too, only I don't like going there. We take the Master there, and he has the coachman gee us up, so the coachman lashes into us with his whip. . . And then there's Alexandrovka as well, and Belozerka, and Kherson Town too. . . But how could you ever understand all that?. . . That, now, is the world – not all of it, I dare say, but anyway, a considerable bit of it.'

And the bay fell silent, though his lower lip still stirred as though he were whispering something. That was due to old age: he was almost seventeen years old, and to a horse that is the same as seventy-seven to a man.

'I don't understand your words of horsy wisdom, and I confess I don't want to try,' said the snail. 'Give me a burdock and that is enough. I have been crawling for the last four days around this one, and there's still no end to it. And after this burdock there's another burdock, and on that burdock, more than likely, sits another snail. And that's it. There's no call to go jumping about – that's a silly waste of time. Just sit and eat the leaf you're sitting on. Crawling's such a bother, or I'd have long since got away from you and your palaver. It gives folk nothing but a headache.'

'No, if you please – why so?' the grasshopper interrupted. 'It's very pleasant to chirrup on, especially about such fine subjects as infinity and suchlike. Of course, there are those practical individuals who care for nothing but cramming their bellies, like you or this charming catepillar here. . .'

'Oh leave me be, I beg you, leave me, let me alone!' cried the caterpillar plaintively. 'I'm doing it for the life to come, only for the life to come.'

'What life to come would that be, then?' asked the bay.

'Surely you know that after I die I shall turn into a butterfly with wings of many colours?'

The bay, the lizard and the snail did not know this, but the insects had some notion of it. And they were all silent for a while, since no one had anything useful to say about the life to come.

'Firm convictions should be treated with respect,' the grasshopper chirruped at last. 'Does no one else wish to say anything? You, perhaps?' he said, turning to the flies.

And the elder of the two replied, 'We can't say we're too badly off. We've just come from the house. The Mistress set out some bowls of fresh-boiled jam and we crawled under the lids and ate our fill. We're satisfied. Our mamma got stuck in the jam, but that can't be helped. She'd lived long enough. We're satisfied.'

'Ladies and gentlemen,' said the lizard, 'I think that you are all absolutely right. But on the other hand –'

But the lizard never did tell them what was to be said on the other hand, for she suddenly felt something pinning her tail firmly to the ground.

Anton the coachman had woken up and come for the bay. He had chanced to tread on the company with his great boot and squashed most of them flat. Only the flies soared off to lick at their deceased and jam-daubed mamma, and the lizard ran away with her tail torn off. Anton took the bay by the forelock and led him out of the orchard, to harness him to the barrel and go for water, saying all the while, 'Come on, Dobbin, come on!' – to which the bay only whispered in reply.

And the lizard was left tailless. True, one did grow again after a while, but it was blackish and stubby forever after. And when the lizard was asked how she damaged her tail, she would answer modestly, 'It was torn off because I had ventured to declare my convictions.'

And she was absolutely right.

1882   *Translated by Liv Tudge*

From the Reminiscences of Private Ivanov

I

I arrived in Kishinyov on the fourth of May 1877, and within half an hour I had got to know that the 56th Infantry Division was passing through the town. I had come with the object of joining one of the regiments and going to the war and so, at four a.m. on the seventh of May, there I was standing in the grey ranks lined up outside the billet of the colonel of the 222nd (Starobelsk) Infantry Regiment. I was wearing a grey greatcoat with shoulderstraps and dark-blue tabs and a forage-cap with a blue band; I had a pack on my back, cartridge pouches on my belt, and a heavy Krynkov rifle in my hands.

The band struck up: the regimental colours were being brought from the colonel's quarters. An order rang out and the regiment noiselessly presented arms. Then there was a terrific roar: the colonel gave a command, and it was taken up by the battalion commanders, company commanders and platoon sergeants. The result of it all was a confused movement of greatcoats that I found utterly bewildering, which ended with the regiment stretching out into a long column and marching off in time to the strains of the regimental band which had struck up a cheerful march. I strode out with the rest, trying to get into step and keep in line with my neighbour. My pack was pulling me back, the heavy pouches were pulling me forward, my rifle kept slipping off my shoulder, the collar of my grey greatcoat was chafing my neck. But despite all these minor discomforts, the band, the precise and massive movement of the column, the freshness of the early morning, and the sight of the bristling array of bayonets and stern, tanned faces, filled me with a calm and resolute spirit.

Though it was early morning, throngs of people gathered outside their houses; half-dressed figures were gazing out of the windows. We marched up a long, straight street, past the market-place where Moldavians with their ox-drawn carts were already converging; the road climbed uphill and led towards the town cemetery. It was a cold, overcast morning, with a slight drizzle; the trees in the cemetery were showing through the mist, and the tops of the tombstones peered out from behind the dank cemetery gate and wall. We skirted round the cemetery, passing it on our right. And I fanced that it was gazing at us through the mist uncomprehendingly. 'Why do you, thousands of you, march for thousands of miles to die on foreign fields, when you can die here, die in peace and lie down beneath my wooden crosses and stone slabs? Stay here!'

But we did not stay. We were drawn on by a mysterious, unfathomable force – there is no greater force in the lives of men. Each one of us, acting alone, would have gone back home, but the mass of us marched on – not from obedience to military discipline, not from any awareness of the righteousness of our cause, not from hatred of an enemy we didn't know, not from fear of punishment, but driven by that unfathomable and unconscious force that will lead men to bloody slaughter for a long time to come – the greatest cause of all manner of agonies and suffering endured by men.

Beyond the cemetery a wide, deep valley spread out, disappearing from sight in the mist. The rain had become heavier, and in the distance the clouds had parted here and there, letting through shafts of sunlight which made slanting and vertical strips of rain sparkle like silver. Through the mists that crept along the green slopes of the valley we could make out the long extended columns marching ahead of us. Every so often bayonets glinted here and there; when a gun entered a patch of sunlight, it would gleam briefly like a bright little star and then fade away. Sometimes the clouds drew together again; then it became darker, and the rain came down faster. An hour after we had set out, I felt a trickle of cold water running down my back.

The first day's march, from Kishinyov to the village of Gaureni, wasn't a long one, no more than eighteen versts. However, I was not used to carrying a load of 25-30 pounds on my body, and when we got to the peasant house we were billeted in, at first I could not even sit down! I just leaned with my pack against the wall and stood there like that in full kit for some ten minutes, with my rifle in my hands. One of the soldiers who was going through to the kitchen to get his dinner felt sorry for me and took my mess-tin with him. But when he came back, he found me fast asleep. I slept till four a.m. when I was wakened by the unbearably piercing sounds of the bugle playing 'Assembly', and ten minutes later I was plodding along a muddy, clay-clogged road under a drizzle so fine that it seemed to be pouring out of a sieve. Somebody's grey back was moving ahead of me with a brown calfskin pack strapped on it, a clanking mess-tin and a shouldered rifle. Identical grey figures walked beside me and behind me. For the first few days I could not distinguish between any of them. The 222nd Infantry Regiment that I had been assigned to was composed in the main of peasants from the Vyatka (they pronounced it Vyachka) and Kostroma Provinces. They all had broad faces with high cheekbones brown from the cold, and small grey eyes; their hair and beards were blond, almost colourless. Though I remembered a few names I did not know whose they were. A fortnight later I found it inconceivable that I could have confused my two neighbours – the one marching alongside me, and the owner of the grey back that was constantly before my eyes. I had been calling them Fyodorov and Zhitkov indiscriminately, constantly mixing them up, even though they were not in the least alike.

Fyodorov, who was a corporal, was a young man of about twenty-two, of average height and a shapely, even refined build. He had a regular-featured, almost chiselled face, with a finely delineated nose, lips and chin covered in a curly blond beard, and cheerful blue eyes. At the call 'Singers to the front!' he would be the leading singer of our company and his strong tenor voice would ring out, rising to a falsetto on the high notes: 'The Senate summons the Tsar!'

A native of Vladimir Province, he had been taken to St Petersburg when still a child. He was a rare enough exception in that Petersburg 'education' had not spoilt him, but had merely given him a polish, teaching him, amongst other things, to read newspapers and utter all manner of weird and wonderful words.

'Of course, Vladimir Mikhaylovich,' he said to me, 'I'm better on the reasoning than Old Zhitkov, because Petersburg had an influence on me. In Petersburg there is civilisation, in that village of his they're ignorant and untamed. But anyway, being as he's an elderly man and, one might say, he's been around, having borne various vicissitudes of fate, I can't bawl at him, you see? He's forty, I am twenty-three. Still, I'm a corporal in this company.'

Zhitkov was a thickset, stocky peasant of exceptional strength who always wore a morose expression. He had a dark face with high cheekbones, and small, sullen eyes. He never smiled and hardly ever spoke. A carpenter by trade, he had been on indefinite leave when our Army was mobilised. He had only a few months to go to get his permanent discharge. Then the war broke out and Zhitkov was called up, leaving behind a wife and five little children. In spite of his unprepossessing appearance and constant moroseness, there was something attractive, kindly and powerful about him. I just cannot comprehend now how I could ever have mixed up these two neighbours of mine, but during the first few days they seemed to be identical to me – grey figures, loaded up, tired and chilled to the bone.

It rained incessantly throughout the first half of May, and we had no tents. The never-ending clayey road climbed up hills and descended into gulleys at virtually every verst. It was hard going. Clumps of mud stuck to our boots, the grey sky hung low, constantly pouring a fine drizzle upon us. And there was no end to it, no hope of drying out and warming up when we reached our night's quarters; the Rumanians would not let us into their houses, not surprisingly – there was nowhere to accommodate such a vast body of men. We would march through a town or village and halt somewhere out on a common.

'Halt . . . Pile arms!'

And so, after having some hot broth, we would have to lie down there and then in the mud. Water from below, water from above: one's entire body seemed to be soaked in water. You shivered, wrapped up in your greatcoat, gradually and slowly began to get warmed by the damp warmth, and you dropped off and slept until you heard the accursed bugle. And again the grey column, the grey sky, the muddy road, and those wet, melancholy hills and dales. It was hard going for the men.

'Heaven's floodgates have opened up,' our half-platoon NCO Karpov said with a sigh. He was an old soldier, and had been on the Khiva Campaign. 'We get drenched and drenched, and it'll never end.'

'We'll dry out all right, Vasily Karpych! The sun will come out and dry us all. We're on a long march: we'll dry out and get drenched again many a time before we get there. Mikhaylych!', my neighbour turned to me. 'How far is it to that Danube?'

'Another three weeks or so.'

'Three weeks! We've already been marching for two . . .'

'To the Devil in Hell, that's where we've been marching,' growled Zhitkov.

'What are you growling for, you old devil? You're upsetting everybody. What do you mean, we're marching to the Devil in Hell? Why do you say things like that?'

'We're not off on holiday, are we?' Zhitkov snapped back.

'Not on holiday, that's for sure. We've got to carry out our oath! Remember what you said when you took the oath? "To spare not life nor limb!" Eh? You're an old fool. You watch what you say.'

'Why, what did I say, Vasily Karpych? I'm marching like the rest of them, aren't I? If we've got to die . . . it's all the same. . .'

'That's better. Don't let's have any more of that from you, then.'

Zhitkov fell silent. His expression became more morose still. Anyhow, no one felt like talking – the going was too hard for that. One's feet kept slipping, and men often fell into the sticky mud. Strong language could be heard throughout the battalion. Fyodorov was the only one not to lose his spirit and he did not tire of telling one tale after another about Petersburg and his village.

Still, nothing lasts for ever. One day, when I awoke in the morning – we were bivouacked near a village when a day's rest had been ordered – I saw a blue sky, little white clay houses and gleaming vineyards bathed in the morning sun, and I could hear cheerful, lively voices. Everybody was already up and about, had dried out and was resting after the arduous ten days' march in constant rain without tents. Tents were brought up during that halt. The men at once got busy stretching the canvas, pitched the tents in proper fashion, drove pegs into the ground and drew the canvas; then most of them lay down in the shade of the tents.

'They didn't help us against the rain, now they'll protect us from the sun.'

'That's right, and the barin will preserve his complexion,' Fyodorov joked, winking slyly in my direction.

II

There were only two commissioned officers in our company: Captain Zaykin, the company commander, and a subaltern, Ensign Stebelkov. Captain Zaykin was of middle-age, a chubby and good-natured little man; Stebelkov, a mere youth, was fresh from the Military Academy. They got on well together. The captain was very protective towards the ensign, saw to it that he had plenty to eat and drink, and during the rainy weather he even shared his own waterproof cloak with him. When the tents were issued, our two officers shared one, and since officers' tents were quite spacious, the captain decided to take me in too.

I was tired after a sleepless night. Our company had been detailed to transport duty on the previous day, and we had spent the whole night dragging the baggage train out of ruts, once even pulling it out of a river that had overflowed, all the while singing 'Dubinushka' for encouragement. I had fallen fast asleep after dinner.

Captain Zaykin's orderly woke me up, tapping me gently on the shoulder.

'Barin Ivanov! Barin Ivanov!' he whispered, as though not really wanting to wake me, but on the contrary, making every effort not to disturb my sleep.

'What do you want?'

'The company commander wants you.' Seeing that I was putting on my belt, with the bayonet attached to it, he added: 'Captain said you were to come just as you are.'

There was quite a gathering in Zaykin's tent. Apart from the two occupants, there were another two officers – Lukin, the regimental adjutant, and Ventzel, commanding officer of the rifle company. In 1877 a battalion had consisted of five companies – not four, as now. When a battalion was on the move, the rifle company brought up the rear, so that the last ranks of our company were now in contact with the first ranks of theirs. I had already marched virtually among the riflemen, and had heard the worst possible comments on Captain Ventzel. The four officers were seated around a box which served as a table. There was a samovar standing on it, as well as crockery and a bottle. They were drinking tea.

'Mr Ivanov! Come in, please!' shouted the captain. 'Nikita! A cup, a mug, a glass, whatever you've got there! Shift over, Ventzel; make room for him to sit by you.'

Ventzel got up and bowed most graciously. He was a lean young man of medium height, pale and tense.

'What restless eyes he's got and how thin his lips are!' it occurred to me. The adjutant gave me his hand without getting up. 'Lukin,' he curtly introduced himself.

I was ill at ease. The officers were silent; Ventzel was sipping tea laced with rum; the adjutant was puffing away at his short little pipe; Ensign Stebelkov nodded to me and went on reading a tattered volume of some foreign novel in translation that had made the journey from Russia to the other side of the Danube and back again in his suitcase, more tattered than ever. Our host poured a large earthenware mug of tea and added a large dose of rum to it.

'There you are, Mister Student! Don't be cross with me: I'm a simple man. In fact, all of us here are simple men, you know? Now you're an educated man, so you have to excuse us. All right?'

And with his enormous hand he clasped mine from above, like a raptor clutching its prey, and gave my hand a few shakes in the air, looking at me gently with his bulging round little eyes.

'Are you a student?' Ventzel asked.

'That's right, sir, I used to be.'

He smiled and raised his restless eyes to look at me. I recalled the soldiers' tales about him, but just then I was not sure I believed them.

'Why this "sir"? Here in this tent you are among equals. Here you are just one of the intelligentsia, among others,' he said quietly.

'One of the intelligentsia, that's right!' Zaykin shouted. 'A student! I'm fond of students, even though they're a rebellious lot. I would have been one myself, if fate had not decreed otherwise.'

'What's so special about your fate, Ivan Platonych?' the adjutant asked Zaykin.

'Well, I just couldn't prepare for examinations. Maths – I could manage that more or less, but the rest, I couldn't do it. Literature, you know, and spelling . . . I didn't even learn to write properly in the Military Academy. That's the truth of it, by God!'

'You know what, Mister Student,' the adjutant said between two enormous puffs of smoke, 'Ivan Platonych manages to make three mistakes in a word like "news".'

'Come on now, old boy, stop making things up,' Zaykin said, with a dismissive gesture of his arm.

'But that's right, I'm not making it up . . . *n, u, z, e* – what do you think of that?' And the adjutant roared with laughter.

'You can shout. A fine adjutant he is. Writes "table" with a "y".'

The adjutant roared still louder. Ensign Stebelkov had just taken a sip of his tea, spluttered some all over his novel and put out one of the two candles which illuminated the tent. I couldn't help laughing either. Zaykin, more pleased with his own witticism than all the rest, went off into peals of deep laughter. Ventzel was the only one who did not laugh.

'So it was literature, Ivan Platonych?,' he asked as quietly as before.

'Literature, that's right, and the rest. You've heard about the fellow who got as far as the equator in geography, and no further than

"era" in history. But no. All that's nonsense, that's not the point. I
had a bit of money to burn and so I just wasted my time. You see,
Ivanov . . . what's your forename and patronymic, by the way?'

'Vladimir Mikhaylych.'

'All right, Vladimir Mikhaylych! . . . I mean, I was a dissolute one
when I was young. What I didn't get up to . . . You know what it
says in the song:

When he had the money, he was quite a lad,

When the money was gone, he went to the bad.

So I joined this glorious regiment – it's actually just one of the line – as
a cadet. I was sent to the Academy and managed to get through it by
the skin of my teeth, and I've been soldiering on for the past twenty
years. And now we're off to have a go at the Turks. Let's drink it
neat, gentlemen! Why spoil it with tea? Let's drink, gentlemen
cannon-fodder!'

'*Chair à canon,*' Ventzel translated.

'All right, *share a cannon* – have it in French if you must. Our
captain is a clever one, Vladimir Mikhaylych. He knows languages
and mugs up German poems by heart. – Look here, young man. I
asked you here to suggest that you move into our tent. It's nasty and
crowded where you are, squeezed in with six privates. Insects, too.
It's better here with us . . .'

'Thank you very much, sir, but please allow me to decline.'

'What for? Rubbish! Nikita! Bring his pack over here. Which tent
are you in?'

'The second from the right. Only, please, let me stay there. I'm
with the soldiers most of the time anyhow. I'd better be with them
altogether.'

Zaykin looked at me attentively, as though trying to read my
thoughts. After a pause he said: 'You mean, you want to be friends
with them?'

'That's right, if it's possible.'

'Right. Don't move in with us, then. I respect your wishes.'

And he seized my hand with his enormous paw and started shaking
it in the air.

A little later I took leave of the officers and left the tent. It was
evening. The men were getting into their greatcoats for the evening
roll-call. The companies lined up so that each battalion formed a
closed square, with the tents and the piled arms inside it. Because of

the day's halt, the entire division was together. The drums beat the Retreat and from somewhere far away we heard the command:

'Regiments, prepare for prayers! Remove caps!'

And twelve thousand men bared their heads. 'Our father, which art in heaven,' our company began. Those beside us began chanting too. Sixty choirs, each of two hundred men, were all singing on their own; there were dissonances, and yet the prayer sounded solemn and moving. Gradually the choirs died down. At last, far away, the last company in a battalion standing at the very end of the bivouac chanted: 'And deliver us from the evil one.' There was a short roll of drums.

'Replace caps!'

The soldiers were settling down for the night. In our tent, in which, as in the other tents, there were six men in a space of two square sazhens, my place was by the entrance. I lay there a long time looking at the stars, at the campfires of troops far away from us, listening to the subdued, confused noise of the camp. In the next tent someone was telling a fairytale, constantly repeating the words 'so then . . .'

'So then, at last, this prince came back to his wife and started telling her all about it. So then, she . . . Lyutikov, are you asleep, or what? . . . Oh well, you sleep, Christ be with you, Lord, Queen of Heaven, father of all the saints,' said the story-teller in a whisper and then fell silent.

There was also talking in the officers' tent. Through the canvas, illumined from inside, I could see the huge, unnatural shadows of the officers sitting inside. Sometimes there was a burst of laughter – the adjutant roaring away. A sentry was going up and down the line. Opposite us, in the nearby artillery bivouac, there was another sentry, with a bared sabre. From there I could occasionally hear the horses stamping, pulling at their tethers, snorting and peacefully chewing their oats with a tranquil, rustling sound I had heard before – not in the war, but at some coaching inn, back at home, on a quiet starlit night like this one. The seven stars of the Great Bear were shining low above the horizon, much lower than at home. As I looked at the North Star I thought that that was the direction where Petersburg must be, where I had left my mother, my friends and all that was dear to me. Overhead, familiar constellations were shining. The Milky Way glowed brightly, a clear and solemnly peaceful strip of light. To the South there were some stars of a constellation that I

didn't know, and which we didn't see at home, one of them glowing
with a red light, the other a greenish one. And I thought: 'When we
go on, across the Danube, over the Balkans, to Constantinople, will I
see any new stars then? And which ones will they be?'

I didn't feel like sleeping. I got up and started strolling across the
damp grass between our battalion and the artillery unit. A dark figure
came up to me, his sabre rattling – the sound made me guess it was an
officer and I stood to attention. The officer came up to me. It was
Ventzel.

'Can't you sleep, Vladimir Mikhaylych?' he asked in a soft, quiet
voice.

'No, sir.'

'I'm Pyotr Nikolayevich . . . Nor can I. I sat there, with your
commanding officer, and it was becoming quite tedious. They
started playing cards, and they all got drunk . . . Ah, what a night!'

He started walking beside me. When we got to the end of the line,
we turned back and walked up and down a couple of times without
saying a word. Ventzel broke the silence.

'Tell me, did you join up of your own free will?'

'Yes.'

'What made you?'

'That's hard to say,' I answered, not wishing to go into details.
'Mainly, of course, to have the experience and to see things.'

'And, no doubt, to study the people in the shape of its representative, the soldier?' Ventzel asked.

It was dark, and I couldn't see the expression on his face, but I
detected the irony in his voice.

'What is there to study? You don't feel like studying when all
you're thinking about is making it to the bivouac and getting some
sleep!'

'No, seriously, though. Tell me, why didn't you move in with
your company commander? Do you really value the opinion of these
peasants?'

'Of course I value it, just as I value the opinion of anyone whom I
have no cause to disrespect.'

'I have no cause to disbelieve you. Anyhow, it's the fashion now.
Even literature is elevating the peasant into a pearl of creation.'

'Who's talking about pearls of creation, Pyotr Nikolayevich?
Acknowledge the human being in them, that's all you need to do.'

'Come on, no more of these piteous phrases, I beg you! Who

doesn't acknowledge it? Human being? Very well, human being. But what kind, that's another question. . . Come on, let's talk about something else.'

We did, in fact, get into a long conversation. Ventzel had clearly read a great deal, and, as Captain Zaykin had said, he knew languages as well. The captain's remark about Ventzel 'mugging up poetry' also proved to be correct. We talked about the French, and Ventzel first chided the Naturalists and then passed on to the poets of the forties and thirties, and even recited Alfred de Musset's *Nuit de décembre* with considerable emotion. He did it well – simply and expressively, with a good French pronunciation. When he had finished, he was silent for a while and then added:

'Yes, that's good. But all the Frenchmen put together aren't worth a dozen lines of Schiller, Goethe or Shakespeare.'

Before taking over the rifle company, Ventzel had been in charge of the regimental library and had also assiduously kept up with Russian literature. He was harsh in his condemnation of what he termed 'the country-bumpkin trend'. This comment brought our conversation back to our previous subject. Ventzel put his views with considerable feeling.

'I was hardly more than a boy when I joined the regiment, and my opinions were different from the ones I'm expressing to you now. I tried to act by the word, I tried to acquire some sort of moral influence. But a year of that sapped all my strength. And when I was confronted with the realities of life, all that was left from reading all those wholesome books turned out to be sentimental nonsense. And now I think the only way to make oneself understood is this!'

He made a gesture with his hand. It was too dark for me to make it out.

'And what's that, Pyotr Nikolayevich?'

'The fist,' he snapped. 'Anyway, good night. . . It's time to get some sleep.'

I saluted and went back to my tent with a feeling of pain and disgust.

Everyone seemed to be asleep in the tent. But a couple of minutes after I had lain down, Fyodorov, who was lying next to me, asked softly:

'Are you asleep, Mikhaylych?'

'No, I'm not.'

'Have you been with Ventzel?'

'That's right.'

'What was he like with you? Quiet?'

'Yes, he was; friendly even.'

'That just goes to show! One barin talking to another! He's not like that with us.'

'What do you mean, is he very fierce with you?'

'I'll say, something terrible! They get their jawbones cracked in the second rifle company. He's a wild beast!'

And Fyodorov immediately dropped off to sleep; the only answer I got to my next question was his calm, steady breathing. I wrapped myself in my greatcoat, everything got confused in my mind and then it all vanished in a deep sleep.

III

The rains were followed by days of intense heat. About that time we left the track where our feet had got stuck in the churned-up mud for the highway from Jassy to Bucharest. The first day's march on that highway, from Tekuch to Berlad, will never be forgotten by those who did it. It was 35 degrees in the shade and we did 48 versts on our first day. The air was still; a cloud of fine limestone dust raised by thousands of marching feet hovered over the highway and got into our mouths and noses, settled like a fine powder on our hair, making its colour indistinguishable, mingled with our sweat and covered all our faces with dirt, turning us all into negroes. For some reason we were marching in full uniform, and not in shirt-sleeves. The black cloth was made hot by the sun, our heads were baked through our black forage-caps. We felt the scorching crushed stone through the soles of our boots. The men were gasping for breath. To make matters worse, the wells were few and far between and there was so little water in most of them that the head of the column – there was a whole division marching – would drink it all and what was left for us, after a terrible crush and jostling around the wells, was a clayey liquid more like mud than water. When there wasn't any of that left, men started to collapse on the march. On that day some ninety men collapsed in our battalion alone. Three died from sunstroke.

In comparison with the others, I got through that torture quite well. Maybe because most of them were from Northern Russia while I had been used to the heat of the steppes, where I had lived as a child.

Possibly there was another reason as well. I frequently observed that the ordinary soldiers tended to be more affected by physical suffering than those from the so-called 'privileged classes' (I'm only talking of those who had gone to war voluntarily). The common soldiers perceived physical distress as a real calamity, which could cause them real anguish and depress them profoundly. As a result of their pampered upbringing and their relatively weaker physiques, etc., those who had joined up voluntarily suffered just as much physically as, and more than, the common soldiers; but inwardly, they were much less troubled. Their peace of mind could not be disturbed by bleeding feet, the unbearable heat or by deadly fatigue. Never before had I experienced such a total inward calm, never had I been so completely at peace with myself, nor had I ever such an unprotesting attitude to life as then, when I suffered all those discomforts on my way to facing bullets and killing people. This may seem very weird and strange, but I'm merely writing down the truth.

Be that as it may, while others collapsed on the way, I managed to stay cool and collected. In Tekuch I had acquired a huge melon-gourd, big enough to hold at least four flaskfuls of water. I replenished it many times during the march; half the water I'd pour into myself, the other half I shared among my neighbours. A soldier marches along, struggling to keep going, but the heat will take its toll: his legs begin to buckle under him, his body reeling as though he were drunk; his face turns purple beneath the layer of mud and dust, his hand clutching his rifle convulsively. A mouthful of water revives him briefly, but finally he flops unconscious onto the harsh, dusty road. 'Orderly!' hoarse voices shout. The orderly's job is to drag him to the wayside and render him assistance: yet that orderly is in almost the same condition. The road-side ditches are strewn with sprawling bodies . . . Fyodorov and Zhitkov are marching beside me, and though they are obviously suffering, they are sticking it out manfully. The effect of the heat on each of them is in accordance with their characters, or rather in contradiction to them. Fyodorov does not say anything, only now and then emitting a heavy sigh, looking up balefully with his fine eyes, now inflamed from the dust. Old Zhitkov is cursing and philosophising.

'Look at that one, flopping down . . . Careful with that bayonet of yours, damn you!', he shouts angrily, swerving to avoid the bayonet of a collapsing soldier, its point almost stabbing his eye. 'Lord Almighty! Queen of Heaven! Why are you doing this to me? I'd be dropping, too, I think, if it weren't for that brute!'

'What brute is that then, Zhitkov?'

'Nemtsev, the staff-captain. He's duty officer today; he's in the rear. You might as well go on marching, or he'll get to work on you. He'll beat you black and blue all over.'

I knew that the men had changed Ventzel's name to Nemtsev.* It was quite similar and had a Russian ring to it.

I stepped out of the ranks. It was easier to walk at the edge of the road, where there was none of the dust and jostling. Lots of us were plodding along the roadside. No one cared about keeping in marching order on that wretched day. I gradually dropped behind my company and soon found myself at the rear of the column.

Ventzel caught up with me, exhausted and panting, but worked up.

'How are you doing?' he asked me in a hoarse voice. 'Let's walk along the edge. I'm totally exhausted.'

'Would you like some water?'

He greedily swallowed a few large mouthfuls from my gourd.

'Thanks, that's better. What a day!'

We walked for a while without speaking.

'By the way, you never moved into Zaykin's tent?'

'No.'

'That's stupid. Sorry for the bluntness. So long, I've got to get to the tail of the column. There's a lot of these tender creatures flopping out.'

A few steps later I looked round and saw Ventzel bending over one of the men who had collapsed and tugging at his shoulder.

'Get up, you scum! Get up!'

I couldn't recognise the civilised man I'd been conversing with. Foul oaths were incessantly pouring from his mouth. The soldier, almost unconscious, opened his eyes and stared despairingly at the officer, who was demented with rage. The soldier's lips were whispering something.

'Get up! Get up this instant! Aha – so you won't? Take that, and that, and that, then!'

Ventzel had seized his sabre and rained one blow after another with the metal scabbard on the helpless man's shoulders, sore and aching from the pack and the rifle. Unable to stand this any longer, I

* See Notes.

went up to him.

'Pyotr Nikolayevich!'

'Get up!' His hand, holding the sabre, was raised for yet another blow. I gripped his arm firmly.

'For God's sake, leave him alone, Pyotr Nikolayevich!'

Ventzel turned his infuriated face towards me. His eyes were rolling and his mouth was twisted convulsively – he was hideous to look at. He wrenched his arm free from my hold with a sharp movement. I thought he would unleash a torrent of anger on me for my impertinence – grabbing an officer by the arm was indeed a major impertinence – but he checked himself.

'Listen, Ivanov, don't you ever do that again! If it wasn't me, but some upstart like Shurov or Timofeyev, you'd pay dearly for that little prank. Just you remember that you're a private and you can be shot out of hand for doing that sort of thing.'

'I don't care. I couldn't watch you and not intervene.'

'All honour to you for your delicate feelings. But they were misplaced. There is no other way of dealing with these . . .' His face expressed contempt, even something worse – sheer hatred. 'I expect that among these dozens who've been collapsing like women, only a few really fainted from the heat. I'm not doing this out of cruelty, there's none of that in me. But you've got to maintain order and discipline. I'd use verbal persuasion if one could talk to this lot. But the spoken word means nothing to them. All they can feel is bodily pain.'

I did not stay to hear the rest of what he had to say and went off to catch up with my company, which was by now far ahead of us. I caught up with Fyodorov and Zhitkov when the battalion had turned off the road, where it was ordered to halt.

'What were you talking to Staff-Captain Ventzel for, Mikhaylych?' Fyodorov asked me as I flopped down beside him, exhausted, only just managing to pile my rifle.

'Talking!' Zhitkov growled. 'That wasn't talking! Grabbed him by the arm, he did. Oh dear, Barin Ivanov, you be careful with that Nemtsev. Just because he enjoys talking to you – he'll get you into real trouble yet.'

IV

We reached Fokshany late that evening, marched through the unlit, silent, dust-covered little town and ended up in open country. By now it was pitch-dark, the battalions were camped in no particular order and the men fell asleep, exhausted and half-dead. Hardly anyone felt like having the 'dinner' that had been made. Soldiers' meals are always 'dinners', whether it's early morning, in the day-time, or at night. Stragglers came in throughout the night. We set off again at dawn, consoling ourselves with the thought that there would be a full day's halt after this march.

Once again, columns on the move: again the pack weighs down on shoulders that have gone numb; again, sore feet, rubbed raw and bleeding. Yet for the first ten versts you're barely aware of anything. The short sleep has not removed the weariness of the previous day and the men are walking as if asleep. I have on occasion marched fast asleep myself, so that when we stopped for a halt I couldn't believe we had already marched ten versts; and I couldn't remember a single one of the places we had passed on the way. It's only when the columns are in reach of the next stopping place and begin to draw up and re-form ready for that halt that you wake up and revel in the thought of a whole hour's rest, when you can unload, boil up some water, have a lie-down at your leisure, and take sips of hot tea. The moment we had piled our rifles and removed our packs, most of us would set about gathering fuel – generally last year's dry maize stalks. Two bayonets are rammed into the ground, a ramrod is laid across them and three mess-tins are hung from it. The dry, brittle stalks burn brightly and merrily; you always build the fire on the windward side; the flame licks the soot-covered mess-tins and ten minutes later the water is boiling vigorously. We would throw the tea straight into the mess-tins and let them stew till it was a potent liquid, almost black. We generally drank it without sugar: the quarter-master issued great quantities of tea (so much that the men smoked it as tobacco when there was none of that), but we were given very little sugar, and we drank huge amounts of tea. One mess-tin held seven glasses of tea, which was the average portion per man.

It may seem odd that I'm so discursive about these trivia. How-ever, a soldier's life on the march is such tough going, there are so many hardships, discomforts and so much suffering to put up with, there is so little hope of it all ending well, that even trifling matters like tea and similar modest luxuries provide enormous pleasure. You should have seen these soldiers, sun-burnt, rough and grim – both young and old (admittedly there was hardly anyone over forty among us), with what serious and happy faces they put little sticks and blades under their mess-tins: they were like children, tending the fire and advising each other:

'Hey, Lyutikov, stick it over there, by the edge! That's right! . . . That's done the trick, she's off! Won't be long before she boils!'

Tea and, occasionally, in cold and rainy weather, a glass of vodka and a pipe of tobacco – these are the soldiers' only pleasures – apart, of course, from all-healing sleep, which brings release from bodily hardships and from thoughts about the dark and frightening future. Tobacco was far from the last among the blessings of life, sustaining and stimulating weary nerves. A well-packed pipe would do the rounds among a dozen men and come back to the owner, who would take a final puff, knock out the ashes, and solemnly tuck the pipe away in the top of his boot. I recall how distressed I had been when one of my friends lost my pipe which I had lent him for a smoke; he was equally distressed and deeply ashamed, as if he had lost a whole fortune that had been entrusted to him.

Long halts (around noon) would give us rests of one-and-a-half to two hours. After drinking tea everyone would normally have a sleep. There was total silence, except for a sentry marching up and down near the regimental standard, and some of the officers wouldn't sleep. You lie there on the ground with your head on your pack, half-asleep and half-awake; the hot sun is burning your face and neck, flies are pestering and biting you and won't let you sleep properly. Dreams and reality mingle: not so long ago my life had been so utterly different from what it was now that, as I drowsed, semi-conscious, I had the sensation that any moment I would wake up to find myself at home, in familiar surroundings, and this plain would disappear, this naked earth with prickly burrs instead of grass, this merciless sun and this dry wind, these thousand men so weirdly attired in white, dust-covered shirts, these piled rifles. It was all like some strange, oppressive dream.

'A-rise!' The powerful voice of Major Chernoglazov, our bearded little battalion commander, gave the harsh, protracted command.

And the prostrate crowd of white shirts would stir, the men rising to their feet, grunting and stretching, putting on their pouches and packs and getting into line.

'To arms!'

We get our rifles from the stack. Even now I can clearly remember my rifle, No. 18635, its butt a shade darker than the others', with a long scratch mark in the dark varnish. Another command, and the battalion strings out and turns off onto the road. Barbarian, the major's mount, a bay stallion, is led by the bridle at the head of the column; his neck arched, he is prancing and pawing the ground. The major rides him only on rare occasions, usually he marches, with the steady stride of the true infantryman, at the head of the battalion alongside his Barbarian. He is showing the men that their commanding officer too is doing his bit, and they love him for it. Always calm and composed, he never jokes and never smiles; in the morning he is the first to get up, and the last to lie down at night; he treats the men in a firm and restrained manner, and never descends to using his fists or shouting without cause. The men say that, but for Major Chernoglazov, Ventzel would be even worse.

It's a hot day, but not as bad as yesterday. And we are no longer marching on the highway, but on a narrow track along a railway line, most of us on grass. There is no dust, clouds are gathering and there are occasional heavy drops of rain. We look up at the sky and put out our hands to test whether it's raining. Even yesterday's stragglers are feeling happier. We don't have much further to go, only some ten versts to the halt, the longed-for break, and we'll be there not for one brief night, but a night plus a whole day, plus another night. The men are in good cheer and feel like singing. Fyodorov, among the lead-singers, breaks into the famous song *It was at the Battle of Poltava*. When he reaches the passage about 'the treacherous bullet landing in the imperial hat', he starts the soldiers' favourite, that senseless and indecent song about Liza who had gone into the forest, found a black beetle and what happened next. Then another historic song, about Peter the Great being summoned to the Senate. On top of all that, the regiment's own creation:

Here comes our noble Tsar, the Sovereign Alexander.
Come on, you lads, and pull yourselves together!
We smartly do our drill, and we get thanked for our skill . . .

Our Battalion Commander, Major Chernoglazov,
He never slept, nor dozed, but drilled us really hard,
All superior and proud, of course, sitting on his splendid horse.

There followed another fifty-odd lines in that vein.

One day I asked Fyodorov why he sang all that nonsense about Liza and mentioned several other songs, all absurd and disgusting to the extent that the very obscenity lost all meaning and became nothing but totally senseless sounds.

'It's a habit, Vladimir Mikhaylych. Anyway, that's not singing. It's just sort of shouting to exercise the chest. And, well, it makes marching more fun.'

The band takes over when the singers get tired. A rhythmic, loud and mostly cheerful march makes the marching much easier. Even those who are most exhausted brace up, get into step and keep in line – the battalion is transformed. I remember one day we covered over six versts in one hour with the music playing, and we felt no fatigue; but when the exhausted bandsmen stopped playing, the stimulation of the music disappeared and I felt I'd drop any moment, and I would have dropped if there had not been a halt just in time.

Five versts after that halt we came up against an obstacle. We were in a valley with a small stream running through it. There were hills on one side and a narrower and fairly high railway embankment on the other. The recent rains had flooded the valley and formed a large pool in our path, some thirty sazhens across. The railway track rose above the water like a dam, and we had to walk along it. The railway guard let the first battalion through and it reached the other side of the pool safely, but then the guard announced that a train was due in five minutes and we should have to wait. We halted and had just piled our rifles when we spied the brigadier's familiar carriage at a turning in the road.

Our brigadier was a dashing fellow. Never have I come across anyone with vocal organs like those he was endowed with, not on the operatic stage, not in a cathedral choir. His rolling bass thundered in the air like trumpet blasts, and his appearance – large fleshy body and thick red head, huge grey whiskers flapping in the breeze, and thick black eyebrows above tiny eyes that glittered like two pieces of coal as he sat on his horse giving an order to the brigade – was inspiring in the extreme. Once, during military exercises on the Khodynka Plain in Moscow, he had cut such a splendid, martial figure that an old gentleman watching in the crowd shouted out: 'Bravo! That's the sort of men we need!' And the nickname Bravo had stuck with him ever since.

He dreamt of performing deeds of heroism. Throughout the

campaign he had several volumes of military history with him. His favourite discourse when talking to the officers was a critique of Napoleon's campaigns. Of course, I knew this only from rumours I had heard, because I very seldom saw our brigadier. Mostly he would drive past us on the march in his carriage drawn by a fine team of three and when he reached the night's bivouac he would go straight to his billet and stay there till late in the morning; during the day he would catch us up again, and the men always took note of the degree of lividness of his face and of hoarseness in his voice as he gave his deafening roar:

'Greetings, men of the Starobelsk!'

'Greetings to your Excellency!' the men would respond, adding, 'Old Bravo's off to have another go at the bottle!'

And the brigadier would drive on, sometimes with no further developments, but sometimes he would give one of the company commanders a thunderous dressing-down.

That particular day, on seeing our battalion halted, the brigadier came charging up to us and leapt out of his carriage as rapidly as his heavy body would allow him. Major Chernoglazov quickly went up to him.

'What's all this? Why have you stopped? Who gave you permission?'

'Your Excellency, the road is flooded and a train is just going to pass along the track.'

'The road is flooded? A train? Nonsense! You are training them to go soft and soppy! You are turning them into women. No halts without orders! I am putting you under arrest, my good sir. . .'

'Your Excellency. . .'

'Don't argue!'

The brigadier's gaze moved on menacingly and fixed on another victim.

'And what's this? Why is the commander of the second rifle company not at his post? Staff-Captain Ventzel, kindly come over here.'

Ventzel went up to him. A torrent of the brigadier's fury poured over him. I heard Ventzel trying to reply, raising his voice, but the brigadier drowned his words, so one could only assume that Ventzel had said something disrespectful.

'You're arguing?! Showing insolence?! roared the brigadier. 'Silence! Remove his sabre. You'll do sentry duty at the money-chest, you're under arrest! A fine example to the men. . . Frightened of a puddle! Follow me, men! Suvorov's way!'

The brigadier rapidly strode past the battalion with the lumbering gait of a man who had long been travelling in a carriage.

'Follow me, men! Suvorov's way!' he repeated and entered the water in his patent-leather jackboots. The major looked back with a scowl and went in at the brigadier's side. The battalion set off behind them. At first the water was knee-high, then it reached the waist, rising higher and higher. The brigadier, a tall man, was striding away easily, while the little major was already floundering and flailing his arms about. The soldiers were like a flock of sheep being driven across a river, they were jostling each other, getting stuck in the mud beneath the water and pulling their feet out of it, flopping from side to side. Captain Zaykin and the adjutant who were on horseback could have crossed the water in great comfort, but with the brigadier's example before them, they rode up to the edge, dismounted and, leading their mounts by the bridle, stepped into the muddy water churned up by hundreds of soldiers' feet. Our company, which comprised the tallest men in the battalion, got across with relative ease, but Eight Company, which was wading along beside us, was made up of very short men, and they were almost up to their ears in water; some of them even clutched at us, gasping for air. One little fellow, a gipsy, his face pale with terror and his black eyes wide open, grabbed Zhitkov by the neck with both arms and threw away his rifle. Luckily for Gipsy, someone caught the weapon before it reached the water. Ten sazhens further on the water became shallower and, with the worst behind us, we were all scrambling to get out, shoving and swearing; many of us were laughing. But Eight Company was not in the mood for laughter – many of their faces had turned blue, and not only from the cold. The riflemen were hard on their heels.

'Come on, toddlers, get on with it! You'll drown!' they shouted.

'We very nearly could have drowned,' was the response from Eight Company. 'It's all very well for him, he's only got his whiskers wet, see that? What a hero he's turned out! Lots of folk could get drowned here, you know.'

'You should have sat in my mess-tin, then I'd have got you across dry as can be.'

'That's right, friend, pity I didn't ask you,' was the good-humoured response to the mocking from the little fellow in

Eight Company.

The man who had caused all this turmoil had by then already dragged his feet out of the viscous mud, got out of the water, and was standing on the bank in a majestic pose, gazing at the mass of bodies flailing about in the water. He was soaked to the skin and really had got his long whiskers wet. Water was dripping from his uniform and the tops of his patent-leather boots were bulging with water, but he kept yelling: 'Onward, men! Suvorov's way!' to encourage the men on.

The officers, soaking wet, looked gloomy as they crowded round Bravo. Ventzel was among them, stripped of his sabre and his face distorted in a scowl. Meanwhile, the brigadier's driver had been walking along the edge of the pool, thrusting his whip into it every so often; he now mounted his box and drove the carriage through the water without mishap, slightly to one side from where we had been wading through. The water barely reached his wheel hubs.

'Your Excellency, that's where we should have forded the pool,' Major Chernoglazov said calmly. 'Will you now give orders for the men to dry out?'

'Why, of course, Sergey Nikolayevich,' the brigadier said equably. The cold water had cooled his fervour. He climbed into the carriage, sat down, but then got up again and yelled at the top of his heroic voice:

'Thank you, men of the Starobelsk! Good lads!'

'Glad to do our bit, your Excellency!' the soldiers roared back in ramshackle fashion. And the sodden brigadier drove off.

The sun was still high, and we had only five versts to go. The major had ordered a long halt. We got undressed, made up some camp fires and dried our clothes, boots, packs and pouches. A couple of hours later we were off again, laughing as we talked about the bath we had just had.

'So Bravo has put Ventzel under arrest!' said Fyodorov.

'That's all right. A couple of days by the money-chest'll do him good,' a rifleman behind us commented.

'Why do you care?'

'Why? Because it'll make life easier for the whole company, not just for me. Things will be better for a couple of days. I just can't take him any more. That's why I care.'

'Patience, Cossack, one day you'll be an ataman.'

'Patience, that's all very well. But we won't be atamans till we're in the next world,' Zhitkov said in his usual gloomy voice. 'If the Turk gets at us.'

'Come on, old man, don't get all miserable,' said Fyodorov. 'Just think: we've dried out now, we're nice and dry, aren't we? And Bravo is sitting in his carriage in his wet clothes!' Everybody laughed.

V

All this time we were marching alongside the railway track; trains, packed with men and horses and supplies, were constantly passing us. The soldiers looked enviously at the goods wagons speeding past us, with horses' heads looking out of the open doors.

'See that? It's horses get the decent treatment. We've got to slog on on foot.'

'A horse is stupid, it can lose its balance. But you're a human being so as you can look after yourself properly,' Vasily Karpych reasoned.

Once, during a halt, a Cossack came galloping up to Battalion HQ with an important message. We were lined up as we were, in our white shirts, without packs and rifles. Nobody knew what it was all about. The officers did an inspection. Ventzel, as ever, was shouting and swearing, tugging at belts that had been put on sloppily and ordering the men with a kick or two to adjust their shirts. Then we were led to the railway track and after much forming and reforming the regiment was strung out in double file along the track. The white line of shirts was a verst long.

'Men!', shouted Major Chernoglazov. 'His Majesty the Tsar will be passing us!'

We started waiting for the Tsar. Our division was from deep in the provinces, and had been stationed far from both St Petersburg and Moscow. No more than one in ten of the men at most could ever have seen the Tsar, and we all waited for the train impatiently. Half an hour went by and still no sign of the train. The men were allowed to sit down and started talking.

'Is he going to stop?' someone wondered.

'Don't count on it! You think he'll stop for every regiment? We'll be lucky if he looks at us from his window.'

'We shan't know which one he is – there's lots of generals travelling with him.'

'I'll know him all right. I saw him on the Khodynka Plain a couple of years ago. That close, I saw him,' and the soldier stretched out his hand to indicate how close he had been to the Tsar.

Finally, after a two hours' wait, we saw a wisp of smoke in the distance. The regiment stood and lined up. First a train passed us with orderlies and a field-kitchen. Cooks and kitchen-boys wearing white caps looked at us out of the windows, laughing at something or other. Some two hundred sazhens behind came the imperial train. Seeing the regiment lined up along the track, the driver reduced speed and the carriages rumbled slowly past before our eyes gazing eagerly at the windows. But all of them had drawn blinds. On the platform of the last carriage stood a Cossack and an officer – they were the only people we saw on the train. We watched it disappearing with increasing speed, stood around for a couple of minutes and then returned to our bivouac. The men were disappointed and gave voice to their feelings.

'It'll be ages before we'll be seeing him now!'

But we did see him very soon. As we approached Ploeshti we were told that the Tsar would review us there.

We marched past before him, straight from the long march, just as we were, in our dirty white shirts and trousers, our dust-covered boots turned rusty-brown, our unshapely full packs piled on our shoulders, ration bags and bottles dangling on bits of string. The soldiers had no dash or swagger about them, each looking more like a simple Russian peasant, but for the rifle and the cartridge pouch that indicated that this Russian peasant was going to war. We were formed in a narrow column, four abreast: that was the only way we could pass through the narrow streets of the town. I was on the outside, trying hard not to trip and to keep in line, and thinking that if the Tsar and his entourage stood on my side of the column I should pass before his eyes and be very close to him. Glancing at Zhitkov marching beside me, his face stern and morose as ever but now also stirred, I perceived that I too was participating in the general excitement, and that my heart was beating faster. And I suddenly felt that everything that would happen to us depended on the way the Tsar would look at us. I was to experience a very similar feeling later, when I came under fire for the first time.

The men constantly quickened their pace and lengthened their stride, their gait becoming easier and firmer. I had no trouble in adapting to the general rhythm – my tiredness had vanished. It was as if we had grown wings that bore us onward to the spot from which the music and the deafening cheering came. I can't remember the streets we marched through, I can't remember if there were crowds standing in them and watching us; I can only remember the excitement that gripped my heart, together with an awareness of the terrible power of the mass to which I belonged and which was carrying us along. I felt that nothing was impossible for this mass, that the tide together with which I was pressing onward and of which I formed a part knew of no obstacles, that it would smash everything, mangle everything, annihilate everything. And each one of us had the thought that the individual before whom this tide was sweeping could with a single word, a single movement of his hand, change its course, turn it back or fling it once more against terrible obstacles, and each one of us hoped to find, in the word or gesture of this one man, that uncomprehended something that was leading us to our deaths. 'You are leading us,' each one of us was thinking, 'to you we give our lives; look at us and be assured: we are ready to die.'

And he knew that we were ready to die. He saw awesome rows of men, firm in their resolve, passing before his eyes almost at the double, men from his own poor country, coarse, poorly clad soldiers. He sensed that they were all going to their deaths, calm and free from all responsibility. He was sitting on a grey, motionless horse, its ears pricked to the music and the frenzied shouts of ecstasy. His splendid retinue stood around him, but I remember no one out of this glittering troop of horsemen but for that one man on the grey horse, wearing a plain uniform and a white peak cap. I remember his pale, weary face, wearied by the gravity of the decision he had taken. I remember the tears running down his face, falling on the dark cloth of his uniform in bright shining drops. I remember the twitching movement of his hand that held the reins, and his quivering lips that were saying something, doubtless a salute to the thousands of young lives about to perish, for whom he was weeping. All this appeared and then vanished, as something briefly illumined by lightning, at the moment when I ran past him, gasping not from the running, but from a frenzied, inhuman ecstasy, holding my rifle high in the air with one hand and with the other waving my cap above my head, yelling a deafening 'Hurrah!' though I could not distinguish my own voice in the general roar.

All this flitted by in an instant and vanished. The dusty streets, bathed in blazing heat; soldiers worn out by the excitement and the march almost at the run for a whole verst, and growing faint from thirst; the shouts of officers ordering us to keep in line and march in step – that was all I saw and heard five minutes later. After marching for another couple of versts through the fetid town we reached a common where we were to bivouac, and I flopped down on the ground, my body and soul utterly shattered.

VI

Arduous marches, dust, heat, fatigue, feet rubbed blood-raw, brief rest periods in the daytime, death-like sleep at night, the hated bugle waking us at the crack of dawn. And all the while, fields unlike those at home, covered in tall green maize, its long silky leaves rustling noisily, or succulent wheat already turning yellow here and there.

Day after day the same faces, the same life of a regiment on the march, the same chats and tales about home, about provincial towns in Russia where the regiment had been stationed, and gossip about the officers.

Only rarely, and reluctantly, did the men speak about the future. They had only the vaguest idea why they were going to war, despite the fact that they had been stationed near Kishinyov for a whole six months, ready for the campaign. That was surely the time when the meaning of the war could have been explained to the men, but this had evidently been considered unnecessary. One soldier, I remember, once asked me:

'What do you think, Mikhaylych, will it be long before we get to the land of Bokhara?'

I thought at first I had misheard, but when he repeated his question I replied that there were two seas between us and the land of Bokhara, which was four thousand versts away, and that we should not be likely ever to go there.

'No, Mikhaylych, you're wrong there. The clerk told me, he said once we've crossed the Danube we'll be in the land of Bokhara.'

'But that's not Bokhara, that's Bulgaria!' I exclaimed.

'Ah, well, Burgaria, Bukharia – whatever you call it. It's all the same, isn't it?'

He fell silent, obviously annoyed.

All we knew was that we were on our way to fight the Turk, because he had shed so much blood. We really did want to fight him, but not so much because of all that blood he had shed – we hadn't the faintest idea whose – but because he had caused so much trouble to so many people, so that we had to endure this long and gruelling march ('We've had to slog God knows how many thousands of versts – all because of him, the dirty heathen!'), and reservists had had to leave their homes and families, and here we were, all of us together having to go somewhere or other to face bullets and cannonballs. We visualised the Turk as a trouble-maker and a rebel who needed to be put down and tamed.

What occupied our minds far more than the war was our domestic concerns, that is to say, regimental, battalion and company matters. In our company all was calm and orderly, but with the riflemen things were going from bad to worse. Ventzel was not easing up, and the men's secret anger grew. After one particular incident which even now, five years later, I cannot recall without feeling deeply agitated, this anger turned into outright hatred.

We had just marched through some town and had reached a meadow where the first regiment, just ahead of us, had already set up camp. It was an agreeable spot – a river on one side, and a neat little grove of old oak-trees on the other, probably a pleasure ground for the local townspeople. It was a fine, warm evening, and the sun was setting. Our regiment halted, rifles were piled. Zhitkov and I started to pitch our tent. We had put up the tent-poles and Zhitkov was driving in the pegs, with me holding one edge of the canvas.

'Draw it tighter, come on, Mikhaylych!' (He had dropped the 'barin' with me a few days before.) 'That's better.'

Just then we heard strange regular clapping sounds behind us. I turned round.

The riflemen were standing at attention. Ventzel was shouting hoarsely and hitting a soldier in the face. The man stood there with his rifle close to his leg, his face pale as death, not daring to dodge the blows, his whole body trembling. Ventzel's small, skinny body was twisted from the effort of the blows which he dealt with both hands, now the left, now the right. Everybody stood in silence around them; all that could be heard were the clapping sounds and the frenzied officer's hoarse muttering. Everything went dark before my eyes, and I made a sudden movement. Zhitkov realised what it signified and gave the canvas a sharp tug.

'Hold it, you clumsy idiot!', he shouted and swore at me in the foulest language imaginable. 'Have your arms dropped off, or what? What are you gawping at? Never seen that before?'

The blows continued to rain. Blood was running down the soldier's upper lip and chin. Finally he collapsed. Ventzel turned away, surveyed the entire company and yelled: 'The next scoundrel who dares to smoke when standing at attention will get a damned sight worse. Pick him up, clean up his ugly mug and put him in his tent. He'll come round. Pile arms!'

His hands were shaking, red, swollen and covered in blood. He got out a handkerchief and went off, leaving the men piling arms in grim silence. Several gathered round the savagely beaten man and picked him up, muttering darkly to each other. Ventzel walked off with a nervous and exhausted gait; he was pale and his eyes glittered; his twitching muscles showed that his teeth were firmly clenched. As he walked past us he met my fixed stare, smiled in a forced, mocking way with his thin lips only, whispered something and went on.

'The blood-sucker!' Zhitkov said with hatred in his voice. 'And you are a fine one, barin! Asking for trouble, you are. Want to get yourself up before the firing squad? You wait, they'll give him what he deserves.'

'Are they going to report him?' I asked. 'Who to?'

'Oh no, they're not going to report him. We'll be in action soon . . .'

And he muttered something half to himself. I didn't dare to understand him. Fyodorov had got in among the riflemen and asked them what it was all about.

'He's torturing those men for no reason,' he said when he came back. 'That soldier, Matyushkin, had been smoking a home-rolled cigarette on the march. When they halted, he had his rifle-butt up against his leg and his cigarette was still in his fingers – he must have forgotten all about it, worse luck for him. Ventzel spotted him.'

'He's a brute!' he added sadly as he crawled into the tent that we had put up by then. 'That cigarette had gone out, it seems he'd forgotten all about it, poor devil.'

A few days later we reached Alexandria, where a very large mass of troops had been assembled. Coming down a high hill we saw a vast area dotted with white tents, black figures of men, long lines of horses and brass cannons here and there glinting in the sun, green gun-carriages and ammunition wagons. Large crowds of officers and men were walking along the main street of the town.

From the open windows of cramped, grubby little hotels came

Hungarian music, both mournful and spirited, the clatter of plates, noisy conversations. The shops were packed with Russian customers. Our soldiers, Rumanians, Germans and Jews were shouting loudly, unable to understand each other; arguments about the exchange rate of paper rubles were heard at every turn.

'What do you mean, giving me *dou galagan**, you black-faced devil? I want ten kopeks. Come on, *domnul†!*'

'*Unde eshte poshta‡?*' an officer was asking a rakish Rumanian, whom he saluted with exaggerated courtesy; he was armed with a military phrase-book which had been issued to the troops. The Rumanian told him; the officer leafed through the phrase-book looking for the unintelligible words and, though he hadn't understood a thing, he thanked him politely all the same.

'Wow, lads, what a rabble! They've got priests like ours, the churches are the same, too, but they don't have a clue about anything! – You want a silver ruble for this?' a soldier, holding up a shirt, shouted to a Rumanian stall-holder. 'For this shirt? *Patru franku*? Four francs?' He took out a coin, showed it to the stall-holder, and the transaction was concluded to mutual satisfaction.

'Stand back there, lads, here comes a general!'

A tall, young-looking general wearing a raffish coat, jackboots and with a whip hanging by the strap from his shoulder strode rapidly along the street. He was followed by his orderly, a few paces behind, a squat little Asiatic wearing a turban and a gaudily coloured gown, with a huge sabre and a revolver on his belt. His head held high, and gazing in a carefree, jaunty manner at the soldiers making way for him and saluting him, the general entered a hotel. Here, huddled in a corner, Captain Zaykin, Stebelkov and I were tucking into some local meat and red pepper dish. The tawdry room, set with little tables, was crowded. The clatter of plates, popping corks, voices sober and drunk, were all drowned by a band ensconced in what resembled a niche shrouded in red calico drapes. There were five musicians: two fiddlers were frenziedly sawing away, a cellist monotonously droned the second part, a bass boomed – but all these instruments were merely providing the background for the fifth

---

* Two coins (corrupt Rumanian).
† Sir, Mister (corr. Rum.).
‡ Where is the post office? (corr. Rum.).

player. A swarthy, curly-haired Hungarian, a mere lad, sat in front of them, with a strange-looking instrument thrust out beyond the wide collar of his velvet jacket: it was an ancient syrinx, just like the one Pan and the Fauns are depicted with, and consisted of a row of wooden pipes of different lengths bound together so that their open ends came together level at the player's lips. Twisting his head now this way, now that, the Hungarian blew into these pipes from which he produced powerful melodious sounds that resembled neither a flute nor a clarinet. He executed the most tricky and difficult passages, constantly shaking and twisting his head, his black greasy hair bobbing on his head and falling on his forehead, his red face sweating and the veins on his neck swelling. He evidently did not find his playing easy . . . Against the discordant background of the string instruments the sounds of the pipes stood out sharply and distinctly, with a wild beauty of their own.

The general chose a place at a table at which sat some officers whom he knew, bowed to everyone who had stood up when he entered and said in a loud voice: 'Sit down, gentlemen!' – this being addressed to the other ranks present. We finished our meal in silence. Zaykin ordered some red Rumanian wine and after the second bottle, when his face had cheered up, his cheeks and nose now a brighter colour, he turned to me, saying:

'Now, tell me, young man – you remember that long march, don't you?'

'I do, Ivan Platonych.'

'You talked to Ventzel then, didn't you?'

'Yes, I did.'

'You seized him by the arm?' the captain asked in an unnaturally solemn tone. And when I replied that I had done that, he gave a long, loud sigh and anxiously blinked his eyes.

'That was a bad thing to do . . . It was a stupid thing to do! You understand, I'm not reprimanding you. It was a fine thing to do . . . I mean, it was against military discipline . . . God knows what I'm trying to say! You must excuse me . . .' He paused, gazing at the floor and puffing heavily. I didn't speak either. Ivan Platonych gulped down half a glassful and slapped me on the knee.

'Promise me you'll not do anything like that again, will you? I do understand . . . It's not easy if you're new. But what can you do with him? He's a mad dog, that Ventzel! Anyway, the point is . . .'

It was obvious that Ivan Platonych couldn't find the right words, and after a long pause he resorted to his glass again.

'I mean to say, the thing is – he's a good chap, really. There's something peculiar about him though, I don't know what it is. I gave a man a clout myself not long ago, you saw it yourself, not a hard one, mind you. I mean, if the idiot doesn't realise what a rotter he is, you know, if he's as thick as two planks . . . I mean, Vladimir Mikhaylych, I do it as if I was a father. Really, I do it without malice, though I admit I do lose my temper sometimes. But Ventzel – he's made it into a system. Hey, you!' he shouted to the Rumanian waiter, '*Oshte vin negru*! More wine! – He'll be court-martialled one day; but what's worse, the men will get angry with him, and the moment we go into action . . . It'll be a shame, because he's really a good chap, don't you see? He's actually quite warm-hearted.'

'Come on!' Stebelkov said in a drawl. 'No warm-hearted man would knock the men about like that!'

'You should have seen what that warm-hearted man got up to the other day, Ivan Platonych.' And I told the captain how Ventzel had laid into the soldier over a cigarette.

'There you have him, that's him all over!' Ivan Platonych turned red, puffed and panted, stopped talking and then continued: 'And yet, he's not a brute. Whose men are the best fed? Ventzel's. Whose are the best trained? Ventzel's. Whose lot has been on hardly any charge? Who never has anyone court-martialled – unless a man has done something really shocking? Ventzel again. If it weren't for this unfortunate weakness of his, his men would carry him shoulder-high.'

'Have you ever spoken to him about it, Ivan Platonych?'

'I have, and quarrelled with him a dozen times over it. But what's the use? "Either this is an army," he says, "or it's a militia." He's always coming out with such stupid things. "War," he says, "is such a cruel business that if I'm cruel to the soldiers, it's just a drop in the ocean. . ." "They stand on such a low rung of evolution," he says. . . . I mean, God knows what to make of him! And yet, he's a fine chap. He doesn't drink, doesn't gamble, does his job conscientiously, supports his old father and his sister, and he's a wonderful comrade! And he's educated, too! There isn't another like him in the regiment. You mark my words: he'll either be court-martialled, or the men' – he nodded towards the window – 'will deal with him. A rotten business. So now you know how it is, my dear Private Ivanov.'

Ivan Platonych gently patted my shoulder-strap, put his hand into his pocket, got out his tobacco-pouch and rolled himself a big fat cigarette. He inserted it into a huge amber-tipped cigarette-holder on which the word 'Caucasus' was inscribed in black enamel on silver, put it into his mouth, then passed his tobacco-pouch round without saying a word. We all three lit up and the captain continued:

'There are times when you have to wallop them. They are just like children. Do you know Balunov?'

Stebelkov suddenly burst out laughing.

'Steady now, Stebelek, what's so funny?' Ivan Platonych growled. 'He's an old soldier, he's been on charges galore. His twenty years is coming up – they won't give him his discharge because he's still got obligations to work off. So there he is, a right old rascal . . . One day – before your time – we were leaving a village outside Kishinyov and HQ ordered us to inspect all the men's second pair of boots. I lined them up and walked behind them to see if the caps of their boots were sticking out of their packs. Balunov didn't have any. "Where are your boots?" – "I put them inside my pack, sir, for safe-keeping." "You're lying!" – "No, sir, I'm not. They're inside my pack, so they won't get wet!" He had a glib tongue, that rogue. "Take off your pack and undo it!" I could see he wasn't undoing the pack, and was pulling his boots out by their tops from under the flap. "Undo it, I said!" – "I can get them out like this, sir!" But I made him undo his pack, and what do you think? Out of the pack he pulled a live piglet by its ears! He'd tied up its snout with a bit of string to stop it squealing! There he stood, pulling ever such a respectful face, right hand at the salute, left hand holding the pig. The rogue had stolen it from a Moldavian peasant-woman. Well, of course, I gave him a bit of a clout then!'

Stebelkov was shaking with laughter and barely managed to say: 'And you know what with, Ivanov? He clouted him with the pig! Ha-ha-ha. . . . He grabbed that pig and clouted him with it!'

'Was there any need for you to do that, Ivan Platonych?'

'Oh, come on with you! What a bore you are, and no mistake. I wasn't going to have him court-martialled for that, was I?'

VII

During the night of the fourteenth and fifteenth of June, Fyodorov woke me:

'Can you hear it, Mikhaylych?'

'Hear what?'

'The shooting. They're crossing the Danube.'

I listened attentively. A strong wind was blowing, driving before it low black clouds that were obscuring the moon. It swooped onto the canvas, slamming it noisily, hummed among the guy-ropes and whistled thinly among the piled rifles. Occasionally through these sounds, dull thuds could be heard.

'There's a lot getting it now,' Fyodorov whispered with a sigh. 'I wonder if we'll be ordered forward or not? What do you think? Hear those bangs! Just like thunder!'

'Maybe it's a thunderstorm?'

'Oh, no! That's no thunderstorm! Those bangs are much too regular. Can't you hear it? One and then another, one and then another.'

Indeed, the bangs did come at regular intervals. I crawled out of the tent and looked in the direction of the shots. There were no light flashes. Occasionally I fancied my straining eyes saw lights from the direction where the guns were roaring, but that was only an illusion.

'So this is it at last!' I thought. And I tried to visualise what was happening over there in the darkness. I fancied I saw a wide black river with precipitous banks, quite unlike the real Danube, as we were to see it later. Hundreds of boats were sailing on it and those frequent and regular shots were aimed at them. Would many of them survive this? A cold tremor ran through my body. 'Would you want to be there?' I was asking myself without meaning to.

I looked at the sleeping camp. All was quiet; above the distant thunder of guns and the roaring wind I could hear the soldiers' peaceful snoring. And an ardent desire arose in me for *that* not to happen, for the march to last for yet a while so that these sleeping men – and I – should not have to go where the gunshots roared.

Sometimes the bombardment grew stronger; sometimes there was another, confused sound, a less loud, muffled sound. 'They're firing rifle volleys,' I thought, unaware that we were still twenty versts away from the Danube, and that those dull thuds were the morbid creations of my straining ear. However, even though they were unreal, those sounds got my imagination working, painting ghastly scenes. I fancied I heard cries and groans of thousands of falling soldiers, desperate, hoarse cries of 'Hurrah!', a bayonet charge, and carnage. And what if they repulsed us, and all this was for nothing?

The dark east had turned grey. The wind was calming down. The clouds had scattered, dying stars could be seen here and there on a pale, greenish sky. Dawn was breaking; in the camp one or two of the men awoke and those who had heard the sounds of battle were waking the others. They spoke little and softly. The unknown had come close to the soldiers: nobody knew what the morrow would bring, and nobody wanted to think or talk about that morrow.

I fell asleep at dawn and slept for quite a while. The guns went on roaring dully and, even though there had been no news from the Danube, rumours spread among us, each more improbable than the last. Some were saying that our men had already crossed the river and were chasing the Turks; others said that the crossing had failed, that whole regiments had been annihilated.

'Some got drowned, and a whole lot have been shot,' someone was saying.

'Stop telling lies,' Vasily Karpych cut him short.

'How am I telling lies if it's the truth?'

'The truth! Who told you?'

'What?'

'The truth! Where did you hear it? We all know there's an artillery bombardment, and that's all.'

'Everyone is saying it. A Cossack's been to the general . . .'

'A Cossack! Did you see the Cossack? What's he look like, then, this Cossack of yours?'

'Just a Cossack, quite ordinary . . . just like a Cossack always looks.'

'"Always looks"! Oh yes! You've got a tongue like an old wife's prattle. Just sit there and shut up. Nobody's come, so there's no way of knowing the news.'

I went to see Captain Zaykin. The officers were sitting quite ready, their tunics buttoned up and revolvers on their belts. Ivan Platonych was as red-faced as ever, hissing and puffing and wiping his nose with a dirty handkerchief. Stebelkov, agitated and radiant, was for some reason trimming up his whiskers that had hung limply before, so that now their sharp points were sticking out.

'Look at our ensign! Got himself all tarted up for the action!' said Ivan Platonych, winking at him. 'My dear old Stebelechek! How sorry I feel for you! Our mess will have to live without those lovely whiskers of yours! They will be the end of you, my dear Stebelechek. . .' The captain was speaking in mock-sorrowful tones.

'Well, are you scared?'

'I shall try not to be,' said Stebelkov in a hearty voice.

'And what about you, warrior, are you scared?'

'I'm not sure, Ivan Platonych. Why is it there's no information?'

'Never mind. God knows what's going on over there,' Zaykin said with a heavy sigh. 'We're moving in an hour,' he added after a pause.

The tent flap was turned back: Lukin, the adjutant, poked his head in; this time he looked grave and pale.

'You're here, Ivanov? You'll have to pledge the oath – not now, when we move off. Ivan Platonych, issue the men their fifth clips of cartridges.'

He declined the invitation to come in and sit down for a bit, saying he was very busy, and ran off. I left the tent too.

Dinner was served about noon. The men didn't eat much. After dinner they were ordered to remove the leather barrel covers from their rifles and the extra cartridges were handed out. Preparing for battle, the soldiers started to go through their packs and throw out everything superfluous. They threw out torn shirts and trousers, sundry rags, old boots, brushes, soiled soldier's books; some of them had carried a multitude of unnecessary things all the way to the Danube. I saw lying abandoned on the ground a fob used for smoothing out ammunition straps before parades and inspections in peacetime, heavy stone jars with hair grease, little boxes and pieces of wood, and even a cobbler's last.

'Come on, get rid of it, lads! It'll make going into action easier. You'll not be needing it all tomorrow.'

'I've been lugging this for five hundred versts, and what do I need it for?' Lyutikov reasoned as he examined an old piece of rag. 'I won't take it with me . . .'

Clearing out our packs and throwing out superfluous possessions became the vogue that day. When we moved off, the area where we had stood, strewn with countless rags and other objects, was a gaudy-coloured rectangle standing out against the dark steppe.

Just before moving off, as the regiment stood ready waiting for the command, several officers and our young regimental chaplain gathered at the head of the column. I was called out of the ranks, together with four volunteer-cadets in other battalions; we had all joined the regiment during the march. We left our rifles with our neighbours, went forward and halted at the regimental standard. My companions, all strangers to me, were agitated; my heart too was beating faster than usual.

'Take hold of the standard,' said the battalion commander. The standard-bearer lowered the standard, his assistants removed the cover. The old faded green silk fluttered in the wind. We stood round it, one hand grasping the staff, the other raised, and repeated the words the chaplain read out from a sheet of paper – an ancient military oath that dated back to Peter the Great. I recalled Vasily Karpych's words on our first day's march. 'Where was that?' I wondered. After a long list of incidents and places where His Imperial Majesty had served – campaigns, offensives, vanguards and rearguards, fortresses, sentry-guards and supply trains – I heard these words: 'To spare not life nor limb', which were loudly repeated in one voice by all five of us; and looking round at the rows of sombre-faced men ready for battle, I felt that these were no empty words.

We returned to our ranks; a tremor went through the regiment, it stirred, extended into a long column and moved off at forced march towards the Danube. The gunshots that we had heard from there had ceased.

I remember this march as in a dream: the dust raised by Cossack regiments overtaking us at a trot, the broad steppe sloping down towards the Danube, whose far bluish bank we had seen some fifteen versts away; the fatigue, the heat, the scuffling and fighting at the well that we reached near Simnitza; the dirty little town filled with troops, some generals waving their forage-caps to us from a balcony and cheering, to which we responded in like manner.

'You've made it! You've made it!' voices intoned all around.

'Two hundred killed, five hundred wounded!'

VIII

It was already dark when, after descending from the bank, we crossed a channel of the Danube by a small bridge and marched across a low, sandy island, still wet from the water that had recently ebbed from it. I can remember the sharp clash of bayonets getting entangled in the dark, the dull rumble of the artillery overtaking us, the black mass of the broad river, little lights on the opposite bank where we were due to be ferried on the following day.

'Better not think of it and get some sleep,' I decided and lay down in the water-soaked sand.

When I opened my eyes, the sun was already high. The sandy bank was crowded with troops, baggage trains and parks of artillery; at the water's edge gun emplacements and trenches for the riflemen had already been dug. On the steep bank on the far side of the Danube we could make out orchards and vineyards where our troops were swarming, and beyond them there were steeply rising stretches of high land which sharply restricted the horizon. On the right, some three versts away on some hills, we saw the town of Sistova with its gleaming white little houses and minarets. A steamer with a barge in tow was ferrying one battalion after another to the other side. There was a little torpedo-boat close by our bank giving out a hiss of steam.

'Safe crossing, Vladimir Mikhaylych!' Fyodorov said cheerfully.

'Same to you. We're not across yet, are we?'

'The steamer will be here any minute now to pick us up. They say there's a Turkish warship not far away – but this little samovar is trained on it.' He pointed at the torpedo-boat. 'Lots and lots have been hit, dear God!' he went on in a changed voice. 'They've been bringing lots of them back from over there.'

And he told me the details of the Battle of Sistova which everyone knew already.

'It's our turn now. We'll get across, and then the Turks will let rip at us. . . Still, we've had a bit of a respite. We're still alive, but the ones over there. . .' He nodded in the direction of a group of officers and men nearby. They had crowded round an invisible object and were all looking at it.

'What is it?'

'They've brought our dead back from over there. Go and have a look, Mikhaylych; it's terrible!'

I went up to the group. They all stood with bared heads, looking silently at the bodies laid out side by side on the sand. Zaykin, Stebelkov and Ventzel were there. Zaykin, frowning angrily, was grunting and puffing; from behind him Stebelkov craned his thin neck with a look of naive horror; Ventzel stood deep in thought.

There were two bodies lying on the sand. One was a strapping, handsome guardsman from the Finland Regiment, from its composite half-company which had lost half its men during the attack. He had been wounded in the stomach and must have been in agonies long before he died. His suffering had left a gentle imprint of something spiritual, graceful and delicately plaintive on his face. His eyes were closed, his arms folded on his chest. Had he adopted this pose just before he died, or had his comrades done it for him? Seeing him aroused in me no horror or disgust, merely an infinite regret for this rich and vigorous life, now ended.

Zaykin bent over the corpse, picked up the forage-cap lying beside the head and read on the cap-band: 'Ivan Zhurenko, Three Company'.

'A Ukrainian, poor devil!' he said quietly.

I visualised his homeland, the hot wind of the steppes, the village in some ravine, meadows with willow trees growing on them in profusion, a little white clay house with red window-shutters . . . Who is waiting there for your return?

The other dead man was an infantryman from the Volhynia regiment. Death had overtaken him very suddenly. He had been charging into the attack in a state of frenzy, choking from shouting. The bullet had struck him on the bridge of the nose, penetrating his head and leaving a gaping black wound. He lay there, his eyes wide-open but now glazed, his mouth open, his face blue and still distorted with rage.

'They've settled their debts in full,' Zaykin said. 'There's nothing at all they need now.'

He turned round, and the soldiers quickly made way for him. Stebelkov and I followed him. Ventzel caught up with us.

'There now, Ivanov,' he said. 'Did you see that?'

'I did, Pyotr Nikolayevich,' I replied.

'What did you think as you stood looking at them?' he asked gloomily.

A sudden surge of malice welled up in me against this vicious man, and the desire to say something really hurtful to him.

'I thought quite a lot. Above all, that those two aren't cannon-fodder any more. They don't need any more drilling or discipline, and nobody is going to bully them to achieve that discipline. They aren't soldiers now, they aren't anybody's subordinates!' I said with a trembling voice. 'They are – human beings!'

Ventzel's eyes flashed angrily. A sound burst from his throat and then broke off; he must have been about to reply, but had checked himself in time. He walked along beside me with lowered head, and after a few paces he said without looking at me:

'Yes, Ivanov, you're right. They are human beings . . . dead human beings.'

IX

We were ferried across the Danube. For a few days we halted near Sistova, waiting for the Turks to come. Then units started to move inland, our regiment included. For a long time we were sent first in one direction and then in another: we were near Tirnovo, another time we were not far from Pleven. Three weeks had passed, and we still had not done any fighting. Finally we were put into a special group those task it was to restrain the advance of a large Turkish army. Forty thousand Russians were stationed along seventy versts, with some hundred thousand Turks facing them. Only our commander's cautious tactics – he would not risk the lives of the men in his charge and contented himself with repulsing the enemy's attacks – and the feebleness of the Turkish Pasha enabled us to carry out our task: to prevent the Turks from breaking through our cordon and cutting our main army off from the Danube.

We were few in number, and our line was very extended; we were therefore able to have only infrequent rests. We passed through a large number of villages and appeared now here, now there, to face the presumed attack. We went to such out-of-the-way places in Bulgaria that our supply column could not find us, and we had to go hungry, having to stretch our two-day rations of hard tack to last for five days or more. Starving soldiers threshed unripened wheat on their spread tents with sticks, and boiled it up together with sour forest apples into a revolting unsalted soup, there being no salt to be had anywhere either, and became ill from eating it. The battalions dwindled, even though they had not been in action.

In the middle of July our battalion, together with some squadrons of cavalry and two gun batteries, reached a Turkish village. It had been half-burned, gutted and abandoned by the inhabitants. We pitched camp on a high precipitous mountain. The village was below, deep in a valley through which a narrow stream wound its way. Steep, high cliffs rose on the other side of the valley. We assumed that that was the Turkish side, though there were no Turks nearby. We halted on our mountain-side for a few days, virtually without any bread, and we even had great difficulty in getting water – we had to descend a long way to a spring gushing from the rock-face. We were completely cut off from the main army and had no idea what was going on in the world. Some fifteen versts ahead of us some Cossack patrols were posted; two or three hundred of them were strung out over twenty versts. There were no Turks there, either.

Even though we could not discover the enemy, our little unit took all precautionary measures. Day and night a chain of outposts surrounded the camp. Because of the nature of the terrain the chain was very extended and several companies were daily engaged in this inactive but very tiring duty. The inactivity, the almost constant hunger, and not knowing what the situation was, adversely affected the men.

The regimental field hospitals were full to capacity; every day men, weakened and exhausted by fever and dysentery, were sent off to the divisional hospital. The companies were down to one-half to two-thirds of their full strengths. Everyone was gloomy, and everyone wanted to go into action. That was at least a way out.

At last the moment came. A mounted Cossack came galloping with the information from the commander of his unit that the Turks had attacked and that he had had to withdraw his men and retreat five versts. Later it turned out that the Turks had not intended to maintain their advance and had turned back. We could therefore just as well have stayed where we were, especially since no one had ordered us to advance. However, the general in command of us, who had only recently joined us from St Petersburg, felt the same as all the men in the unit did. They found it intolerable to be sitting around with nothing to do or doing sentry-duty for days on end on the look-out for an invisible and, as we were all convinced, non-existent foe, eating vile food and waiting for their turn to be ill. They were all eager to go and fight. The general gave the order to attack.

We left half the unit in the camp. We knew so little about the overall situation that attacks could be expected from other directions too. One afternoon fourteen companies, some hussars and four cannons moved off. Never before had we marched so quickly and in such spirits, apart from the day when we had paraded before the Emperor.

We marched along a valley, passing through one deserted Turkish or Bulgarian village after another. We encountered not a single human being, not one head of cattle, not a dog; in the narrow lanes skirted with tall wattle-fences higher than a man's head, only some hens cackled and fluttered off before us onto fences and roofs, and a few geese ponderously rose into the air with a screech and tried to fly off. Branches that seemed to have ripe plums of every conceivable kind stuck all over them peeped out at us from the little orchards. We were given a half-hour break in the last village, five versts from where the Turks were supposed to be. Half-naked soldiers shook down a vast quantity of plums, ate their fill and packed the remainder into their food-pouches. Some, but only a very few, busied themselves with catching geese and killing them; they plucked them and took them along. I remembered how before the crossing at Sistova these same soldiers, expecting to go into battle, had thrown all their possessions out of their packs. I mentioned this to Zhitkov, who was plucking an enormous goose.

'Ah well, Mikhaylych, we've not been in action, but we have got used to waiting. You get the feeling we're just passing through here. It'll be the luck of the draw. There's no harm in having some supplies if we do get into action. And if you don't get killed, you've got a bit of food.'

'Are you scared?' I asked almost mechanically.

'Maybe nothing's going to happen,' he replied after a pause, screwing up his eyes and plucking the last tufts of white down.

'But supposing something does happen?'

'If it's going to happen it'll make no difference whether you're scared or not, you've just got to go in. They aren't going to ask the likes of us. Just go on, with God's help. Lend me your knife, will you? You've got a rare one there.'

I handed him my large hunting-knife. He split the goose down the middle and held one half out to me. 'You take it, go on, it may come in handy. But about being scared or not – it's best not to think about it, barin. It's all God's will. You can't get away from that.'

'If a bullet comes flying at you, or a shell, you'll not dodge it,' Fyodorov, who was lying beside us, confirmed. 'This is what I think, Vladimir Mikhaylych: there's more danger in running away. Because a bullet has to fly along a trajectory like this' – he demonstrated with his finger – 'and it's in the rear that you get the really big fry-ups!'

'That's right,' I said, 'especially with the Turks. They say they aim high.'

'A proper scholar, aren't you?' Zhitkov said to Fyodorov. 'Go on, tell us more! They'll show you a trajectory all right! Of course,' he said after a moment's thought, 'you're best off out in front . . .'

'Where the officers are,' Fyodorov said. 'Ours will be out in front, they'll not be cowards.'

'That's right, they'll be there. Nemtsev will be there as well.'

'Zhitkov,' Fyodorov asked, 'what do you say? Will he be alive after today or not?'

Zhitkov lowered his eyes.

'Why do you have to go and talk about that?' he asked.

'Come off it, will you? Have you seen him? He's all worked up, you know.'

Zhitkov's expression became even gloomier.

'You're talking rubbish,' he said in a flat voice.

'Remember what they were saying before we got to the Danube?' Fyodorov retorted.

'Before the Danube! . . . They were furious, beside themselves, they thought of all kinds of things. They couldn't take any more, you know that. Do you think they're criminals or something?' Zhitkov turned round to Fyodorov and looked him straight in the face. 'You think they don't have God inside them? They don't know where they are going! Maybe some of them will have to answer to God today, and you think they could think of doing a thing like that? Before the Danube! I once said it myself to the barin here' – nodding in my direction – 'before the Danube. That's right, I did say it, because it was sickening to look at what he was doing. Oh yes, I remember all right – before the Danube!'

He felt inside the top of his boot and got out his tobacco-pouch, and went on growling as he filled his pipe and lit it. Then he put the pouch away, got into a more comfortable position and, clasping his knees, fell to intense brooding.

Half an hour later we moved out of the village and started climbing out of the valley. The Turks were on the other side of the high ground that we had to cross. We reached the crest of the ridge. Before us lay a broad hilly expanse with a gradual downward slope covered in wheat and maize fields as well as huge thickets of elms and cornelian cherries. In two places we could see the white minarets of villages hidden between the green hills. We had to take the village on the right. Beyond it, on the horizon, we could just make out a whitish strip – the highway which had previously been held by our Cossacks. Soon all this vanished from view, and we entered a dense thicket broken here and there by a few small clearings.

I do not remember clearly how the fighting began. We had come into the open on top of the hill where the Turks could clearly see us and watch our companies emerging from the bushes, forming up and extending into a line, when there was a solitary shot. The Turks had fired a shell. The men shuddered, everyone's eyes fixed on the little white puff of smoke already dissolving and gently rolling down the slope. Just then the resounding, screeching sound of the shell that seemed to be coming at us just above our heads made us all duck. The shell flew overhead and hit the ground near the company coming up behind us; I can remember the dull thud as it exploded, followed by a piteous cry: a splinter had torn off the Sergeant-Major's leg. I learnt this later; at the time I could not make sense of that cry – my ear had heard it, and that was all. Everything merged in that blurred emotion that cannot be put into words, which grips you when you are under fire for the first time. They say that there is nobody who is not scared in battle; everyone who is honest and not a braggart, when asked whether he is scared, will answer: Yes, I am scared. But there was none of that physical terror that seizes you when you come face to face with a robber at night in some deserted alley. What you felt was a clear and total recognition of the inevitability and the proximity of death. And – strange and crazy as it may sound – that recognition did not make a man stop, did not make him think of running away, it urged him to go ahead. No bloodthirsty instincts were aroused, he didn't want to press on in order to kill somebody; but there was an irresistible impulse to go on regardless, and thoughts of what had to be done in battle could be rendered not by the words 'You've got to kill', but rather 'You've got to die'.

While we crossed that clearing the Turks fired a number of shots. All that lay now between us and them was the last, large thicket that rose slowly to the village. We entered the bushes. There was silence all around.

Progress was made difficult by the dense, intertwining bushes, many of them prickly; we had to skirt round them or else force our way through them. The riflemen ahead of us had already scattered into a dispersed line and occasionally called to each other softly so as not to lose touch. We stayed together in company formation for the time being. Deep silence reigned in the forest.

Then came the first, subdued rifle-shot, as quiet as the tap of a wood-cutter's axe. The Turks started firing random shots in our direction. Their bullets whistled in varying tones high in the air, then noisily pierced the bushes and tore off branches, without hitting anyone. The sound of wood-felling was becoming more frequent and finally merged into a single undifferentiated crackle. One could no longer hear isolated screeches and whistling sounds: the whole air was now whistling and wailing. We hurried onwards, all those near me unharmed, as was I myself, a fact that surprised me greatly.

Suddenly we emerged from the bushes. A deep gulley with a stream in it cut across our path. The men rested briefly and drank their fill of water.

From here each company went off in a different direction in order to outflank the Turks. Our company was held back in reserve in the gulley. The riflemen were ordered to move straight on through the bushes and storm the village. The Turks kept up their heavy fire unabated; the shooting was now much louder.

Clambering out of the gulley on the far side, Ventzel formed up his company. He said something to his men that I didn't catch.

'We'll do our best, we will!' the riflemen's voices rose in reply.

I looked up at Ventzel from below. He was pale and, I thought, sad-looking, yet reasonably calm. When he caught sight of Zaykin and Stebelkov he waved his handkerchief at them, then his eyes started gazing over our company, looking for something. I guessed he wanted to say good-bye to me, and I stood up so that he could see me. Ventzel smiled, nodded a couple of times in my direction, and then ordered his company into battle formation. Groups of four went off to the right and to the left, spreading out in an extended line, and disappeared into the bushes all at once except for one man, whose body abruptly bounded forward with raised arms and slumped heavily to the ground. Two soldiers leapt out of the gulley and recovered his body.

There was half an hour of agonising suspense.

The fighting now intensified. The rifle-fire became more frequent, fusing into an unbroken, menacing howl. Guns started roaring on the right flank. Men covered in blood started appearing, crawling or walking out of the bushes; at first there were only a few, then their numbers increased by the minute. Our men helped them down into the gulley, gave them water and laid them on stretchers to await the medical orderlies. A rifleman with one of his wrists shattered came up unaided and sat down by the stream, groaning terribly and rolling his eyes, his face turned blue from loss of blood and from the pain. Men strapped his arm and laid him on a stretcher; his blood stopped flowing. He was feverish, his lips were trembling and he was sobbing nervously and convulsively.

'Brothers! Brothers! My dear fellow countrymen! . . .'

'Many got hit?'

'Masses – lying everywhere.'

'Is the company commander all right?'

'So far. If it weren't for him we'd have been beaten back. We'll take the village. With him we shall,' the wounded man said in a feeble voice. 'Three times he led us, we were driven back. He led us a fourth time. They're sitting in a gulley. They've got loads of ammunition – they're firing away, firing away like mad . . . Ah no!' the wounded man suddenly shouted with great malice, sitting up and waving his injured arm. 'No you won't, no you won't, damn you!'

And with his eyes rolling wildly, he yelled out some awful, foul oath and collapsed unconscious.

The adjutant, Lukin, appeared on the brow of the gulley.

'Ivan Platonych!' he shouted in a voice not his own. 'Bring your men on!'

Smoke, crackling, groans, frenzied 'Hurrah!'s. The smell of blood and gunpowder. Smoke-swathed strange alien men with pale faces. A savage, inhuman mêlée. Praise be to God that such moments are only remembered in a haze.

When we came up, Ventzel was leading what was left of his company into action for the fifth time, to be showered with lead by the Turks. This time the riflemen stormed the village. A few of the Turks who were defending it at this point managed to run away. In two hours of fighting the Second Rifle Company had lost fifty-two men out of a total of just over a hundred. Our company which had been in action only briefly had lost several men.

We did not stay in the position we had taken, even though the Turks had been driven back along the entire line. When our general saw that one battalion of theirs after another was coming out of the village and heading for the highway, and masses of cavalry and long convoys of guns, he was horrified. Clearly the Turks had not known the size of our forces, concealed in the bushes. Had they known that they had been driven out of the deep-lying roads, gulleys and wattle-fences surrounding the village by a mere fourteen companies, they would have come back and smashed us. They were three times our number.

In the evening we were back in our old position. Zaykin invited me to take tea with him.

'Have you seen Ventzel?' he asked.

'Not yet.'

'Go to his tent and ask him to come along. The poor fellow's taking it very badly. "Fifty-two! Fifty-two!" – that's all you hear from him. Go and see him.'

A meagre candle-stub lit Ventzel's tent. Huddled in a corner, his head down on a box, he was uttering stifled sobs.

1882   *Translated by Peter Henry*

The Red Flower

To the memory of Ivan Sergeyevich Turgenev

I

'In the name of His Imperial Majesty, the Sovereign Emperor Peter the First, I hereby proclaim an inspection of this lunatic asylum!'

These words were spoken in a loud, sharp, resonant voice. The hospital clerk, who had been registering the new patient in a large, ragged ledger that lay on an ink-drenched desk, could not suppress a smile. But the two young men who were escorting the patient found nothing to laugh at; they could barely stand after two sleepless days and nights closeted with the lunatic whom they had just brought in by train. At the last station but one, his violent attacks had worsened; they had procured a straitjacket from somewhere and, calling the guards and a policeman to help, got the patient into it. And thus they brought him to the town; and thus they delivered him to the hospital.

He was frightful to behold. Over his grey garment that he had ripped to shreds during his attacks, a coarse canvas jacket, slashed deeply at the neck, clipped his frame, and the long sleeves trussed his arms crosswise to his breast and were tied behind. His inflamed, widely dilated eyes (he had not slept in ten days) burned with a torrid, fixed glister; the edge of his lower lip twitched nervously; his tangled, curly hair fell in a mane over his forehead; with rapid, heavy strides he paced from one corner of the office to the other, casting probing looks at the old cupboards full of papers and the oil-cloth chairs, and giving his travelling companions an occasional glance.

'Take him to the Section. On the right.'

'I know, I know. I was here with you last year. We inspected the hospital. I know everything and you'll be hard put to outwit me,' said the patient.

He turned towards the door. A warder opened it for him; with the same rapid, heavy, purposeful step, his demented head held high, he walked out of the office and all but ran off to the right, in the

direction of the mental section. His escorts could scarcely keep up
with him.

'Ring the bell. I can't. You've tied my arms.'

A porter opened the door and the travellers entered the hospital.
It was a large stone edifice, built in the old governmental style.
Two large rooms – a dining-hall and a common room for the quieter
patients – a wide corridor with a french window that looked out onto
a flower-garden, and some twenty separate rooms allocated to the
patients, occupied the ground floor; and here there were also two
dark rooms, one with padded walls and one panelled with wood, to
which violent patients were consigned, and a huge, dismal, vaulted
chamber that was the bathroom. The upper storey was for the
women. A babble of sound, broken by howling and wailing, carried
down from there. The hospital had been built to accommodate
eighty, but, since it served several neighbouring provinces, the roll
could be anything up to three hundred. The small rooms contained
four or five beds each; in winter, when the patients were not allowed
out into the garden and all the windows were locked tight behind
their iron bars, the hospital grew unbearably stuffy.

The new patient was led into the room where the baths were. Such
a place would have oppressed even a sane person, but on a distraught,
agitated imagination its effect was all the more oppressive. It was a
large room with a vaulted ceiling and a sticky stone floor, whose sole
source of light was a corner window; the walls and the vaulted ceiling
were coated with dark-red oil-paint; set flush into the grime-
blackened floor were two stone bath-tubs that resembled oval pits
brim-full with water. A huge copper stove with a cylindrical boiler
for heating the water and a whole system of copper pipes and taps
occupied the corner opposite the window. To the distraught mind, it
all had an uncommonly dismal and bizarre air, and the gloomy
expression on the face of the warder in charge of the baths – a stocky,
eternally taciturn Ukrainian – made it worse still.

And when they led the patient into this fearsome chamber, to
bathe him and, in accordance with the senior doctor's mode of
treatment, to put a large blistering plaster on his nape, he was
terrified and infuriated. Absurd thoughts, each more grotesque than
the last, whirled into his head. What was this? The Inquisition? A
place of secret execution, where his enemies had determined to do
away with him? Perhaps Hell itself? Finally it occurred to him that
this was some kind of trial by ordeal. He was undressed, against his

desperate resistance. His strength redoubled by his malady, he easily wrested himself from the hands of several warders, pitching them onto the floor. At last four of them brought him down, seized hold of his arms and legs, and lowered him into the warm water. To him it was boiling, and in his deranged mind flickered the disjointed, fragmentary thought that this was an ordeal by boiling water and red-hot iron. Choking in the water, convulsively thrashing his arms and legs, which were still in the warders' firm grasp, and gasping for breath, he screeched out a disjointed tirade unimaginable to anyone who had not actually heard it. It was a jumble of prayers and maledictions. He shouted until his strength was gone and finally, with scalding tears in his eyes, he made a quiet announcement that was wholly at odds with the harangue that had gone before.

'Saint George, thou holy martyr, into thy hands I commend my body. But my spirit – no, oh no!'

The warders were still holding him, although he was calm now. The warm bath and the ice-pack placed on his head had done their job. But when they drew him, almost unconscious, from the water and sat him on a stool to apply the blistering plaster, the remnants of his strength and his lunatic thoughts exploded once more.

'Why? Why?' he cried. 'I've never wished evil on anyone. Why kill me? O-o-oh! Oh my God! Oh you who were tortured before me! Deliver me, I pray you. . .'

A searing sensation on his neck made him flail about desperately. The attendants could not cope with him, and did not know what to do.

'This is hopeless,' said the soldier who was performing the operation. 'It'll have to be taken off.'

These simple words made the patient shudder. 'Taken off!. . . What's to be taken off? Who's to be taken off? Me!' he thought, and closed his eyes in mortal terror. The soldier took hold of both ends of a coarse towel and, pressing down hard, quickly drew it across the nape, scraping off the plaster and the top layer of skin and leaving a raw, red wound. The pain of this procedure, which would have been unendurable for even a calm and sane man, seemed to the patient like the end of all things. Beside himself, he wrenched himself bodily from the warders' clutch, and his naked body rolled upon the flagstones. He thought they had cut off his head. He wanted to cry out, and could not. They carried him to his bed in a swoon which passed into a long, deep, death-like sleep.

II

He awoke in the night. All was quiet; the breathing of sleeping patients carried from the large room next door. Somewhere far away, a patient put into a dark room for the night was talking to himself in a peculiar monotone, and from the women's section upstairs came a hoarse contralto singing a wild refrain. The patient listened hard to all these sounds. He felt fearfully weak and ached in every limb; his neck was very painful.

'Where am I? What's wrong with me?' he wondered. And suddenly, with extraordinary vividness, the past month of his life rose up before him, and he understood that he was sick and what his sickness was. A succession of absurd thoughts, words and deeds recurred to him, sending shudders through his whole being.

'But that's all over, thank God, all over!' he whispered, and fell asleep again.

The open window with its iron bars looked out onto a secluded corner between the big buildings and a stone wall. No one went to that corner, and it was densely overgrown with uncultivated shrubs and with lilac which was blooming lushly at that time of year. . . Behind the bushes, directly facing the window, loomed the high dark wall; the high crowns of trees, bathed and suffused with moonlight, peered over it from the main grounds. On the right rose the white hospital building with its iron-barred windows lit from within; on the left, vivid in the moonlight, was the blank, white mortuary wall. Moonlight poured through the window-bars into the room, dipping to the floor and illuminating part of the bed and the patient's pale, exhausted face with its closed eyes; there was not a sign of insanity about him now. This was the deep, heavy sleep of an exhausted man, dreamless, motionless, almost breathless. For a few moments he awoke, in full possession of his faculties, as if he were normal, only to rise from his bed in the morning as mad as ever.

III

'How do you feel?' the doctor asked him the following day.

The patient had just woken and still lay under his blanket.

'Very well indeed!' he replied, leaping up, putting on his slippers and snatching up his dressing-gown. 'Excellent! There's just one thing – this!'

He pointed to his nape.

'I can't turn my head without pain. But it's nothing. Everything is good if you understand it. And I understand.'

'Do you know where you are?'

'Of course, doctor! I'm in a lunatic asylum. And yet, if you understand it, it's decidedly all the same. Decidedly all the same. . .'

The doctor stared into his eyes. His handsome, well-groomed face with its exquisitely trimmed golden beard and tranquil, light-blue eyes behind gold-rimmed spectacles was immobile and inscrutable. He was observing.

'Why are you staring at me? You'll not read what's in my soul,' the patient continued. 'But I can clearly read what's in yours! Why do you do evil? Why have you collected this crowd of unfortunates and why do you keep them here? It's all the same to me; I understand everything and I am calm – but the others? Why all these sufferings? When a man has arrived at the point where his soul harbours a great thought, a universal thought, it's all the same to him where he lives, what he feels. Even whether to live or not to live. . . Is that not so?'

'Perhaps,' replied the doctor, seating himself on a chair in the corner of the room so that he could watch the patient, who was rapidly pacing from corner to corner, scuffing his huge horse-hide slippers and waving the flaps of his cotton dressing-gown, with its broad red stripes and enormous flowers. The assistant and the supervisor who had accompanied the doctor were still standing at attention by the door.

'And I have one!' the patient exclaimed. 'And when I hit upon it, I felt I had been reborn. My feelings have become more acute and my brain functions as never before. Things that before could be attained only by a long process of reasoning and conjecture, I now know intuitively. I have attained in reality what philosophy has only postulated. I experience in my own self the great concept that space and time are mere fictions. I live in every age. I live where space does not exist, everywhere or nowhere, as you will. And therefore it's all the same to me whether you confine me here or give me my liberty, whether I am free or bound. I have noticed that there are several more like me here. But for all the rest of them, this situation is terrible. Why don't you set them free? What's the use –'

'You said,' the doctor interrupted him, 'that you are living outside time and space. However, you are bound to admit that you and I are in this room and that now' – the doctor drew out his watch – 'it is half past ten on the sixth of May 18 –. What do you think about that?'

'Not a thing. It's all the same to me where I am and when I live. If it's all the same to *me*, then doesn't that mean that I am everywhere and always?'

The doctor grinned.

'A rare turn of logic,' he said, getting to his feet. 'You could well be right. Goodbye. Would you like a cigar?'

'Thank you very much, I would.' He stopped, took the cigar and feverishly bit off the end. 'This is an aid to thought,' he said. 'This is the world, a microcosm. At one end alkalis, and at the other acids. . . Such too is the equilibrium of the world, in which opposing principles are neutralised. Goodbye, doctor!'

The doctor continued his rounds. Most of the patients were waiting for him, standing at attention by their beds. No one in authority commands such reverence from his subordinates as that accorded a psychiatric doctor by his charges.

But the patient, left on his own, continued to pace fitfully from corner to corner of the room. Tea was brought; still on his feet, he drained the large mug in two gulps and bolted a big hunk of white bread in a trice. Then he left his room and for several hours ceaselessly paced with his rapid, heavy step right from one end of the building to the other. It was a rainy day, and the patients were not allowed out into the garden. When the doctor's assistant came to look for the new patient, he was sent to the end of the corridor; and there he stood, his face pressed to a pane of the french windows that gave onto the garden, staring at a flowerbed. His attention had been caught by an extraordinarily vivid scarlet flower, a variety of poppy.

'Please come and be weighed,' said the assistant, touching his shoulder.

And when the patient turned to face him, the assistant almost recoiled in fear, so wild was the malice and hatred that burned in those demented eyes. But seeing the assistant, he promptly changed his expression and obediently followed him, saying not a word, as if plunged in deep thought. They went into the examination room, and the patient stood on the small decimal scales without being asked to. The assistant weighed him and entered against his name in the ledger: 109 pounds. The next day it was 107, and the day after that, 106.

'If he continues like this, he'll not survive,' said the doctor, and ordered the best possible diet for him.

But despite this and despite the patient's uncommon appetite, he grew thinner each day, and each day the number of pounds that the assistant entered in the ledger decreased. The patient hardly slept and was constantly in motion for days on end.

IV

He was aware of being in a lunatic asylum; he was even aware that he was sick. Sometimes, as on the first night, he would wake in the hush, after a long day of tumultuous motion, with a wrenching ache in every limb and a frightful heaviness in his head, but in full possession of his faculties. Perhaps it was the absence of sensations in the nocturnal calm and the dim light; perhaps it was the reduced brain activity of a man barely awake – but at such moments he clearly understood his situation and seemed to be sane. Then daybreak would come, and with the light and the arousal of life in the hospital he would once again be engulfed in a surge of sensations; his sick brain was overwhelmed and he was mad once more. His condition was a peculiar blend of accurate judgements and absurdities. He understood that all around him were sick, but at the same time he saw in each of them someone concealed or trying to conceal himself, someone he knew from before or whom he had read or heard about. The hospital was inhabited by people of all times and all lands. Here were the living and the dead. Here were the famed and the mighty of this world and also soldiers killed in the last war and risen from the grave. He saw himself in some occult, enchanted circle, which had gathered within itself all the power of the earth, and in an ecstasy of pride he placed himself at the centre of that circle. All of them, all his fellows in the hospital, had gathered there to perform a task which his clouded comprehension saw as a titanic venture aimed at the annihilation of evil on earth. He did not know what that task would entail, but he felt within himself sufficient strength to perform it. He could read the minds of others; in any object he saw all its history; the great elms in the hospital garden recounted to him entire legends from the past; he believed that the building, which was in fact quite old, had been built by Peter the Great, and he was sure that the Tsar had lived there at the time of the Battle of Poltava. This he read in the walls, in the crumbling stucco, in the fragments of brick and tile that he found in the garden; all the history of that house and its garden was inscribed on them. He populated the small mortuary building with dozens, with hundreds of the long-deceased, and would gaze fixedly into its little cellar window that looked onto the corner of the grounds, seeing in the light glancingly reflected in the grimy, rainbow-hued old pane familiar features that he had glimpsed once in life or in portraits.

Meanwhile, the weather had turned bright and fair, and the patients spent days on end taking the air in the garden. Their section of the garden was not large but it was thick with trees, and flowers had been planted in every conceivable spot. The supervisor had every more or less able-bodied inmate working there; day after day they swept and sanded the pathways, weeded and watered the beds of flowers, cucumbers, water melons and musk melons that they had dug and planted with their own hands. In a corner of the garden was a dense stand of cherry-trees, flanked by an avenue of elms. In the middle, on a low, man-made mound, was set the most lovely flowerbed in the entire garden; gorgeous flowers grew around its upper level, and at the centre, in all its glory, stood a great big rare dahlia whose yellow petals were dappled with red. In that elevated position it was the focal point of the whole garden, and evidently many of the patients accorded it some cryptic significance. The new patient also viewed it as something out of the ordinary, as a kind of Palladium of the garden and the hospital building. All the paths had also been lined with flowers by the patients. Here were all the flowers that might ever be encountered in a Ukrainian garden: tall roses, vivid petunias, tall tobacco plants with pink blossom, mint, marigolds, nasturtiums and poppies. And here too, by the porch, grew three clumps of an unusual kind of poppy which was much smaller than the familiar variety and differed, too, in being an exceptionally vivid shade of scarlet. This was the flower that had so struck the patient when he had looked through the french windows into the garden on the day after his admission to the hospital.

Going out into the garden for the first time, even before descending the porch steps, he looked at those vivid flowers. There were only two of them; as it happened, they grew apart from all the other flowers, on an unweeded patch, where they were surrounded by a dense growth of goosefoot and some kind of steppe-grass.

As the patients filed past the warder in the doorway, he handed them each a thick white knitted-cotton cap with a red cross on the brow. These caps had been to war and had been bought at an auction. But the patient, needless to say, endowed the red cross with a particular cryptic significance. He removed his cap and looked at the cross, then at the poppies. The flowers were the brighter.

'It's winning,' the patient said, 'but we shall see.'

And he stepped down from the porch. Glancing round but failing to notice the warder standing behind him, he strode across the flowerbed and stretched his hand towards one of the flowers, but could not bring himself to pluck it. He felt heat and a stabbing pain in his outstretched hand and then throughout his body, as if a powerful current of some force unknown to him were emanating from the red petals and striking through his entire body. He moved nearer and stretched his hand right up to the flower, but it seemed to him that the flower, in self-defence, was exhaling a lethally venomous miasma. His head began to spin; he made a last desperate effort, and had actually seized its stem when suddenly a heavy hand fell on his shoulder. The warder had seized hold of him.

'No picking,' said the old Ukrainian. 'And don't walk on the flowerbeds. There's a lot of you lunatics here – one flower each and you'll strip the whole garden,' he urged, still gripping the patient's shoulder.

The patient looked him straight in the face, silently shook off his hand, and walked down the path in agitation. 'Oh, you poor unfortunates!' he thought. 'You cannot see, you're so blind now that you even defend him. But whatever the cost – I shall do away with him. If not today, then tomorrow we shall match our strength. And if I perish, it's really all the same. . .'

He walked in the garden until evening, making new acquaintances and holding strange conversations in which each of his interlocutors heard nothing but replies to his own lunatic thoughts, couched in absurd and cryptic words. The patient walked with one fellow-inmate after another, and by the end of the day was even more convinced that 'all was ready', as he put it to himself. Soon, soon the iron bars would fall asunder, all those now incarcerated would rush to the ends of the earth, and all the world would shudder, cast off its threadbare covering, and show itself in a marvellous new beauty. He had almost forgotten about the flowers, but mounting the porch as he left the garden, in the densely darkening grass that was already touched with early dew, he saw once again the likeness of two red embers. Then the patient lagged behind the crowd and, placing himself behind the warder, bided his time. No one saw him spring across the flowerbed, seize a flower and hastily hide it down the front of his shirt against his breast. When the fresh, dewy leaves touched his body, he turned pale as death and opened his eyes wide in horror. A cold sweat broke out on his forehead.

The lamps were lit in the hospital. Most of the patients lay on their beds, waiting for supper – all but a few restless ones who hurriedly paced the corridors and the main rooms. The patient with the flower was among them. He paced about with his arms convulsively pressed crosswise to his breast; he seemed to be trying to crush, to obliterate the flower that was hidden there. He veered widely around the other patients he encountered, afraid to let even the hem of his garment touch them. 'Don't come near, don't come near!' he cried. But few in the hospital paid any attention to exclamations of that sort. And he walked faster and faster, with longer and longer strides; he walked for an hour, for two hours, in a paroxysm of rage.

'I'll wear you out, I'll throttle you!' he repeated in a hollow, savage voice.

Now and then he would grind his teeth.

Supper was served in the dining-room. On large tables without cloths were set a few wooden bowls, painted and gilded, that contained a watery millet gruel. The patients sat on benches; each was given a hunk of dark rye bread. They ate with wooden spoons, eight to each bowl. The few who were on an improved diet were served separately. Our patient gobbled down the portion brought to him by the warder, who had called him to his room, but was not satisfied with that and went into the dining-room.

'Let me sit here,' he said to the supervisor.

'Haven't you had yours?' asked the supervisor as he poured second helpings of gruel into the bowls.

'I'm very hungry. And I need to build up my strength. Food is my only support. You know that I don't sleep at all.'

'Then eat, my dear man, and welcome. Taras, give him a spoon and some bread.'

He found a place near one of the bowls and ate an enormous extra helping.

'That's enough, now, that's enough,' the supervisor said at last, when all the others had finished their supper but our patient was still sitting over a bowl, scooping up gruel with one hand and clasping the other tightly to his breast. 'You'll turn your stomach.'

'Ah, if only you knew how much strength I need, how much strength! Farewell, Nikolay Nikolaich,' said the patient, getting up from the table and giving the supervisor's hand a hard squeeze. 'Farewell.'

'Where are you off to?' the supervisor asked with a smile.

'Me? Nowhere. I'm staying here. But perhaps we'll not see each other tomorrow. I thank you for your kindness.'

Once more he gripped the supervisor's hand hard. His voice trembled and tears welled in his eyes.

'Calm yourself, my dear man, calm yourself,' the supervisor replied. 'Why such gloomy thoughts? Go to bed and get a good night's sleep. You should sleep more. If you sleep well, you'll soon be on the mend.'

The patient was sobbing. The supervisor turned to tell the warders to hurry and clear away the remnants of supper. Within half an hour all the hospital slept, save one man, who lay fully clothed on his bed in the corner room. He was shivering as if in a fever, and convulsively clutching his breast, which he believed to be impregnated with an unearthly, death-dealing poison.

V

He did not sleep all night. He had picked the flower because he perceived that deed as the act of heroism which he was bound to perform. At the first glance through the french windows, the scarlet petals had attracted his attention and from that moment he believed he had comprehended perfectly what he was to accomplish on earth. In that vivid red flower all the evil of the world had accumulated. He knew that opium is derived from poppies; perhaps it was that thought, ramifying and taking on grotesque forms, which had prompted the creation of this frightful, bizarre spectre. In his eyes, the flower embodied all evil. It had soaked up all the innocent blood ever spilled (which was why it was so red), all the tears, all the bile of mankind. This frightful, mysterious entity was the antithesis of God; it was Ahriman, in humble and innocent guise. It had to be picked and killed. But more than that – it must not be allowed to pour out all its evil upon the world as it expired. That was why he had it hidden on his breast. He hoped that by morning the flower would have lost all its power. Its evil would have passed into his breast, his soul, and there would be conquered or conquer – then he would perish, but perish an honourable warrior, the foremost warrior of mankind, because no one hitherto had dared to grapple with all the evil of the world at once.

'They didn't see it. I saw it. How can I let it live? Death is better.'

And he lay, his strength ebbing in an illusory, spectral combat, but ebbing nonetheless. In the morning the assistant found him close to death. Yet in spite of this, restiveness overcame him after a while, and he jumped up from his bed and began to rush about the hospital again, talking to the other patients and to himself more loudly and incoherently than ever. They would not allow him out into the garden; the doctor, seeing that he was continuing to lose weight, was still not sleeping and kept roaming about, prescribed a sizable injection of morphine. He did not resist; fortunately, his deranged thoughts now somehow concurred with this procedure. He was soon asleep; his frenzied movements ceased and the loud refrain that constantly accompanied him – the fitful rhythm of his footsteps – no longer assailed his ears. He was unconscious, and thought no more about anything, not even about the second flower which had yet to be picked.

He did pick it, however, three days later, right under the nose of the old man, who was not quick enough to stop him. The warder chased after him. With a loud, triumphant howl, the patient ran into the hospital, rushed to his room and hid the plant on his breast.

'What are you picking the flowers for?' asked the warder, who had run after him. But the patient, who was by now lying on the bed in his usual pose with his arms crossed, started raving so nonsensically that the warder just silently removed the cap with its red cross, which he had forgotten about in his hurried flight, and left him. And the spectral combat was joined once more. The patient felt long, serpentine streams of evil writhing from the flower; they coiled around him, squeezing and crushing his limbs, and saturating his entire body with their hideous substance. He wept and prayed to God between curses at his enemy. By evening, the flower had withered. The patient trampled on the blackened plant, picked up the remains from the floor and took them into the bathroom. He threw the misshapen little knot of vegetation onto the blazing coals in the stove, and watched for a long time as his enemy hissed, shrivelled, and finally turned into a delicate, snowy-white pellet of ash. He blew and it all vanished.

Next day the patient took a turn for the worse. Frightfully pale, with sunken cheeks and burning eyes receding deep into their sockets, he continued his frenzied pacing in a faltering gait, stumbling frequently, and talked and talked endlessly.

'I would prefer not to resort to force,' the senior doctor said to his assistant.

'But all this exertion simply must be stopped. His weight is 93 pounds today. If this continues, he'll be dead in two days.'

The senior doctor pondered this.

'Morphine? Chloral?' he said in a half-questioning tone.

'The morphine had no effect yesterday.'

'Have him restrained. Though I doubt if he'll come through this.'

VI

And the patient was restrained. He lay on his bed in a straitjacket, lashed firmly with broad canvas straps to the iron cross-pieces of the bed. But this, far from limiting his frenzied movements, actually spurred them. For many hours he stubbornly strained to free himself from his tethers. At last, with one powerful heave, he tore one of the straps, freed his legs and, slipping out of the other bonds, began to ramble round the room with his arms still tied, screeching out a wild, incomprehensible tirade.

'Oh, away wi' 'ee!' a warder cried, coming into the room. 'T'divvil looks after his own! Gritsko, Ivan! Shape up, a's got loose.'

The three of them pounced on the patient and a long struggle ensued which was exhausting for the attackers and agonising for the one defending himself as he expended what remained of his depleted strength. They finally tumbled him onto the bed and strapped him down more firmly than before.

'You don't realise what you're doing!' the patient shouted, panting. 'You are doomed men! I saw a third one, just coming into bloom. It's ready now. Let me finish my task. It must be killed, killed, killed! Then it will all be over, all will be saved. I would send you, but I alone can do this. You would die from the merest touch!'

'Be quiet, master, be quiet!' said the old warder, who had stayed to watch at the bedside.

The patient suddenly fell silent. He had decided to trick the warders. They kept him under restraint all day and left him thus for the night. Having fed him his supper, the warder spread something on the floor by the bed and lay down. A moment later he was sound asleep, and the patient went to work.

He curved his whole body until he could touch the iron side-bar of his bed and, having groped for it with a hand wholly enveloped in the long straitjacket sleeve, he began to rub the sleeve rapidly and forcefully against the metal. After some time the thick canvas yielded, and he freed a forefinger. Then things proceeded more rapidly. With an agility and litheness that would have been quite beyond belief in a sane man, he untied the knot at his back that held the sleeves tight, and unlaced the jacket; then he listened long and hard to the warder's snoring. But the old man was sleeping soundly. The patient took the straitjacket off and unloosed himself from the bed. He was free. He tried the door; it was locked from the inside and the key was, most likely, in the warder's pocket. Not daring to search the man's pockets for fear of waking him, he decided to leave the room by the window.

It was a quiet, warm, moonless night; the window stood open; the stars glimmered in the black sky. He looked at them, recognising familiar constellations and rejoicing that they seemingly understood him and sympathised with him. Blinking, he beheld the unending beams of light they dispatched to him, and his lunatic resolve grew. He had to bend a thick bar in the iron grid, squeeze through the narrow opening, drop into the corner that was overgrown with bushes, and climb over the high stone wall. There the last battle would take place, and after that – if death, so be it.

He tried to bend the thick bar with his bare hands, but the iron would not yield. Then he twisted the sturdy sleeves of his straitjacket into a rope which he hooked over the forged spike at the top of the bar and hung on it with his whole weight. After desperate efforts which all but sapped his remaining strength, the spike bent; a narrow gap opened up. He pushed through it, skinning his shoulders, elbows and bare knees, forced his way through the bushes and stopped in front of the wall. All was quiet; night-lights feebly lit up the windows of the huge building from within; there was no-one to be seen there. Nobody would notice him; the old man on duty by his bed was doubtless sound asleep. The stars blinked affectionately, the beams piercing to his very heart.

'I'm coming to you,' he whispered, looking up at the sky.

At his first attempt he fell with torn finger-nails and bloodied hands and knees; then he searched for a better place. Where the garden and mortuary walls met, some bricks were missing from both. The patient felt out the gaps and made use of them. He scaled the wall, clutched hold of the branches of an elm on the other side and quietly climbed down the tree to the ground.

He ran to the spot by the porch that he knew so well. The head of the flower was dusky, its petals infolded; it stood out distinctly against the dewy grass.

'The last one!' the patient whispered. 'The last one! Today – victory or death. But it's all the same to me now. Wait a little,' he said, looking up at the sky. 'I shall be with you soon.'

He pulled up the plant, tore it to pieces, crushed it and, holding it in his hand, returned to his room the way he had come. The old man still slept. The patient barely reached his bed and collapsed on it insensible.

In the morning he was found dead. His face was clear and serene; his emaciated features, with the thin lips and deep-sunken, closed eyes, bore an expression of prideful joy. As they laid him on the stretcher, they tried to unclench his hand and remove the red flower. But the hand had stiffened, and he bore his trophy to the grave.

1883   *Translated by Liv Tudge*

The Tale of the Toad and the Rose

Once upon a time there was a toad and a rose.

The rose bloomed on a bush that grew in a small semi-circular garden in front of a country house. The flower garden was very neglected; the old beds were overgrown with a rank mass of weeds and had sunk to the level of the paths, which no-one had swept or sanded for a long time. The wooden trellis fence with palings shaped like four-sided lances had once been painted green: now the paint had peeled off and the fence had cracked and collapsed. The palings had all been taken by village boys to play soldiers with, and peasants who used them when they came up to the house to ward off the savage guard dog and the other dogs that accompanied it.

But the flower garden was none the worse for this destruction. What was left of the trellis was a tangle of hops, of bindweed with its large white flowers, and vetch which hung in large pale-green clumps with pale-lilac bunches of flowers here and there. On the bed's rich moist soil (there was a big shady garden around it) the welted thistles reached such a size that they seemed almost like trees. The yellow Aaron's rods raised their arrow-heads of flowers even higher than the thistles. Nettles had taken over a whole corner of the flower garden; even though they were stinging nettles their dark green colour could still be admired from afar, especially when it formed the background for a gorgeous delicate pale rose.

The rose had opened on a fine May morning: as it unfolded its petals the morning dew left a few pure, transparent teardrops on them. It looked as though the rose had been crying. But everything was so beautiful, so pure and clear around it on that fine morning when it first saw the blue sky and first felt the fresh morning breeze and the shining rays of the sun, with their rosy light penetrating its fine petals, and it was so peaceful and still in the flower-bed then that, had the rose been able to weep, it would have been for the joy of living, not from grief. It could not speak; it could only bow its head and diffuse a fine fresh scent, and this scent was its speech, its tears and its prayer.

But beneath, on the damp earth among the rose-bush's roots, there

sat a fat old toad with its flat belly apparently stuck to the ground; it
had been hunting grubs and midges all night and had settled down at
daybreak to rest from its labours, choosing as shady and damp a place
as it could. There it sat, its hooded toad's eyes closed, barely seeming
to breathe as it puffed out its dirty-grey, warty, clammy sides,
leaving just one ugly foot sticking out: it could not be bothered to
tuck it under its belly. It was not pleased by the morning, the sun or
the good weather; it had eaten its fill and now meant to rest. But
when the breeze died down for a minute and the rose's scent was no
longer wafted away, the toad smelled it and was vaguely disturbed by
it; however, some time passed before it bothered to look for the
source of the fragrance.

For a long time nobody had come into the flower garden where the
rose grew and the toad squatted. The previous autumn, the day the
toad had found a nice crack under one of the stones in the foundations of the house and was about to clamber in to hibernate there, a
little boy had come into the flower garden for the last time; throughout the summer he had spent every fine day there underneath the
window. A girl, his grown-up sister, sat by the window; she read a
book or sewed and occasionally glanced at her brother. He was a
little boy aged about seven with large eyes and a large head on a thin
little body. He was very fond of his flower garden (it was his, for
apart from him almost nobody came to this deserted spot) and he
would come and sit in the sun on an old wooden seat on a dry sandy
path which had survived beside the house because it was used when
the shutters were closed, and he would start reading a book he had
brought with him.

'Vasya, would you like me to throw you the ball?' his sister would
ask from the window. 'You could run about with it.'

'No Masha, I'm happy with my book.'

And he would sit there reading for a long time. When he was bored
with reading about the Swiss Family Robinson, savage lands or
pirates he would put down the open book and make his way into the
thick of the flower garden. Here he knew every shrub and almost
every stalk. He would squat in front of a thick Aaron's rod three
times his height with its shaggy whitish leaves sprouting all over it,
and spend a long time watching the ants running up to milk their
cows, the grass aphids, observing an ant carefully touch the delicate
tubes sticking out of the aphid's back and pick up the tiny droplets of
sweet fluid that formed on the ends of the tubes. He would gaze at a

dung beetle labouring somewhere with its ball, at a spider weaving a cunning colourful net and trapping flies, at a lizard opening its flat mouth and sunning itself, the green scales shining on its back; once as evening fell he had seen a hedgehog. He was so overcome by joy that he all but shouted and clapped his hands; however, fear of scaring the prickly animal made him hold his breath, and with wide-open, joyful eyes he was delighted to see the hedgehog snort and sniff at the roots of the rose bush with its piggy snout as it searched for worms, working away comically with its fat little bear-like paws.

'Vasya, come in now, darling, it's getting damp,' his sister called out loudly.

Frightened by the human voice, the hedgehog quickly pulled its thick coat of prickles over its head and hind paws and rolled itself into a ball. The boy gently touched its prickles; the animal curled up even tighter and gave out a short muffled hiss like a little steam engine.

Later the boy had made friends with the hedgehog. He was such a frail, quiet and meek boy that even the smallest wild creatures seemed to realise this and soon got used to him. What joy he felt when the hedgehog tasted some milk from a saucer that the master of the flower garden had put out!

This spring the boy could not go out to his favourite spot. His sister watched over him as before, this time not from the window, but at his bedside. She was reading a book, but not to herself; she was reading it aloud to him, since he found it too hard to lift his emaciated head off the white pillows and hold even a very small book in his wasted hands; moreover, reading soon tired his eyes. It was clear that he would never go out to his favourite spot again.

'Masha,' he suddenly whispered to his sister.

'What is it, dear?'

'Is it nice in the garden now? Are the roses out?'

His sister bent over, kissed his pale cheek and furtively wiped away a tear.

'It is nice, darling, very nice. And the roses are out. We'll go out there together on Monday. The doctor will let you go out.'

The boy did not answer and sighed deeply. His sister began reading to him again.

'That's enough. I'm tired. I'd better sleep now.'

His sister straightened his pillows and the little white blanket; laboriously he turned his face to the wall and fell silent. The sun was shining through the window that looked out onto the flower garden, and threw its bright beams onto the bed and the little figure that lay there, lighting up the pillows and the blanket, gilding the child's cropped hair and thin little neck.

The rose knew nothing of this; it was growing and displaying its beauty: the next day it would open out fully and the day after that it would begin to fade and shed its petals. Such is a rose's life. But even this brief life had much fear and grief in store for it.

The toad had seen the rose.

When the toad's ugly evil eyes first spotted the flower, something strange stirred in its toadish heart. It could not take its eyes off the tender rose petals and kept staring and staring. It liked the rose very much and felt a desire to be as near as it could to such a fragrant and beautiful thing. The best it could think of to express its tenderness was a hoarse croak:

'You wait, I'll gobble you up!'

The rose shuddered. Why was it attached to a stalk? The free birds twittered around it, hopping and flying from branch to branch; sometimes they would leave for somewhere far away, the rose knew not where. The butterflies were free, too. How it envied them! Had it been like them, it would have fluttered away, flown away from the evil eyes that oppressed it with their stare. The rose did not know that toads sometimes lurk in waiting for butterflies too.

'I'll gobble you up!' the toad said again, trying to speak as sweetly as it could, though only sounding more horrible still, as it crawled nearer the rose.

'I'll gobble you up,' it repeated, its eyes fixed on the rose. And the poor flower saw to its horror the foul clammy paws clutching the branches of the bush on which it was growing. But the toad found the climb hard going; its flat body could crawl and leap freely only on even ground. After each effort it looked at the rose swaying gently above it, and the rose froze with fear.

'Lord,' it prayed, 'grant me a different death.'

The toad clambered higher and higher. But when it got to where the old stems ended and new twigs began it had to put up with a good deal of pain. The smooth dark-green bark of the rose bush was studded with strong sharp thorns. They lacerated the toad's feet and belly and it tumbled to the ground, covered in blood. It glared at the flower with hatred.

'I said I'd gobble you up!' it repeated.

Evening came: supper had to be thought about and the wounded toad staggered off to pounce on unwary insects. Its anger did not prevent it from filling its belly as always; the scratches were not serious and it decided that after a rest it would try again to get to the flower which it found so attractive and so hateful.

It had quite a long rest. Morning came, noon went by, and the rose had almost forgotten about its enemy. It had opened out completely and was the most beautiful sight in the flower garden. There was nobody to come and admire it – the young master lay motionless in his little bed and his sister stayed by his side and did not appear at the window. Only the birds and butterflies fluttered around the rose and the bees perched buzzing inside its open corolla and flew out again, shaggy with yellow pollen. A nightingale came flying to the rose bush, perched inside it and began its song. How unlike the toad's croaking this song was! The rose listened and was happy; it felt, and perhaps rightly, that the nightingale was singing for it alone. The rose did not see its enemy stealthily making its way up the branches. This time the toad did not spare its feet or its belly: it was covered in blood and yet it kept bravely climbing upwards. Suddenly, through the nightingale's sweet and ringing song, the rose heard the familiar wheezing sound:

'I said I'd gobble you up and I will!'

The toad's eyes stared at it from a neighbouring branch. The evil creature needed to make only a single movement to grab the flower. The rose realised it was doomed . . .

The young master had been lying motionless in bed for some time now. Sitting in an armchair at the bed-head, his sister thought he was asleep. An open book lay on her lap but she was not reading. Little by little her head drooped with tiredness: the poor girl had gone several nights without sleep, constantly beside her sick brother, and now she dozed off.

'Masha,' he suddenly whispered.

His sister awoke with a start. She had been dreaming that she was sitting by the window and her little brother was playing in the flower garden as he had the year before, and was calling her. She opened her eyes, and seeing him in his bed, weak and drawn, she gave a deep sigh.

'What it it, dear?'

'Masha, you told me the roses are out. May I . . . have one?'

'Of course you may, darling.'

She went to the window and looked at the bush. There was only one rose on it, but it was a magnificent one.

'A rose has come out just for you, and wat a lovely one it is! Shall I put it in a glass for you on the table? Would you like that?'

'Yes, please. . . I would.'

The girl took a pair of scissors and went out into the garden. She had not been out of the room for a long time. The sun dazzled her and the fresh air made her a little giddy. She went up to the bush at the very moment that the toad was going to grab the flower.

'Ugh, how nasty!' she cried out. She took hold of the branch and shook it vigorously. The toad tumbled and its belly hit the ground with a plop. In its rage it tried to leap at the girl but could jump no higher than the hem of her dress and was immediately sent flying by the toe of her shoe. It did not dare to try again, and had to look on from a distance as the girl carefully cut the flower and took it into the room.

When the boy saw his sister with the flower in her hand, he smiled his first smile for a long time, and with an effort he made a movement with his thin little hand.

'Give it to me,' he whispered. 'Let me smell it.'

His sister put the rose into his hand and helped him move it to his face. He inhaled the sweet smell and whispered with a happy smile:

'Oh, how lovely . . .'

Then his little face became grave and motionless, and he fell silent – for ever.

Even though it had been cut before its petals had begun to fall, the rose felt it had not been cut in vain. It was placed in a glass vase by itself beside the little coffin. There were whole bouquets of other flowers, but truth to tell, nobody paid the least attention to them. When the young girl placed the rose on the table, she raised it to her lips and kissed it. A teardrop fell from her cheek onto the flower, and that was the best thing that happened in the rose's life. When it began to fade it was laid inside a thick old book and dried, and then, many years later, it was given to me. That's how I came to know this story.

1884   *Translated by Donald Rayfield*

Haggai the Proud

An ancient legend retold

In a certain land there lived a king; his name was Haggai. He was mighty and renowned: the Lord had given him full power over the land; his enemies feared him, friends he had none, but the people lived quietly and obediently throughout his domain, knowing the strength of their ruler. Now this king became smitten with pride, and he believed that there was no one in the world mightier and wiser than he. He lived in great splendour; he had much wealth, and many servants, too, but he never spoke to them, for he thought them unworthy. With his queen he lived in full accord, but her, too, he treated strictly: she did not dare address her husband, but would wait until he had asked her a question or had spoken to her first.

Such was Haggai's life – a lonely life, like a hermit atop a high tower. Below him were the common people gazing up at him; Haggai wished acquaintance with none as he stood on his lowly podium; he believed this was the only place worthy of him – a lonely place, but a lofty one.

One day – it was a feast day – Haggai went to church with his queen. Both of them wore splendid garments – cloaks woven in gold, belts adorned with precious jewels – and they walked under a canopy fashioned from brocade. Ahead of them and behind them marched warriors carrying swords and hatchets. They escorted Haggai with his queen into the church and led them to their place, where they stood to hear the service. Around them stood the army-chiefs and ministers. And Haggai listened to the service, and thought his own thoughts, wondering whether what was written in the Holy Scriptures was true or false.

The arch-priest started reading from the Holy Book. He reached the place where it is written: 'And the rich shall become poor, and the poor shall become rich.' Hearing these words, Haggai was much angered.

'What made you, priest, take it into your head to read out such a falsehood?' he said. 'Or don't you know how renowned and wealthy I am? How shall I become poor and some pauper become as rich as I am?'

But the arch-priest did not heed Haggai's words; he went on reading from the Holy Book, continued the service to the end, and made no reply to his question.

The king waxed furious indeed: he ordered the arch-priest to be put in irons and cast into a dungeon, and that the page on which these words were written be torn out of the Book.

The arch-priest was taken off to the dungeon, and the page was torn from the Book. And Haggai went to his palace; he held a feast, ate and drank and made merry.

A youth chanced to be walking across the open land. He spied a stag mightier and more beautiful than he had ever seen before. And wishing to please the king, the youth ran off to the city and into the palace, and told the servants about the stag. They reported this to their master, and he gave orders for a hunt to be prepared.

The hunting party rode off into the open land; they spied the stag and swiftly rode towards it. The stag stood there, raised its head and looked round at the hunters, as though waiting for something to happen. Never before had Haggai seen so noble a beast: so mighty and sleek it was, with a fine and intelligent face; its antlers spread like the branches of a tree, a whole sazhen they spanned. Its hide was a reddish brown and glistened as though it had been burnished; its haunches were white as snow. Haggai rode towards the stag and wondered why it did not run away, why it stood there looking at him with its large eyes, as though it wanted to tell him something. Now he was quite close to the stag and had already resolved to hurl his spear at the animal. The stag turned its head, shook its spreading antlers, took a huge leap forward, a full three sazhens, and ran off across the plain. Haggai's mount was a fine and priceless steed, yet it could not catch up with the stag: the gap between them became greater and greater. Haggai looked round to see where his huntsmen were, but he could scarcely see them. Then he looked ahead of him again and saw that the stag was now running less fast. 'Now I'll surely catch up with it,' he thought. And he rode on, urging his steed to go as fast as ever it could; he kept catching glimpses of the stag with its white haunches ahead of him as he came closer and closer to the beast. Just as he was about to hurl his spear, the stag turned its head round to look at him, then it set off again at a greater speed, and once again Haggai was left far behind. The other hunters had long been out of sight, and the stag and Haggai on his steed were on their own, galloping across the plain.

Half a day long Haggai pursued his prey; at last he saw the stag making for a river. 'If it heads to the right,' he thought, 'it will get away; if it heads to the left, it shall be mine!' There was a bend in the river on the left, and there the stag could not possibly escape: a huntsman behind it, and a river ahead of it so wide that neither man nor beast could swim across it. The stag turned to the left; Haggai's heart trembled with great joy. As he rode on, he thought: 'Soon you will reach the river, and you shall not be able to escape.' The stag reached the river bank. There was a little island in the river not far from the bank, with dense bushes and young trees growing on it. The stag took a mighty leap into the water, vanished below the surface, then reappeared and swam on towards the island. Haggai reached the river's edge and saw the stag disappearing among the bushes. Then he urged his horse into the water.

The horse stepped into the water and took three paces, until the water came up to its neck; after that it could no longer touch bottom. Haggai turned his mount and rode back to the bank. 'That stag shall not escape me,' he thought. 'But my horse would drown in such swift-flowing water.' He dismounted, tied his horse to a bush, took off his fine clothes and entered the water. He swam on and on, and the current all but carried him away. At last he could touch bottom. 'I shall surely catch the stag now,' he thought and went off into the bushes.

But the Lord was angry with Haggai. He summoned an Angel and bade him assume the guise of Haggai, put on his clothes, mount his horse and ride off into the city. And the Angel carried out the will of the Lord.

For a long time Haggai looked for the stag among all the bushes, but nowhere could he see it. He walked around the entire island, crawled through all the bushes – it was gone. Haggai could not think where the stag might be: ahead of it was the river, so wide that no beast could have swum across it; and he would surely have seen it had it thought to try to cross it. Haggai became sorely vexed, but there was nothing for it, he had to turn back. He went back to the water's edge and threw down his spear, lest it hamper him as he swam back to the river bank. When he reached it, he looked up and saw that both his horse and his clothes had gone. The king grew exceedingly angry, for he thought that they had been stolen, and he resolved to punish the thief most harshly. He climbed out of the water and mounted the steep bank – there was no one to be seen on the bare, wide plain. All he could do was walk on, naked as he was. As he walked, the grass cut his feet; he was not accustomed to walking unshod. The sun scorched his bare head and his naked body. On and on he walked. Then he reached a little hillock; from there he saw a cowherd in a hollow, minding his cows and calves. Haggai stopped and waved his hand at the cowherd.

'Hey, you,' he said, 'come here!'

The cowherd looked at him in wonderment: 'Wherever can this naked man have come from out here on the open plain?' He went up to him slowly, holding a long whip in one hand and a horn made from birch bark in the other. He had bast shoes on and wore a tattered home-spun coat, and a sack for his bread was slung across his shoulder.

Haggai shouted at him: 'Why don't you come when I call you?'

'Who are you, anyhow?' the cowherd asked him. 'What do you want?'

'Did you see who took my clothes and rode away on my horse?'

'Who are you?' the cowherd asked again.

'Do you mean you don't know me? I am Haggai, your king.'

The cowherd looked at him and laughed out loud. 'What nonsense you talk! Our master has just ridden by, returning to the city from the hunt. The huntsmen had been looking for him hereabouts for a long time and then they found him; they rode off together.'

'How dare you, you slave and scoundrel!' shouted Haggai.

'Be off with you, do you hear?' said the cowherd. 'Or you'll get a taste of my whip.'

The king was beside himself with rage. Forgetting that he was naked and unarmed, he flung himself at the cowherd. He grasped him by the shoulder and meant to strike him, but the cowherd was the stronger of the two: he flung Haggai to the ground and began to belabour him with his wooden horn. He went on beating him and stopped only when all the birch bark had come apart, and then his anger was spent.

'There,' said the cowherd, 'that's for talking to me like that. Be gone with you!'

Haggai got up from the ground, sore all over from the beating, and slowly dragged himself away. But the cowherd thought a while, then he felt sorry for the man. 'I did wrong,' he thought, 'to hurt that man so badly: perhaps his mind is unhinged, a madman, maybe.'

Haggai had gone some distance away; then he heard the cowherd calling him: 'Hey, you, come back!'

Haggai turned round and saw the cowherd holding up something in one hand; with the other he was beckoning to him. 'Come back!' the cowherd shouted. 'Where will you go, naked as you are? Have this sack, at least.'

Haggai stopped walking and stood motionless. He felt wretched and ashamed at heart. The cowherd took his knife from his belt, cut three holes in the sack – one for the head, two for the arms – and went up to Haggai.

'There's nothing in my sack: I've eaten all the bread. But no man should walk about naked; put this on instead of a shirt.'

And he helped Haggai put the sack on. Haggai went off towards the city without saying a word. And as he walked, he pondered on his misfortune and why it should have befallen him. Some knave and impostor who looked like him must have taken his clothes and his horse. And the longer he walked, the angrier he became. 'I'll show him that I am Haggai, a true and dreaded ruler. I shall have him taken out to the public square and beheaded. And I shall deal with that cowherd, too' – but then Haggai suddenly remembered about the sack the cowherd had given him, and he felt ashamed.

He walked till evening came, but he was still a long way from the city. He would have to spend the night on the open plain; so he crawled into a hayrick and slept there all night. He arose at sunrise and continued on his journey, and not far from the city he reached the highway. A multitude of people were going along it, some walking, some riding in carts – they were all going to the market. A string of carts overtook him, and the drivers asked him who he was and why he was wearing a sack.

Haggai remembered the blows the cowherd had given him and he was afraid to speak the truth.

He said: 'I am not from these parts. I was riding through your city on my affairs, and some footpads attacked me on the road; they beat and robbed me, they took my clothes and my horse, and my money, too. Then they dressed me in this sack and let me go.'

The good people took pity on him: one of them gave him a shirt, another a pair of trousers; yet another gave him some worn old shoes, another gave him a kaftan, and yet another a hat. Haggai thanked them all and he asked for their names and where he could find them. Then he walked on into the city, much happier at heart.

'Soon my torments will be at an end,' he thought. 'I shall punish the villain and reward those who have helped me.'

He went straight on to the city square, where stood his palace. He meant to enter it through his own gate, but the guards did not recognise him and would not let him pass. Fearing that he might be beaten again he went away, wondering what he should do. He could not enter his own home: until that impostor was unmasked, he would surely be beaten, put in jail, perhaps be put to death. 'I shall have to be patient awhile,' he thought. He went to the market-place where labourers were hired and he stood among the crowd of men waiting there. He was hired at a low wage to carry bricks to where a house was being built. The work was hard indeed; his shoulders were rubbed sore till they bled: he was unaccustomed to such labour, and completely worn out. Towards evening he received his wages and divided them into three portions: with one he bought some bread, the second he put aside to buy a night's shelter, and with the third he bought some writing paper to write a letter to his wife. He and his queen shared a great secret; only the two of them knew it, and in order that she should know that the letter had been written by him, he mentioned that secret in it. He went to his own home and seeing one of the queen's servants, handed the letter to her to take it to her mistress. But even the queen's servant did not recognise him in his poor clothes. Haggai went to stand not far from the gate and waited for a reply.

But the queen could not believe that Haggai had written the letter, since here was her husband living with her. She thought that her husband had foolishly told someone their secret, and that that evil person was trying to confound her. She lived in fear of her severe and dreaded husband, and she knew that if he found out that such letters were being brought to her, he would surely punish her without asking how it had happened. And she decided to chase away the man who had written the letter and frighten him enough never to dare trouble her again, so she bade her men-servants seize him, take him into the courtyard and thrash him savagely. The servants did as they were told; then they let Haggai go, more dead than alive. He staggered to an inn for a night's shelter, and lay all night in torment: he did not fall asleep till morning. His body was in pain, and his soul even more so; he was tormented by his powerless anger, than which there is no greater torment.

The next day was a feast day, and the innkeeper and his wife made ready to go to church. The wife arrayed herself in all her finery and went into the street; the innkeeper lingered awhile in the courtyard. His wife called him.

'Come along,' she shouted, 'or the king will have entered the church, and we shall miss seeing him.'

Hearing this, Haggai asked: 'Who is your ruler?'

'You must be a stranger here, seeing you do not know that,' said the woman. 'Haggai is our ruler. For twenty years he has reigned over this city and the entire land. Mighty and severe is our king: I saw him passing through the street yesterday – I nearly fell over with fright.'

The innkeeper and his wife went off to church, and Haggai did not know what to think. Then he shrugged his shoulders, saying to himself: 'Things cannot be worse than they are now, whatever happens. I may be punished harshly, put to death even, but I will go and find that scoundrel.' And he followed the innkeeper and his wife to the church, and stood in the crowd gathered on the church steps, waiting to see their ruler pass by.

And Haggai saw his own bodyguards with their hatchets and swords, and his army-chiefs and ministers in their festive clothes. And the king and queen passed by under the canopy fashioned of brocade; their clothes were woven with gold, their belts adorned with precious jewels. And Haggai looked at the king's face and was terrified: the Lord had opened his eyes, and he recognised the Angel of the Lord. And Haggai fled the city in terror.

He ran for a long time – he did not know where he was or where he was going. At last he saw that he was in a dense forest, and he dropped down exhausted beneath a tree. He lay there a long time; all his strength was gone, and he was unconscious; it was as though for a time his soul had abandoned him.

It was night when he awoke, and he felt frightened and ill at ease. He had forgotten all that had happened in the past three days, and he could not understand why stars were gazing at him through the branches, why above him there were trees rustling in the wind, why he felt cold and was lying not in his soft and downy bed but on damp grass. He tried to recall the past and then it all came back to him.

And bitterly did Haggai weep. He recalled his whole life, and understood that the Lord had punished him not for the page torn from the Holy Book, but for his whole life. 'I have angered the Lord,' he thought. 'Can there be mercy and salvation for me now?'

Thus he lay for a long time and wept, repenting of his sins and begging the Lord for help and strength. And the Lord sent him strength.

Daylight came: Haggai rose and walked out of the forest, and went into the wide and radiant world, to the common people.

A year passed, then another, and the queen still believed that the man living with her in the palace was her wedded spouse. One thing only did she wonder at – why was it that her husband had become meek and kindly: he chastised or punished no one; he did not ride to the hunt, but went to church, resolved quarrels and conflicts, and made peace between men who had fallen out with each other. She saw him but rarely; he would look at her not as he had been wont to do, but gently, he would say a kindly word to her and then go off into his chamber, lock himself in and sit there alone.

At last she went up to him and said: 'Tell me, my lord and master, what I have done to offend you so much that you are keeping your wife away from you? I know of no wrong that I have done: why have you shunned me these two years?'

The Angel looked at her with a kindly smile and said: 'You have done nothing to offend me, my gentle wife; but I made a vow to the Lord not to know you for three years. The third year is approaching now, and soon you shall live with your husband as before.'

Having said this, he went to his chamber and locked himself in. The wife wept and then she, too, went to her apartment.

This was how they lived for three years. A week before the fourth year began, the king gave orders to gather all the poor and the needy from the entire land. There was to be a great feast for them at the court with much hospitality, and the king was to present gifts to them all. The heralds rode out to all the towns, from the towns they sent out the order to the villages and hamlets, and from all parts of the land the paupers came. No one had known till then that there were so many paupers in the realm; they filled all the roads – the lame, the legless, the armless, and the blind, the weak and the crazed, the feeble-minded, old and young. Those of the paupers who could see mostly came singly; the blind came in brotherhoods. They assembled in the city; so many of them had come that there was not room for all of them in the king's courtyard, and they filled the entire square as well.

The king entered the church, and those of the paupers who managed to find room crowded in too; the others stood in a throng on the square outside the church. Then servants put out tables on the square, covered them with cloths and set on them pies, soups and meat, wine and mead. And there were places enough for all the many poor and needy that had come.

Then the king came out of the church. He stood on the church steps, made a sign with his hand, and the crowd fell silent.

'I am glad to see you all here, good people: I invite you to eat and drink. Please be seated. When you have done, I shall come to see you again.'

Having said this, he retired into his palace. The guests settled at the tables. One brotherhood of blind men occupied an entire table. These blind men had come from afar; they could walk only slowly and it had taken them a long time. There were twelve of them and they had a guide who walked in front; two of them held on to him, and the rest also came in twos, each holding on to the two ahead of him. Their guide seated them in their places and himself served them: he gave them bowls of soup and handed them pies, cut meat for them and put spoons into their hands. The blind men ate and the guide went from one man to the next and served them all.

At the end of the meal the king came out of his palace and walked round all the tables. Some of his guests he asked a question, to others he said a kindly word; his servants followed him, carrying money and clothes, and each of the guests received a gift. He went round all the tables and reached the last, where the brotherhood of blind men was seated. Their guide saw the king, trembled and turned pale.

The king went up to him and asked him: 'Are you a pauper, too?'

'No, great ruler, I am not a pauper. I am these paupers' servant.'

'You have spoken well, my man. What is your name?'

The guide lowered his eyes to the ground and said: 'The people call me Aleksey.'

The Angel looked into his eyes, smiled and said: 'Not every untruth told is reckoned a lie. Come with me.'

The guide left his blind men and followed the king into the palace. As they walked through the crowd, all men marvelled at them – it was as though two blood-brothers were walking past them. Both were tall and stately, they were both black-haired, and of like face; but there were silver-grey streaks in the dense curly hair of Aleksey, the blind men's guide, and the wind and the sun had darkened his face, whereas the king's face was white and pure.

The people made way for them, and the two went into the palace. The Angel led Aleksey the guide into the farthest chamber and locked the door behind them. Then he said: 'I have recognised thee, Haggai. Dost thou know me?'

'I know, Master, that thou wert sent to punish me. I repent my sin and my entire life.'

And Haggai wept and wept bitterly. Before him stood the Angel, his face serene, and he was smiling. Haggai raised his head and he stopped weeping – never had he seen so wondrous a smile.

'Thy punishment is over,' said the Angel. 'Put on the ruler's cloak, take up thy sword and the ruler's staff and crown. Remember for what thou hast been punished. Rule thy people gently and wisely, and be a brother to thy people henceforth.'

'No, my Master, I shall not obey thy command, I shall not take up the sword, nor the staff, nor the crown, nor yet the cloak. I will not leave the blind, my brothers: I am their light and their nourishment, their friend and their brother. For three years have I lived with them and worked for them, and my soul clings to the paupers and the needy. Forgive me and allow me to return to the world of the people. For long I used to stand, alone among the people, as on a pillar of stone, high above them I stood, but I was lonely; my heart became embittered and my love for the people died. Let me go.'

'Well hast thou spoken, Haggai,' the Angel replied. 'Go in peace!'

And Aleksey, the guide of the blind, went off with his twelve men, and he worked all his life for them and for others who were poor and feeble and oppressed, and thus he lived for many years until his death.

After three days the Angel left the body of the king. His body was laid to rest, and the people mourned their ruler, who had first been proud, and then had become meek and gentle.

And the Angel appeared before the face of the Lord.

1886   *Translated by Peter Henry*

The Travelling Frog

Once upon a time there was a frog living in a bog. He sat there catching gnats and midges, and in spring-time he and all his fellow-frogs would croak away for all they were worth. And he would have gone on living there happily all his life – naturally as long as the stork didn't eat him. However, a certain incident occurred.

One day this frog was squatting on a branch that stuck out of the water; he was revelling in a gentle warm drizzle.

'Ah, what lovely wet weather we are having today!' he thought. 'What a delight it is to be alive!'

The rain drizzled on his speckled glossy back; raindrops trickled down his belly and the back of his legs, and this was so pleasant, so delightfully pleasant, that he very nearly let out a croak. But luckily he remembered that it was autumn and frogs don't croak in the autumn – spring is the season for that – and he felt that by croaking now he might well lose his frogly dignity. So he kept silent and went on basking in the drizzle.

Suddenly he heard a soft, intermittent sound up in the air above him. There is a kind of duck whose wings, in flight, cleave the air making a sound like singing, or rather whistling. 'Phew-phew-phew' is what you hear when a flock of these ducks flies high above you in the air, so high that you can't see them. On this occasion the ducks flew in a great semi-circle and came down in the very swamp where our frog lived.

'Quack, quack!' said one of the ducks. 'We still have a long way to fly; we must get something to eat.'

The frog hid himself at once. He knew that the ducks would not eat him, being such a big, fat frog, but he dived under the branch nonetheless, just in case. But then he thought the matter over and decided to stick his pop-eyes out of the water – he was very curious to find out where the ducks were flying to.

'Quack, quack!' said another duck. 'It's getting cold! We must get to the South! We must get to the South!'

And all the ducks quacked their agreement.

'Most respected ducks!' the frog plucked up the courage to say.

'What is this South you are flying to? Begging your pardon for disturbing you.'

The ducks gathered round the frog. At first they felt a desire to eat him, but on thinking it over each decided that he was too big to swallow. Then they all started quacking and flapping their wings.

'It's lovely in the South! It's warm there now! There are some marvellous swamps down there! And what worms! It's lovely in the South!'

They made such a noise that the frog was nearly deafened. He had great difficulty in persuading them to be quiet so that he could ask one of the ducks, the one which seemed to be the fattest and cleverest among them, to explain what exactly the South was. When the duck told him about it, our frog went into raptures, but, being a cautious creature, he nevertheless asked the duck:

'Are there many gnats and midges in the South?'

'Oh yes! Clouds of them!' replied the duck.

'Croak!' said the frog and instantly looked round to see whether any other frogs were around who might have heard him and would reprimand him for croaking in autumn. He hadn't been able to stop himself giving just that one little croak.

'Please take me with you!'

'What a strange idea!' the duck exclaimed. 'How can we take you along? You don't have any wings.'

'When are you flying?' asked the frog.

'Soon, soon!' all the ducks quacked. 'Quack, quack, quack, quack! It's cold here! To the South! To the South!'

'Please allow me just five minutes to have a think,' said the frog. 'I'll be back right away, I'm sure I can come up with a good idea.'

And he flopped off the branch onto which he had just clambered back again. He dived into the slime and completely buried himself in it, so that nothing whatever should distract him from thinking. Five minutes passed and the ducks were all set to fly off when suddenly the frog's face popped out of the water again near the branch on which he had sat; and on that face was the most radiant expression that a frog was capable of wearing.

'I've got it! I've thought of something!' he said. 'Two of you each take one end of a twig in your beaks, and I'll hang onto it in the middle. You'll do the flying, and I'll be getting a ride. The important thing is that you mustn't quack, and I mustn't croak – and everything will be perfect!'

Goodness knows, it's no great pleasure not being able to talk and carrying even a little frog for three thousand versts, but the ducks were so delighted at the frog's cleverness that they agreed unanimously to take him along. They decided to take turns every two hours; and as there were as many ducks again, then a half and still a quarter as many again, as the riddle says, and as there was only one frog, the turns to carry him would not come round too often. The ducks found a good strong twig, two of them took it in their beaks, the frog caught hold of it in the middle with his mouth, and the whole flock became airborne. The tremendous height to which they rose nearly took his breath away; to make matters worse, the ducks did not fly evenly and kept jerking the twig. Our poor frog bobbed about in the air like a Jack-pudding made of paper, and he had to clench his jaws as tight as he could so as not to let go and come tumbling to the ground. Nonetheless, he soon got used to being in this position and even started looking around. Fields, meadows, rivers and hills rapidly passed by below; however, the frog found it difficult to look at them, because hanging from the twig he could only see backward and a little upward. Still, he could see something and felt very pleased and proud of himself.

'What a superb idea of mine this was,' he thought to himself.

The ducks that flew behind the leading pair carrying the frog quacked their praises.

'That frog of ours is really awfully clever,' they said. 'There can't be many as clever as that, even among us ducks.'

The frog nearly gave in to the temptation of thanking them, but remembering that if he opened his mouth he would go hurtling down from that tremendous height, he clenched his jaw even tighter and resolved to bear it in silence. He went on dangling in the air in this way all day. The ducks that carried him changed over in flight, the new pair deftly catching hold of the ends of the twig; this was most terrifying, and several times the frog nearly croaked with fright. Presence of mind was needed, and this our frog had. In the evening the company halted in a swamp. They set off again at dawn, the frog still with them; but this time, to get a better view, the passenger hung onto the twig with his back and head in front, belly to the rear. The ducks flew over harvested cornfields, forests that had turned golden, villages full of corn-stacks from which came the hubbub of people talking and the thudding of flails threshing the rye. The villagers would look up at the flock of ducks, and noticing there was something odd about them they pointed their hands up at them. The frog was dying to fly closer to the ground so as to display himself and hear what they were saying about him. At the next halt he said:

'Couldn't we fly a little lower? The height is making my head dizzy and I'm afraid I may fall if I suddenly feel sick.'

The kind ducks promised to fly lower. The following day they flew so low that they could hear voices.

'Look, look!' some children shouted in one village. 'Those ducks are carrying a frog!'

The frog heard this and his heart thumped with pride.

'Look, look!' some grown-ups cried in another village. 'There's a wonder for you!'

'But do they know that *I* thought of this and not the ducks?' the frog wondered.

'Look, look!' was the cry in the third village. 'There's a wonder, and no mistake! Who can have thought of such a clever trick?'

By now the frog could stand it no longer, and throwing all caution to the winds, he cried out at the top of his voice:

'It was me! Me!'

And with that he came tumbling down to earth head over heels. The ducks quacked loudly; one of them tried to catch their poor passenger in mid-air, but missed its aim. The frog fell rapidly towards the earth, kicking his four little legs in the air. But as the ducks were flying so fast, he did not land in the spot above which he had cried out and where there was a hard road, but much farther on – which was lucky for him, because he came down plop into a muddy pond on the outskirts of the village.

He soon popped up out of the water to shout at the top of his voice again:

'It was me! *I* thought of it!'

But there was nobody nearby. Frightened by the sudden splash, all the resident frogs had hidden in the water. When they gradually emerged again, they looked at the newcomer in astonishment.

Our frog told them the wondrous tale of how he had been thinking all his life and had finally invented an extraordinary new way of travelling by duck; how he had ducks of his own, which carried him wherever he wanted to go; and how he had been in the wonderful South where it was so lovely, with such wonderful warm swamps and such a lot of gnats and all kinds of other edible insects.

'I've just dropped in on you to see how you are getting on,' he told

them. 'I'll stay with you until spring, when my ducks come back –
I've given them a spot of leave.'

But the ducks never returned. They believed that the frog had been
smashed to death when he fell, and felt very sorry for him.

1887   *Translated by Peter Henry*

The Signal

Semyon Ivanov was a lineman on the railway. His cabin was twelve versts away from the nearest station in one direction and ten versts in the other. The previous year a large spinning mill had been opened some four versts away; its tall chimney stood out darkly from behind a wood. Apart from the other linemen's cabins, there were no dwellings nearby.

Semyon Ivanov was a sick, broken-down man. He had been in the war nine years before; he had been an officer's batman and remained with him throughout the campaign. He had gone without food, been frozen by the cold, roasted by the sun, and he had made marches of forty and fifty versts a day in both hot weather and cold. He had been under fire, but no bullet, thank God, had got him. Once his regiment had been in the front line, and there had been an exchange of fire with the Turks that lasted a whole week. Our men were on one side of a glen and the Turks on the other, and the firing went on from morning till night. Semyon's officer was in the firing line, too; three times a day Semyon brought him his meal and a hot samovar from the regimental kitchen in a ravine in the rear. He carried that samovar across open space, with bullets whistling by and smacking into the rocks; he was terrified, he wept, but kept going. The officers were pleased with him, because they always had hot tea. He returned from the campaign unharmed, but with pains in his arms and legs. Thereafter he suffered many hardships.

When he reached home he found that his old father had died; his little son, a four-year old, had also died – his throat had been diseased. Semyon and his wife were alone in the world. They could not look after their piece of land: Semyon found it hard to do the ploughing, with his swollen arms and legs. Life in their home village became more than they could endure; and so they went off to seek their fortune elsewhere. They went to the borderlands, to Kherson, and to the Don; but they had no luck anywhere. His wife went into service, while Semyon kept on wandering from place to place. One day he happened to get a lift on a locomotive, and the station-master at one of the stations seemed to be someone familiar. Semyon looked at him, and the station-master peered closely at Semyon. They recognised each other. It turned out that the station-master had been one of the officers in his regiment.

'You are Ivanov?' he said.

'Yes, sir, that's me, sir.'

'How do you come to be here?'

Semyon told him what had happened.

'Where are you going now?'

'I don't know, sir.'

'You fool – how do you mean you don't know?'

'That's right, sir, I've nowhere to go. I'm looking for a job, sir.'

The station-master looked at him, thought a bit, and said:

'Look here, old chap, you can stay here at the station for a while. You are married, I believe? Where's your wife then?'

'That's right, sir, I am married. My wife is in Kursk, in service with a merchant.'

'Well then, you write to your wife and tell her to come here. I'll get a free ticket for her. There's a lineman's cabin that will be vacant soon. I'll have a word with the divisional director about you.'

'I'm ever so grateful, sir,' Semyon replied.

He stayed at the station. He helped in the station-master's kitchen, chopped firewood, swept the platform and the yard. Two weeks later his wife arrived, and the two went off to the cabin on a hand-trolley. It was a new cabin, it was warm, and there was as much firewood as they wanted. There was a small vegetable plot left over from earlier linemen and about half a desyatin of arable land on either side of the permanent way. Semyon was overjoyed; he started thinking about doing some farming, and buying a cow and a horse.

He was given all the necessary tools and equipment – a green flag, a red flag, lanterns, a horn, a hammer, a wrench for tightening up the nuts, a crowbar, spade, brooms, bolts and rail-spikes; and he was given two books of regulations and a timetable. At first Semyon could not sleep at night, learning the timetable off by heart. Two hours before a train was due he would go over his section of the track, then he would sit down on a bench by his cabin, looking out all the time and listening for the humming of the rails and the rumble of the train. He also knew all the regulations by heart; he was a poor reader, having to spell out each word, but he managed in the end.

It was summer and the work was not arduous – there was no snow to clear and there were few trains on that line anyhow. Semyon would go over his section twice a day, testing a nut every so often and tightening it up, levelling down the bed, looking at the water-pipes, and then going home to see to his household. The only trouble there was that he had to get the traffic inspector's permission for the slightest thing he wanted to do; the inspector reported everything to the divisional director and much time would pass before his request was dealt with. Semyon and his wife were getting tired of it.

Two months went by. Semyon got to know the other linemen. One of them was a very old man whom the authorities were meaning to replace. He could barely move out of his cabin; his wife did all his rounds for him. The other lineman, the one nearer to the station, was a young man, skinny but strong. He and Semyon first met on the track, midway between the two cabins, when they were both doing their rounds. Semyon took off his hat and bowed.

'How do you do, neighbour?' he said.

The neighbour looked at him askance.

'Hello,' he said.

He turned round and went off. Later the two wives met each other. Semyon's Arina passed the time of day with her neighbour, but she did not say much either. One day Semyon met her.

'That husband of yours isn't much of a talker, is he?' he said to her.

The young woman said nothing at first, then she replied:

'Why, what's he got to talk to you about? Everyone has his own affairs to mind. You go your way, and God be with you.'

However, about a month later they did get to knew each other. Semyon and Vasily would meet on the permanent way, and they would sit down on the embankment, smoke their pipes and talk about life. Vasily did not say very much, but Semyon talked about the village he came from and the war.

'I've had my share of trouble in my time all right, and God knows I'm not that old. God didn't give me any luck. But still, you've got to accept whatever lot He sends you. That's what I say, friend Vasily Stepanych.'

Vasily Stepanych knocked out his pipe against the rail, stood up and said:

'It's not God's lot that's plaguing us, it's people. There's no animal on earth more greedy and vicious than man. Wolf doesn't eat wolf, but man gobbles up man alive.'

'Steady on, friend, don't you say that. Wolf does eat wolf, you know.'

'That's just my way of putting it. Anyway, there's no beast crueller than man. If it weren't for man's spite and greed, we could all get by all right. Everyone's for ever trying to snap at you, bite off a piece of you or swallow you up.'

Semyon pondered for a while.

'I don't know, friend,' he said. 'Maybe that's the way it is, and if it is, then it must be God's will.'

'If that's what you think,' said Vasily, 'then there's no sense in my talking to you. If you blame God for everything nasty and sit there and put up with it all, then you're just a dumb animal and not a human being. That's what I say.'

He turned and went off without saying good-bye. Semyon also got up.

'Neighbour!' he shouted. 'Why are you so angry?'

The neighbour did not turn round but went on. Semyon watched him go until he was out of sight in the cutting at the turn. Then he went home and said to his wife:

'That's a fine neighbour we've got, Arina, He's poison, he's not human.'

However, the two men did not quarrel. They met again and had another talk like the time before, about the same things.

'Ah friend, if it weren't for human beings,' Vasily said, 'you and I wouldn't be stuck in these cabins.'

'What's wrong with them? They're all right, they're not too bad.'

'Not too bad, not too bad. . . Get away with you! You've lived long and learnt nothing, clapped eyes on everything and seen nothing. It's a great life for a poor man, in these cabins or anywhere else! Those skin-flints eat you up. They squeeze the life-blood out of you. When you're old they'll throw you out like the husks they feed to pigs. What pay do you get?'

'Not a lot, Vasily Stepanych. Twelve rubles.'

'I get thirteen fifty. Can you tell me why? By the regulations the management is supposed to pay us the same amount – fifteen rubles a month, plus heating and lighting. Who's decided then that you and I get twelve or thirteen fifty? Who's supposed to get the fat, who's pocketing those other three or one-and-a-half rubles? Answer me that, can you? . . . "Not too bad," you say! Don't you see – I'm not just talking about one-and-a-half or three rubles. They should pay us the full fifteen. Last month I was at the station when the director came through. I saw him; I had that honour. Travelled in a carriage all to himself; he came out on the platform, stood there with his gold chain spread across his belly, with his red, overblown cheeks . . . He's got bloated on our blood. Oh, if I only had the strength and the power! . . . I'm not hanging around here much longer, I'm going somewhere else, I don't care where.'

'But where will you go, Stepanych? It's all right here, you'll not find anything better. You've got a home, warmth, a patch of land. Your wife's a good worker. . .'

'A patch of land! You should see my patch. There's not a stick growing on it. Last spring I was planting out some cabbages when the inspector comes along. "What's this then?" he says. "How come you've not reported this? Why didn't you get permission first? Dig them up, the whole lot of them!" He had some drink inside him. Any other time he wouldn't have said anything, but this time something had got into his skull and he says: "Three rubles fine!"'

Vasily paused, sucking at his pipe, and then he said quietly: 'I was close to knocking his brains out.'

'Now then, neighbour, you're really hot-tempered, you know.'

'I'm not hot-tempered, I only say what's true and what I think. He's got it coming to him, with that red face of his. I'm going to complain about him to the divisional director. We'll see what happens!'

And he really did lodge his complaint.

One day the divisional director came to inspect the track. Some important gentlemen from St Petersburg were due to travel along the line three days later. They were doing a tour of inspection, and everything had to be put in proper order before they passed through. So the bed was ballasted and levelled out, all the sleepers were examined, the spikes rammed home, nuts tightened, sleepers painted, and yellow sand was sprinkled at the level crossings. The neighbouring lineman's wife even got the old man out to trim the grass. Semyon worked for a whole week, put everything in order, mended his coat, and polished his brass badge with crushed brick till it gleamed. Vasily also worked away. The divisional director arrived in a trolley, with four men working the handles. It came racing along with its six wheels whirring, doing twenty versts an hour. It came flying up to Semyon's cabin; Semyon leapt out and reported in soldierly fashion. All was found to be in good order.

'How long have you been here?' the director asked him.

'Since the second of May, sir.'

'Very well. Thank you. – Who's at Number 164?'

The track engineer, who was travelling with the divisional director on the trolley, replied:

'Vasily Spiridov.'

'Spiridov, Spiridov . . . isn't that the one you reported last year?'

'That's the one, sir.'

'Very well, then, let's take a look at Vasily Spiridov. Get moving.'

The workmen laid to the handles and the trolley moved off.

Semyon watched it go and thought: 'There's going to be trouble over there.'

He went on his round a couple of hours later. Then he saw somebody coming out of the cutting along the track; he seemed to have something white on his head. Semyon looked closer – it was Vasily; a stick in his hand, a little bundle on his back, his cheek bandaged with a piece of cloth.

'Where are you off to, neighbour?' shouted Semyon.

Vasily came up quite close. He looked deathly pale, white as chalk, his eyes blazing. When he spoke his voice was choking.

'To the city,' he said, 'Moscow, to Head Office.'

'Head Office . . . I know: you're going to complain, I suppose. Don't do it, Stepanych, forget it . . .'

'Oh no, my friend, I'll not forget it. It's too late for that. See where he hit me in the face so hard that I bled. I'll not forget this as long as I live, I'm not going to leave it at that. They need to be taught a lesson, those bloodsuckers . . .'

Semyon grabbed him by the arm.

'Don't do it, Stepanych! Believe me, you'll not make things any better.'

'Better! I know I won't make things any better. You were right about fate. I'll not make things any better for myself, but I've got to stand up for what's right.'

'But how did all this happen?'

'Well . . . He inspected everything, got off the trolley and looked in the cabin. I knew he was going to be strict, so I'd got it all in good shape. He was just going to leave when I made my complaint. He started shouting. "This is a government inspection," he said, and such like, "and you are lodging a complaint about a vegetable patch. There's Privy Councillors here, and you go on about your cabbages!" I answered back – I couldn't help it. I didn't say that much, but he took it amiss all right. Then he hit me, really hard. . . It's that damned patience of ours! I ought to have gone for him, and yet there I stood as if that's how it should be. Off they went. I came to, washed my face, and then off I went.'

'But what about the cabin?'

'The wife is staying. She'll look after things. To hell with the railway!'

Vasily got up to go.

'Good-bye, Ivanych. I don't know whether I'll get amends.'

'Surely you're not going all the way on foot?'

'I'll get on a goods train at the station. I'll be in Moscow tomorrow.'

The neighbours said good-bye to each other. Vasily walked off, and he was away for a long time. His wife did his job for him, and did not sleep night or day. She wore herself out waiting for her husband to return. On the third day the commission passed through – a locomotive, a luggage van and two first-class carriages – but there was no sign of Vasily. Semyon saw his wife on the fourth day; her face was swollen from crying and her eyes were red.

'Is he back yet?' he asked. The woman shrugged her shoulders, and went her way without uttering a word.

In boyhood Semyon had learnt how to make willow pipes. He would burn the pith out of a rod, drill some holes and make a mouthpiece at one end, then he would tune it so well that any tune he liked could be played on it. Now he made lots of these pipes in his spare time, and the guard on a goods train with whom he was friendly took them to the market in town, getting two kopeks apiece for them. Three days after the inspection he went off to the wood with a knife to cut some willow rods, leaving his wife at the cabin to meet the six o'clock evening train. He went to the end of his section where the line made a sharp turn, then he went down the embankment and downhill through the wood. There was a big marsh half a verst away where there were some excellent willows for his pipes. He cut a big bundle of rods and started back home through the wood. The sun was already low in the sky, there was a death-like silence – all he could hear was the birds twittering and the crackle of dead twigs underfoot. He walked a little further, getting nearer to the track, when he fancied he could hear something like the clang of iron striking iron. He quickened his pace. No repairs were being done on his section. What could it mean? He reached the edge of the wood and the railway embankment rose before him. There was someone squatting on the top, doing something to the track. Semyon crept up quietly, thinking that it was someone stealing the nuts. The man stood up, and Semyon could see that he had a crowbar in his hands. He had put it under the rail and was twisting it to one side. Everything went dark before Semyon's eyes. He wanted to shout, but could not. Then he saw it was Vasily. He ran, and Vasily, with the crowbar and a wrench in his hands, went tumbling headlong down the other side of the embankment.

'Vasily Stepanych! My dear friend! For goodness' sake, Vasily! Come back! Give me that crowbar! We'll put the rail back, nobody will know. Come back! Save your soul from this sin!'

Vasily did not look back and went off into the wood.

Semyon stood by the torn-up rail, dropping his sticks. The next train was a passenger train. And he had nothing to stop it with – he didn't have a flag with him. He could not put the rail back – he could not have driven the spikes in with his bare hands. He must run, run back to his cabin to get some tools. 'God help me!' he muttered.

Semyon ran towards his cabin. He was out of breath, but ran on, stumbling and nearly falling. He ran out of the wood – the cabin was no more than a hundred sazhens away. Then he heard the factory hooter – six o'clock. In two minutes the train would come. 'Oh Lord! Spare those innocent souls!' Semyon saw in his mind's eye the locomotive's left wheel striking the twisted rail, the whole locomotive shuddering, tilting over, tearing up the sleepers and smashing them to smithereens, and at the curve in the line, the embankment with an eleven-sazhen drop, the whole train toppling down it, the third-class coaches packed full with people, little children . . . They were all sitting in the train now without a worry in their heads. 'Oh God, tell me what to do! . . . Oh no, I won't manage to run to the cabin and back in time . . .'

Semyon did not run on to the cabin, but turned back and ran even faster than before. He was almost out of his mind as he ran, not knowing what would happen next. He reached the torn-up rail; his sticks lay there in a heap. He bent down, picked up one of them without knowing why, and ran on. He thought he could hear the train already coming. He heard the distant whistle, then the quiet steady tremor of the rails. He had no strength to run any further; he stopped about a hundred sazhens away from the dreadful spot; then a light flashed in his mind. He removed his cap, took his cotton handkerchief out of it, drew his knife out of the top of his boot and crossed himself, mumbling 'God bless me!'

With the knife he gashed his left arm above the elbow; the blood spurted out in a hot stream; in it he soaked the handkerchief, spread it and smoothed it out, tied it to his stick and put out his red flag.

There he stood, waving his flag. The train was already in sight. The driver of the locomotive wouldn't see him, he would come up too close – he wouldn't be able to pull up the heavy train in a hundred sazhens!

And the blood kept flowing. He pressed his gashed arm against his side to stem the flow, but the blood went on pouring; he had evidently cut his arm very deeply. His head began to reel, black spots started dancing before his eyes, then everything went dark; there was a ringing sound in his ears. He did not see the train and did not hear its rumbling; he had only one thought in his mind: 'I won't keep my feet, I'll fall, I'll drop the flag. The train will run over me . . . Help me, oh Lord, send someone to relieve me . . .'

All went black before his eyes and his mind a blank; he dropped the flag. But the blood-soaked banner did not fall to the ground – a hand seized it and raised it high before the oncoming train. The driver of the locomotive saw it, shut off the governor and reversed steam. The train came to a standstill.

People jumped out of the carriages and gathered in a crowd. They saw a man lying unconscious, drenched in blood. Another man stood beside him with a blood-stained rag on a stick.

Vasily cast his eyes over the crowd and hung his head.

'Take me,' he said. 'I tore up the rail.'

1887   *Translated by Peter Henry*

NOTES

by Peter Henry and Liv Tudge

FOUR DAYS

Four Days (Chetyre dnya) was first published in the St Petersburg journal *Notes of the Fatherland (Otechestvennyye Zapiski)*, No. 10 (October), 1877. It had the subtitle 'One of the Episodes of the War' and was dated 'Bela, August 1877'. Garshin had been wounded in an engagement on 11/23 August near Yaslar and was taken to a field hospital at Bela (Byala) on the River Yantra, Bulgaria, where he began writing the story. From there he was sent back to Russia with other wounded men, arriving in September in Kharkov, where he completed *Four Days*.

Notes of the Fatherland (1839-84), the most influential democratic journal of the 1870s and early 1880s, was from 1877 under the editorship of M. E. Saltykov-Shchedrin, N. K. Mikhaylovsky and G. Z. Eliseyev. It was the first 'thick' journal to take a stand against the Russo-Turkish War. Garshin published the greater part of his stories in it. In 1884 it was closed down by government decree for 'propagating harmful ideas and having members of secret societies as its closest collaborators'.

Four Days had a phenomenal success and when its author arrived in St Petersburg at the end of the year he was given an enthusiastic welcome by the capital's democratic intelligentsia. The story is based on the fate of Vasily Arsenyev, a soldier in the 138th (Bolkhov) Regiment. Severely wounded in an engagement on 12/24 July 1877, Arsenyev was left on the field of battle for several days beside the corpse of an enemy soldier. He was finally discovered by a Russian search party and taken back to camp, but subsequently died of his wounds.

Concurrently with his work on *Four Days* Garshin wrote a documentary account (*ocherk*) of the action in which he was wounded, and an unfinished story in which the campaign is described as viewed by a dog.

Page 28: *Ivanov, Volunteer Private.* The term *vol' noopredelyayushchiysya* was used for persons with secondary education who volunteered for service in the Imperial Army; such volunteers enjoyed a number of privileges over common enlisted soldiers. As a student, Garshin-Ivanov was exempted from military service (actually, at twenty-two, he was above call-up age).

Page 29: *fellah.* Egyptian peasant. The Turkish Army, under Abdul Kerim Pasha, comprised numerous contingents conscripted from non-Turkish nationalities in the Ottoman Empire.

Page 29: *from Istambul to Rustchuk*. The Turkish Army was moved into Bulgaria via the Black Sea port of Varna or from the capital, Istambul (Constantinople). Rustchuk (Ruse), on the southern bank of the Danube, was a Turkish fortress. It was heavily bombarded from Giurgevo (Giurgiu) on the northern bank before the Russians' long-delayed crossing of the Danube. Thereafter, Rustchuk became the base for the Eastern Army Group ('the Rustchuk Army') before its advance into the Balkans.

Page 29: *his patented English Peabody-Martini rifle*. These rifles were superior to the Krnka rifles with which most of the Russian infantry regiments had recently been equipped. The former had a range of 1,800 yards, against the latter's 600-1,200 yards.

Page 31: *that thousand-verst march*. Roughly equivalent to 1,000 kilometres. A verst (*versta*) was equal to 1,067 kilometres or 3,500 English feet.

Page 31: *Kishinyov*. Town in Bessarabia, now capital of the Moldavian SSR. Bessarabia, part of the Principality of Moldavia, lies between the River Dniester in the east and the River Pruth in the west. Formerly under Turkish rule, it was incorporated into the Russian Empire in 1812. A large Russian army was marshalled at Kishinyov from the autumn of 1876 in readiness for the impending war with Turkey (Russia declared war on 12/24 April 1877); it moved into Rumania following the railway line, which involved a major detour to the north-west, and reached the Danube in May.

Page 33: *Bashi-bazouks*. From the Turkish *başıbozuk* (literally 'wild-head'). The term denoted irregular units in the Turkish Army, but was widely used for the Turkish forces generally, notably by Russians and British and other foreign war correspondents with the Russian Army.

Page 33: *Cossacks*. Cossack units enjoyed a degree of independence in the Tsarist Army. In 1881 they accounted for almost 45 per cent of the Army's total cavalry complement of 92,000 men. In some Cossack units the officers were not Cossacks themselves.

Page 34: *Barin Ivanov*. Barin (from *boyarin*) denoted members of the Russian land-owning aristocracy; the term was also used in the nineteenth century of members of the propertied classes and the intelligentsia, and by the lower classes as a respectful form of address, roughly equivalent to 'sir'.

AN INCIDENT

An Incident (Proisshestviye) was first published in *Notes of the Fatherland*, No. 3, 1878. Garshin had feared that the radical *Notes* would not welcome it, since 'my fragment does not even touch upon the war, or upon social, political or other issues. Simply two broken souls in torment' (letter, 16 February 1878). He called it 'something in the Dostoyevsky vein'; although he had no particular admiration for Dostoyevsky, as man or writer, the urban prostitute, the petty clerk, St Petersburg's 'white nights' and city-scapes, high passion and suicide were indeed characteristically Dostoyevskian motifs. *An Incident* was well received. Indeed, seven years later, the prominent critic N. K. Mikhaylovsky was calling it 'the best thing to appear during the seventies'. 'This story,' he added, 'was rightly instrumental in firmly establishing Garshin's literary reputation.'

Page 36: *the Eldorado and the Palais de Crystal*. Two of St Petersburg's *cafés chantants*, risqué establishments where food and spirits were served and there was music and dancing.

Page 36: *'The Dragonfly'*. See the introductory note to *A Very Brief Romance*.

Page 37: *the Yekaterinovka*. One of the many canals of St Petersburg.

Page 37: *on the Nevsky!* Nevsky Prospekt (Avenue), the main street of St Petersburg – a place to see and be seen, and the pivot of many a work of Russian literature.

Page 37: *cousine Olga Nikolayevna*. She chooses not to use the normal Russian word for 'cousin', preferring the Frenchified *kuzina*.

Page 37: *à la Capoule*. Hairstyle named after the French singer Victor Capoul [sic] (1839-1924): the hair was given a centre parting, carefully separated across the forehead and formed into two little ringlets in the middle.

Page 38: *our Russian philosopher*. We have been unable to identify this 'philosopher', but the concept of 'safety valves' suggests the influence of the 'subjective sociology' of Herbert Spencer (1820-1903), as developed in Russia by N. K. Mikhaylovsky. While still at school, Garshin had considered Spencer obligatory reading, describing him as 'another formidable monster . . . I wonder if I'll finish him by Shrovetide' (letter, 12 December 1874).

Page 39: *the Lithuanian Castle*. This splendid edifice with seven towers was built in 1787 as the barracks for the Lithuanian Regiment. From 1823 it served as a prison; hence our heroine's familiarity with it. It was burnt down in the February Revolution of 1917, presumably because it housed political prisoners as well as common criminals.

Page 40: *our General*. The Head of the Department. In the Tsarist Civil Service, senior officials had military ranks, e.g. *shtatskiy general*.

Page 44: *But what are you chasing me away for?* Hitherto Ivan Ivanovich has been pointedly addressing Nadezhda Nikolayevna with the polite pronoun and verb, a normal form of respect between acquaintances. Now he uses the familiar form, effectively emphasising her lack of social respectability.

Page 47: *'today is my name-day.'* The feast-day of the saint after whom he was named. In pre-revolutionary Russia, a name-day was more important than a birthday. Ivan Ivanovich is here weaving a fabrication; his name-day (Ioann-Ivan-John) on the Orthodox calendar is, in fact, 26 September.

Page 48: *in various dens of iniquity*. The Russian word is *priton*, which generally means 'a den of thieves', 'a low dive'. However, in nineteenth-century usage, a *taynyy* [secret] *priton* was also an apartment regularly used by an 'independent' prostitute who did not reside in a brothel.

A VERY BRIEF ROMANCE

A Very Brief Romance (Ochen' koroten'kiy roman) was first published in *The Dragonfly (Strekoza)*, Nos 10 and 11 (March), 1878, under the pen-name 'L'homme qui pleure'. *The Dragonfly* was a weekly 'artistic and humorous journal' with a mildly satirical tone which appeared from 1875 to 1908; its sequel was the more hard-hitting *Satirikon* (1908-13), followed by *The New Satirikon*, whose anti-Bolshevik stance brought it to grief in 1918. Garshin's impish dig at the magazine and its 'typical' reader could hardly have gone unnoticed by readers of this story.

The story is both a bitter-sweet sequel to *Four Days* and an experiment in the confessional style. A personal immediacy contributes to its tight-lipped impact: Garshin had had his share of military hospitals, and knew only too well the discomfort of 'hobbling half a verst or so on my stick' (letter, 5-6 December 1877). Time has scarcely blunted the pun in the title, the same in Russian as in English.

Page 52: *the dark bulk of the ornate palazzo*. The setting is St Petersburg; the *palazzo* is the Winter Palace, on the left bank of the Neva.

Page 52: *the Fortress Cathedral*. The Peter and Paul Fortress, on an island almost opposite the Winter Palace, was the first large structure built in St Petersburg. By the time of the story, it was used mostly to house political prisoners.

Page 52: *'Our Mutual Friend'*. Garshin wrote the title in English in his text; mistakenly as *Our Common Friend*.

Page 53: *like the time Feigin's flour-mill burnt down*. This refers to an actual event – the 'Ovsyannikov Affair', a financial scandal which had all St Petersburg agog in March 1875.

Page 55: *the attendant, a kind-hearted old soldier*. Veteran soldiers were commonly employed in hospitals and other institutions, as attendants, guards and even medical assistants. See *The Red Flower* for another instance.

AN ENCOUNTER

An Encounter (Vstrecha) was first published in *Notes of the Fatherland*, No. 4, 1879; its subtitle – 'A Fragment' – perhaps reflects Garshin's abiding reservations about his story. '. . . When I told Shchedrin [the editor, and Garshin's crusty mentor] that I had been afraid for this story, he gave me the rough edge of his tongue.' The story is set in a resort on the Black Sea.

Page 66: *a sazhen*. Here probably a nautical sazhen, or Russian fathom (1.83 metres).

Page 66: *many hundred poods*. 1 pood = 36 pounds avdp.

Page 68: *as Krylov put it, you've all got fluff on your snouts?* This phrase is taken from Ivan Krylov's fable 'The Vixen and the Marmot', in which the marmot cannot understand why she has been dismissed so summarily from her post of judge in the hen-house. Has the vixen, she asks, ever seen her abusing her authority? 'No, dearie,' the vixen replies. 'Though I've often seen feathers on your snout.' The second stanza relates this directly to hidden graft in officialdom. Vasily Petrovich's 'quotation' is oddly inaccurate, considering that he is a Russian language teacher.

Page 69: *let's have done with this 'accursed question'*. The 'accursed questions' to which Kudryashov sarcastically refers were the vast, practically insoluble moral dilemmas which writers and thinkers such as Dostoyevsky – to give the most salient example – were wont to place before their readers.

Page 73: *Freedom for the free.* The complete version of this old Russian saying is: 'Freedom for the free, paradise for the saved, the plains for the possessed, the bog for the devil.'

THE COWARD

The Coward (Trus) was first published in *Notes of the Fatherland*, No. 3, 1879. A first version was unacceptable to the censor – Garshin's first encounter with 'the scissors', and he felt that the story, as published, had been 'spoilt to a significant degree'. Kuzma is modelled on a student friend of Garshin's, Semyon Kuzmich Kvitka, who contracted gangrene in 1876 and was treated by the Scotsman G. L. Carrick; unlike Kuzma in the story, Kvitka 'miraculously' survived.

Page 74: *The war.* The Russo-Turkish War of 1877-78.

Page 74: *The Tiligul railway disaster.* The River Tiligul is north-east of Odessa. In December 1875, during a blizzard, a troop train bound for Odessa was derailed here, while repair work was being carried out on the line. The train hurtled into the Tiligul Ravine, and some one hundred soldiers were killed.

Page 74: *I've been put in the reserves. Opolcheniye* between 1874 and 1917 signified a home-based reserve made up of both men liable for call-up and older men, who were not drafted into the Army proper but performed a variety of auxiliary duties in the rear, roughly equivalent to a Home Guard.

Page 76: *the third battle of Plevna* of 30-31 August 1877 failed to dislodge the Turkish forces dug in on the Plevna Heights and was followed by a three-month siege.

Page 76: *a mountain of corpses used as a pedestal for grandiose deeds.* Here we have a verbal equivalent of V. V. Vereshchagin's painting *Apotheosis of War*, a pyramid of countless skulls.

Page 86: *had left the village of Markovka for the Amur in Eastern Siberia.* This refers to the migration from central Russia and the Ukraine settling in Siberia and the Far East; at first more or less illegally, towards the end of the century with government encouragement. The River Amur is the frontier between the Soviet Far East and Manchuria.

Page 88: *They'd marched from Kishinyov.* See note to *Four Days*, page 31.

Page 88: *Anna Karenina* had been published in 1876-77. Lvov's reference to the novel is doubly topical in that the concluding part includes the departure of Russian volunteers to fight in Serbia against the Turks in 1876, Vronsky among them.

Page 90: *you, the great toe of this assembly*. From Memenius's tale of the Belly and Other Members in *Coriolanus* Act I, Scene 1.

ARTISTS

Artists (Khudozhniki) was first published in *Notes of the Fatherland*, No. 9, 1879. It had proved a troublesome piece, politically as well as artistically. 'It would, of course, be going rather less haltingly,' he wrote, 'if in the course of writing one were concerned with *what to write* instead of *what not to write*' (letter, 25 April 1879).

Garshin was familiar with the artistic life of St Petersburg, being close friends with the 'brotherhood' of 'progressive' writers there and, while still a student, had published four art reviews in *The News (Novosti)*, a middle-of-the-road daily 'newpaper for all' (see Introduction, page 8). Much effort has been devoted to identifying the models of Ryabin, Dedov, Professor N., the art critics V. S. and Alexander L., the painter K., the rivet-bucker. Did Garshin 'see' him first in Yaroshenko's painting *The Furnaceman* (1878), or was the initial encounter more direct and dramatic? 'Yes,' Garshin is quoted as saying, 'I did visit a factory.' The promise of a sequel to the story was never fulfilled.

Page 93: *Kronstadt* was established by Peter the Great in 1703. It is some fifteen miles west of the city, on an island in the Gulf of Finland.

Page 93: *laivas* were large two-masted boats of Finnish origin, common in the Baltic Sea and elsewhere.

Page 95: *Mr V. S.* The art critic and historian V. V. Stasov (1824-1906), idealogue of the Itinerants.

Page 97: *bast shoes, leg-cloths and sheepskin coats*. Items of Russian peasant costume that had acquired, by the time this story was written, an almost symbolic significance.

Page 98: *Fifteenth Street, off Sredny Prospekt*. Ryabin lives on Vasilevsky Island, where the Academy of Fine Arts and various other cultural and educational institutions were located. The point of the Island served as the port of St Petersburg until 1880.

Page 99: *those stone-lugs*. The word that Dedov uses here *(glukhar')* is the common name for *tetrao urogallus* (capercaillie), the largest species of the old-world grouse. The imputation of deafness in its Russian name arises from the common belief that the male is deaf during its mating call.

Page 101: *Repin's infamous 'Volga Boatmen'*. Ilya Repin (1844-1930) was a leading figure among the Itinerants, and his grimly realistic *barge-haulers on the Volga* (1870-73) had caused a sensation in the Russian art world. Repin went on to paint vast canvasses like *The Religious Procession in Kursk Province* and *Zaporozhian Cossacks Writing a Reply to the Turkish Sultan*, as well as portraits of contemporary writers, composers and others. On his relations with Garshin, see Introduction, page 8.

Page 102: *Who summons me?* Ryabinin quotes, slightly inaccurately *('Wer ruft mich?')* from Goethe's *Faust*. '*Earth Spirit*: Who summons me? *Faust*: Horrifying vision!'

Page 103: *The art critic L.* A. Ledakov, art critic of *The St Petersburg Gazette*.

Page 107: *à la Klever.* Yu. Klever – doubtless the K. mentioned earlier in the story by Dedov – was a prolific and popular artist of the time. Garshin had been singularly caustic in his regard in an art review of 1877: 'A sweet little piece by a fashionable painter. Paint your pieces, Mr Klever, so that they will come out "sweet" . . . Ensure, in brief, that, halting before that piece of yours, elegant ladies shall without fail declare: "Ah! C'est joli".'

Page 109: *He'll just go to waste, he'll perish out in the countryside.* Dedov, glib representative of 'pure art' and opponent of the Itinerants, is scornful of realistic, socially purposeful art. He cannot understand how a man of talent like Ryabinin can abandon his art and 'go to the People' to engage in educational work among the peasants (and, quite possibly, illegal revolutionary activity as well).

ATTALEA PRINCEPS

Attalea princeps was first published in the populist journal *Russian Wealth (Russkoye Bogatstvo)*, No. 1, 1880, with the subtitle 'A Fairytale'. Garshin had originally submitted it to *Notes of the Fatherland*, but it was rejected by the editor, Saltykov-Shchedrin, for 'preaching the most merciless fatalism'. Garshin's fairytale certainly touched a live chord among the democratic intelligentsia, who read it as an inspiring call for individual heroism. It was seen as a prophetic allegory of the revolutionaries' brief moment of triumph when, in the following year, The People's Will succeeded in assassinating Alexander II on 1 March 1881, which so many Russians saw as heralding the end of autocracy. The literary historian S. D. Durylin expressed this mood of exhilaration by paraphrasing the climactic passage in *Attalea princeps*: '. . . a metallic bang rang out. A stout iron band had snapped. Glass splinters rained down with a ringing noise . . . Alexander II was killed.'

Russian Wealth, founded in Moscow in 1876, transferred to St Petersburg in 1880, where it was initially run by an *artel'* of writers with populist *(narodnik)* sympathies, including, briefly, Garshin (before his mental collapse later that year). After the débâcle of March 1881, the journal went into decline, but rose to prominence in the 1890s, publishing Leonid Andreyev, K. M. Stanyukovich, the early Maxim Gorky, Ivan Bunin and A. I. Kuprin.

A NIGHT

A Night (Noch') was first published in *Notes of the Fatherland*, No. 6, 1880. Garshin wrote this story shortly before the event that triggered off his mental breakdown – Mlodetsky's attempt on Count Loris-Melikov and the terrorist's public execution, despite Garshin's dramatic pleas for his pardon (see Introduction, page 13). The story not only expresses the states of existential despair and crises of identity into which Garshin could sink, but also illustrates the pessimism and scepticism (including the numerous suicides among the intelligentsia at the time) that were regarded by the Establishment as manifestations of 'sedition'.

N. K. Mikhaylovsky, one of the editors of *Notes of the Fatherland*, read the ending as showing that Aleksey Petrovich had in fact killed himself, overlooking the telling detail that the gun was still loaded. Turgenev, who rated the story highly, also complained that the ending was 'unclear'. Section V is autobiographical; Garshin here reminisces about his life with his father after his mother had eloped with his tutor, the radical student P. V. Zavadsky, leaving the five-year-old boy alone with his father near Starobelsk for three years.

Page 118: '*Martha*'. Friedrich von Flotow's opera of 1847, which was very popular throughout Europe in the nineteenth century. The tune played by the organ-grinder is extremely light, not to say trivial, and as such contrasts poignantly with the suicidal despair of Garshin's hero. The Russian words ('*U devits/Est' dlya ptits/Strely kalyonyye*') fit the music of '*Wohlgemuth, junges Blut, über Weg, über Steg . . .*' (commonly rendered in English, extremely loosely, as 'Come away, maidens gay, to the fair all repair . . .'). It is the opening of a 'Chorus of Maid-Servants'.

Page 122: *the Tenginsk Regiment*. Formed in 1796 as Grand-Duke Alexander's own regiment; it distinguished itself in the Patriotic War of 1812-14 and in the Caucasian campaigns later in the century.

Page 123: *the Turkish campaign*. Presumably the Russo-Turkish War of 1877-78.

Page 128: *Wait, stop a while, it's good here*. Cf. Goethe's *Faust*: 'Verweile doch, du bist so schön.' There are other Faustian echoes in the story, notably the Easter bells that save the hero from suicide.

Page 131: *Except ye be converted . . .* Matthew XVIII.3.

ORDERLY AND OFFICER

Orderly and Officer (Denshchik i ofitser), first published in *Russian Wealth*, No. 3, 1880, was originally conceived as one of several 'episodes from the war' based on Garshin's first-hand observations of army life. The story rapidly became, in Garshin's mind, the nub of a huge saga. 'As you can see,' he wrote to a friend in April 1880, 'the plot is extensive, yet I have the "intrigue", the clashes, crises and finale all prepared . . . [The sections for the] July, Aug., Sept., and Oct. [issues of *Russian Wealth*] are already written, though for May I have nothing and for June nothing.' He saw this epic, which he had provisionally entitled *People and War*, growing to three volumes. But all this, tragically, was taking place during a hyper-active phase which led to his mental collapse. All that remains of this ambitious project is *Orderly and Officer* and, perhaps, *From the Reminiscences of Private Ivanov*.

Page 134: *The title*. It was and is a convention in the Russian/Soviet armed forces to mention the socially inferior rank first: 'soldiers and officers'. 'Orderly' is really too grand a word for *denshchik* – 'batman' – but fits better here than the more exact but clumsier English term.

Page 135: *Have they sheared thee?* Prior to this date, the peasant's forehead used to be shaved when he was officially conscripted. Under serfdom, landlords even had the right to 'shear' unruly serfs for the army as a punishment. By the 1870s the custom had fallen into disuse, but the term lingered among the peasantry.

Page 135: *Taken thine, have they, Ivan?* Firm social distinctions existed in pre-revolutionary Russia at all levels. The prosperous peasant Ilya Savelich uses the familiar form of address in speaking to the poorer man, while the latter uses the formal 'you' in the following conversation.

Page 135: *If tha'd've adopted him afore now . . .* By law an only son could not be conscripted. This was the sole exemption for an able-bodied man and, since Nikita was a foster-child who had never been legally adopted, he did not qualify.

Page 141: *a volunteer cadet*. See note to *Four Days*, page 28.

Page 146: *Aunt Paraskovya*. Nikita's wife was also named Paraskovya. This Paraskovya, however, was probably his foster-mother, Ivan's wife. When applied by adults to a woman older than they, the designation implies friendly familiarity.

WHAT NEVER WAS

What Never Was (To, chego ne bylo) was first published in *Foundations (Ustoy)*, No. 3/4, 1882. This liberal-oppositionist 'literary and political' monthly lasted for less than two years.

During his lengthy convalescence on his Uncle Akimov's estate near the Black Sea coast, Garshin at first feared that he would never be able to write again. However, he began to learn French and tried his hand at translation. Early in 1882, the children of his friend in St Petersburg, the naturalist and educationist A. Ya. Gerd, implored him to contribute to their family magazine. He intended to let them have *What Never Was*, a new version of a fable he had begun in 1879 for *Russian Wealth*. He sent the reworked story to his mother, requesting her to pass it on to Gerd's children. On discovering that she (and his brother) had offered it to *Foundations* instead, he was dismayed but realised that it was too late to protest.

A passage in Turgenev's *On the Eve* (1859) reads: 'What strikes me most forcibly in ants, beetles and other insect gentry is their astonishing seriousness; they run to and fro with such important physiognomies, as though their life actually had some significance! And, so please you, the king of creation, the highest being, looks at them, and they pay him no heed.' Other possible literary forbears of this tale are Pushkin's 'Gathering of Insects' *Sobraniye nasekomykh)*, a lampoon of certain acquaintances in insect guise, and the poem recited by Captain Lebyadkin in Dostoyevsky's *Devils*, in which a cockroach falls into a glass full of flies, and, while they are complaining loudly about the intrusion, a house servant comes and dumps them all unceremoniously into the pig-pail.

Reaction to the tale irritated Garshin greatly; no one seemed able to resist interpreting it as an 'Aesopian' political satire. 'I swear to you by all that I can swear by,' he wrote to his brother, 'that until I received your letter it never even entered my head that this tale could say anything about constitutions, caretakers, village constables, socialists, peasants, i.e. in general, about present-day topics of conversation.' That admittedly disingenuous disclaimer, oft-repeated as it was, has been affably discounted by editors and critics ever since.

Page 147: *28 degrees Réaumur* is the equivalent of 35° Centigrade, 95° Fahrenheit.

Page 147: An *arshin* equals 71 centimetres, or about 28 inches. This makes the dog's tongue a gloriously hyperbolical 12 inches long or more.

Page 149: *Luparyovka . . . Kislyakovka . . . Svyato-Troitskoye . . . Bogoyavlensk, etc.* For most of the time that Garshin was on his uncle's estate near Yefimovka, these hamlets, villages and towns formed the limits of his world too. The coachman, Anton, was one of the Akimov family servants.

FROM THE REMINISCENCES OF PRIVATE IVANOV

From the Reminiscences of Private Ivanov (Iz vospominaniy ryadovogo Ivanova) was first published in *Notes of the Fatherland*, No. 1, 1883. Garshin wrote this work on Turgenev's estate at Spasskoye-Lutovinovo where, on Turgenev's invitation, he spent the summer and autumn of 1882. Turgenev had intended to meet Garshin there, but ill-health prevented him from leaving Paris, and the two writers were never to meet. The sustained epic narrative of *The Reminiscences* shows the extent to which Garshin had recovered from his mental collapse in 1880 and his nearly two-year absence from writing and the literary world.

Page 151: *Kishinyov*, in Bessarabia, was where the Russian Army assembled prior to the outbreak of the Russo-Turkish War. See note to *Four Days*, page 31.

Page 151: *the 222nd (Starobelsk) Infantry Regiment.* The Garshin family estate was near Starobelsk, a small town in Lugansk Province (now Voroshilovgrad Oblast') in the Ukraine.

Page 151: *a heavy Krynkov rifle in my hands.* Re-equipping Russian infantry regiments with Krnka (Krenke) rifles had begun in 1870; at the beginning of the Russo-Turkish War, 27 out of the 48 infantry divisions had been issued with these rifles. It was a breech-loader, still something of a novelty then, and weighed 11 (Russian) pounds, or 4.5 kilograms, without the bayonet. It was less satisfactory than the Snider and Peabody-Martini rifles of the Turkish Army (see note to *Four Days*, page 29). By the end of the war all regiments had been equipped with the American Berdan rifle.

Page 153: *peasants from the Vyatka . . . and Kostroma Provinces . . . Vladimir Province.* These peasant-soldiers came from areas located from 200 to 800 kilometres from Moscow.

Page 154: *the Khiva Campaign.* Russian expansion into the Central Asian khanates of Khiva and Bukhara, begun in the 1860s, culminated in the storming of Khiva in 1873. Thenceforth, Khiva and Bukhara were vassals of the Russian Empire. Their territories are in present-day Soviet Uzbekistan and Kirgizistan.

Page 154: *Vasily Karpych!* The full form of the patronymic is Karpovich; the fact that it is here shortened to Karpych indicates that the speakers are on informal terms. Similarly, the narrator, previously addressed in the formal style as 'Vladimir Mikhaylovich', is here addressed simply as 'Mikhaylych', that is, with the shortened form of his patronymic and omitting his forename altogether, a common practice in rural communities; later he is addressed as 'Vladimir Mikhaylych', all of which shows nuances in the degree of familiarity developing between the peasant-soldiers and the volunteer private. Nevertheless, the soldiers also used the respectful *barin* when speaking to or referring to him. (On *barin* see note to *Four Days*, page 34.)

Page 156: *Dubinushka.* An old Russian work-song sung by the barge haulers *(burlaki)* as they dragged boats upstream. *Dubina* was the wooden bar, with the ropes attached to it, which the haulers gripped or pressed their chests against.

Page 159: *two square sazhens.* 4.5 square metres.

Page 162: *Jassy* (Iaşi), a large town in Bukovina in north-eastern Rumania, is some 320 kilometres from Bucharest as the crow flies. *Tekuch* (Tecuci) is 150 kilometres south of Jassy, at the northern end of the Wallachian Lowlands. *Berlad* (Bîrlad) is another 40 kilometres further south. Garshin's otherwise highly accurate memory must have failed him here: the Army must have gone from Tekuch to Berlad, not vice versa. *Bucharest*, the capital of Rumania, is 45 kilometres north of the Danube.

Page 162: *35 degrees in the shade*, or 95° Fahrenheit; *48 versts*, just over thirty miles.

Page 164: *Nemtsev.* A surname coined from *nemets/nemtsy* (German/s). Ventzel's name (Wenzel), upbringing and general demeanour suggest that he was a Russianised German, possibly descending from a German baronial family in the Baltic Provinces.

Page 166: *Fokshany* (Fokşani) is 25 kilometres south-west of Tekuch.

Page 168: *It was at the Battle of Poltava.* The opening line of a poem by I. E. Molchanov (1809-1881) which became a very popular song. It extols Peter the Great's victory over the Swedes under Charles XII at Poltava, in the Ukraine, in 1709.

Page 169: *Khodynka Plain (Khodynskoye polye).* A large open space in Moscow where major public events were held.

Page 170: *sentry duty at the money-chest.* Military units had money with them to cover necessary expenses during the campaign. Ventzel is temporarily stripped of his rank and compelled to do sentry duty as a common soldier.

Page 171: *Suvorov's way!* Count Alexander Vasilyevich Suvorov (1729-1800), celebrated Russian general who put down the Pugachov Rebellion and defeated the Turks in several major campaigns, was the founder of Russian military training and discipline. (Doubtless Brigadier Bravo had been studying Suvorov's victory at the Battle of Fokshany in 1789.) Suvorov defeated Napoleon in Italy in 1798 and led his army across the Alps in the following year.

Page 174: *Ploeshti* (Ploieşti), in southern Rumania, 55 kilometres due north of Bucharest, now the centre of the Rumanian oilfields, was the headquarters of the Danube Army until after the crossing.

Page 176: *the land of Bokhara.* The soldier may have heard of (or fought in) the Central Asian Campaigns of the 1860s and early 1870s.

Page 177: *reservists,* known as *biletnyye* (from *bilet,* ticket, pass), were soldiers on temporary discharge, but liable to be recalled at any time.

Page 178: *Alexandria,* south-west of Bucharest, is 35 kilometres north of the Danube.

Page 182: *'Caucasus'.* The cigarette-holder was doubtless a souvenir that Zaykin had acquired during active service in the Caucasus. The 'Caucasian War' lasted from 1817 until 1864, when the whole territory was finally subjugated by the Russians.

Page 182: *During the night of the fourteenth and fifteenth of June.* This was, in fact, when the five-day crossing of the Danube at Simnitza began, according to the Old Style Julian Calendar.

Page 184: *My dear old Stebelechek!* Zaykin has coined an affectionate diminutive from the ensign's name, deriving from *stebel'* (stem, stalk); he has here anticipated Kipling, the diminutive being roughly equivalent to 'Stalkie'.

Page 186: *Simnitza* (Zimnicea), on the northern bank of the Danube, was situated opposite Sistova (Svishtov), mentioned below. The main body of the Danube Army, totalling 185,000 men, crossed into Bulgaria here (see second note to page 182).

Page 188: *the Volhynia regiment.* It was, in fact, a Volhynian regiment that led the vanguard of the Russian Army across the Danube under heavy fire. Volhynia is in the north-west of the Ukraine, bordering on Poland.

Page 189: *Tirnovo* (Tйrnovo), 60 kilometres south of the Danube, the ancient capital of the Kingdom of Bulgaria, was the site of the Army's HQ in July and August. From here, General I. V. Gurko made his foray into the Balkan Highlands ahead of the Main Army. *Pleven* (Plevna), north-west of Tirnovo, was the scene of some of the most bitter fighting of the war. The Turks had made this a fortification, which the Russians captured after a five-month siege in December 1877.

THE RED FLOWER

The Red Flower (Krasnyy tsvetok) was first published in *Notes of the Fatherland*, No. 10, 1883. In this work Garshin externalises and, perhaps, exorcises the memory of his incarceration three years earlier in the Saburov *dacha*, the asylum in Kharkov. He had been brought there, violent and bound, by train. While in the asylum he demonstrated that he could create electricity by touching his hair to his nose, and tried to absorb the destructive force of a thunderstorm through a stick thrust against his chest and stuck out of the window to rest against the roof. He also had periods of complete and agonising lucidity. He wrote in July 1883 that the story 'relates to the time I spent in the Saburov *dacha*; what resulted is something bizarre yet rigorously real.' The response to *The Red Flower* was, predictably, polarised on political lines, for this harrowing tale of a deluded hero locked in a chimeric battle with all the world's evil could not but stir deep emotions in the fraught political atmosphere of the 1880s.

Page 197: *To the memory of Ivan Sergeyevich Turgenev*. Turgenev had died in August of 1883.

Page 198: *to put a large blistering plaster on his nape*. 'Blister compound' was a staple item in the nineteenth-century medical cupboard. The wing covers of the Spanish fly *(Lytta vesicatora)* were crushed and mixed into a paste, and this potentially lethal substance was used to blister the skin, as a 'counter-irritant'.

Page 199: *Saint George, thou holy martyr*. St George, a great fourth-century saint of the Eastern Church and patron of soldiers, was martyred for his faith. He was closely associated with the rulers of Early Russia and the Russian Empire. (His exploit with the dragon was a later addition to his legend.)

Page 207: *Ahriman*. The major evil spirit in the Zoroastrian religion of Ancient Persia, the chief opponent of Ahura Mazda (Ormazd, or Sovereign Knowledge).

Page 209: *93 pounds*. 6 stone 10 lb. The Russian *funt* was just over 14½ oz.

THE TALE OF THE TOAD AND THE ROSE

The Tale of the Toad and the Rose (Skazka o zhabe i roze) was first published in Litfond's first jubilee volume in 1884. The charitable organisation Litfond

(Literaturnyy fond) had been set up in 1859, its primary objective being to assist needy writers, scholars and artists and their families. Litfond had the support of most leading writers of the time and in the 1880s became a major publishing enterprise. Beneficiaries included Dostoyevsky, Nadson, Garshin, Uspensky and, later, Maxim Gorky. In the last years of his life Garshin was an active and conscientious member of Litfond's committee.

As his staunch friend, the Professor of Zoology V. A. Fausek, recorded, the idea of this fairy-tale took shape in Garshin's mind during a piano recital at the home of the poet Ya. P. Polonsky. 'Anton Rubinstein [1829-94] was playing, and opposite him and staring at him sat a person whom Garshin heartily disliked, a senior official of a disagreeable appearance . . . As the antitheses of Rubinstein and his loathsome listener, the idea of the toad and the rose arose in Garshin's mind. It was to the sounds of Rubinstein's music that his simple story and the touching words of his little fairy-tale took shape in his head.' Garshin wrote his story that very night, dating it 'the night of 1 January 1884'.

THE LEGEND OF HAGGAI THE PROUD

Haggai the Proud. An Ancient Legend Retold (Skazaniye o gordom Aggeye. Pereskaz starinnoy legendy) was first published in *Russian Thought (Russkaya Mysl')*, Book IV, 1886. It is based on an old Russian legend, *The Edifying Tale of King Aggey, Who Suffered for His Pride*, first published in A. N. Afanasyev's *Narodnyye russkiye legendy (Russian Folk Legends)* in 1860. Garshin changed the end of the legend where Aggey, after suffering his punishment, is forgiven by the Lord and returns to his throne, and thenceforth is a just and kind ruler.

Garshin's work is very close in form and spirit to Leo Tolstoy's folk legends, and it was originally intended to be published by the Tolstoyan publishing house Posrednik (The Mediator), which produced cheap, widely distributed editions of moral tales, modern parables and other works for the common reader. Permission to publish the story in book form was not granted to Posrednik until 1895, doubtless because of its veiled strictures on absolutist rule. Simultaneously with, but independently of Garshin, Tolstoy had been writing a dramatisation of the same legend, but abandoned his work on hearing of Garshin's story.

The fact that the work had been intended for Posrednik accords with Garshin's 'downgrading' of the title of the central character. In the legend Haggai is a *tsar*; in Garshin's story he is merely a 'ruler' *(pravitel')*, and his spouse is his 'wife' *(zhena)* as against *tsaritsa* in the legend. This change reflects the democratic (or anarchistic) disregard and contempt for all official institutions, ranks and titles which Tolstoy and his followers advocated at that time. In this translation the words 'king' and 'queen' have been preferred to the literal but bland-sounding 'ruler' and 'wife', as being more in keeping with the idiom of folk-tale, while preserving Garshin's respectful distance from the dangerous terms *tsar* and *tsaritsa*.

Russian Thought, published in Moscow from 1880 till 1918, had a liberal orientation. After the closure of *Notes of the Fatherland* in 1884, a number of its contributors transferred to *Russian Thought*; Garshin had here also published his longest work, *Nadezhda Nikolayevna*. In the 1890s Chekhov published several stories in *Russian Thought* and assisted with the editorial work.

This is the first published English translation of the story. A French version by Yvan Loskovtoff, *Histoire de l'Orgueilleux Aggée*, illustrated in the stylised manner of Ivan Bilibin, was published in 1983.

THE TRAVELLING FROG

The Travelling Frog (Lyagushka-puteshestvennitsa) was first published in *The Spring (Rodnik)*, a magazine for children, Book VII, 1887. It is possible that Garshin may have known an ancient Indian fable about a tortoise that is taken on a similar flight by two geese and, of course, La Fontaine's *La Tortue et les deux canards*. The story, the last publication in his life-time, is very popular with younger present-day readers in the Soviet Union.

THE SIGNAL

The Signal (Signal) was first published in *The Northern Herald (Severnyy Vestnik)*, Book I, 1887. This journal, edited until 1890 by Anna M. Evreinova, to some extent continued the tradition of *Notes of the Fatherland* after its closure in 1884. Contributors to the latter transferred partly to *Russian Thought*, and partly to *The Northern Herald*. Chekhov published several works here, notably his innovatory impressionistic story *The Steppe* (1888); Garshin, who read this story a few days before his death, spoke enthusiastically about its beauty and originality, amidst a generally sceptical response to it in the literary world of the capital. In the 1890s *The Northern Herald* became effectively the journal of the early Russian Symbolists – Minsky, Merezhkovsky, Gippius, Sologub and Balmont.

Page 233: *He had been in the war nine years before*. The Russo-Turkish War of 1877-78. It is probable that Garshin intended here to continue the story of Nikita Ivanov, the batman in *Orderly and Officer* (1880); in an early draft, he is, in fact, called Nikita Ivanov.

Page 233: *They went to the borderlands, to Kherson, and to the Don*. The Russian phrase *na Linii* referred to frontier fortifications, such as the Caucasian Line and the Black Sea Line.

Page 234: *half a desyatin*. A desyatin *(desyatina)* was equal to 24,000 square sazhens, 1.09 hectares or 2.7 acres. In the eighteenth and nineteenth centuries, a larger, 'proprietary' desyatin was also in use, amounting to 32,000 square sazhens.